# Once upon a time...

# HEARTLESS PRINCE

### A GRAPHIC NOVEL

STORY & ILLUSTRATIONS BY
## ANGELA DE VITO

WRITTEN BY
## LEIGH DRAGOON

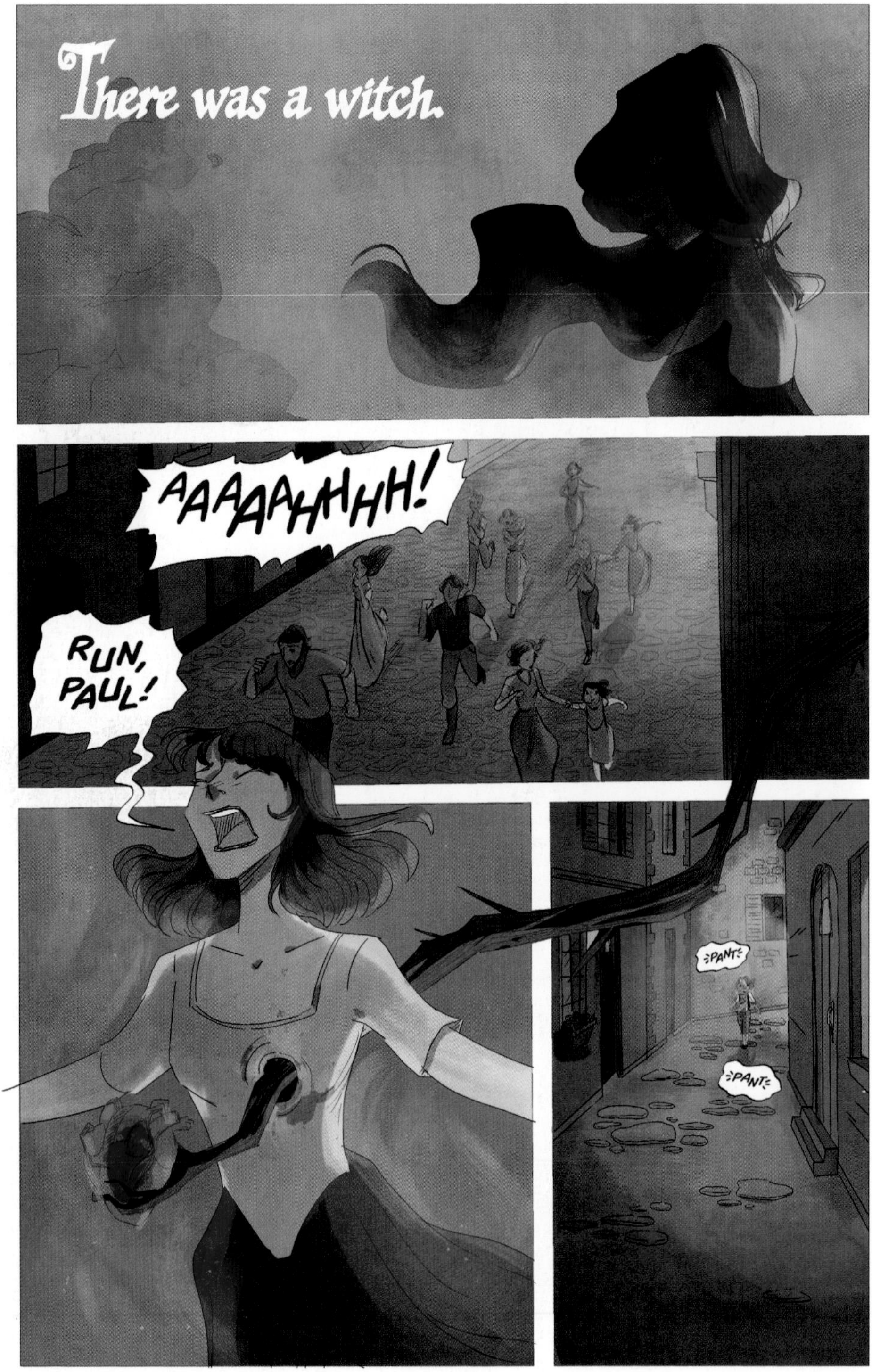
There was a witch.
AAAAAHHHH!
RUN, PAUL!
PANT
PANT

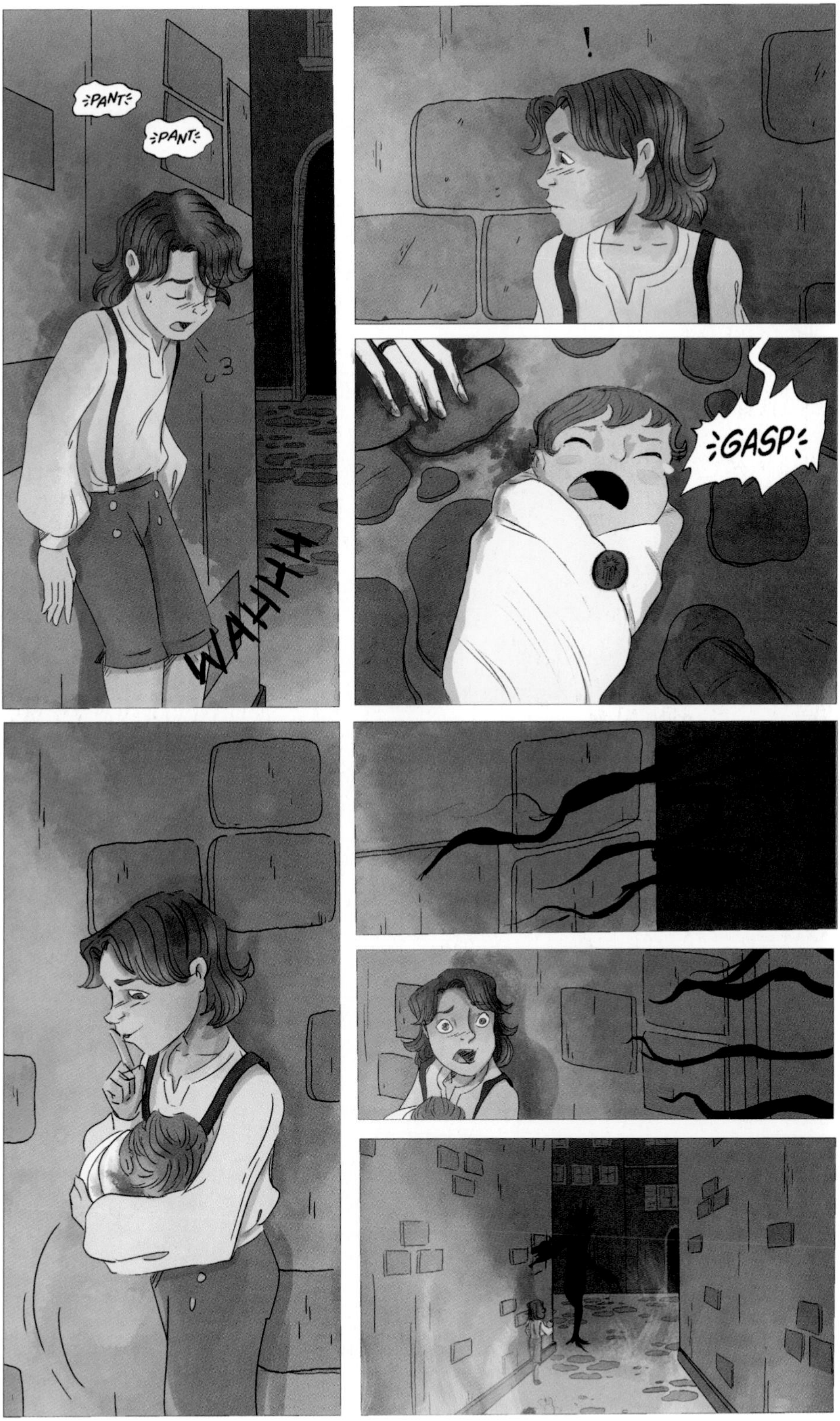
PANT
PANT
WAHHH
!
GASP

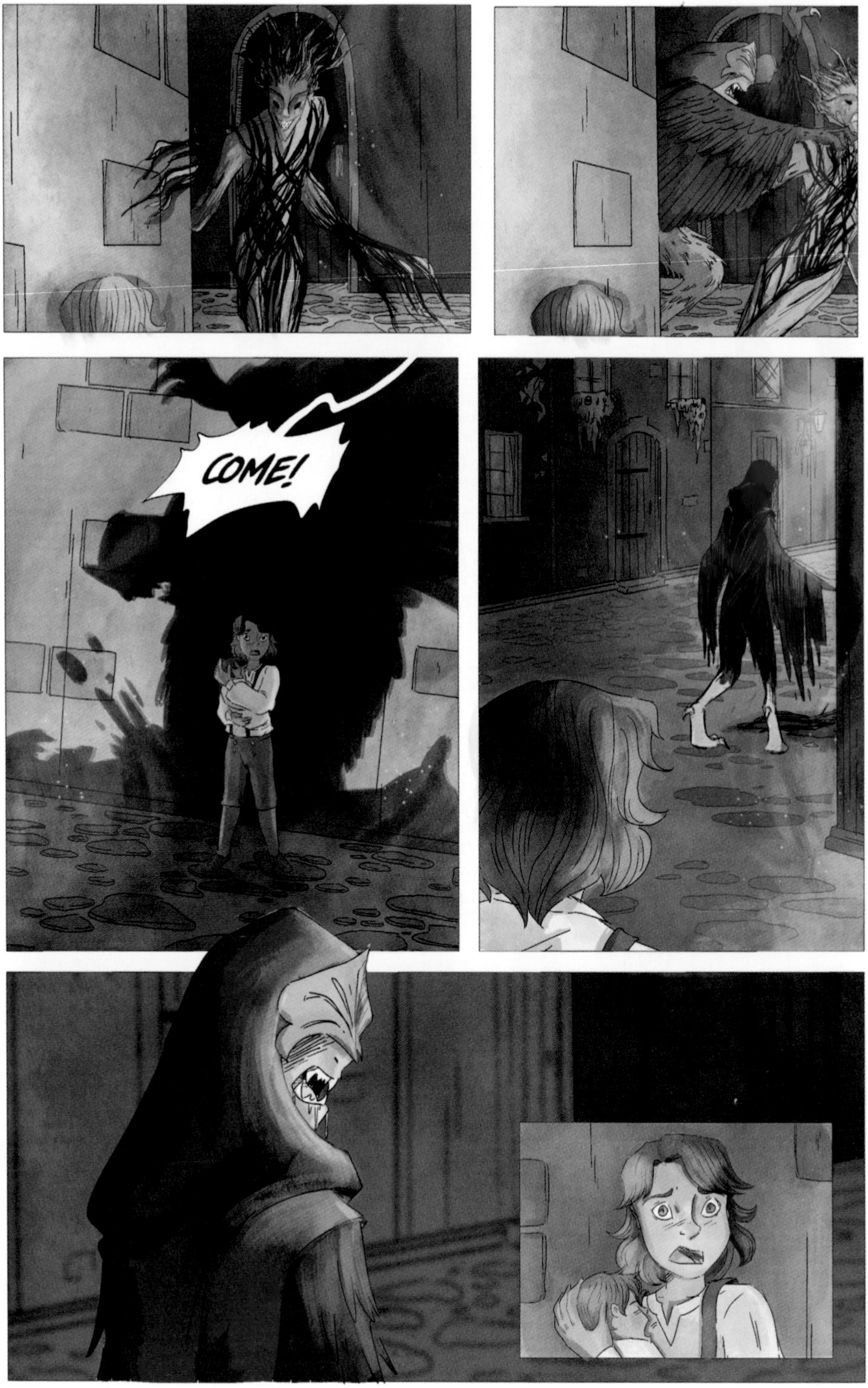
COME!

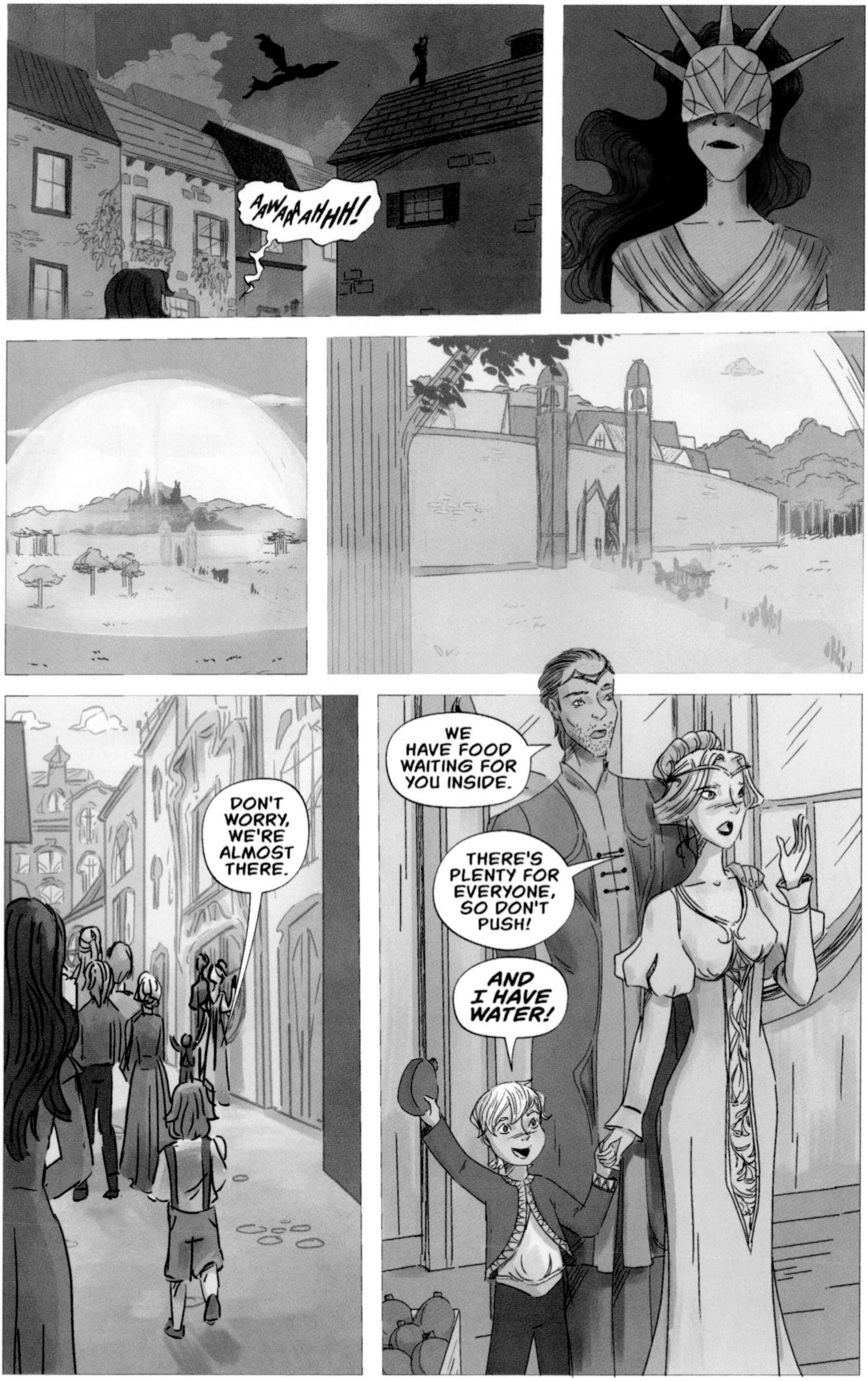
AWAAAAHHH!
DON'T WORRY, WE'RE ALMOST THERE.
WE HAVE FOOD WAITING FOR YOU INSIDE.
THERE'S PLENTY FOR EVERYONE, SO DON'T PUSH!
AND I HAVE WATER!

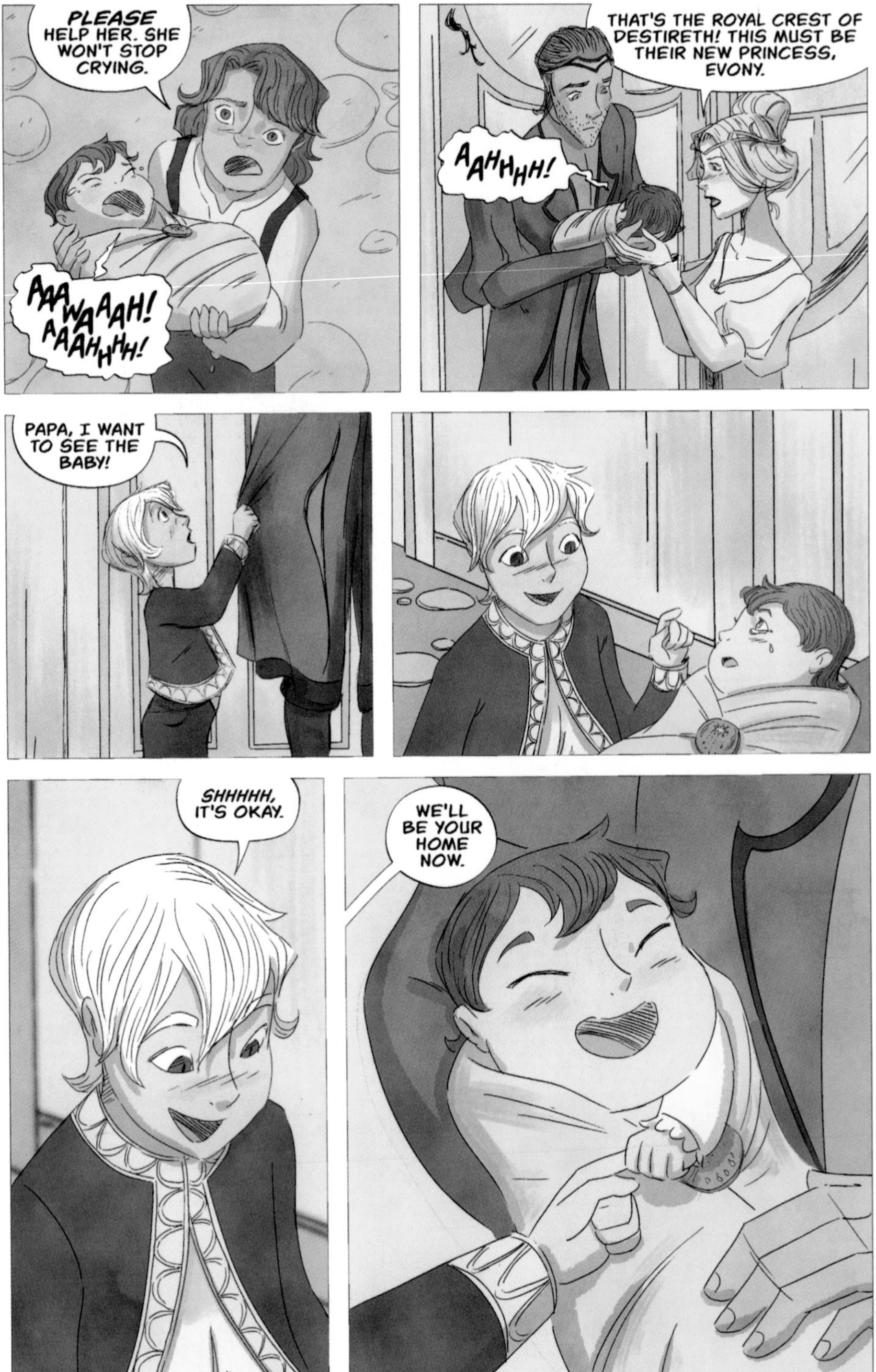
PLEASE HELP HER. SHE WON'T STOP CRYING.
AAAWAAAH! AAAHHHH!
THAT'S THE ROYAL CREST OF DESTIRETH! THIS MUST BE THEIR NEW PRINCESS, EVONY.
AAHHHH!
PAPA, I WANT TO SEE THE BABY!
SHHHHH, IT'S OKAY.
WE'LL BE YOUR HOME NOW.

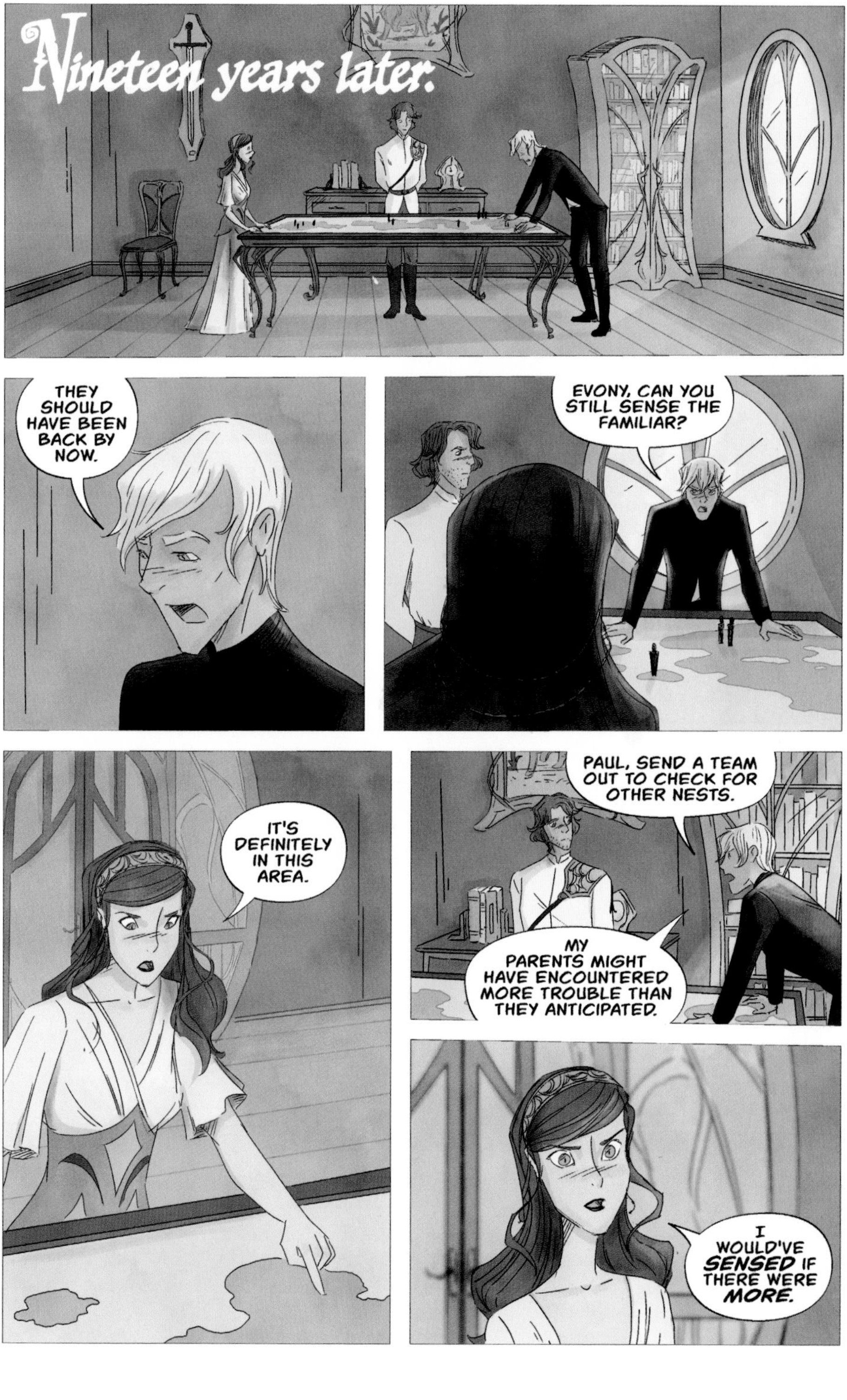
Nineteen years later.
THEY SHOULD HAVE BEEN BACK BY NOW.
EVONY, CAN YOU STILL SENSE THE FAMILIAR?
IT'S DEFINITELY IN THIS AREA.
PAUL, SEND A TEAM OUT TO CHECK FOR OTHER NESTS.
MY PARENTS MIGHT HAVE ENCOUNTERED MORE TROUBLE THAN THEY ANTICIPATED.
I WOULD'VE SENSED IF THERE WERE MORE.

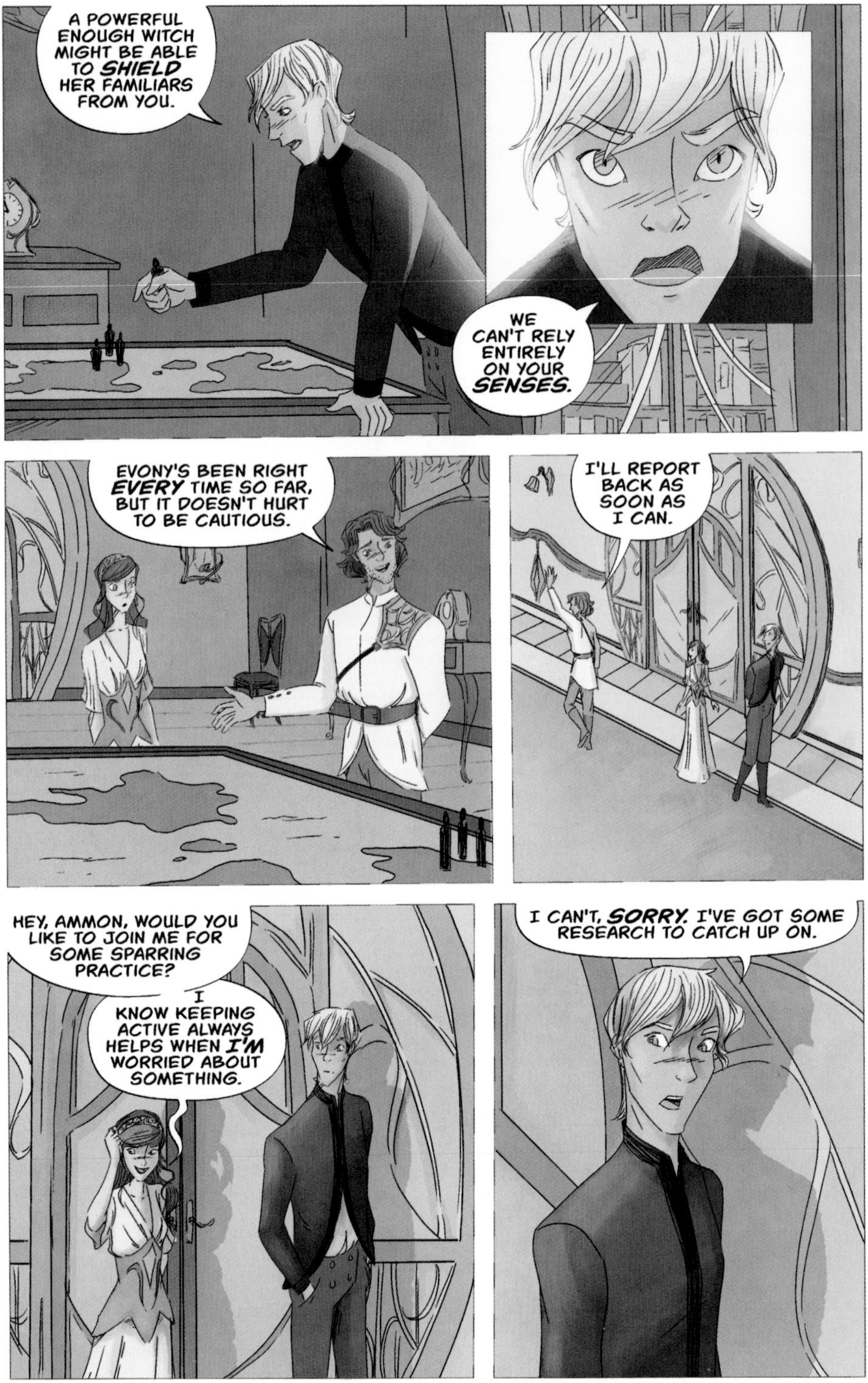
A POWERFUL ENOUGH WITCH MIGHT BE ABLE TO SHIELD HER FAMILIARS FROM YOU.
WE CAN'T RELY ENTIRELY ON YOUR SENSES.
EVONY'S BEEN RIGHT EVERY TIME SO FAR, BUT IT DOESN'T HURT TO BE CAUTIOUS.
I'LL REPORT BACK AS SOON AS I CAN.
HEY, AMMON, WOULD YOU LIKE TO JOIN ME FOR SOME SPARRING PRACTICE?
I KNOW KEEPING ACTIVE ALWAYS HELPS WHEN I'M WORRIED ABOUT SOMETHING.
I CAN'T, SORRY. I'VE GOT SOME RESEARCH TO CATCH UP ON.

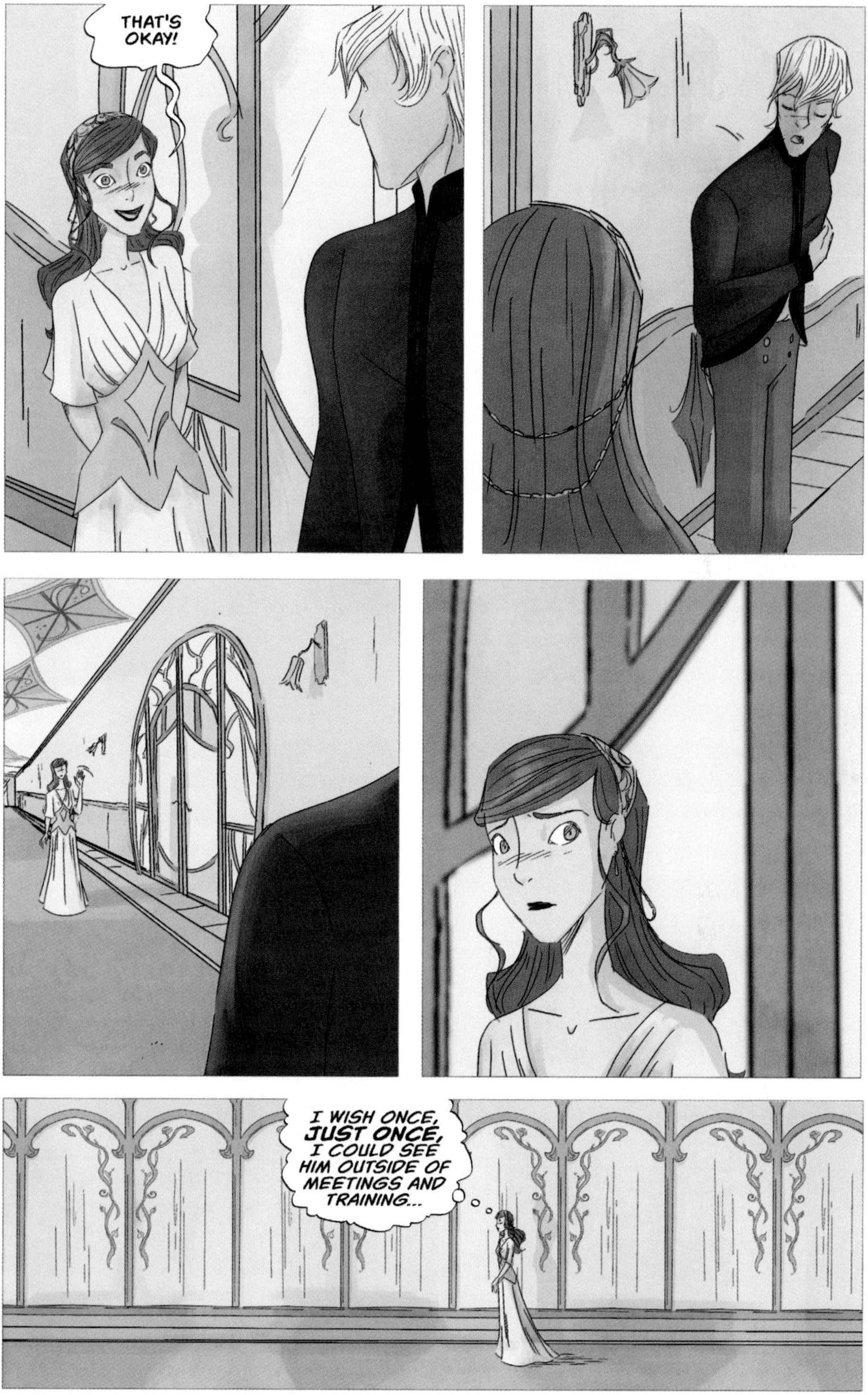
THAT'S OKAY!
I WISH ONCE, JUST ONCE, I COULD SEE HIM OUTSIDE OF MEETINGS AND TRAINING...

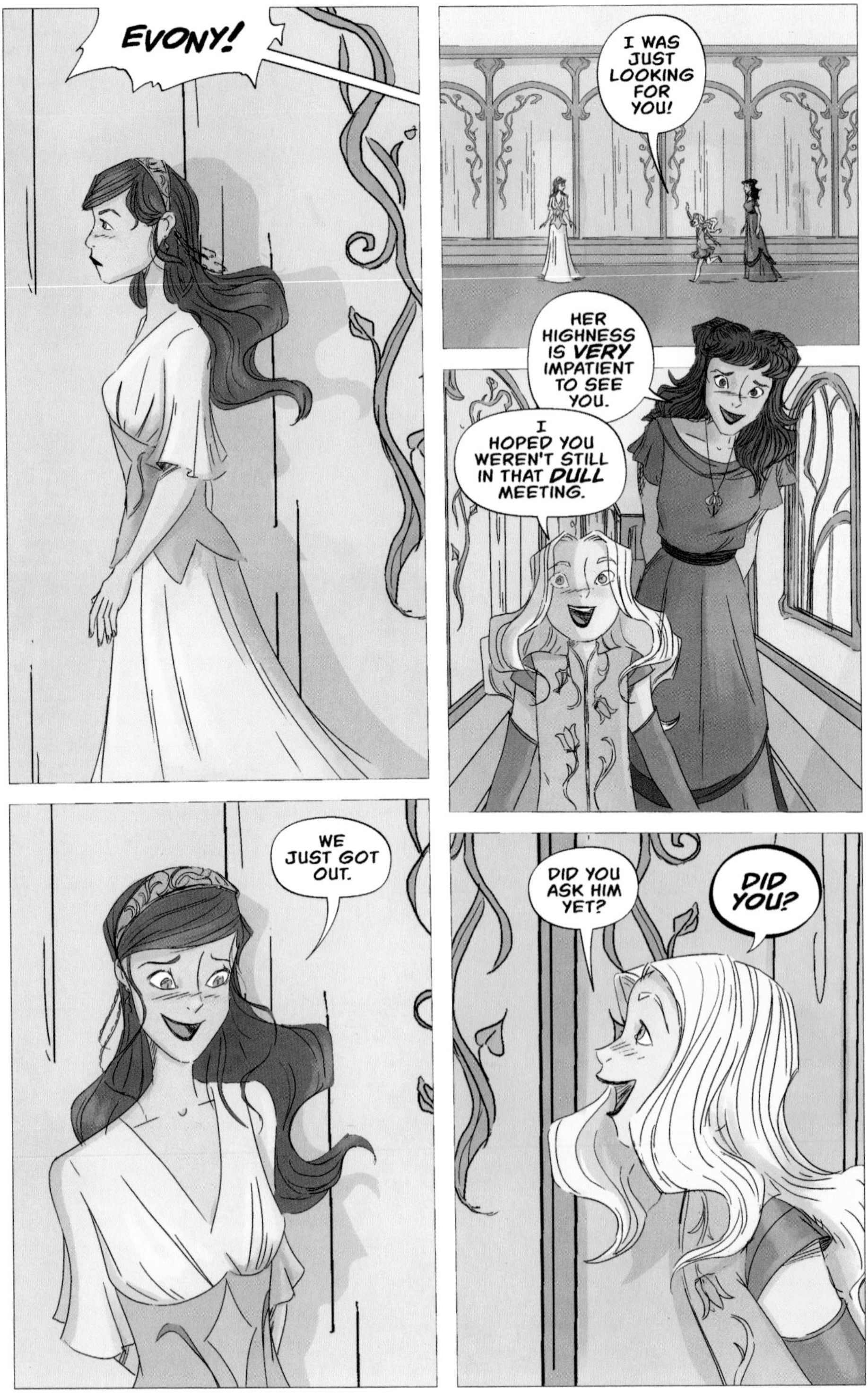
EVONY!
I WAS JUST LOOKING FOR YOU!
HER HIGHNESS IS VERY IMPATIENT TO SEE YOU.
I HOPED YOU WEREN'T STILL IN THAT DULL MEETING.
WE JUST GOT OUT.
DID YOU ASK HIM YET?
DID YOU?

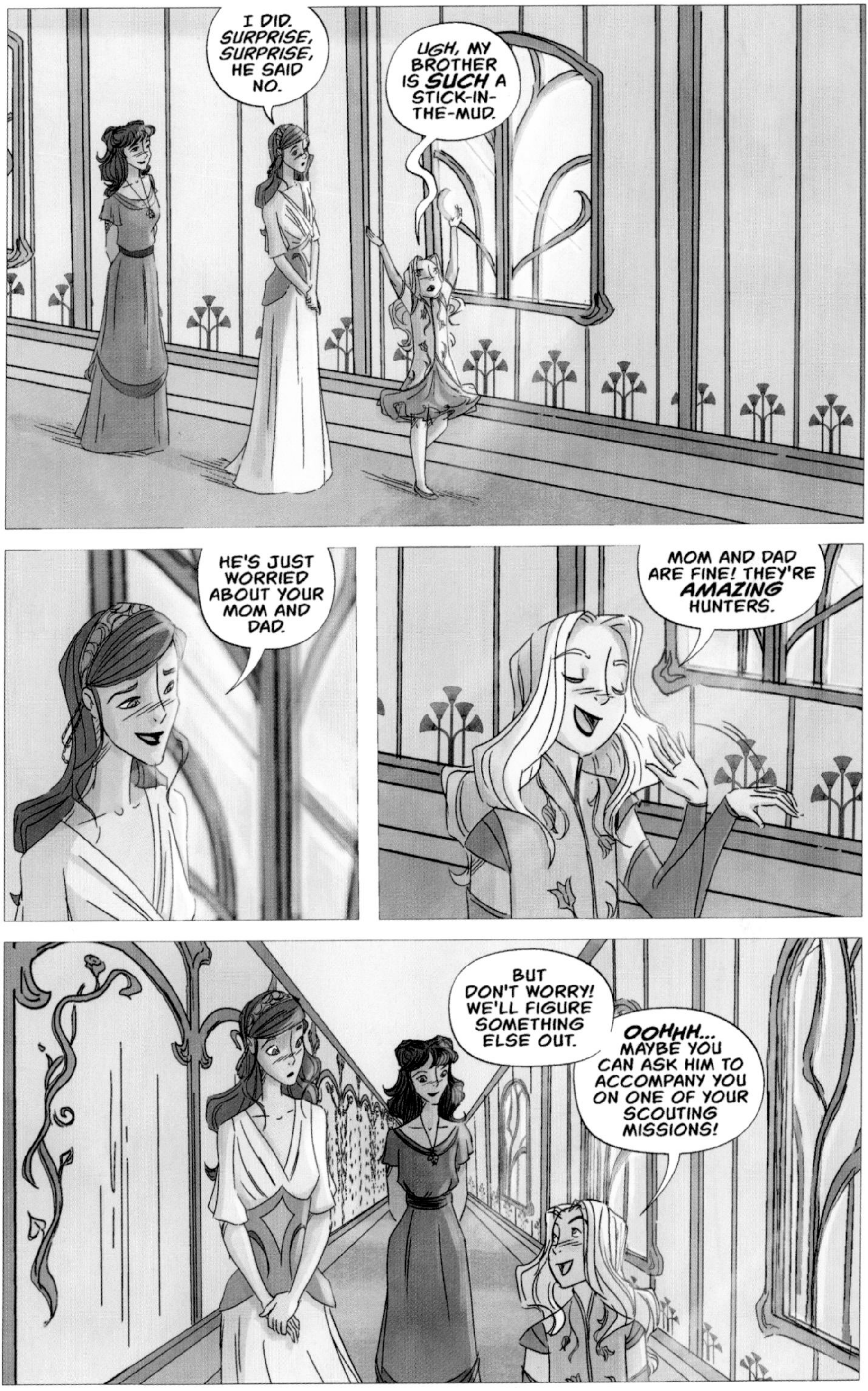
I DID. SURPRISE, SURPRISE, HE SAID NO.
UGH, MY BROTHER IS **SUCH** A STICK-IN-THE-MUD.
HE'S JUST WORRIED ABOUT YOUR MOM AND DAD.
MOM AND DAD ARE FINE! THEY'RE **AMAZING** HUNTERS.
BUT DON'T WORRY! WE'LL FIGURE SOMETHING ELSE OUT.
**OOHHH...** MAYBE YOU CAN ASK HIM TO ACCOMPANY YOU ON ONE OF YOUR SCOUTING MISSIONS!

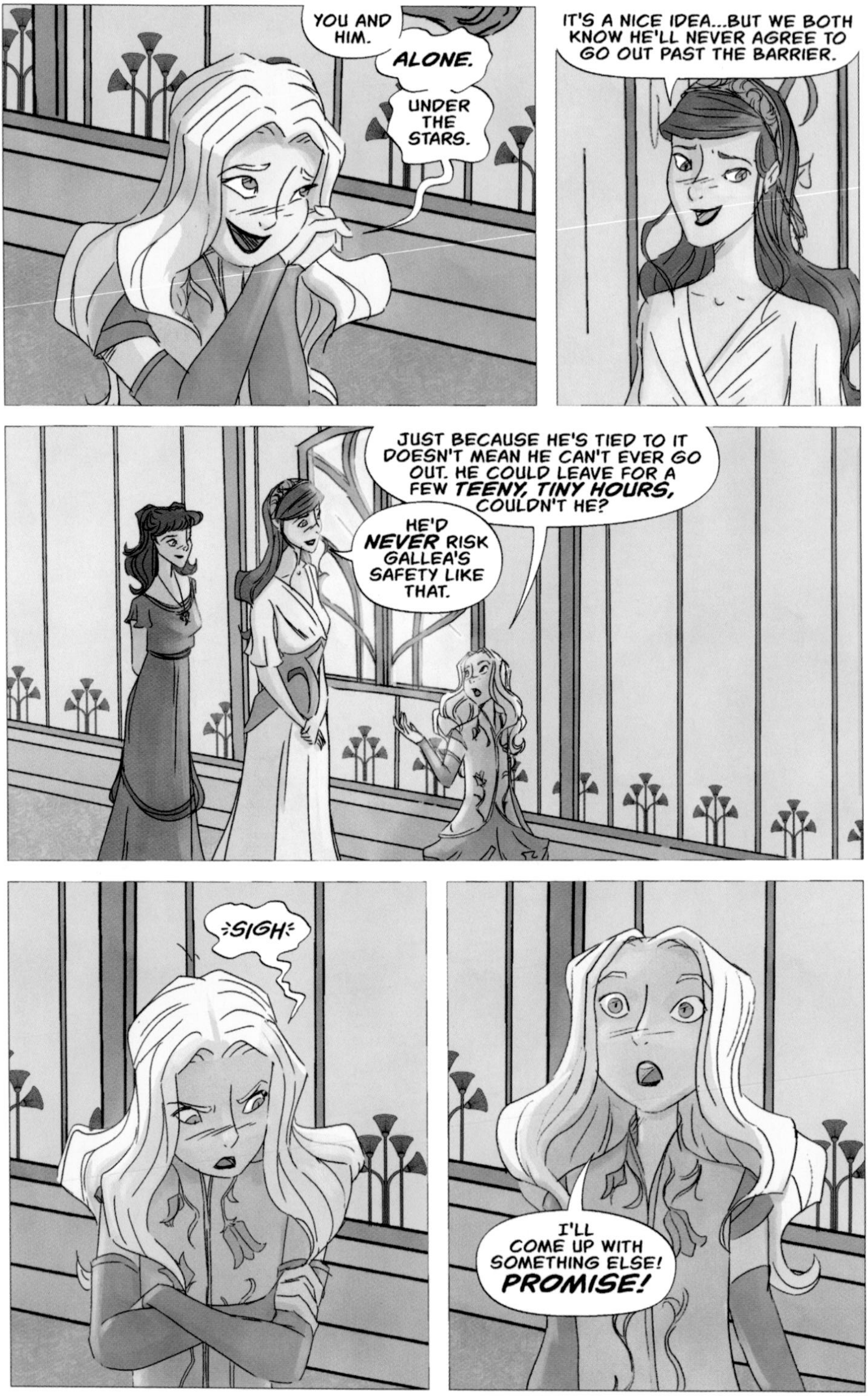
YOU AND HIM.
ALONE.
UNDER THE STARS.
IT'S A NICE IDEA...BUT WE BOTH KNOW HE'LL NEVER AGREE TO GO OUT PAST THE BARRIER.
JUST BECAUSE HE'S TIED TO IT DOESN'T MEAN HE CAN'T EVER GO OUT. HE COULD LEAVE FOR A FEW TEENY, TINY HOURS, COULDN'T HE?
HE'D NEVER RISK GALLEA'S SAFETY LIKE THAT.
SIGH
I'LL COME UP WITH SOMETHING ELSE! PROMISE!

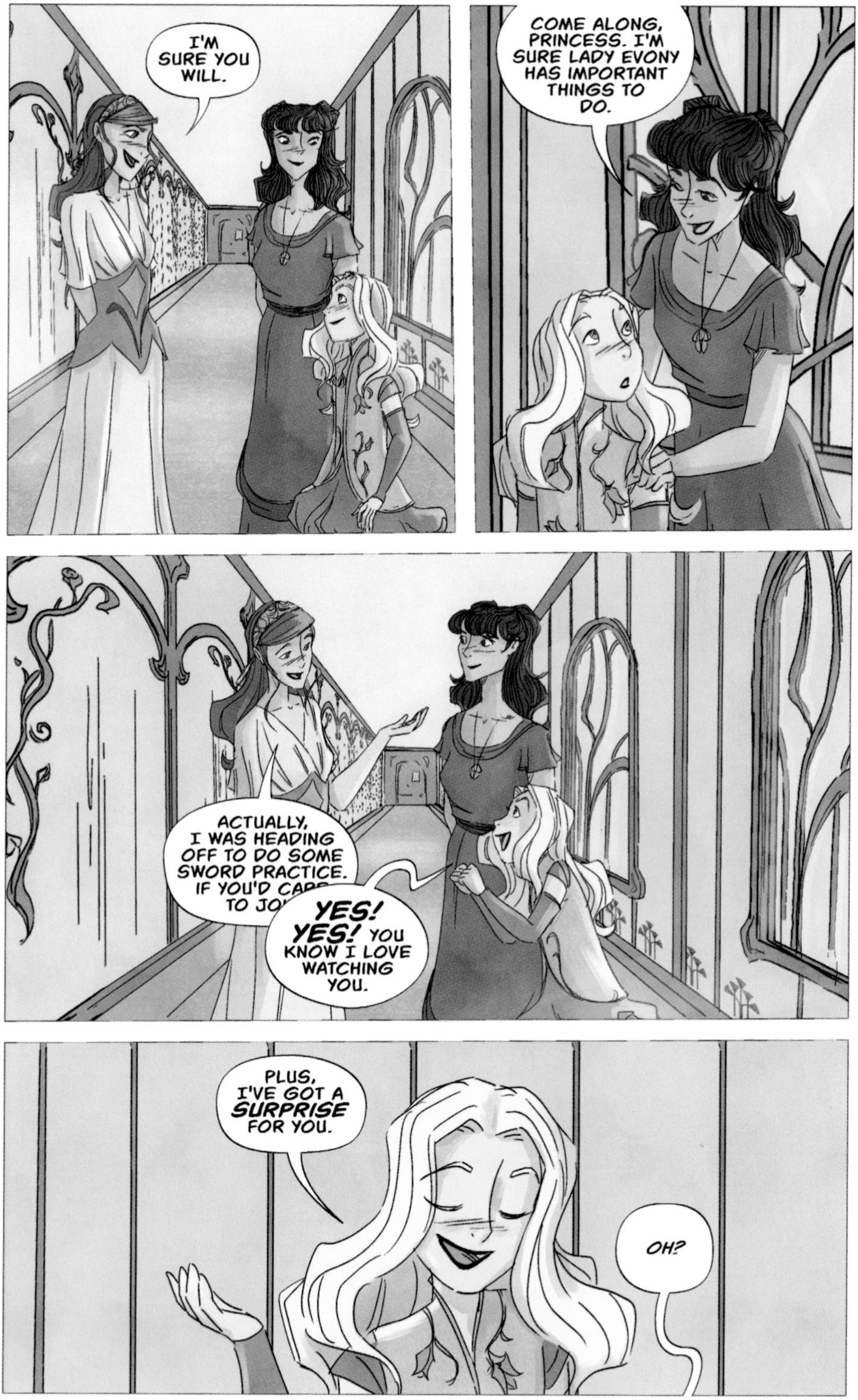
I'M SURE YOU WILL.
COME ALONG, PRINCESS. I'M SURE LADY EVONY HAS IMPORTANT THINGS TO DO.
ACTUALLY, I WAS HEADING OFF TO DO SOME SWORD PRACTICE. IF YOU'D CARE TO JOI
YES! YES! YOU KNOW I LOVE WATCHING YOU.
PLUS, I'VE GOT A SURPRISE FOR YOU.
OH?

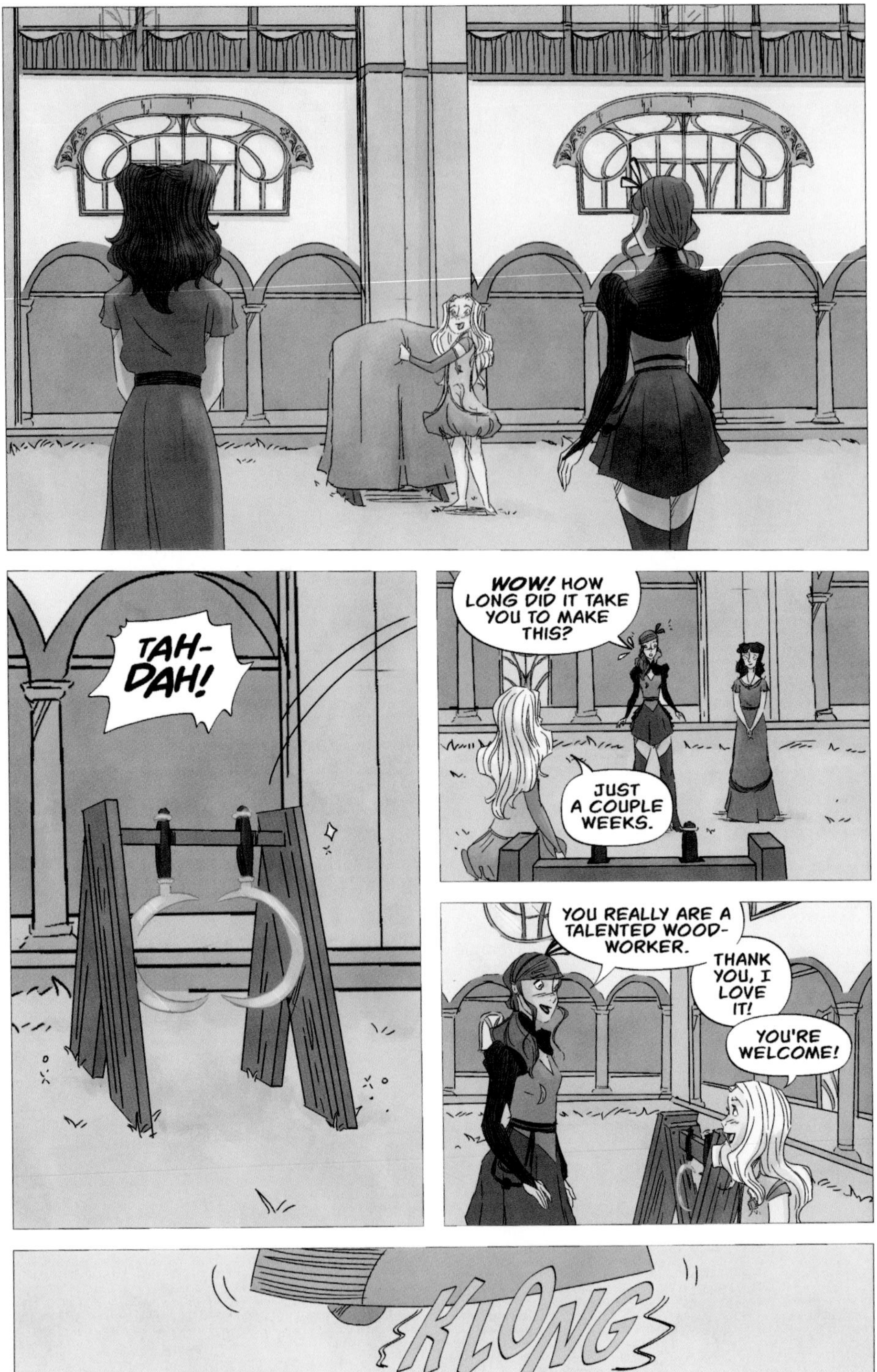
TAH-DAH!
WOW! HOW LONG DID IT TAKE YOU TO MAKE THIS?
JUST A COUPLE WEEKS.
YOU REALLY ARE A TALENTED WOOD-WORKER.
THANK YOU, I LOVE IT!
YOU'RE WELCOME!
KLONG

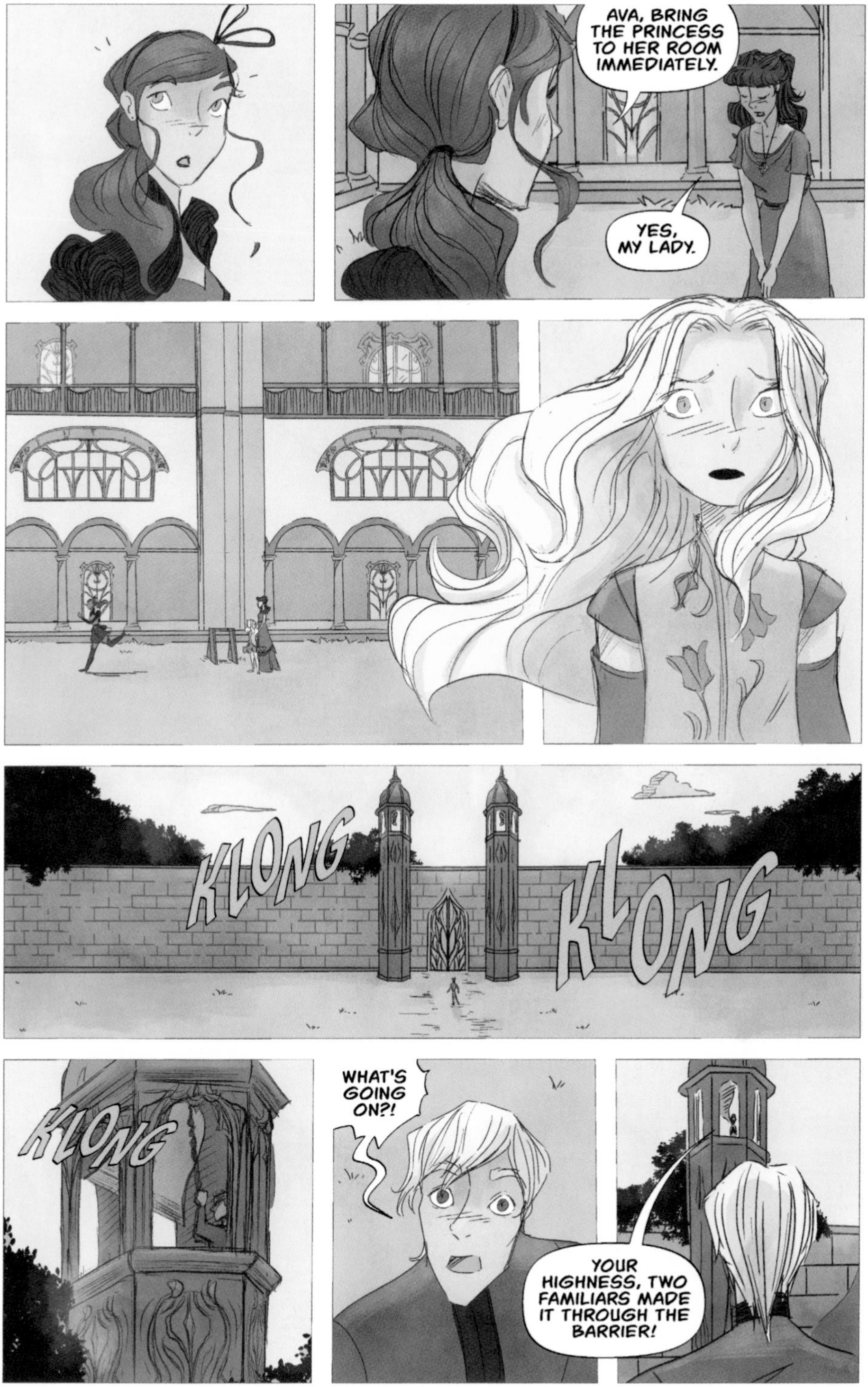
AVA, BRING THE PRINCESS TO HER ROOM IMMEDIATELY.
YES, MY LADY.
KLONG
KLONG
KLONG
WHAT'S GOING ON?!
YOUR HIGHNESS, TWO FAMILIARS MADE IT THROUGH THE BARRIER!

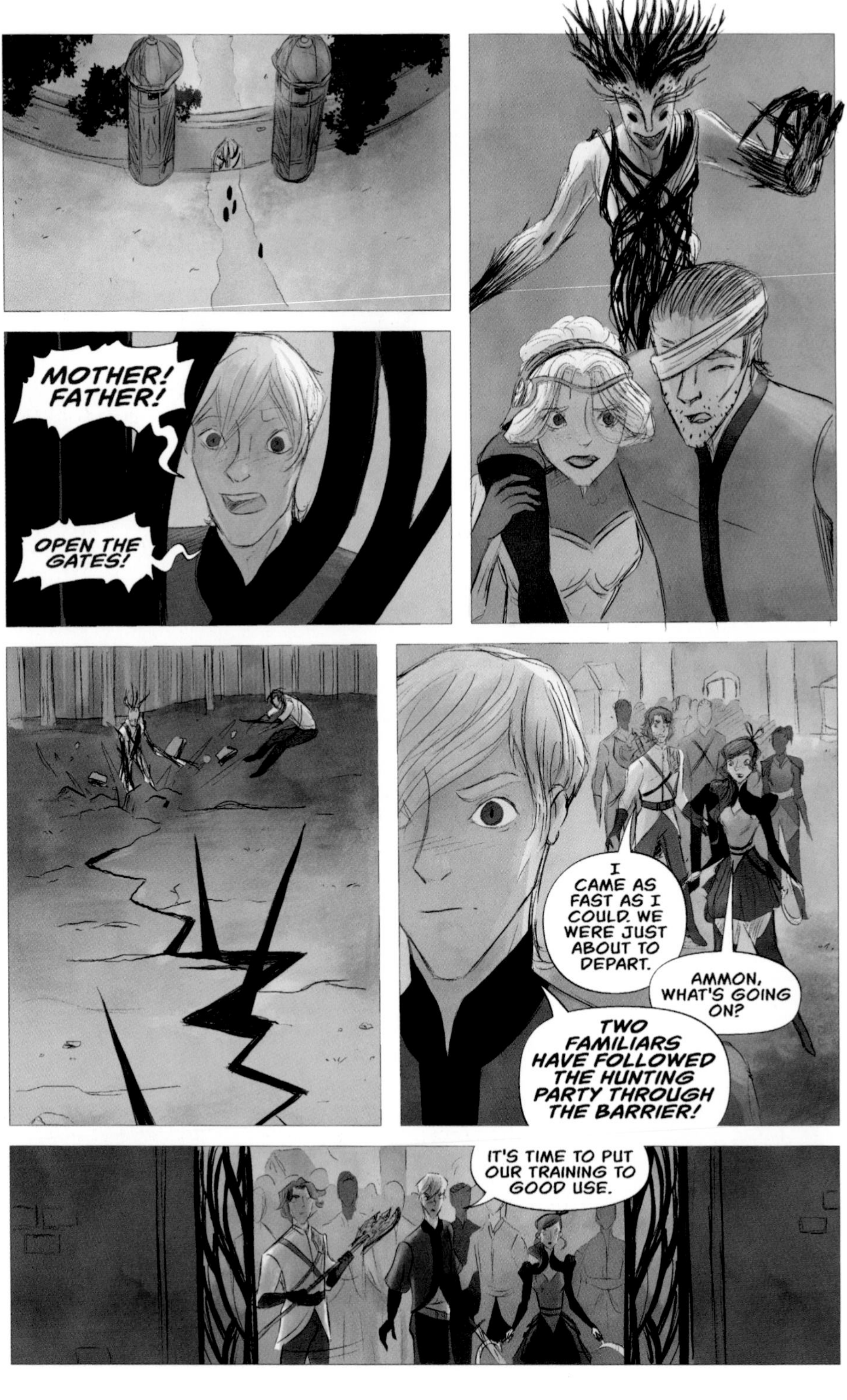
MOTHER! FATHER!
OPEN THE GATES!
I CAME AS FAST AS I COULD. WE WERE JUST ABOUT TO DEPART.
AMMON, WHAT'S GOING ON?
TWO FAMILIARS HAVE FOLLOWED THE HUNTING PARTY THROUGH THE BARRIER!
IT'S TIME TO PUT OUR TRAINING TO GOOD USE.

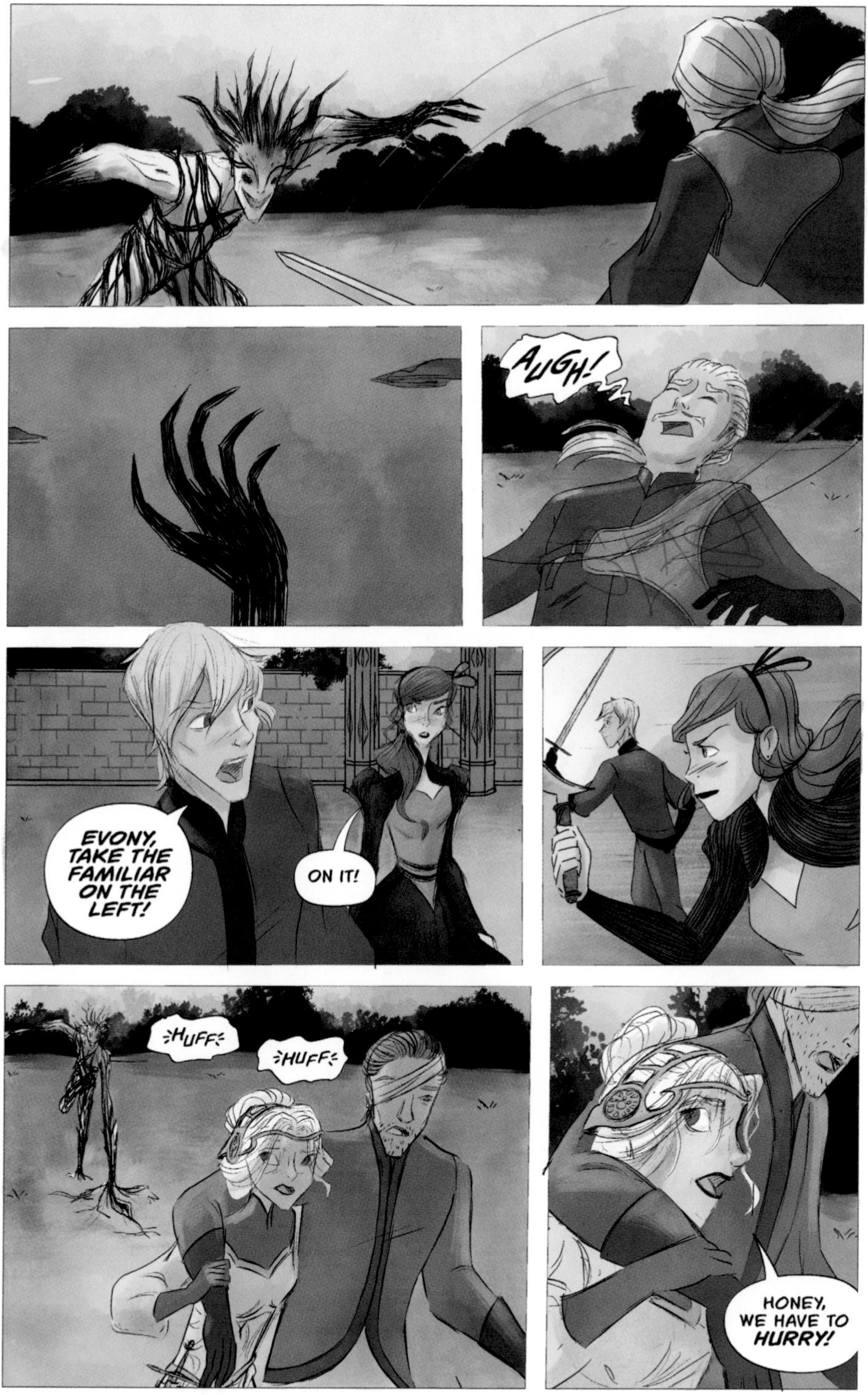
AUGH!
EVONY, TAKE THE FAMILIAR ON THE LEFT!
ON IT!
HUFF
HUFF
HONEY, WE HAVE TO HURRY!

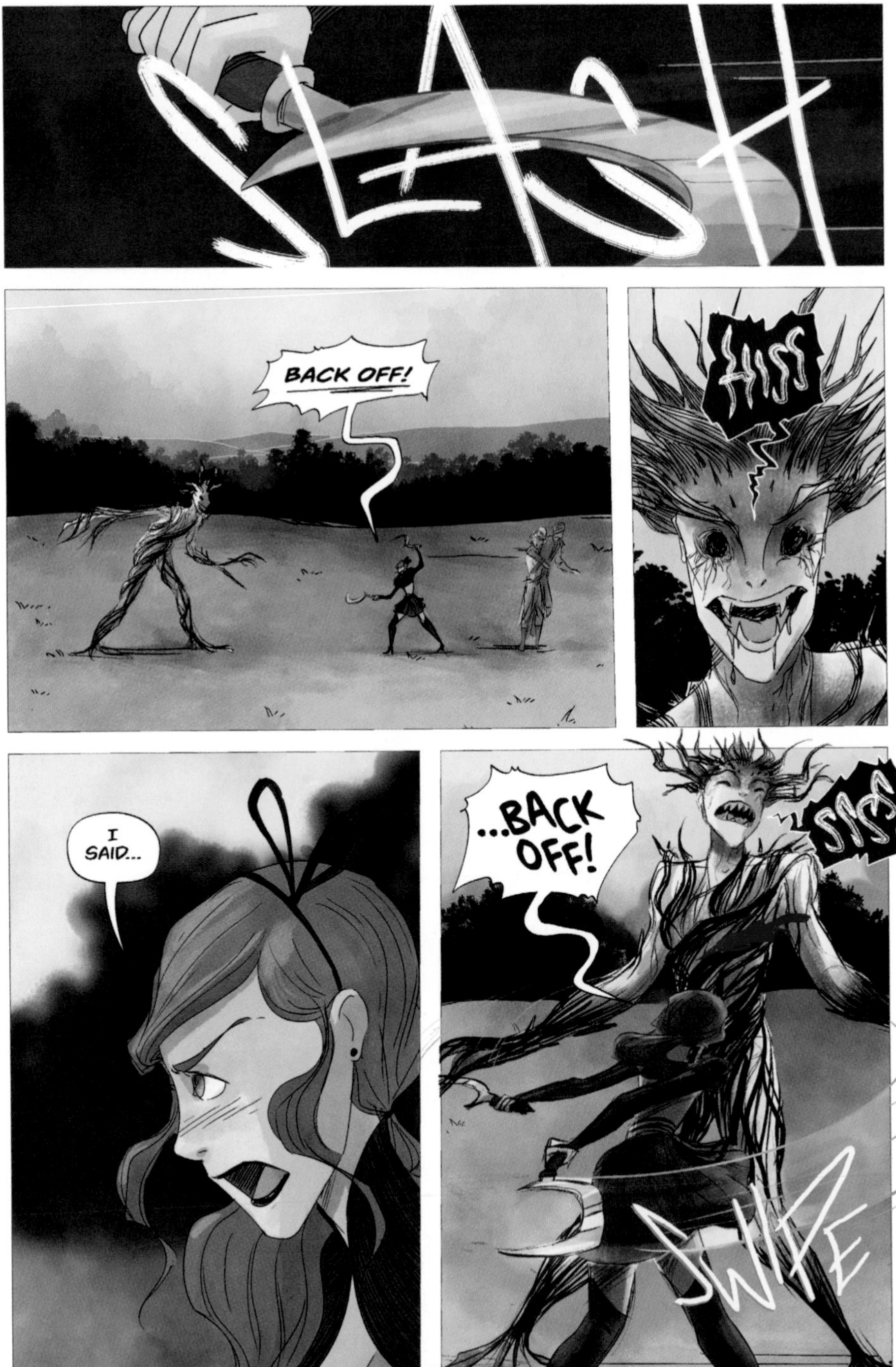
SLASH
BACK OFF!
HISS
I SAID...
...BACK OFF!
SISS
SWIPE

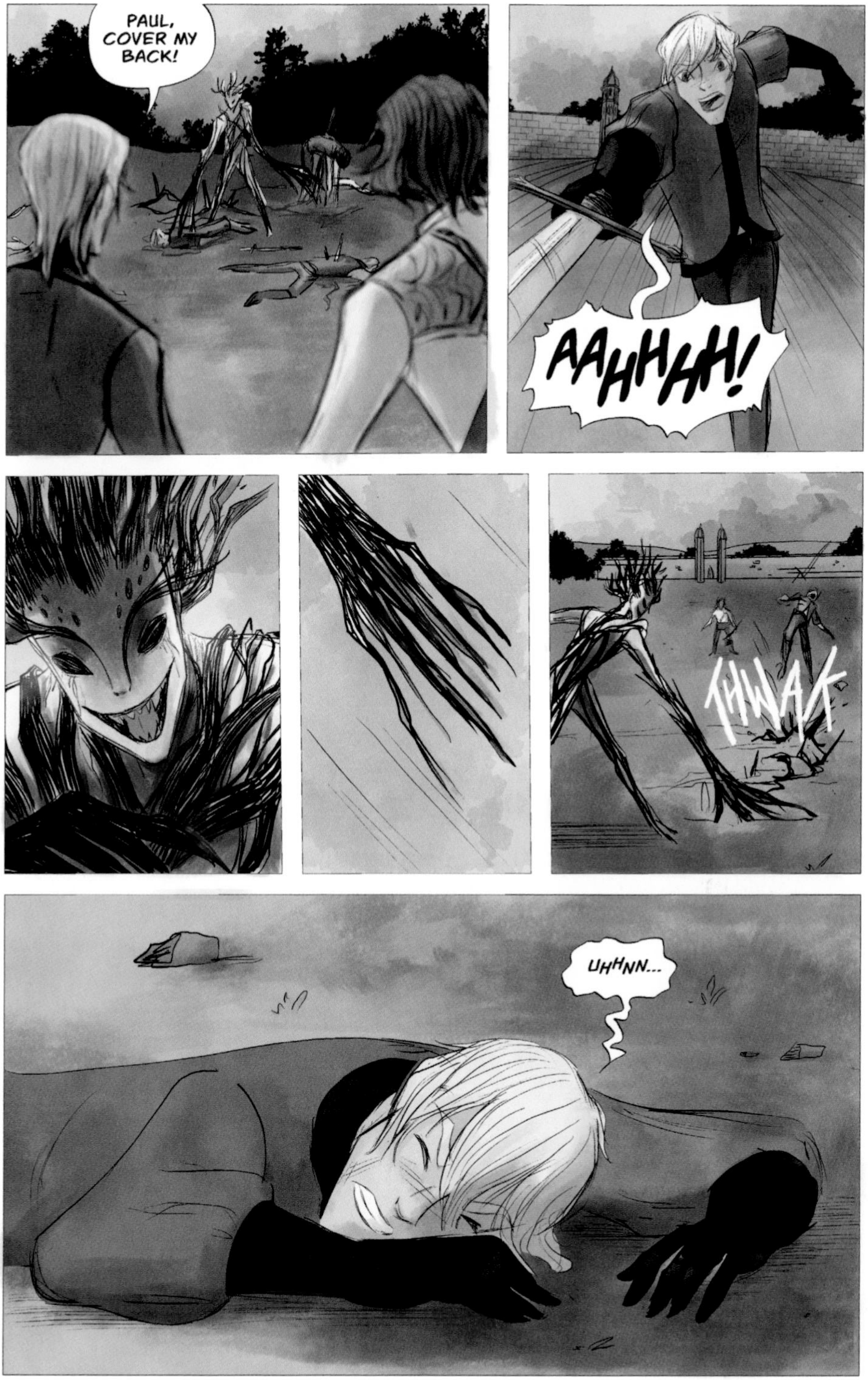
PAUL, COVER MY BACK!
AAHHHH!
THWAK
UHHNN...

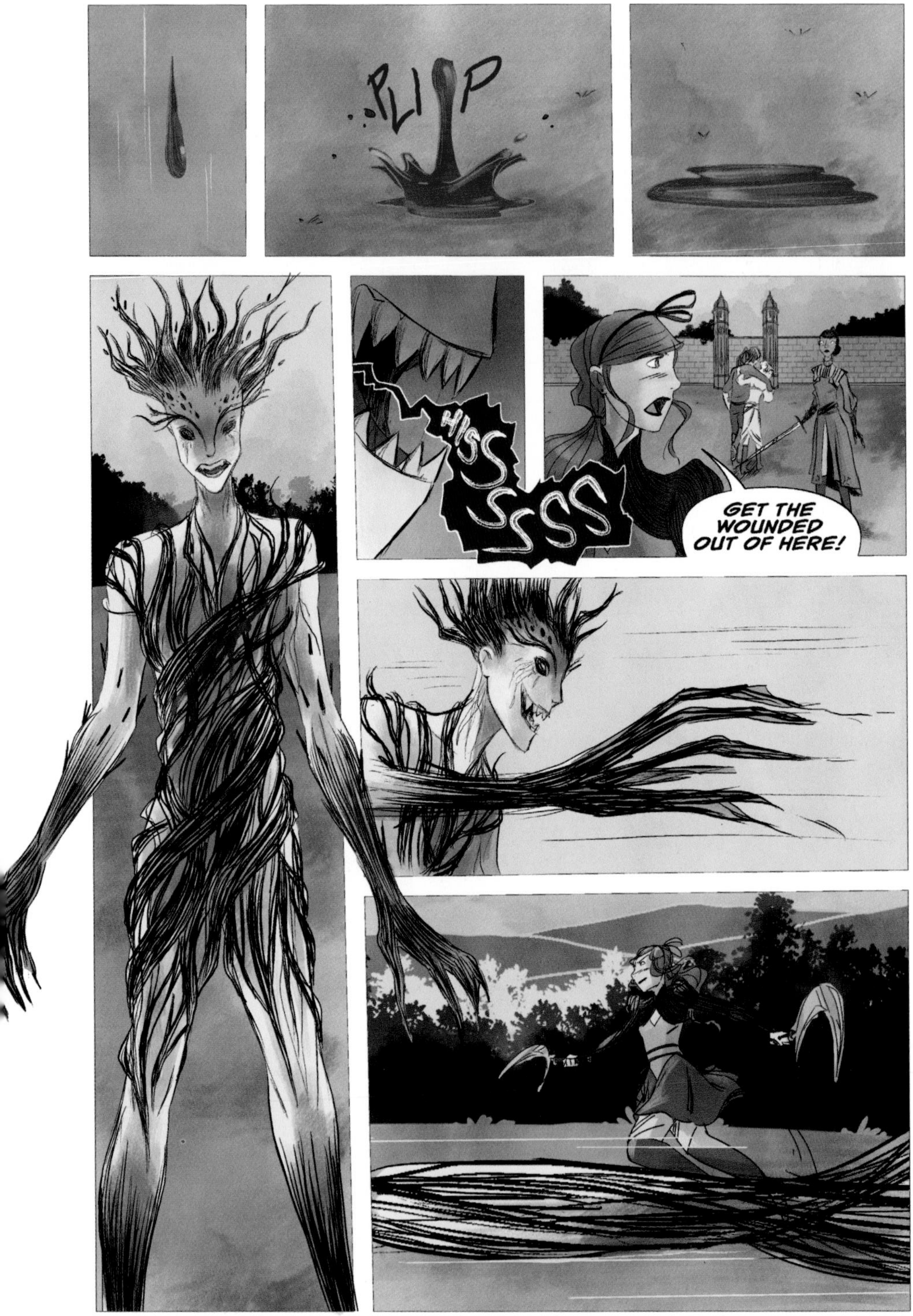
PLIP
HISSSSSS
GET THE WOUNDED OUT OF HERE!

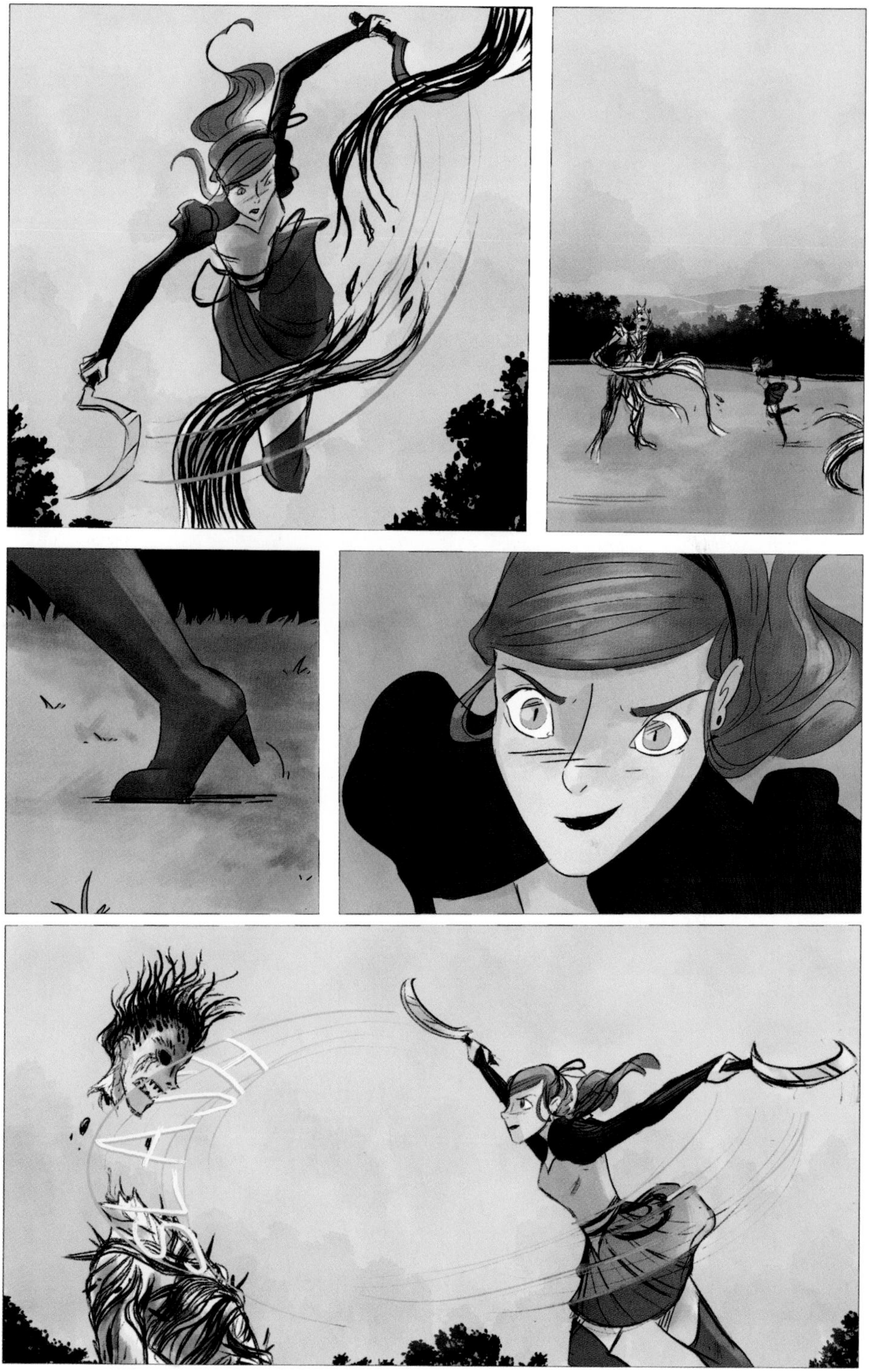
SLASH

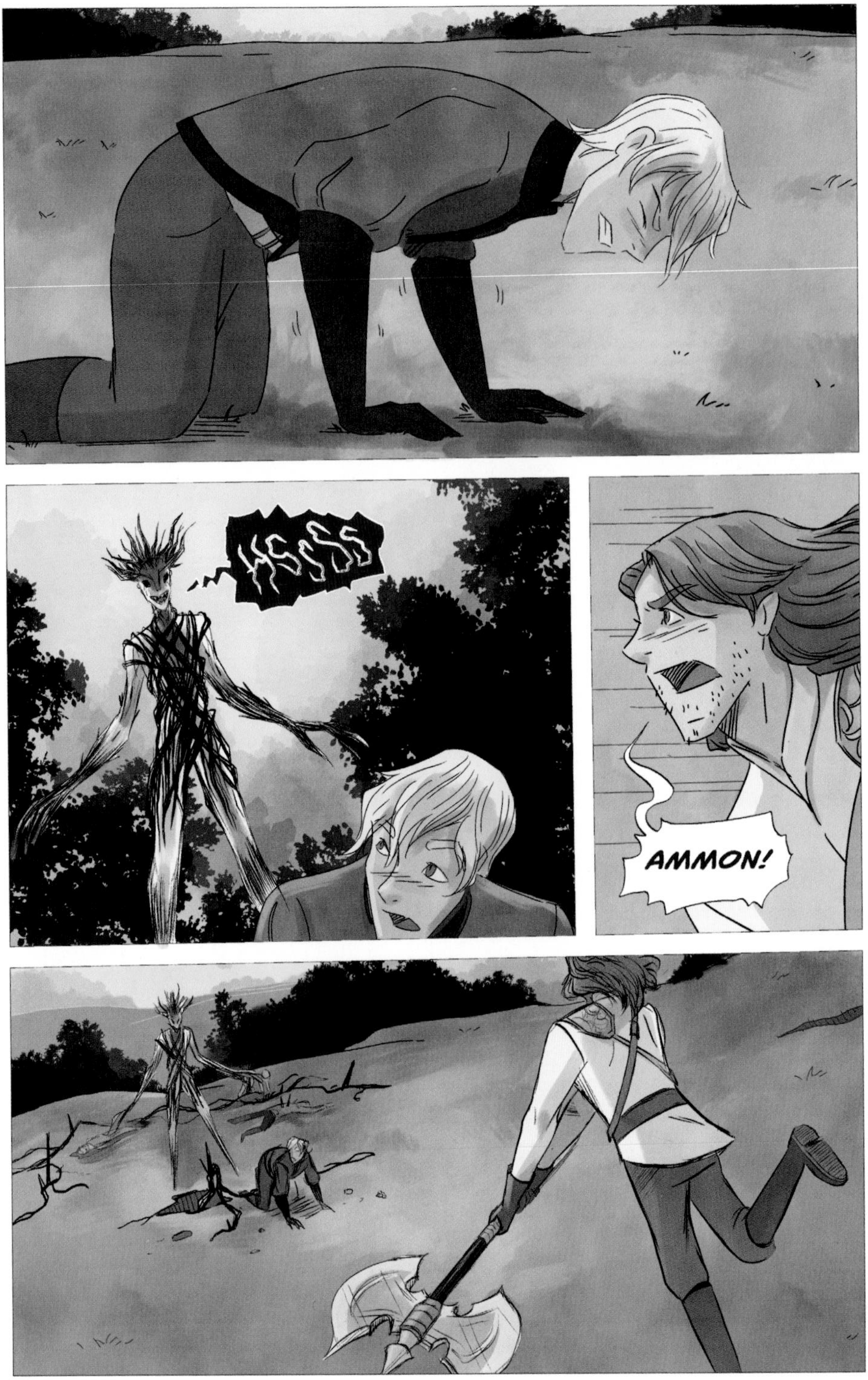
HSSSS
AMMON!

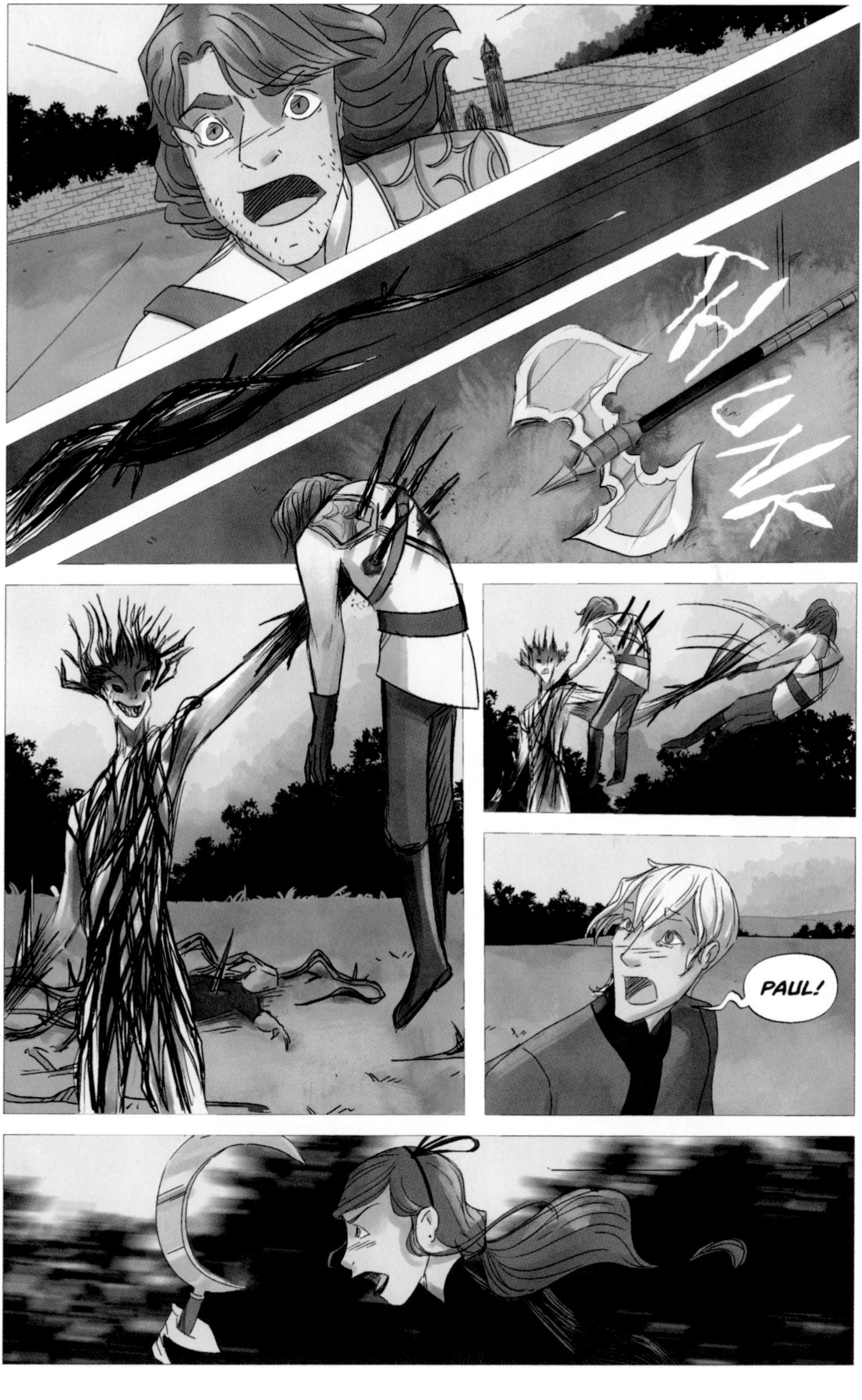
THUNK
PAUL!

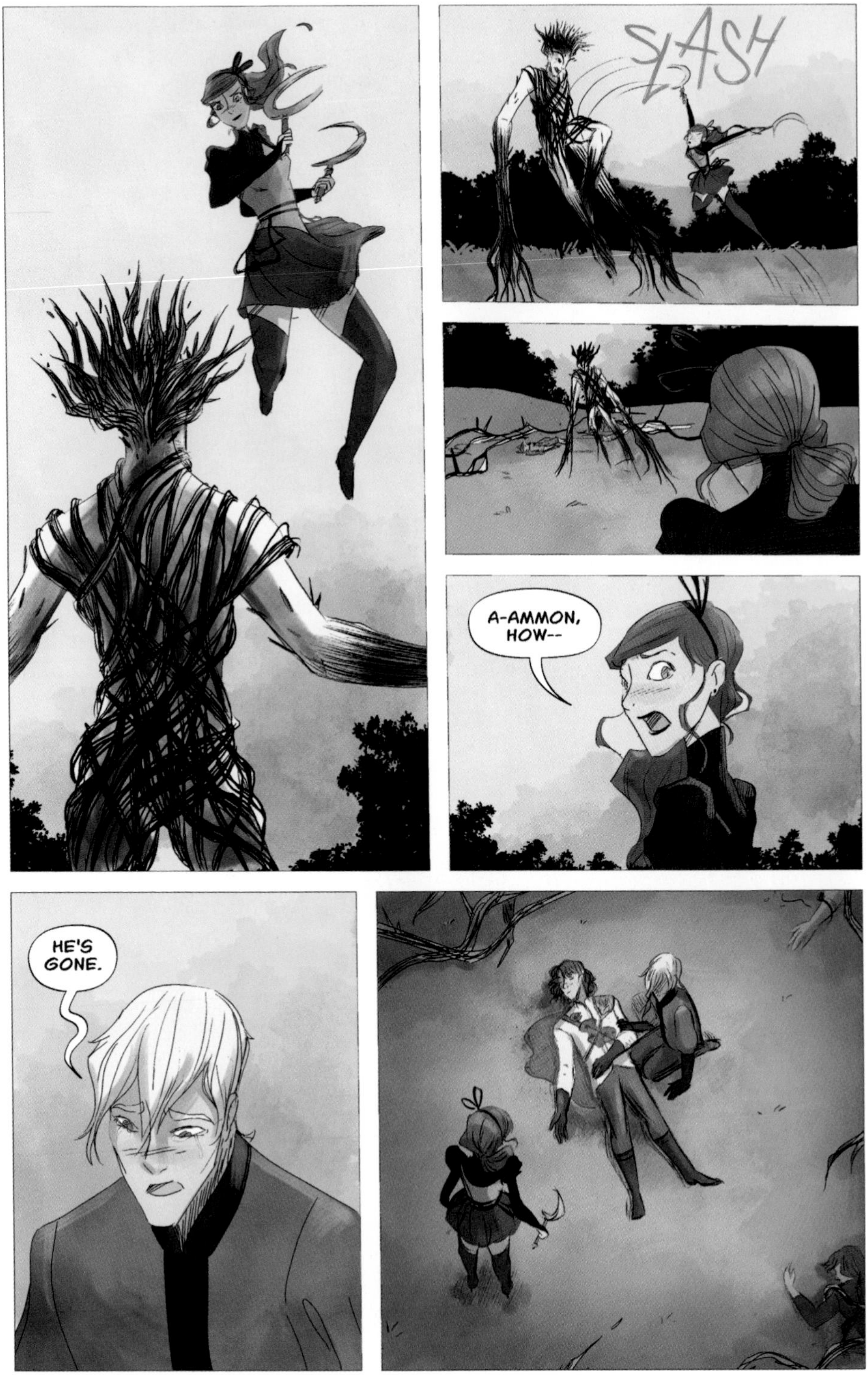
SLASH
A-AMMON, HOW--
HE'S GONE.

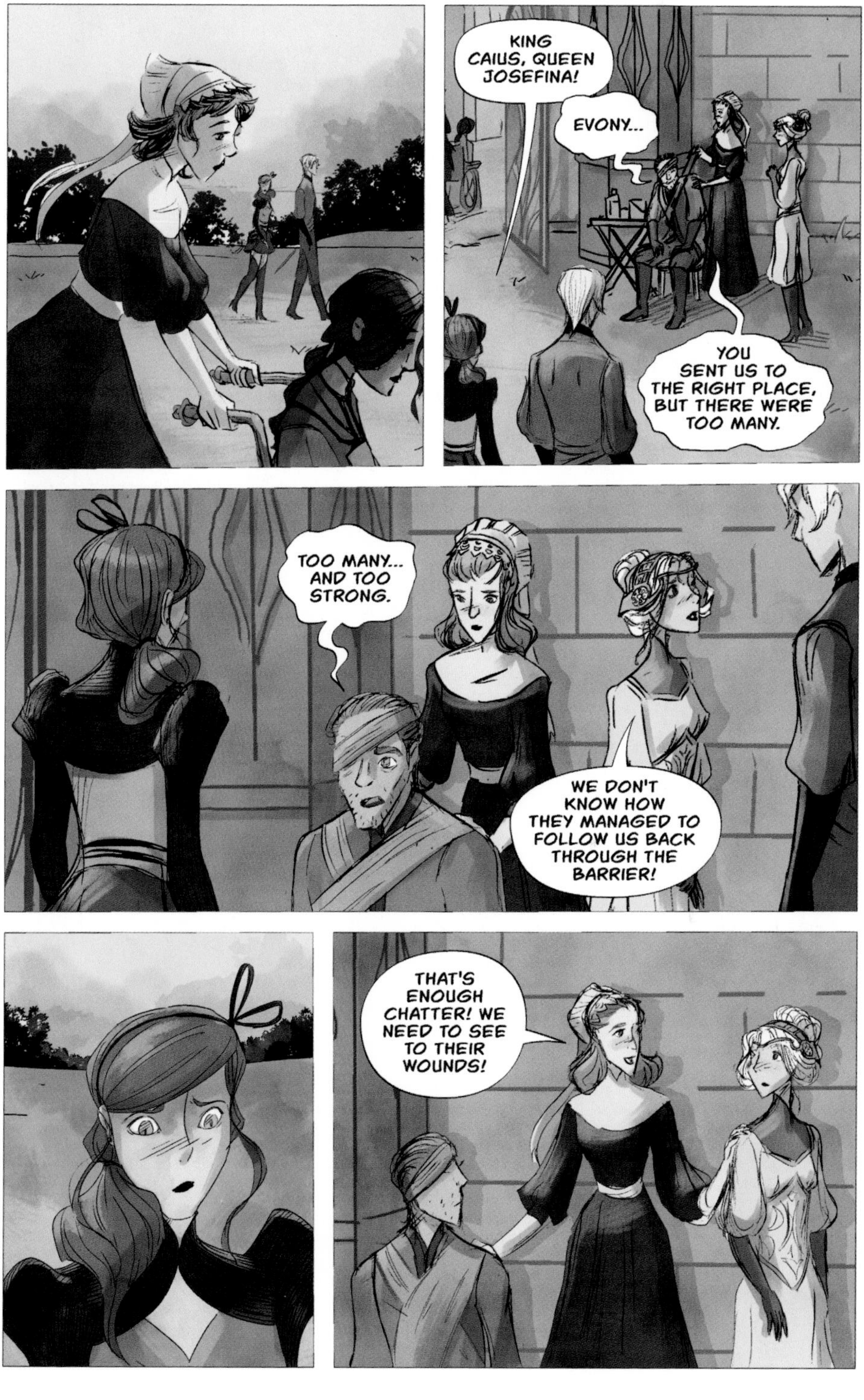
KING CAIUS, QUEEN JOSEFINA!
EVONY...
YOU SENT US TO THE RIGHT PLACE, BUT THERE WERE TOO MANY.
TOO MANY... AND TOO STRONG.
WE DON'T KNOW HOW THEY MANAGED TO FOLLOW US BACK THROUGH THE BARRIER!
THAT'S ENOUGH CHATTER! WE NEED TO SEE TO THEIR WOUNDS!

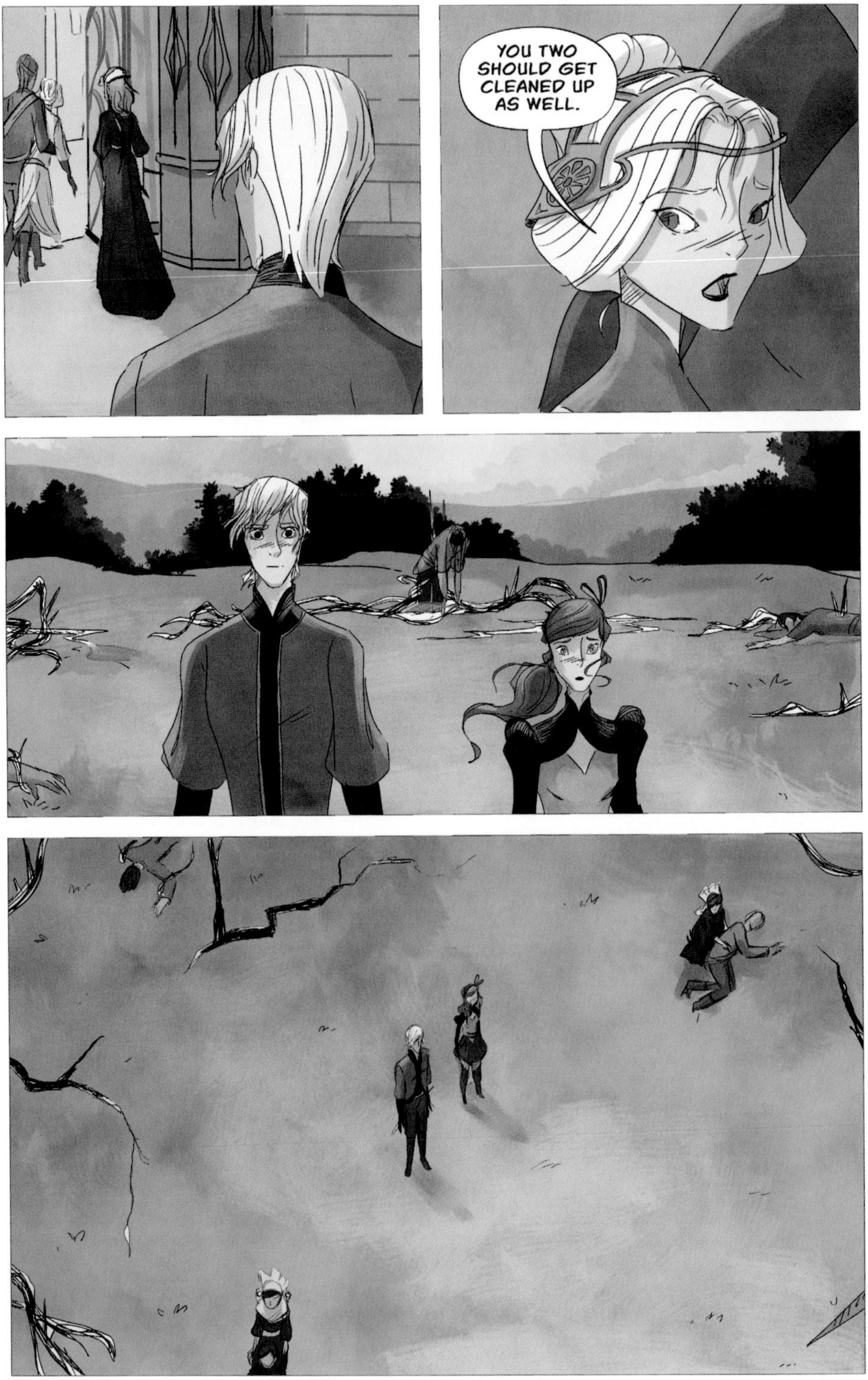
YOU TWO SHOULD GET CLEANED UP AS WELL.

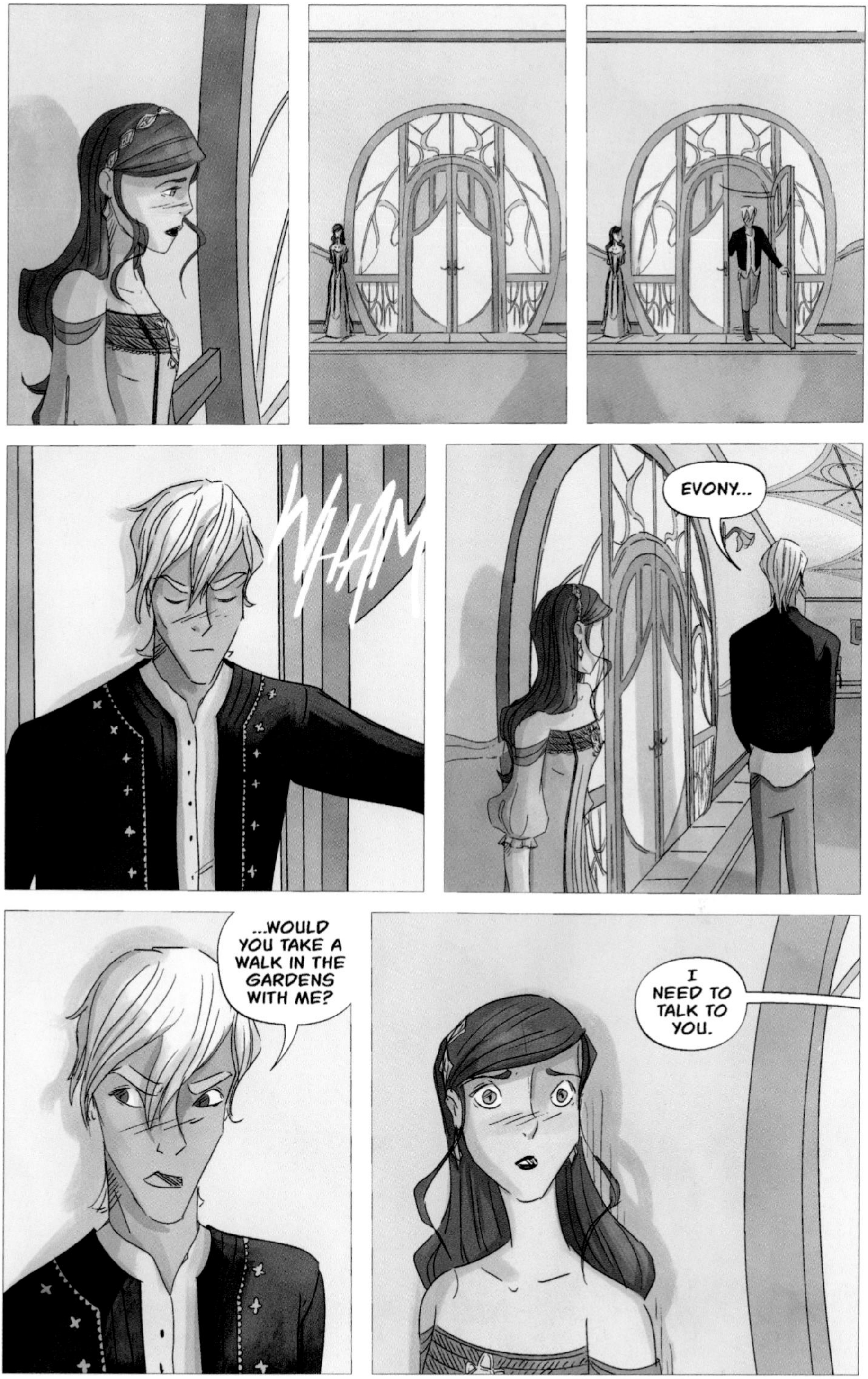
WHAM
EVONY...
...WOULD YOU TAKE A WALK IN THE GARDENS WITH ME?
I NEED TO TALK TO YOU.

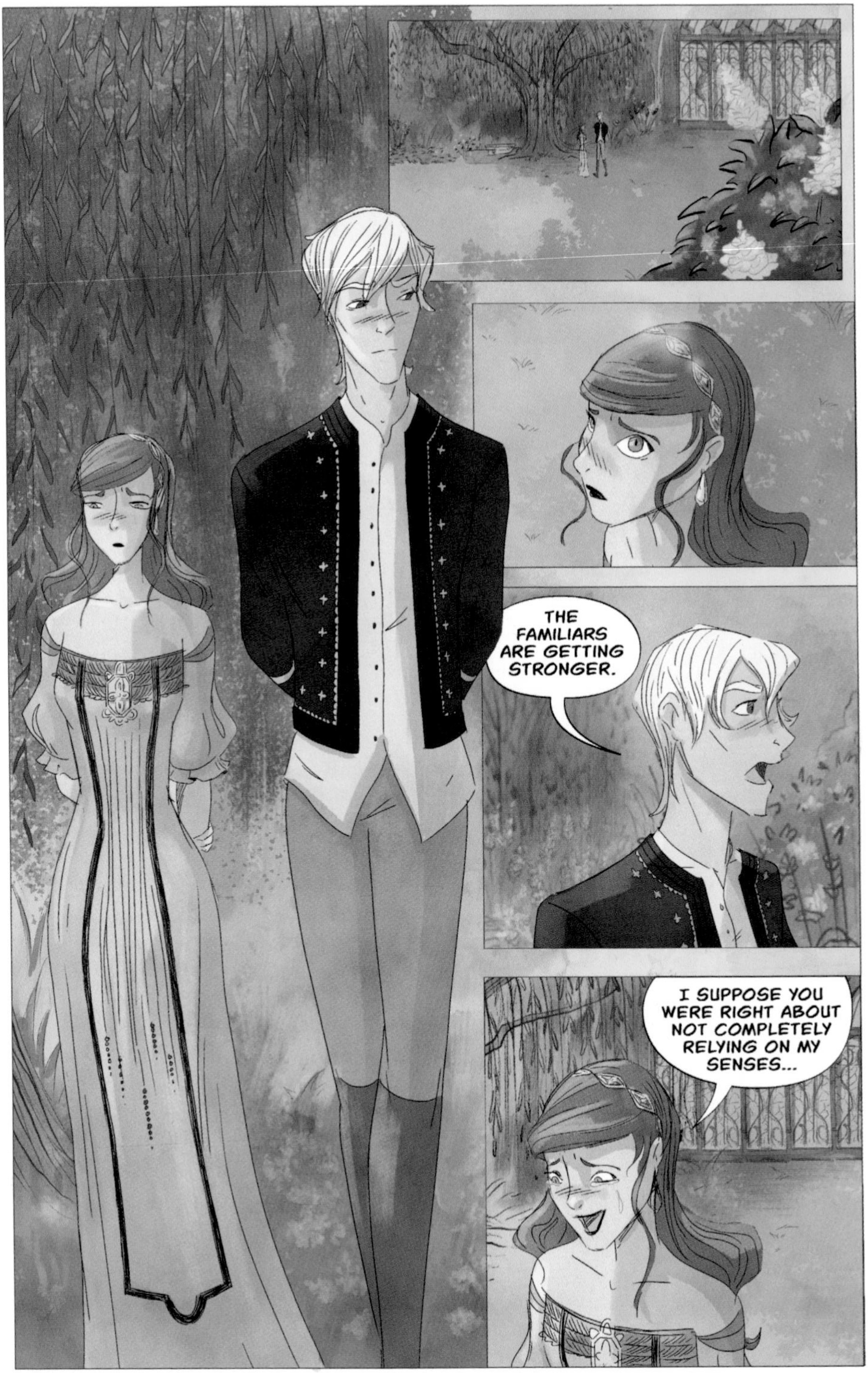
THE FAMILIARS ARE GETTING STRONGER.
I SUPPOSE YOU WERE RIGHT ABOUT NOT COMPLETELY RELYING ON MY SENSES...

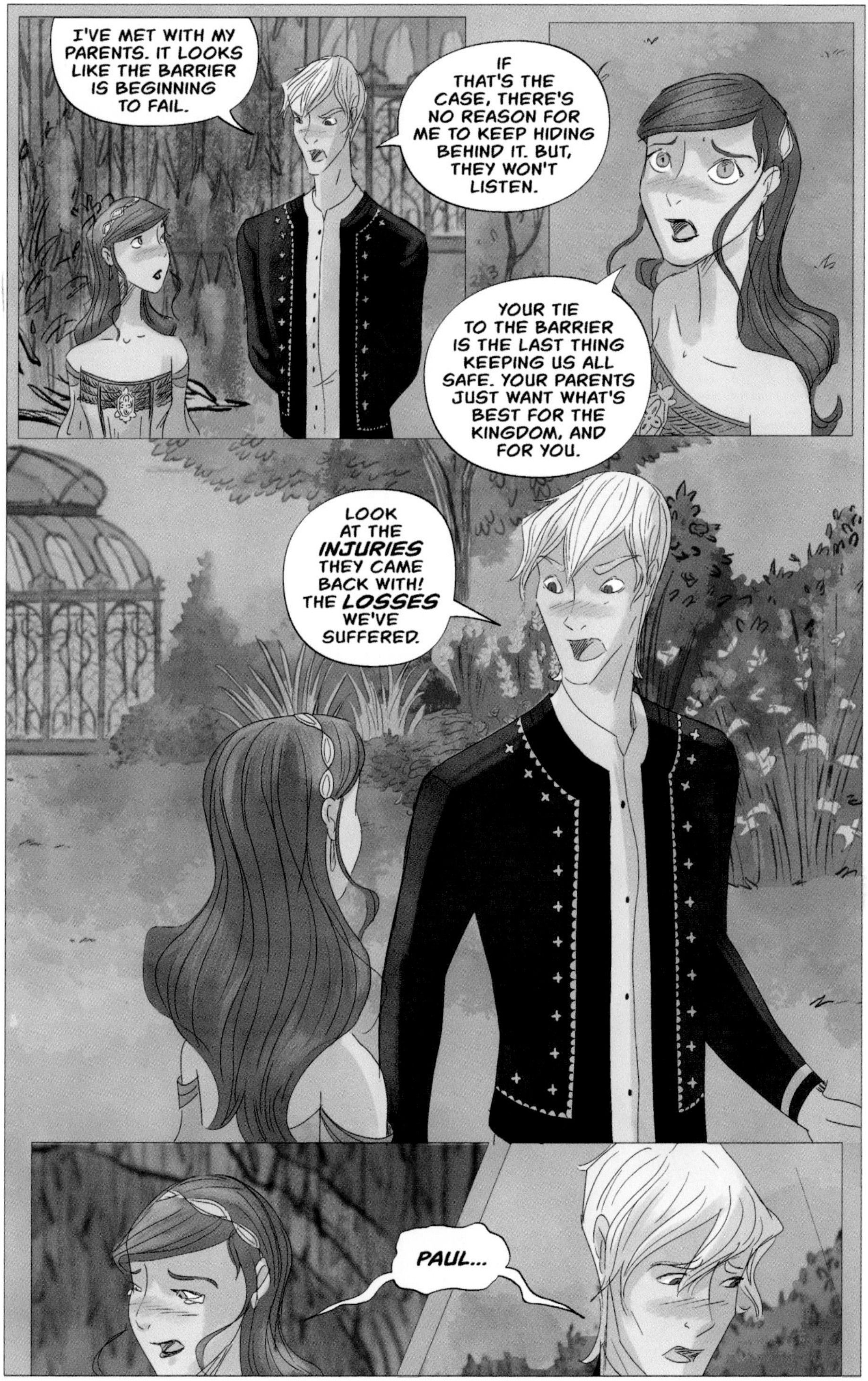
I'VE MET WITH MY PARENTS. IT LOOKS LIKE THE BARRIER IS BEGINNING TO FAIL.
IF THAT'S THE CASE, THERE'S NO REASON FOR ME TO KEEP HIDING BEHIND IT. BUT, THEY WON'T LISTEN.
YOUR TIE TO THE BARRIER IS THE LAST THING KEEPING US ALL SAFE. YOUR PARENTS JUST WANT WHAT'S BEST FOR THE KINGDOM, AND FOR YOU.
LOOK AT THE *INJURIES* THEY CAME BACK WITH! THE *LOSSES* WE'VE SUFFERED.
PAUL...

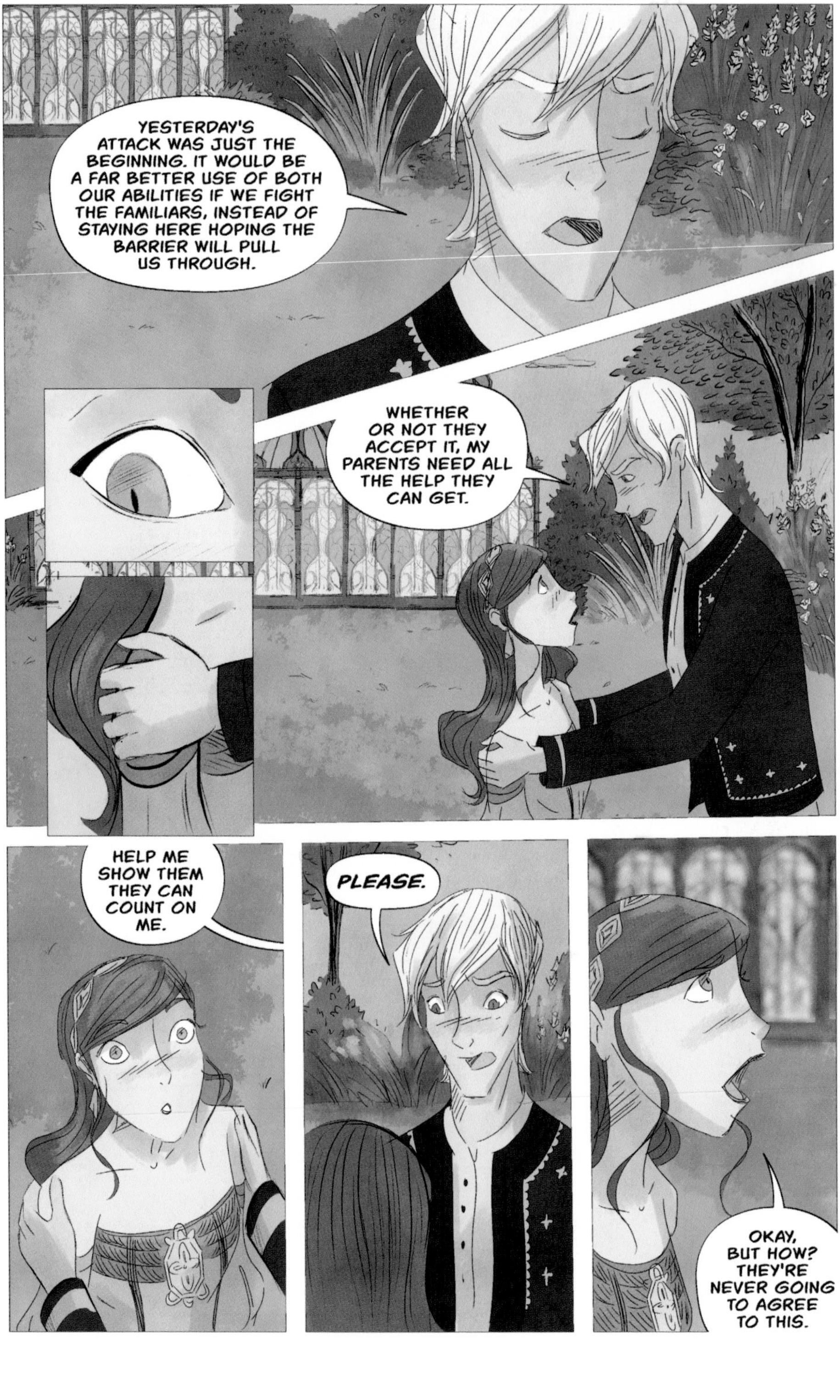
YESTERDAY'S ATTACK WAS JUST THE BEGINNING. IT WOULD BE A FAR BETTER USE OF BOTH OUR ABILITIES IF WE FIGHT THE FAMILIARS, INSTEAD OF STAYING HERE HOPING THE BARRIER WILL PULL US THROUGH.
WHETHER OR NOT THEY ACCEPT IT, MY PARENTS NEED ALL THE HELP THEY CAN GET.
HELP ME SHOW THEM THEY CAN COUNT ON ME.
PLEASE.
OKAY, BUT HOW? THEY'RE NEVER GOING TO AGREE TO THIS.

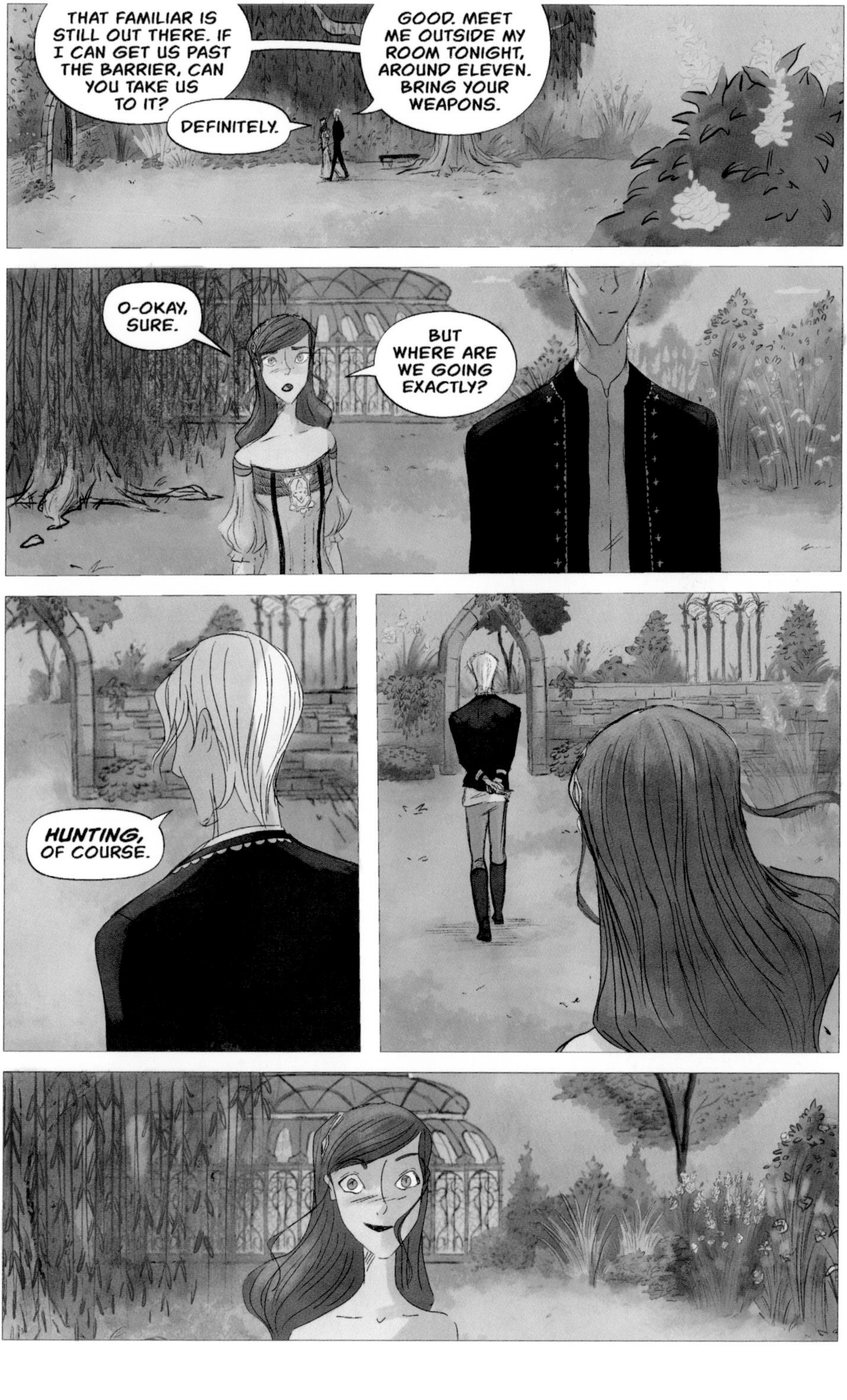
THAT FAMILIAR IS STILL OUT THERE. IF I CAN GET US PAST THE BARRIER, CAN YOU TAKE US TO IT?
DEFINITELY.
GOOD. MEET ME OUTSIDE MY ROOM TONIGHT, AROUND ELEVEN. BRING YOUR WEAPONS.
O-OKAY, SURE.
BUT WHERE ARE WE GOING EXACTLY?
HUNTING, OF COURSE.

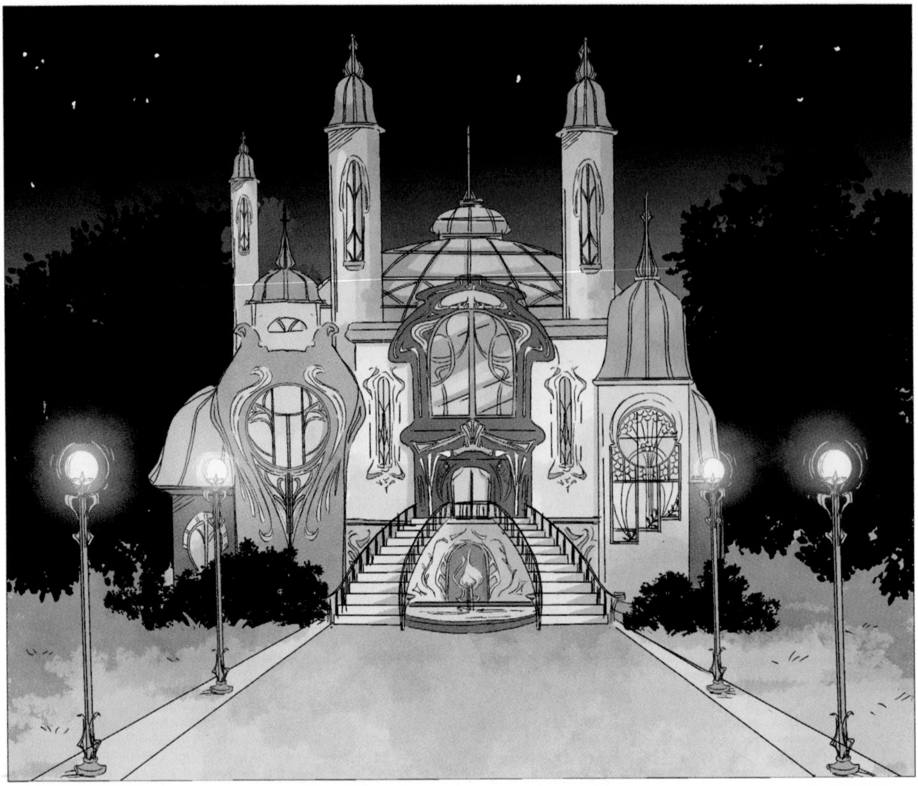
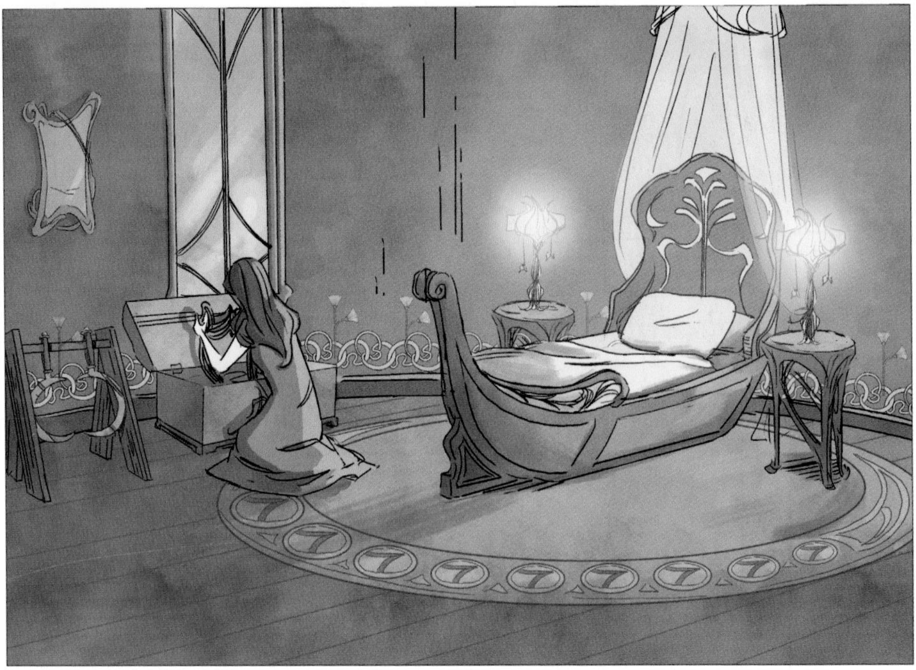

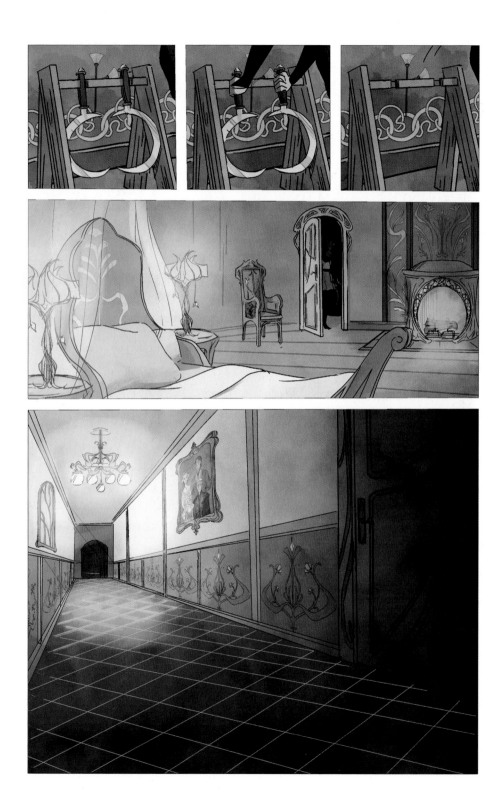

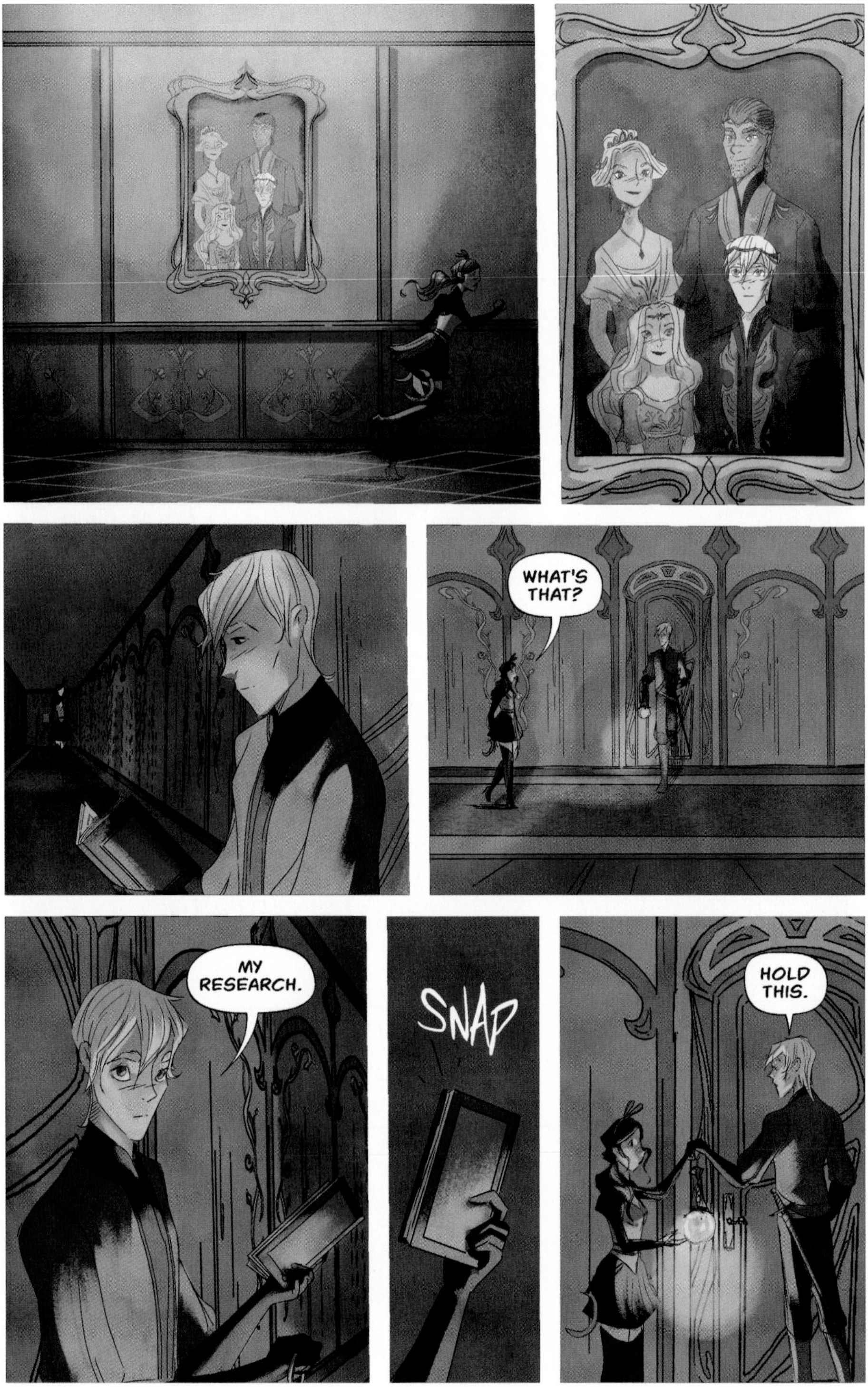
WHAT'S THAT?
MY RESEARCH.
SNAP
HOLD THIS.

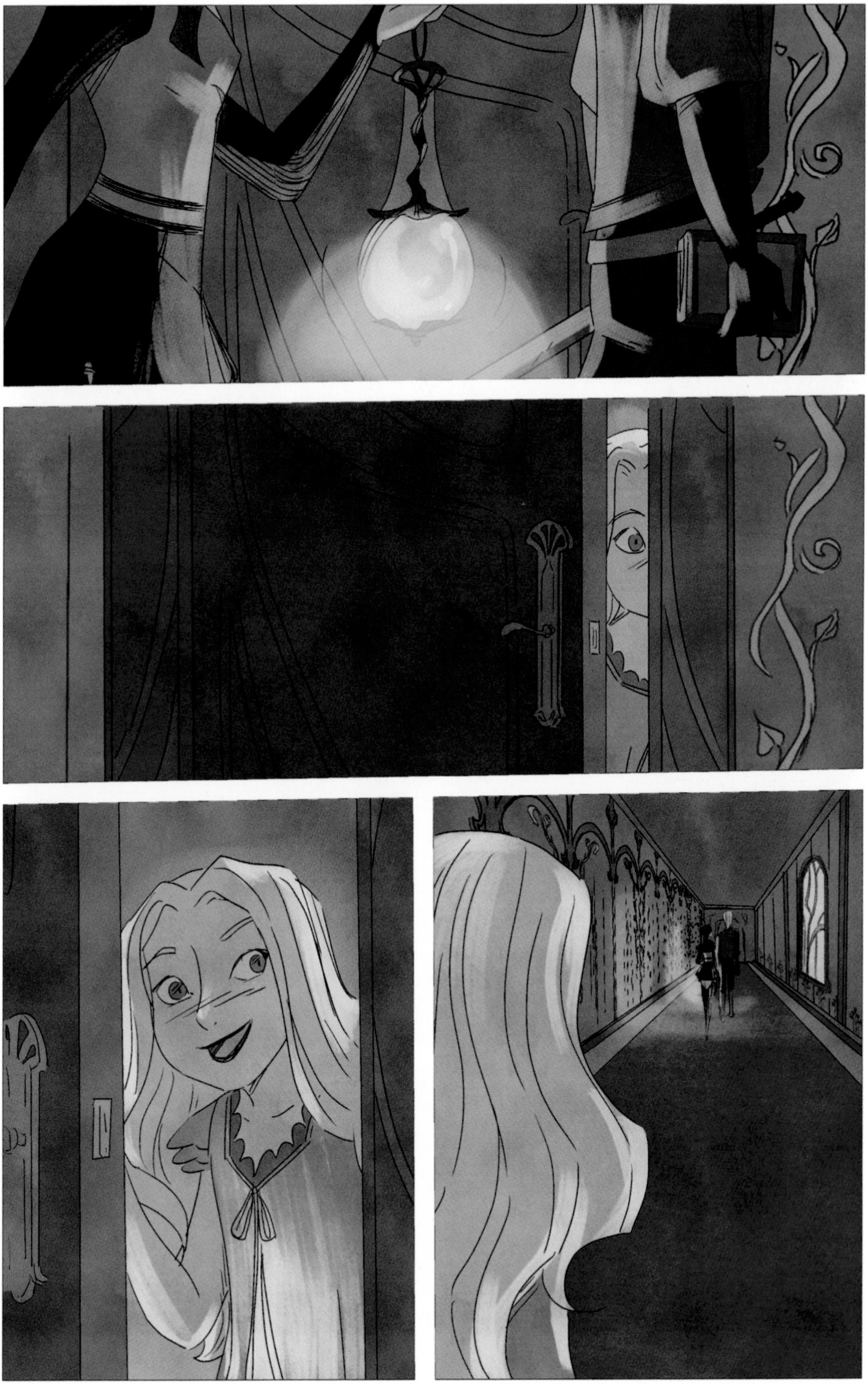

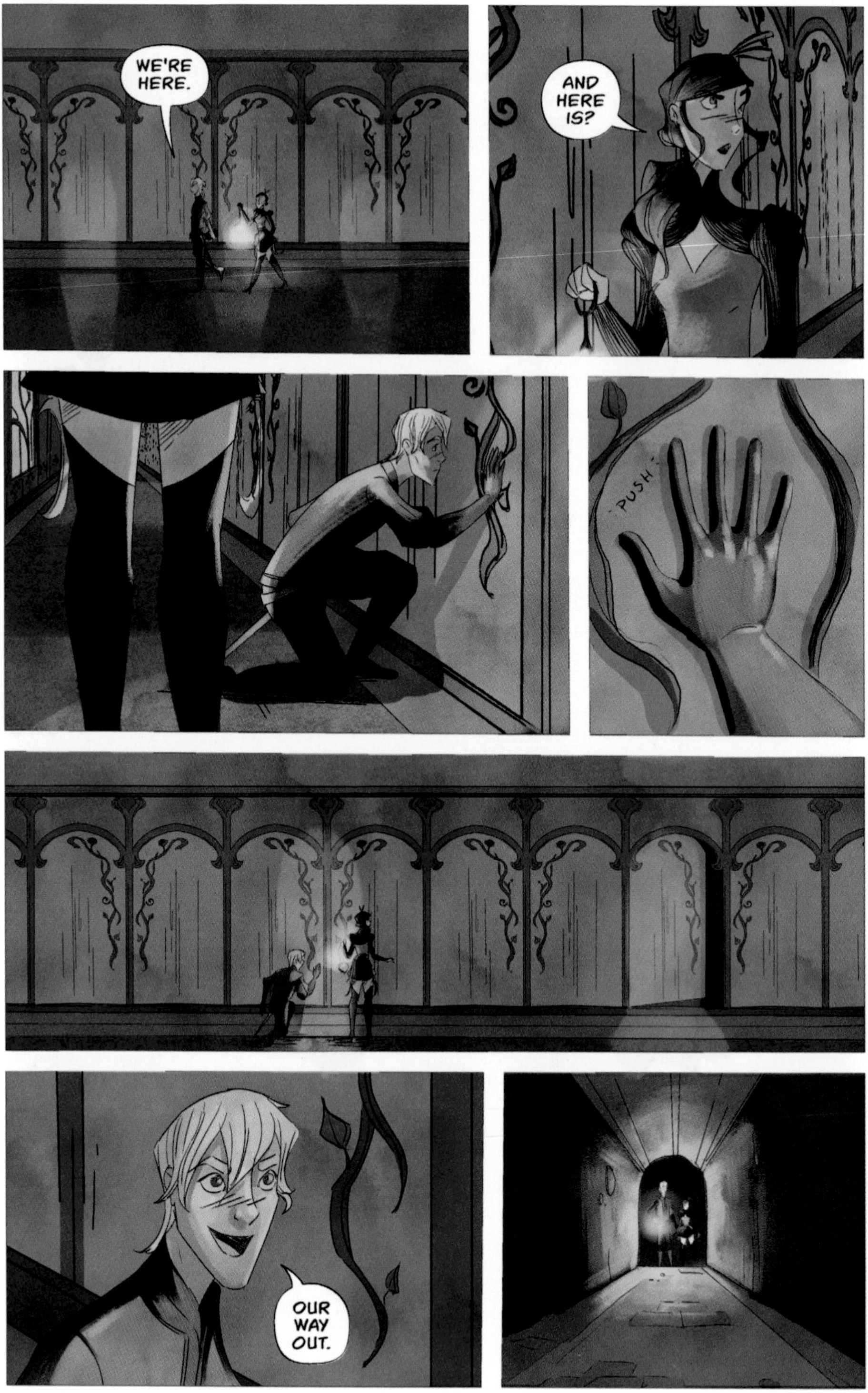
WE'RE HERE.
AND HERE IS?
PUSH
OUR WAY OUT.

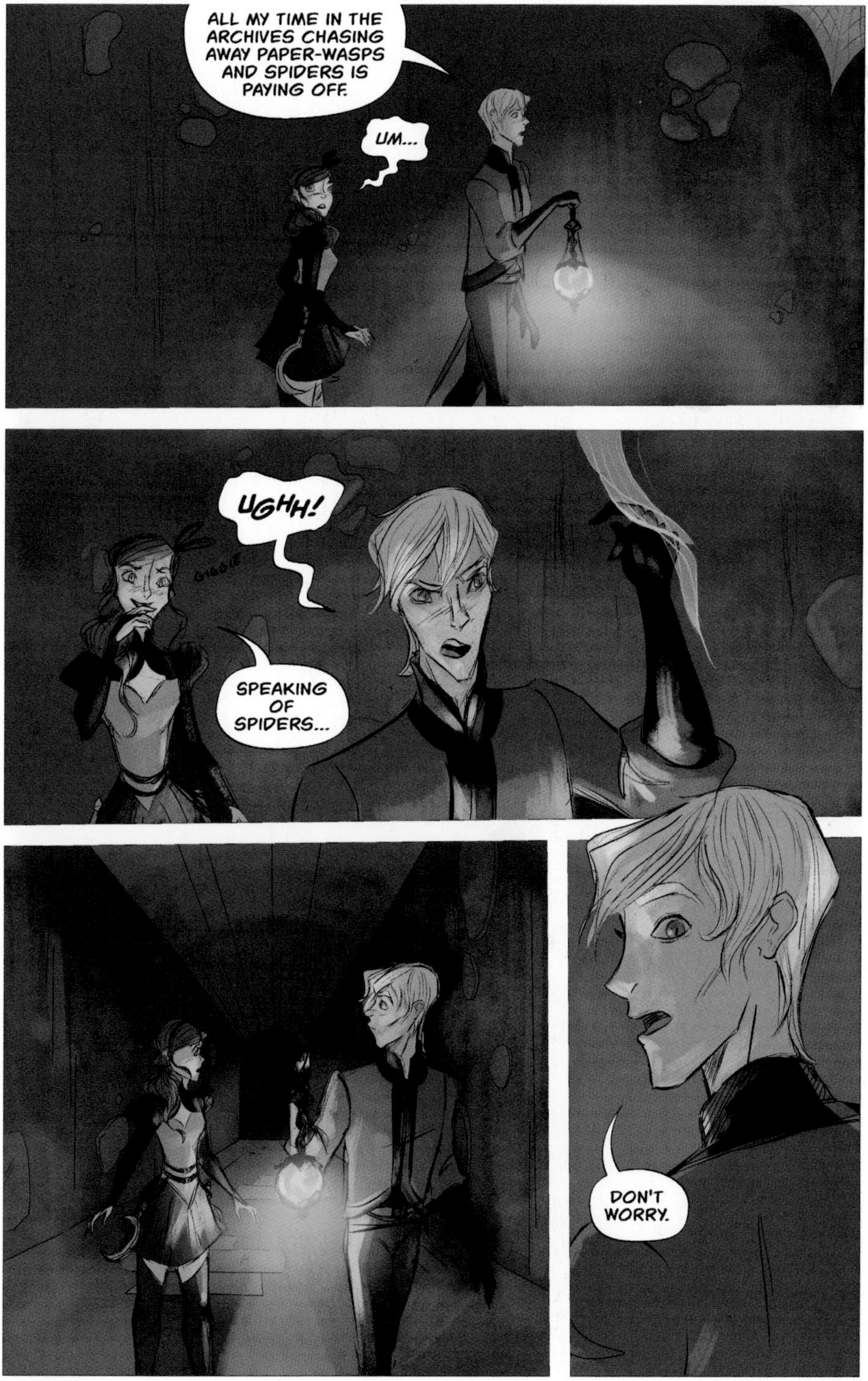
ALL MY TIME IN THE ARCHIVES CHASING AWAY PAPER-WASPS AND SPIDERS IS PAYING OFF.
UM...
UGHH!
GIGGLE
SPEAKING OF SPIDERS...
DON'T WORRY.

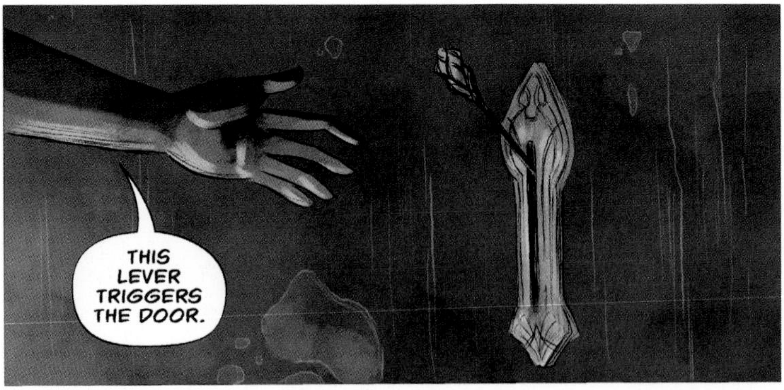
THIS LEVER TRIGGERS THE DOOR.

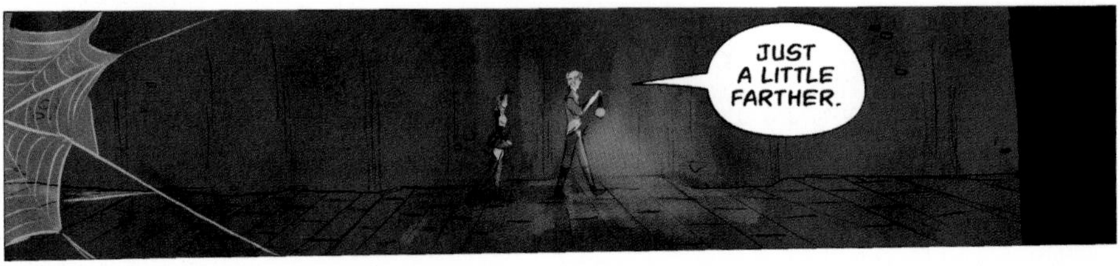
JUST A LITTLE FARTHER.

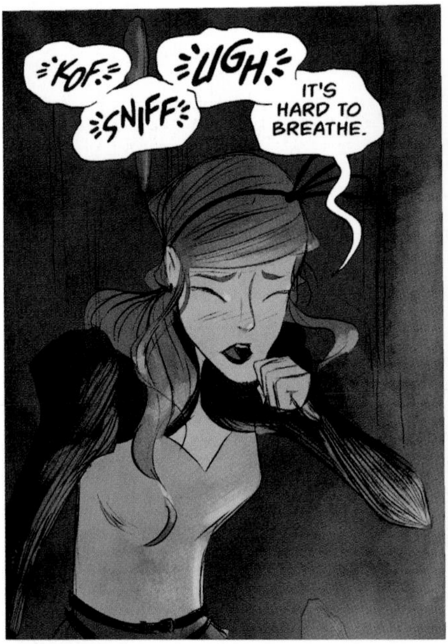
KOF
SNIFF
UGH
IT'S HARD TO BREATHE.

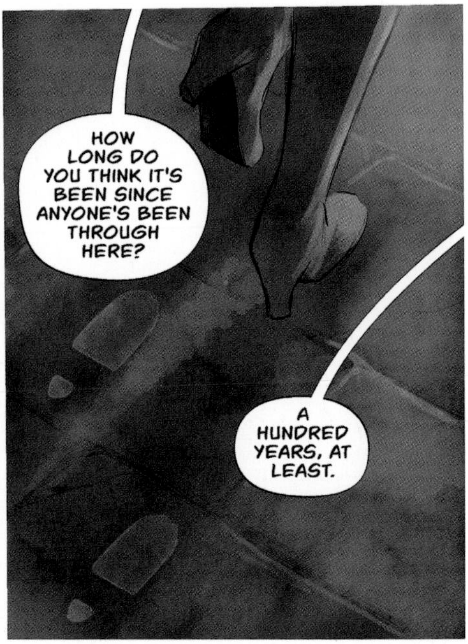
HOW LONG DO YOU THINK IT'S BEEN SINCE ANYONE'S BEEN THROUGH HERE?
A HUNDRED YEARS, AT LEAST.

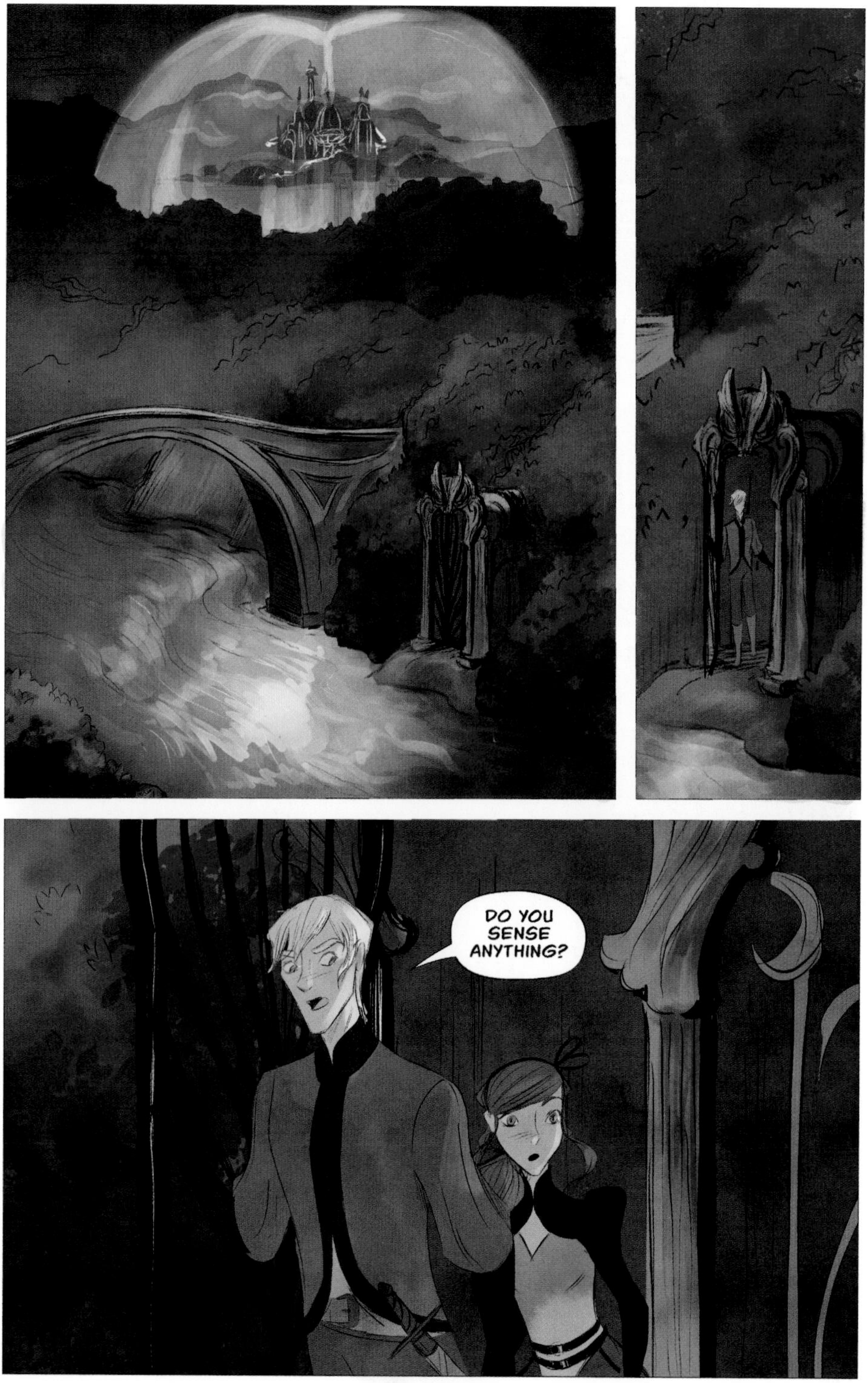
DO YOU SENSE ANYTHING?

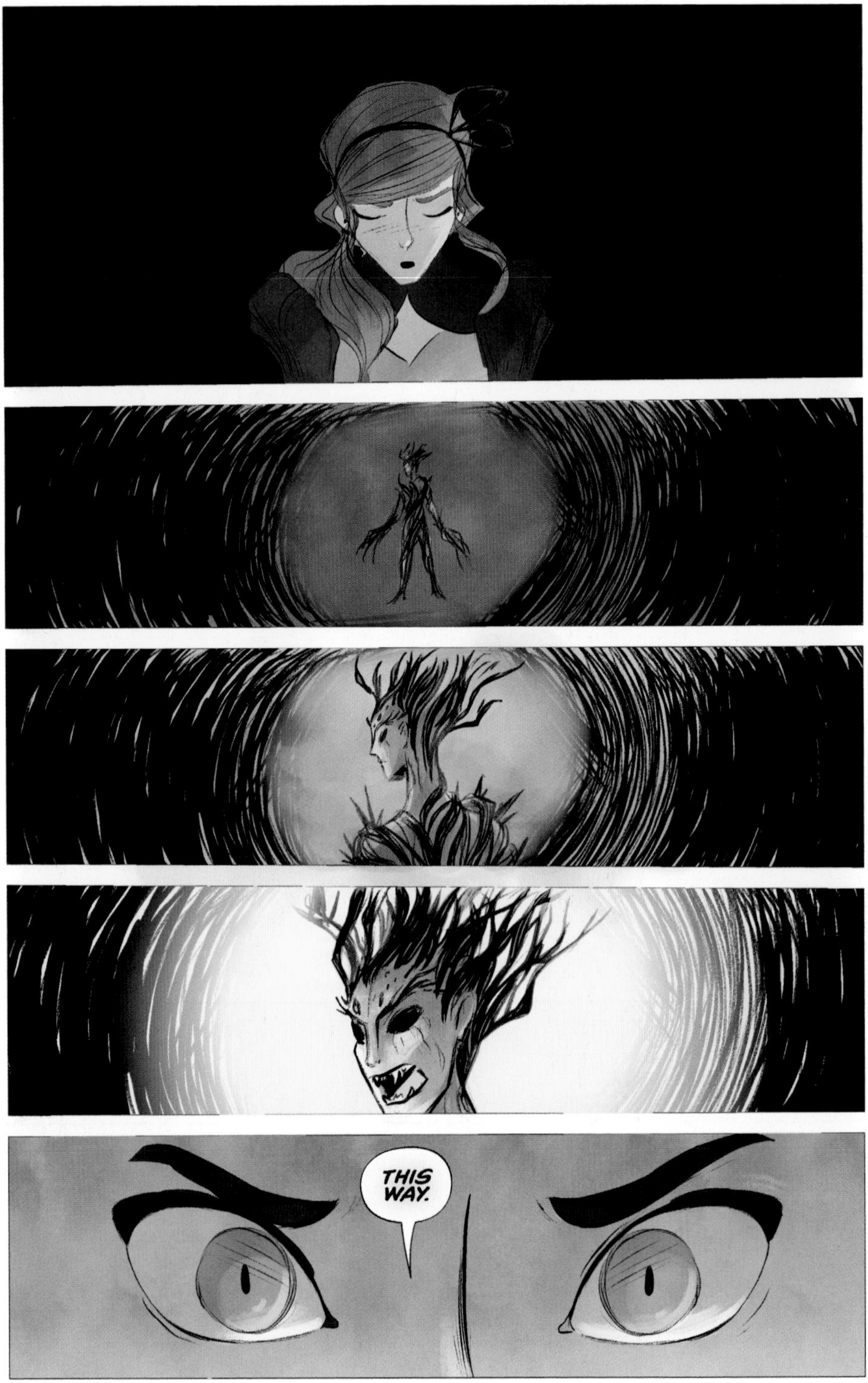
THIS WAY.

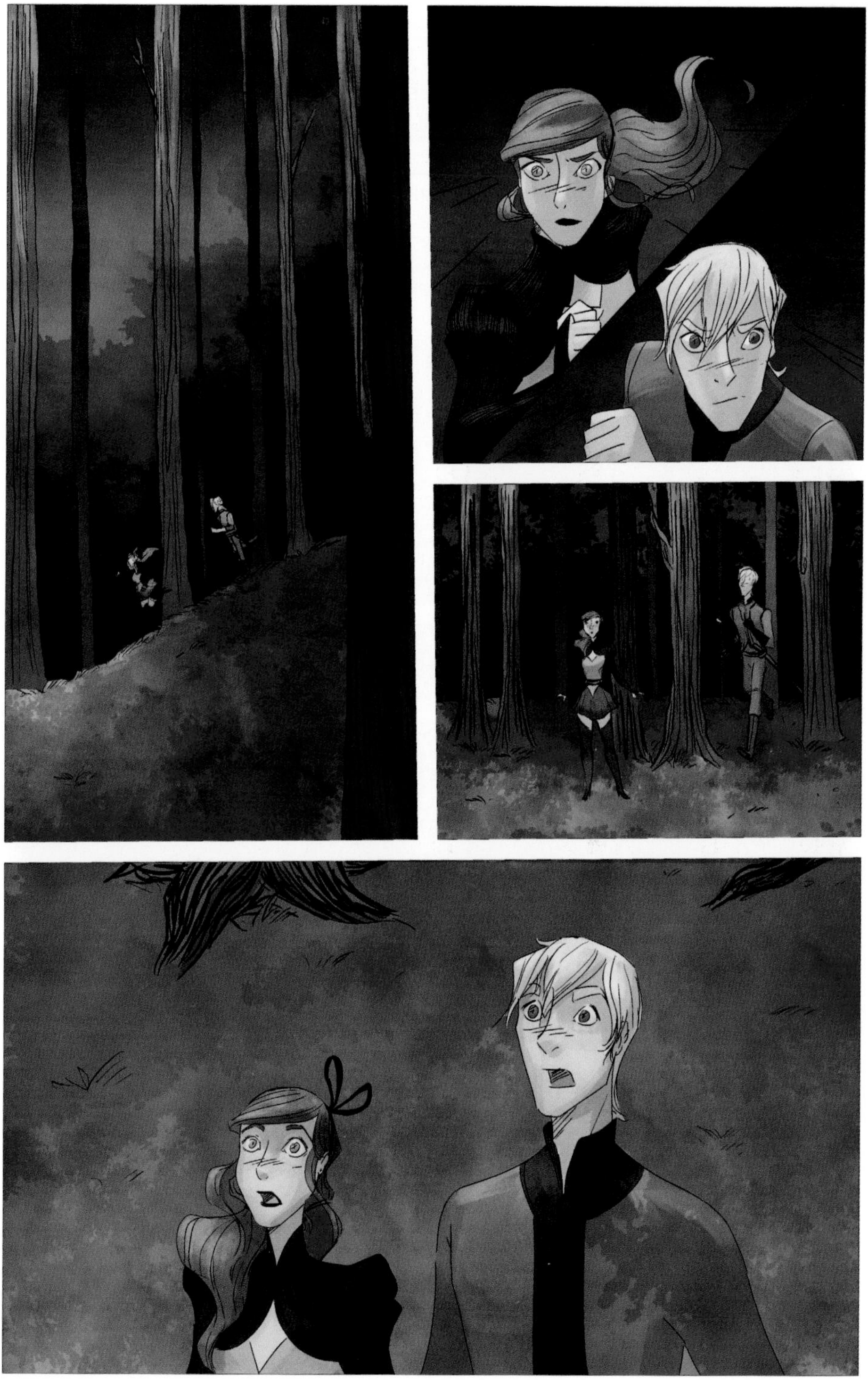

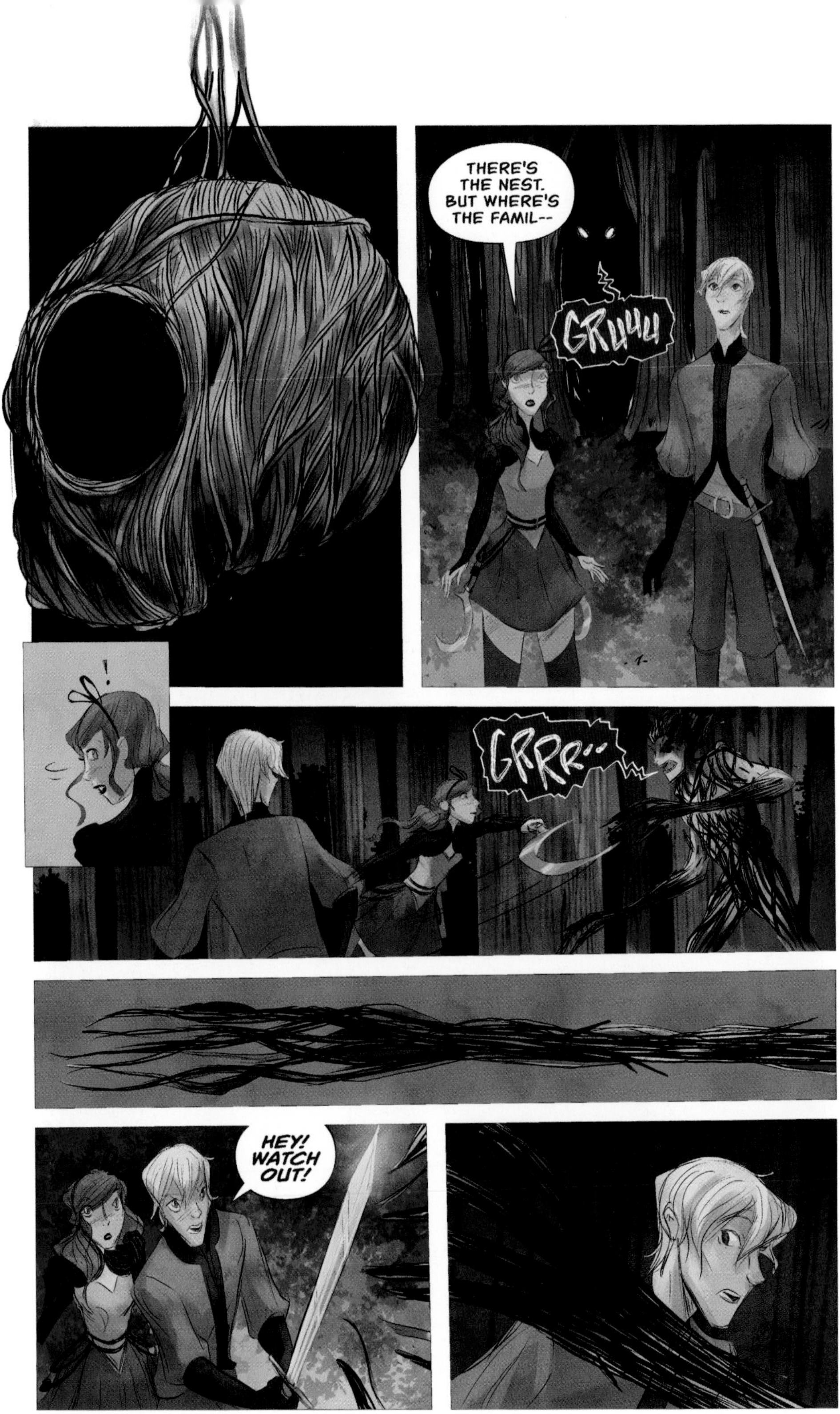
THERE'S THE NEST. BUT WHERE'S THE FAMIL--
GRUUU
!
GRRR..
HEY! WATCH OUT!

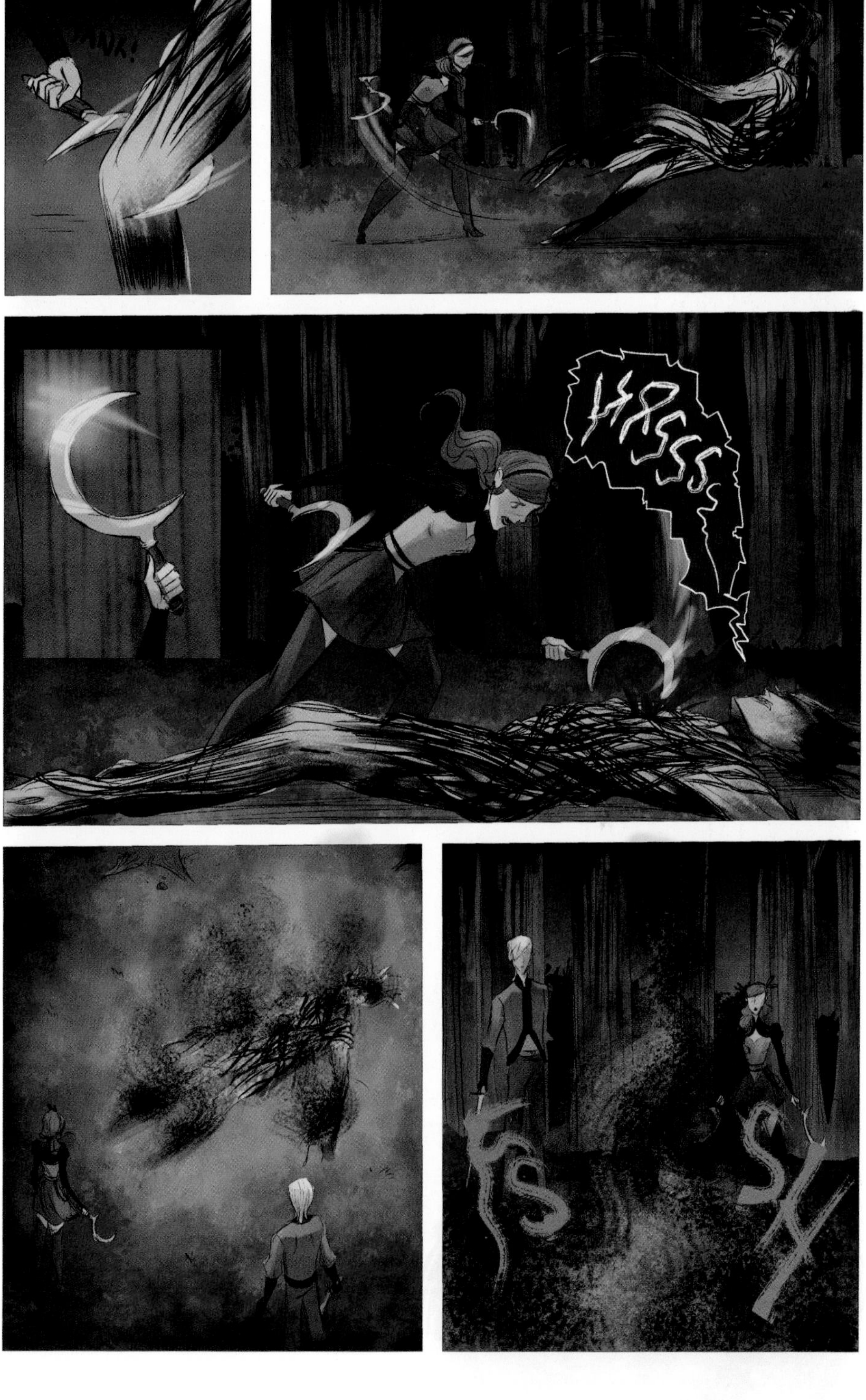
HSSSSS

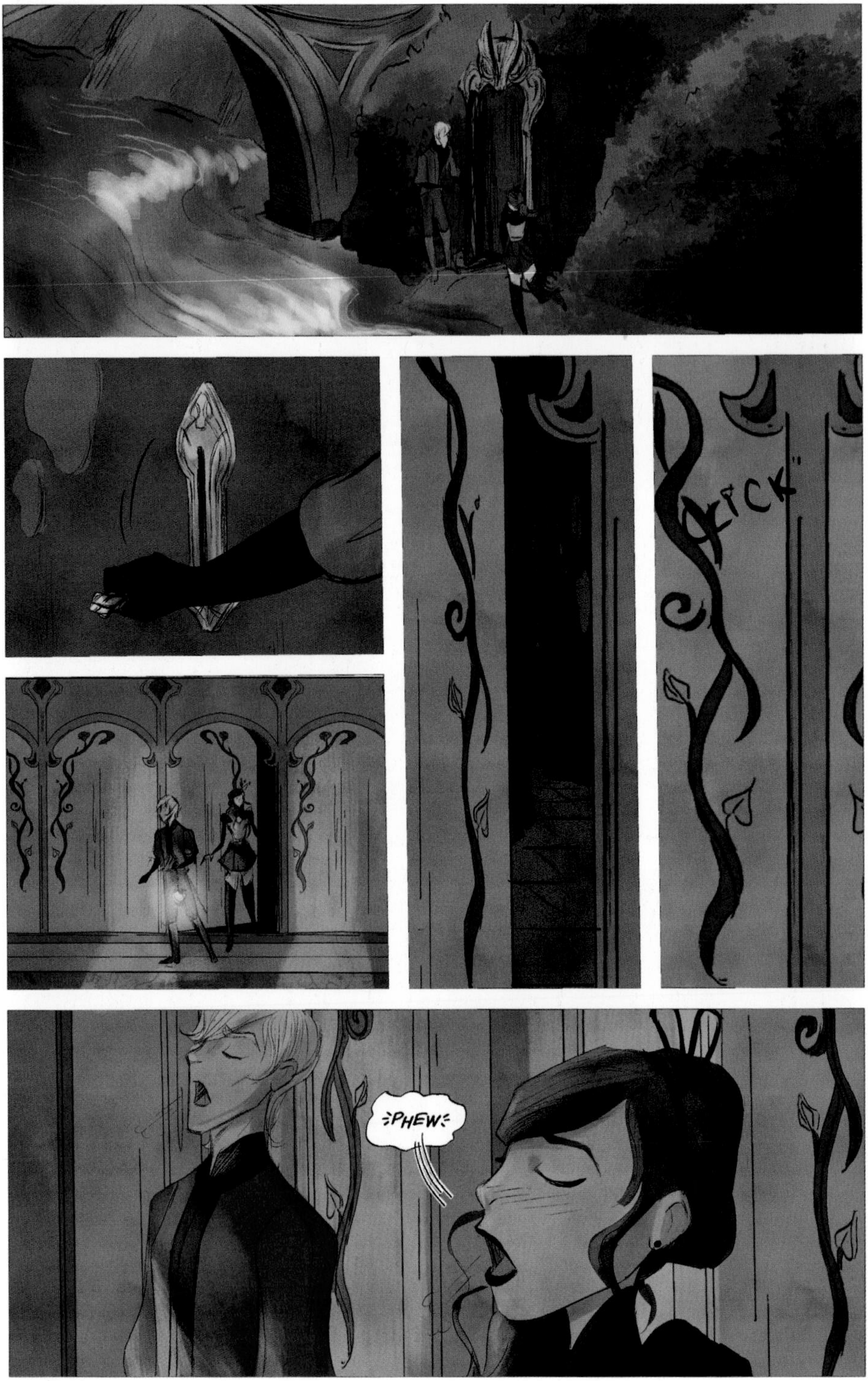
CLICK
PHEW

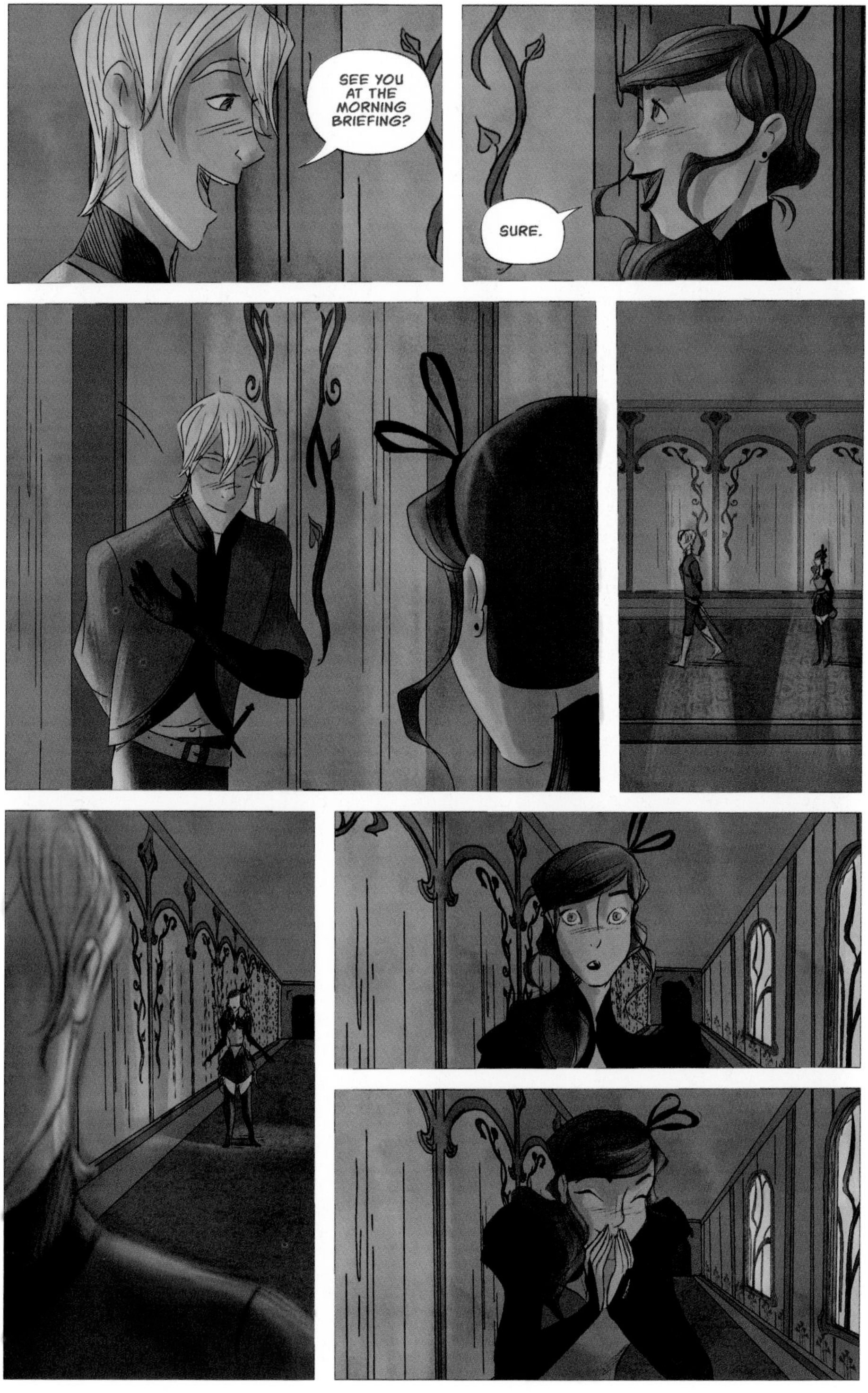
SEE YOU AT THE MORNING BRIEFING?
SURE.

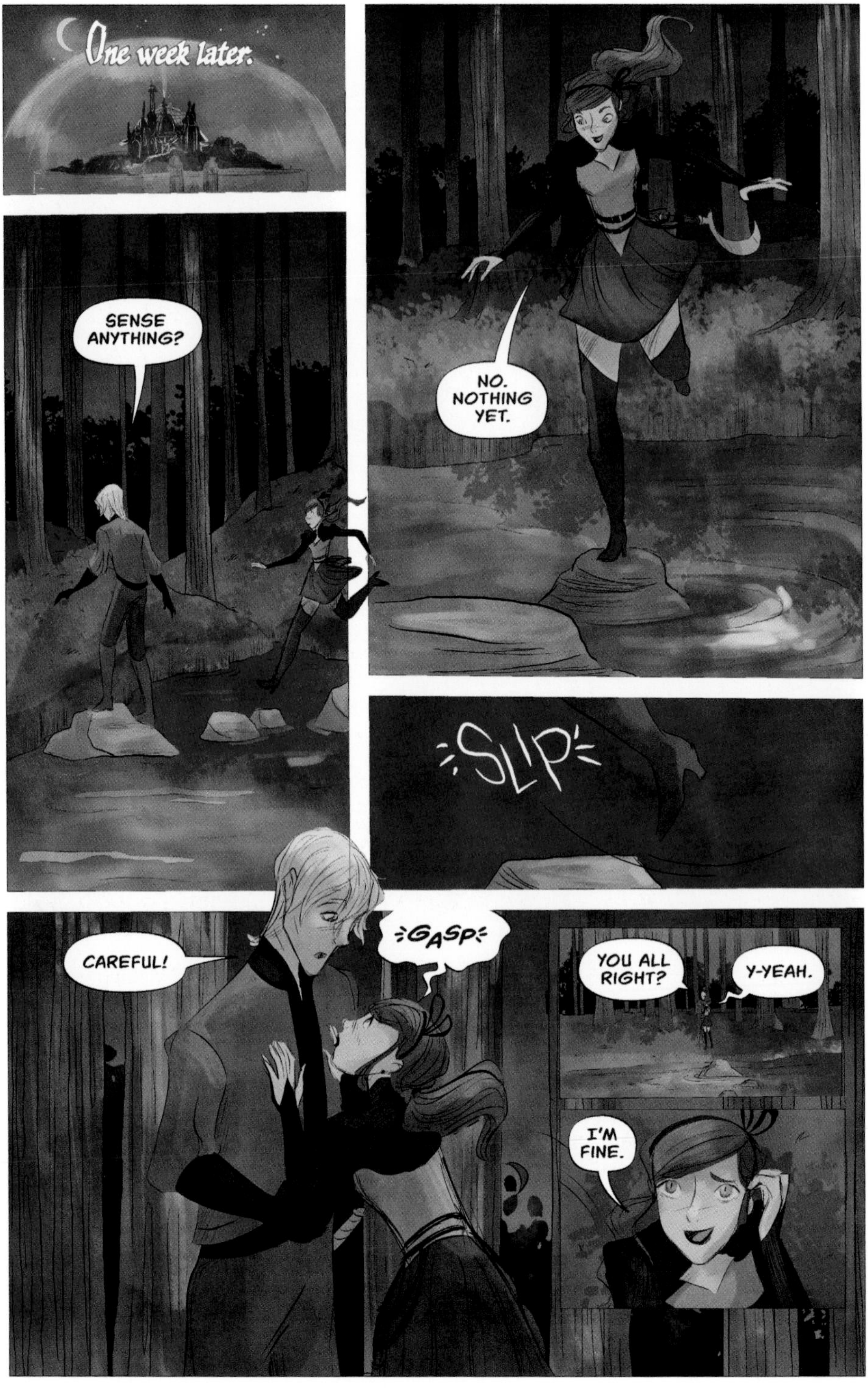
One week later.
SENSE ANYTHING?
NO. NOTHING YET.
SLIP
CAREFUL!
GASP
YOU ALL RIGHT?
Y-YEAH.
I'M FINE.

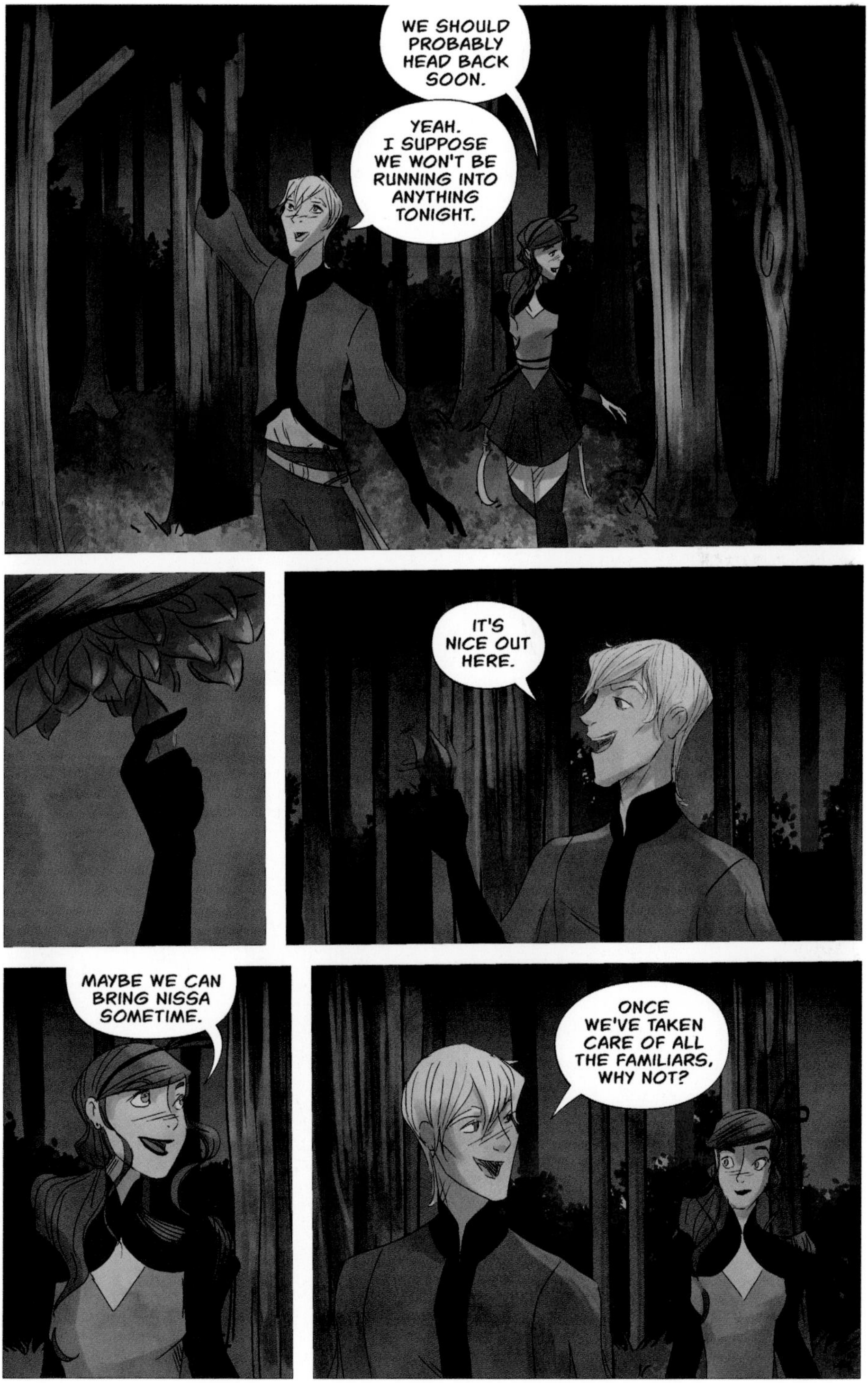
WE SHOULD PROBABLY HEAD BACK SOON.
YEAH. I SUPPOSE WE WON'T BE RUNNING INTO ANYTHING TONIGHT.
IT'S NICE OUT HERE.
MAYBE WE CAN BRING NISSA SOMETIME.
ONCE WE'VE TAKEN CARE OF ALL THE FAMILIARS, WHY NOT?

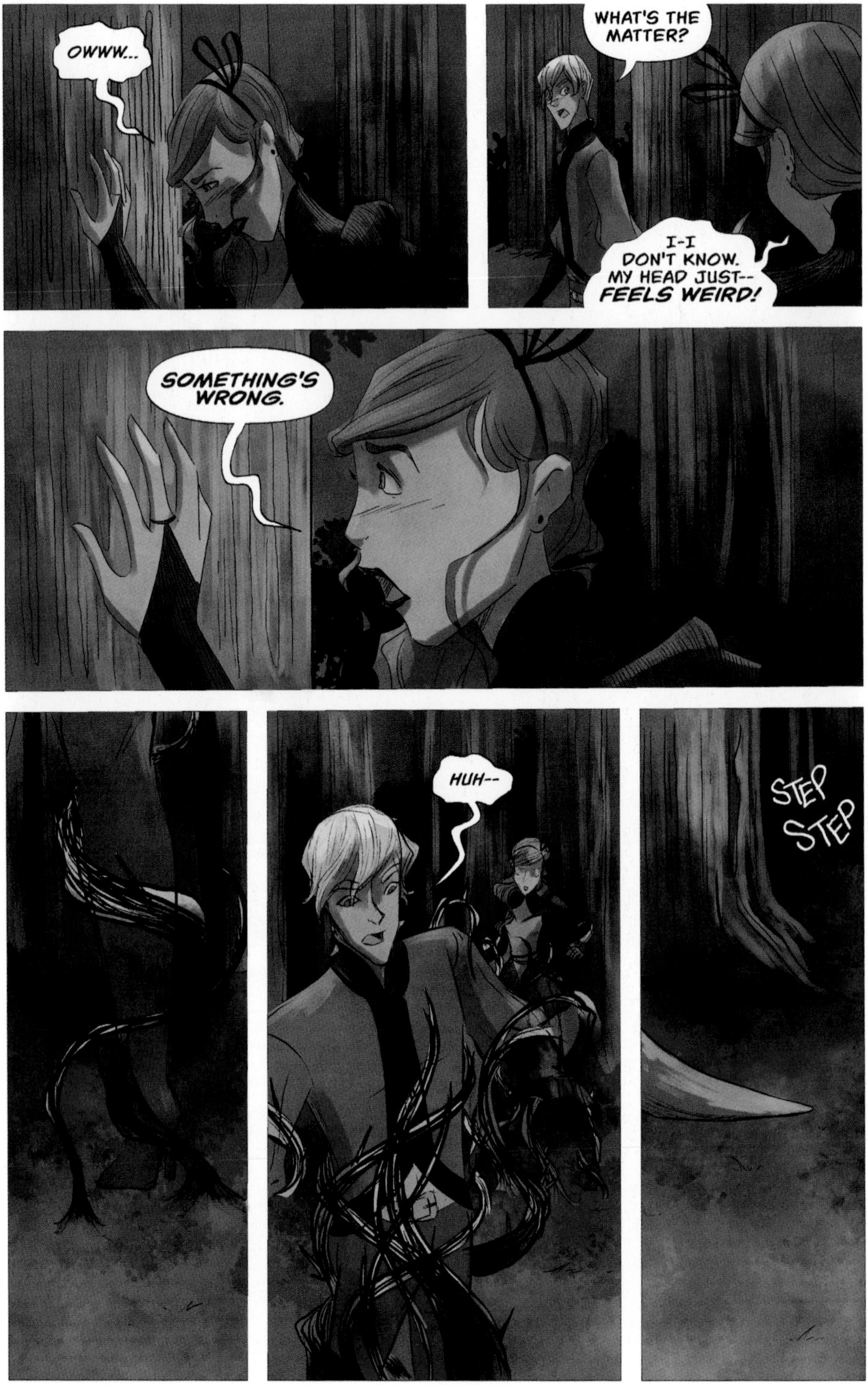
OWWW...
WHAT'S THE MATTER?
I-I DON'T KNOW. MY HEAD JUST-- FEELS WEIRD!
SOMETHING'S WRONG.
HUH--
STEP STEP

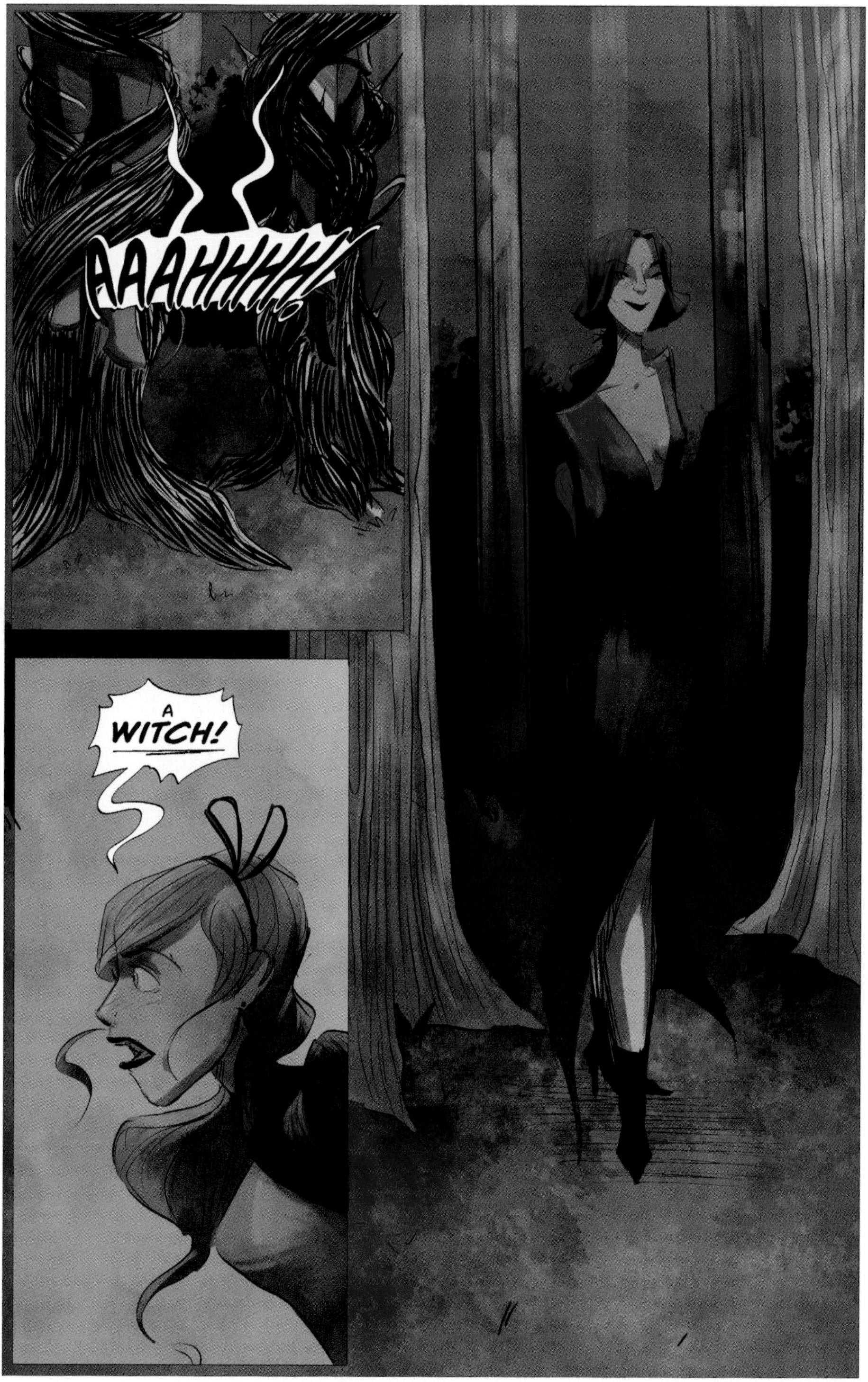
AAAHHHH!
A WITCH!

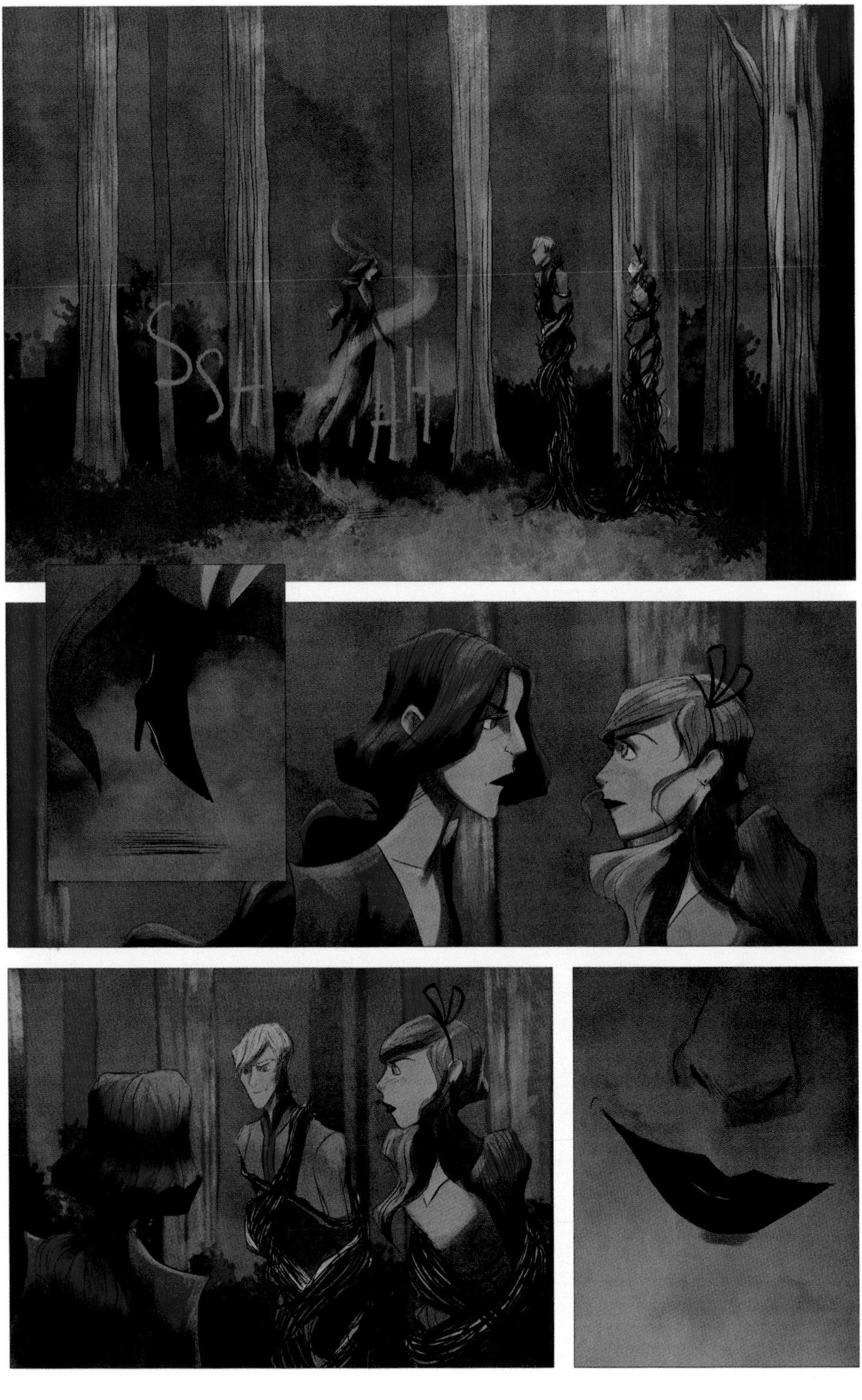
SSH AH

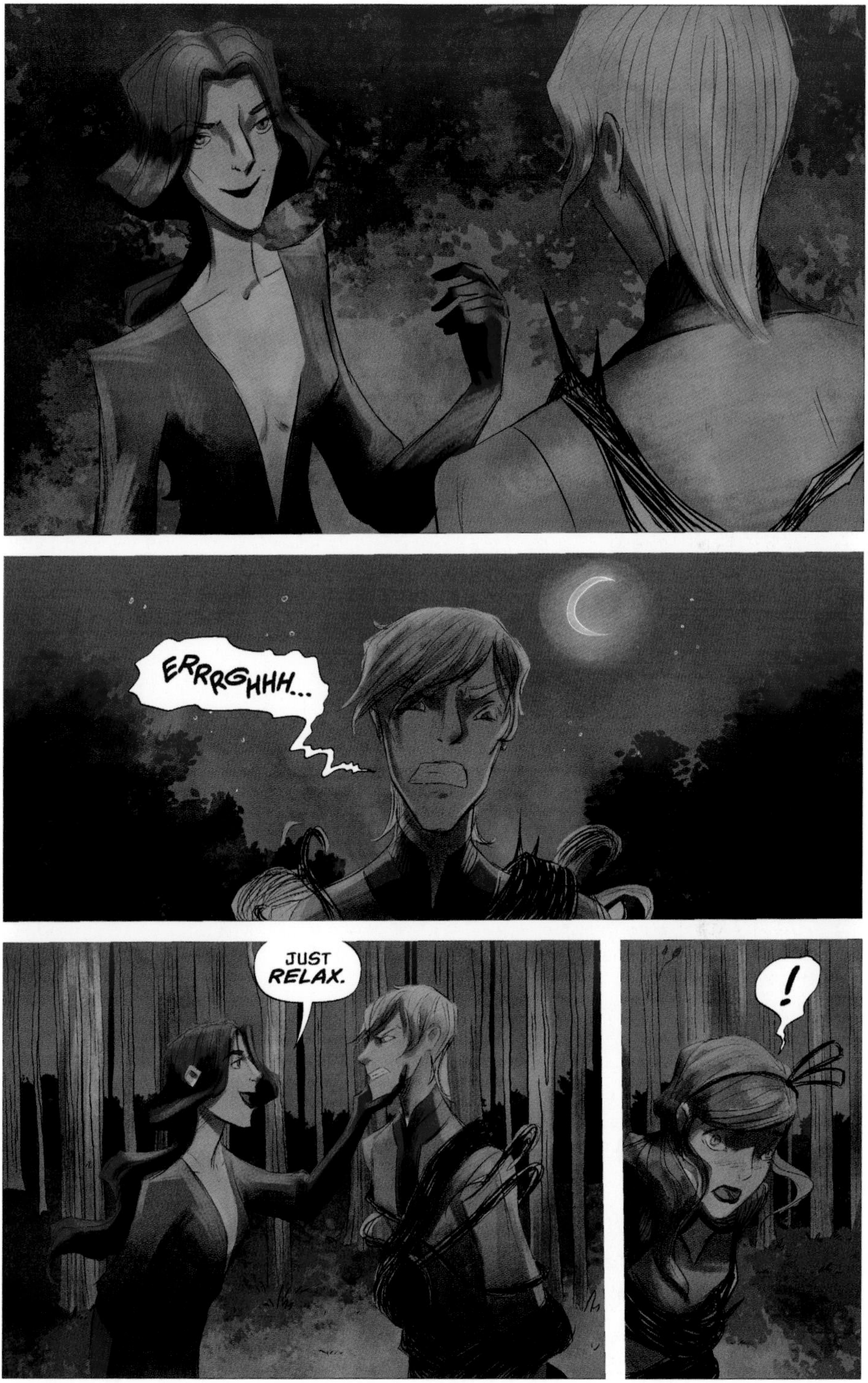
ERRRGHHH...
JUST RELAX.
!

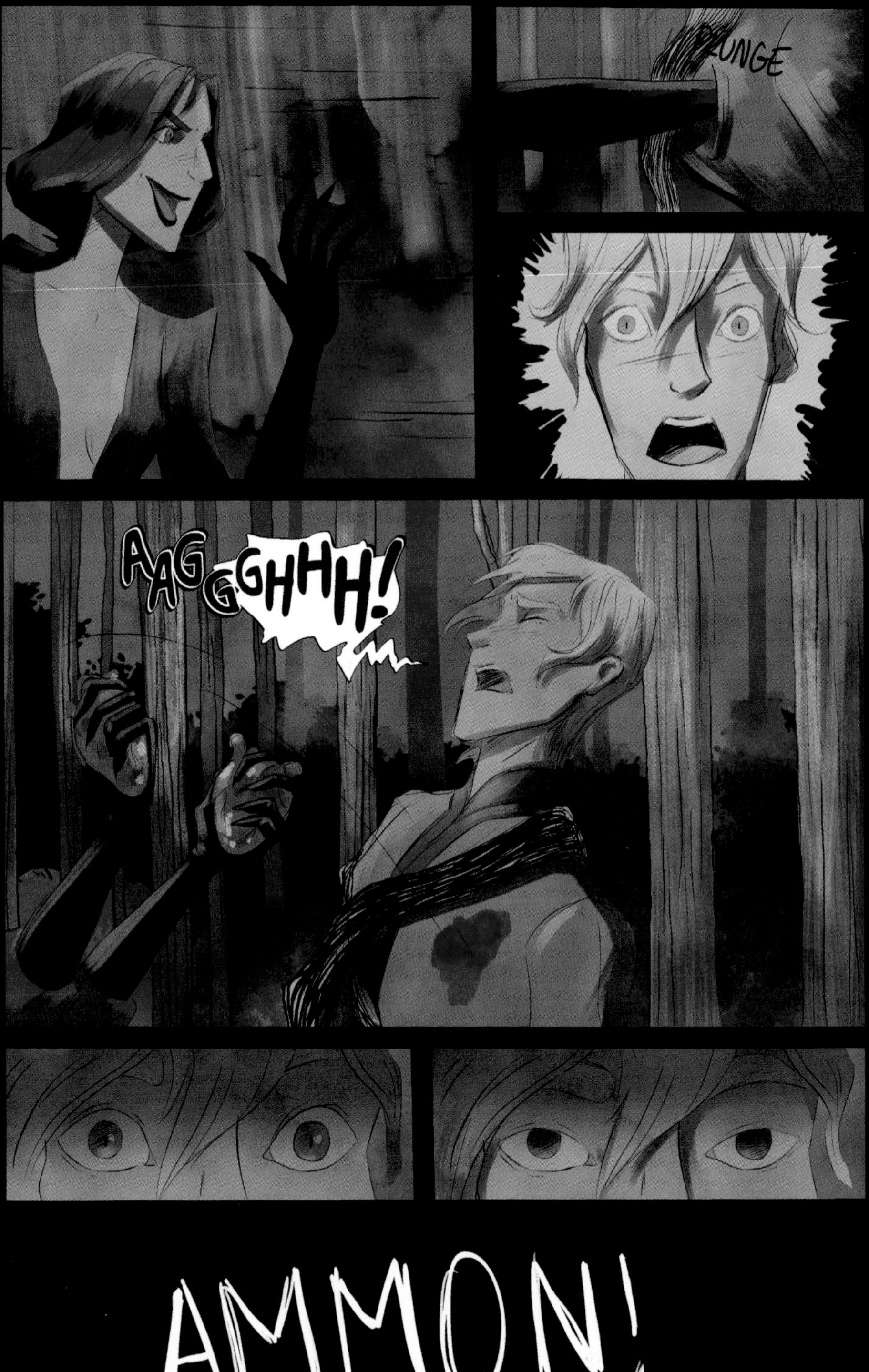
PLUNGE
AAGGHHH!
AMMON!

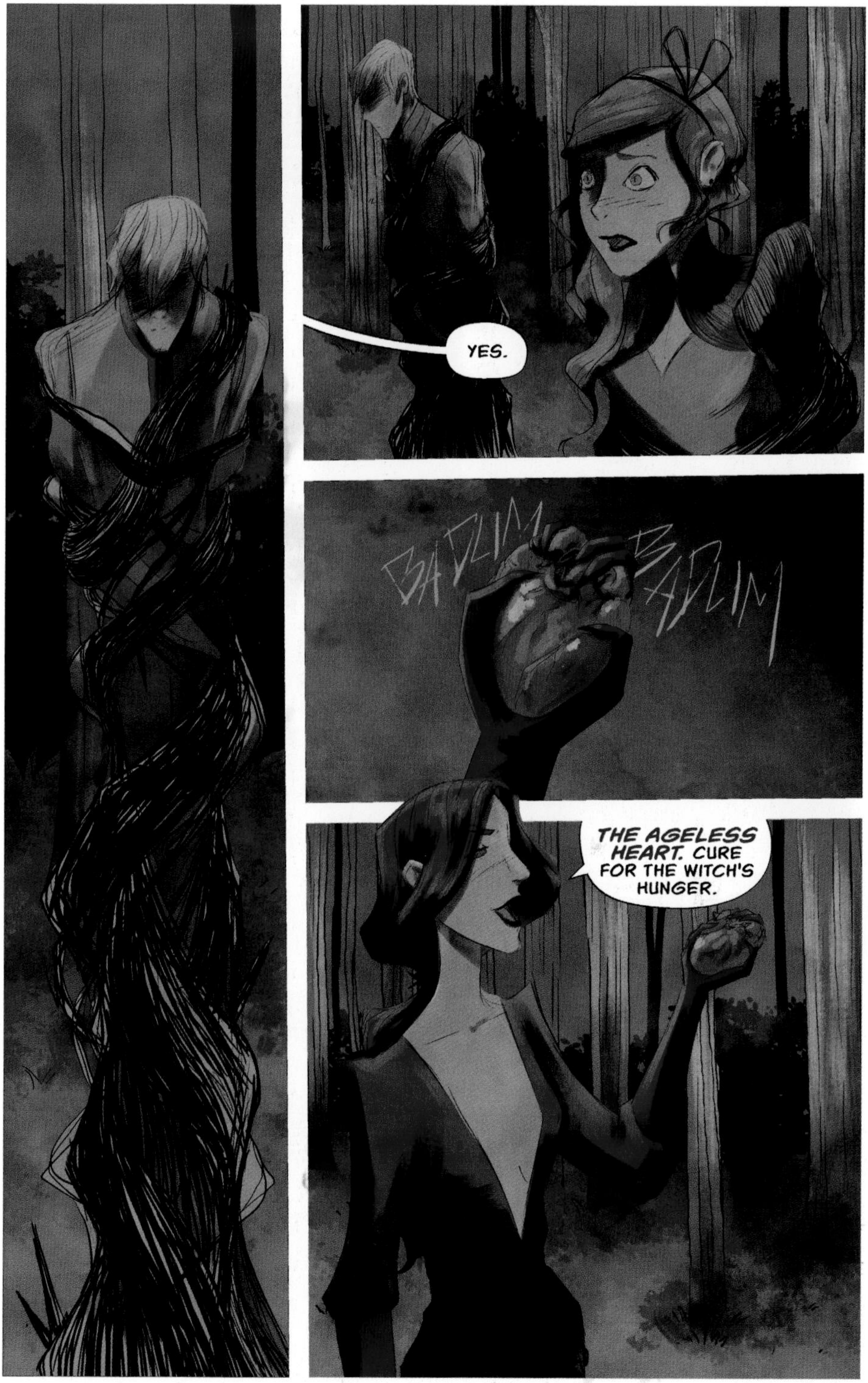
YES.
BA DUM BA DUM
THE AGELESS HEART. CURE FOR THE WITCH'S HUNGER.

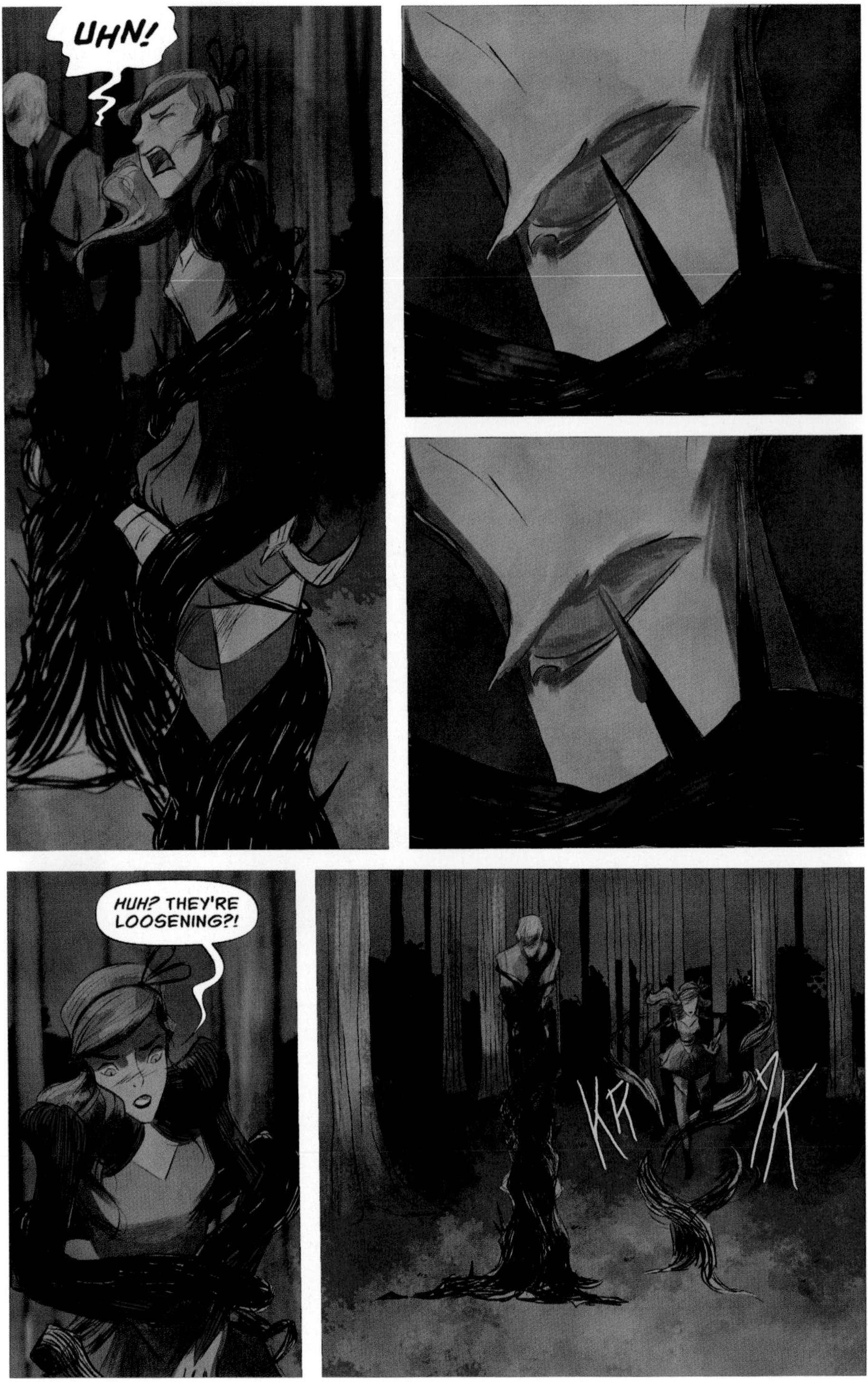
UHN!
HUH? THEY'RE LOOSENING?!
KR
ZK

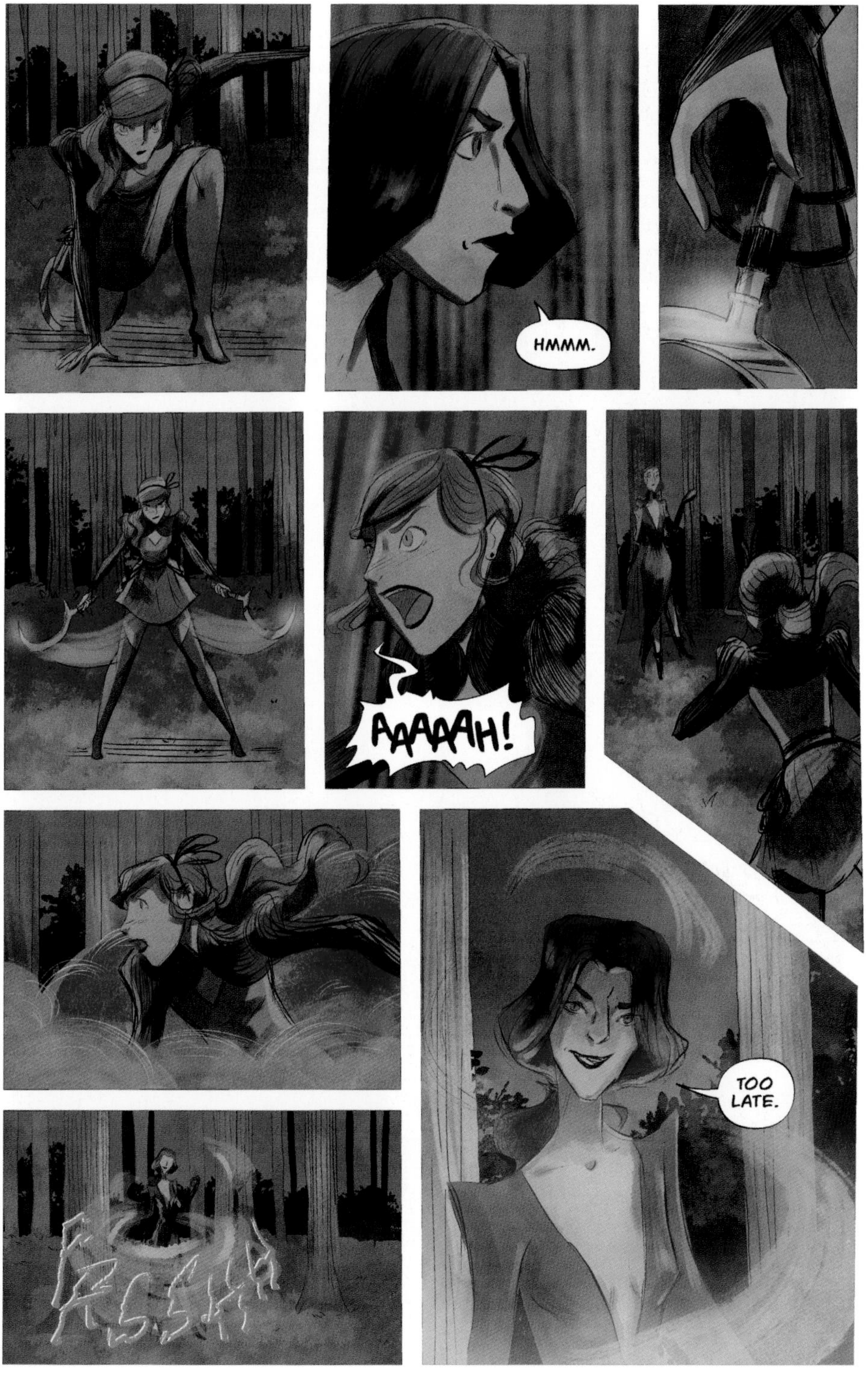
HMMM.
AAAAAH!
TOO LATE.

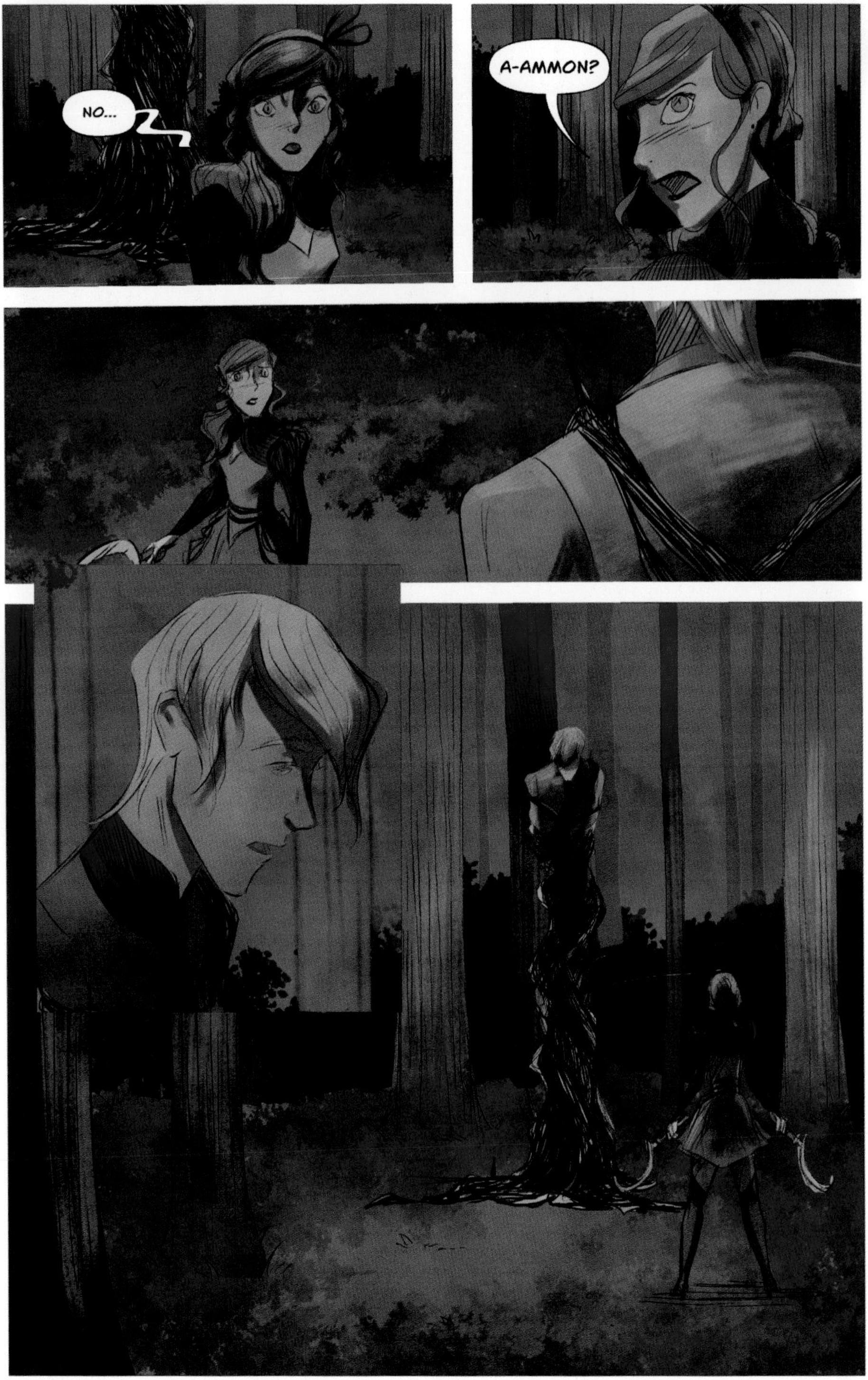
NO...
A-AMMON?

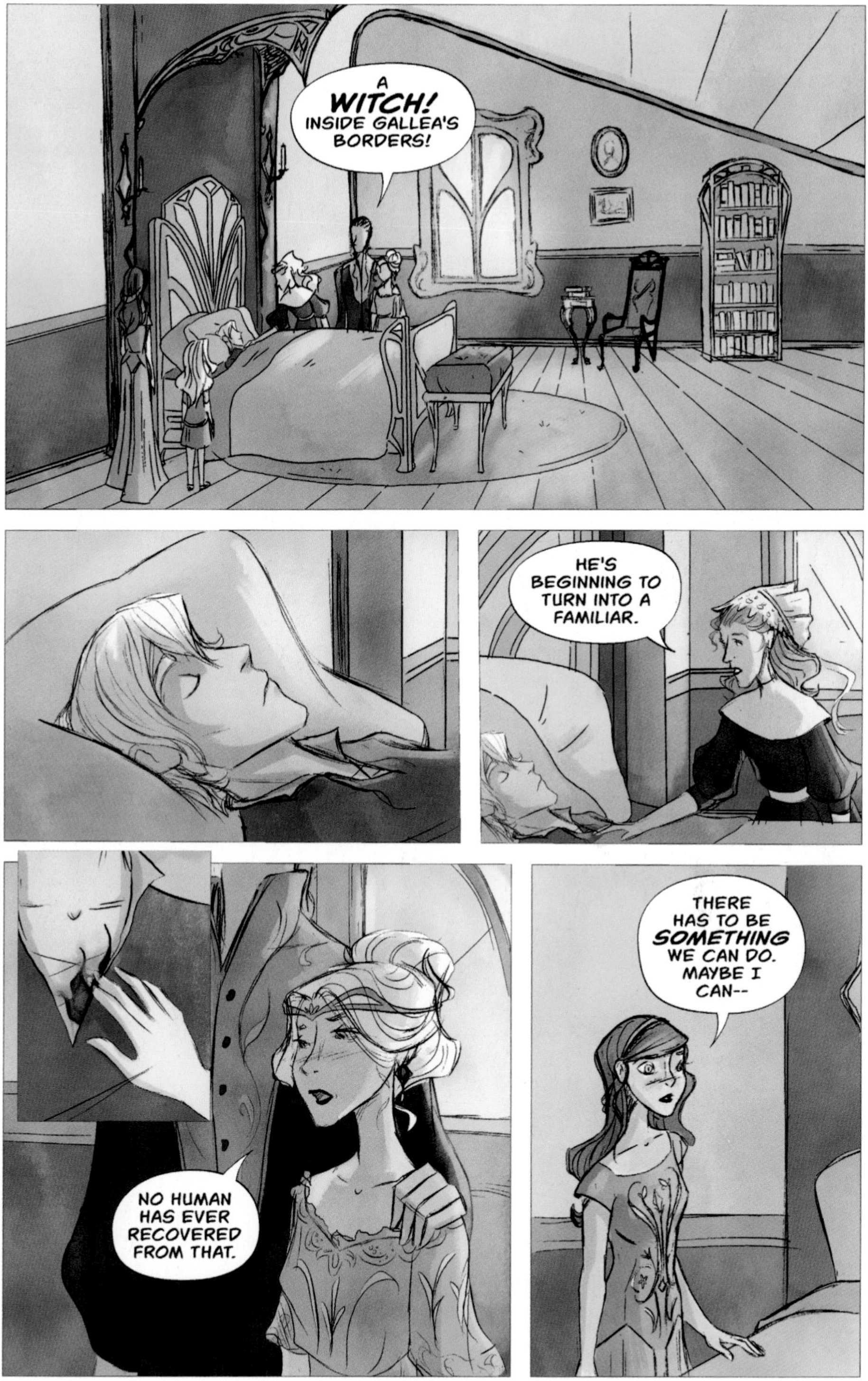
A WITCH! INSIDE GALLEA'S BORDERS!
HE'S BEGINNING TO TURN INTO A FAMILIAR.
NO HUMAN HAS EVER RECOVERED FROM THAT.
THERE HAS TO BE SOMETHING WE CAN DO. MAYBE I CAN--

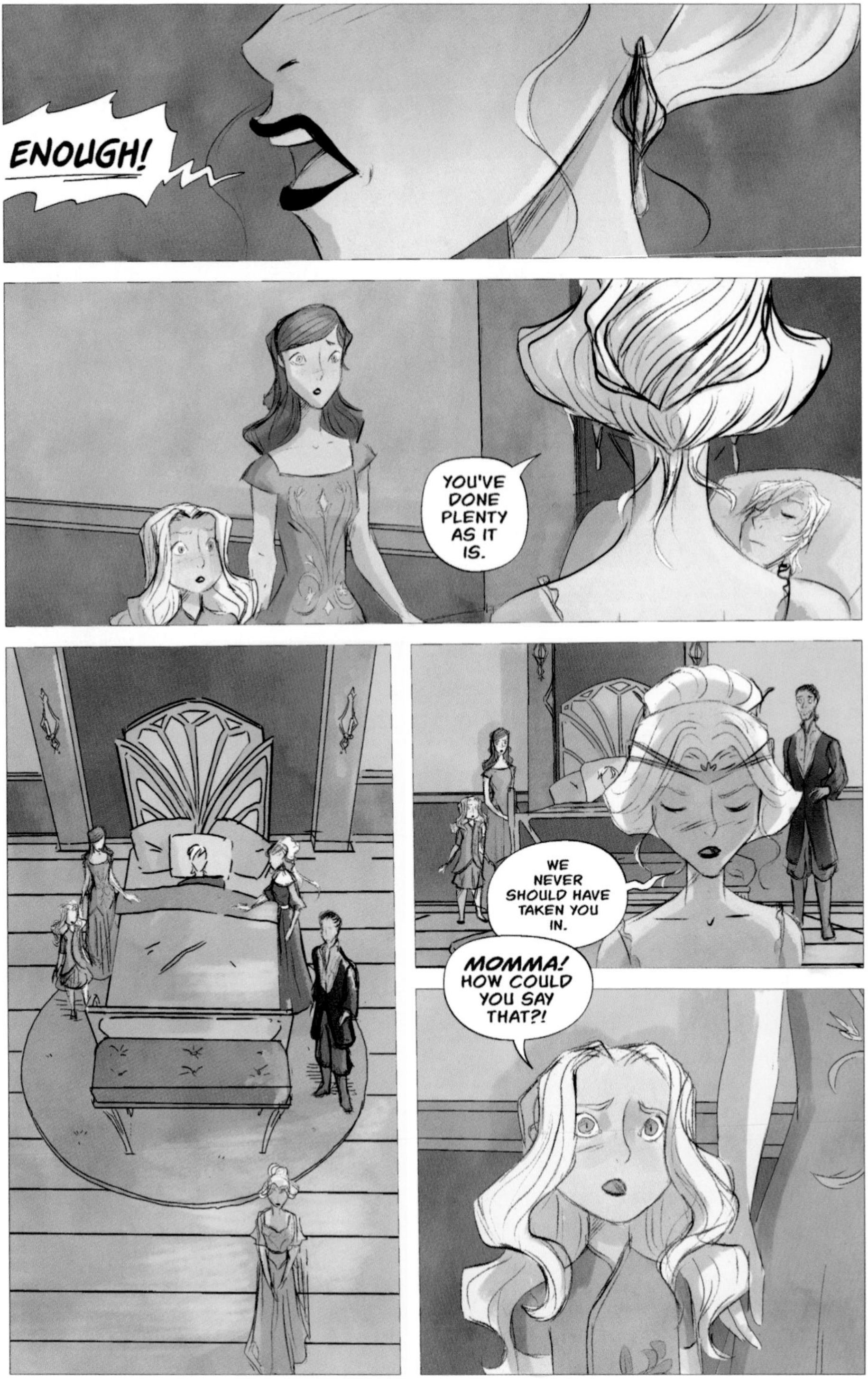
ENOUGH!
YOU'VE DONE PLENTY AS IT IS.
WE NEVER SHOULD HAVE TAKEN YOU IN.
MOMMA! HOW COULD YOU SAY THAT?!

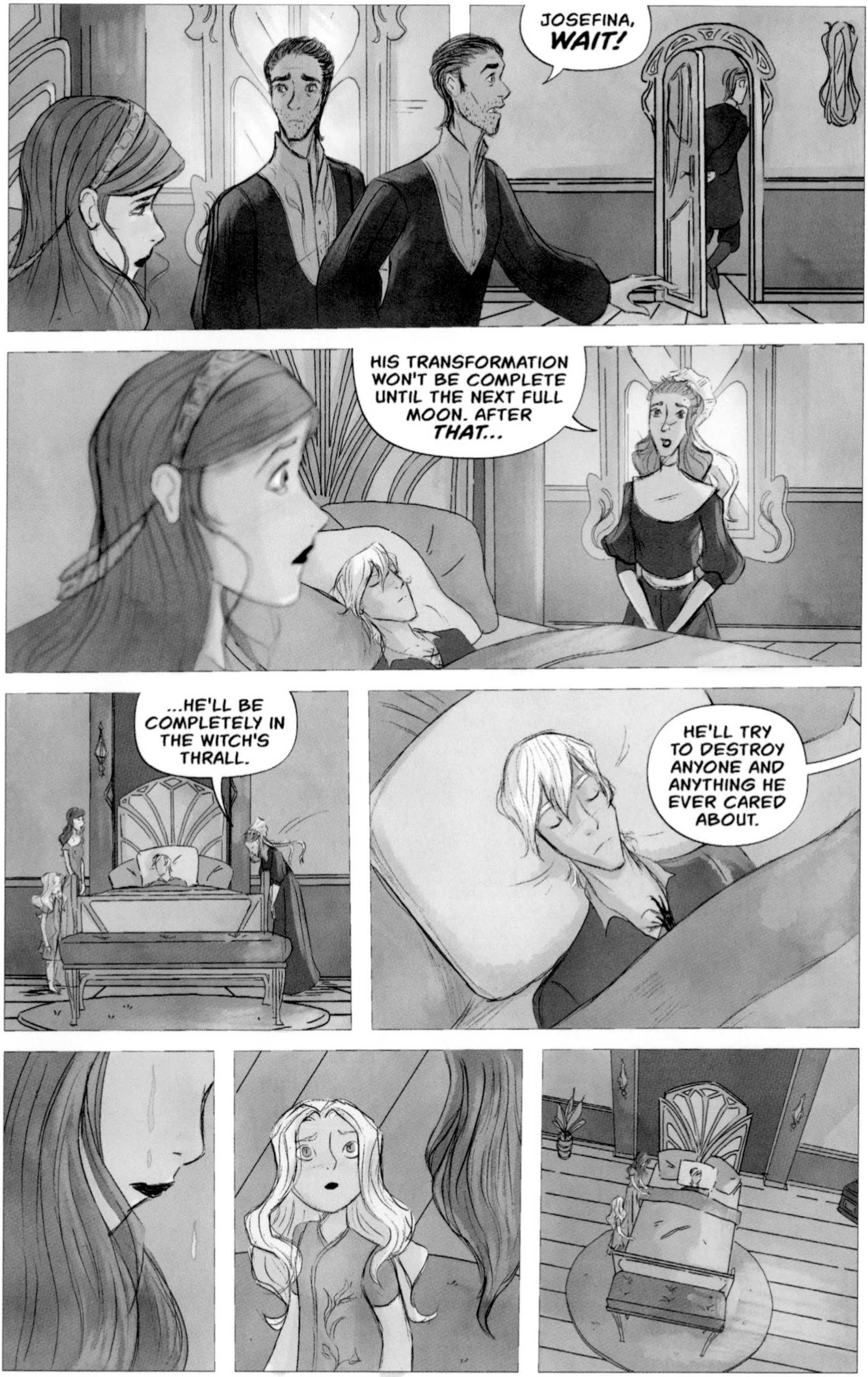
JOSEFINA, WAIT!
HIS TRANSFORMATION WON'T BE COMPLETE UNTIL THE NEXT FULL MOON. AFTER THAT...
...HE'LL BE COMPLETELY IN THE WITCH'S THRALL.
HE'LL TRY TO DESTROY ANYONE AND ANYTHING HE EVER CARED ABOUT.

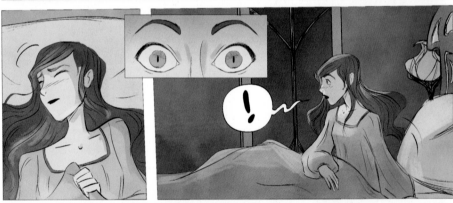

A FAMILIAR...

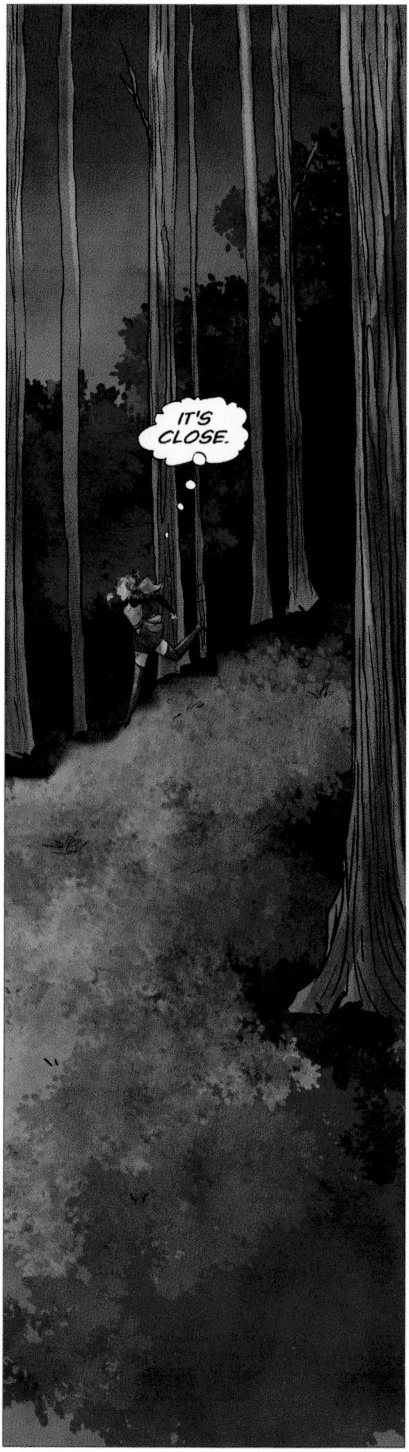
IT'S CLOSE.
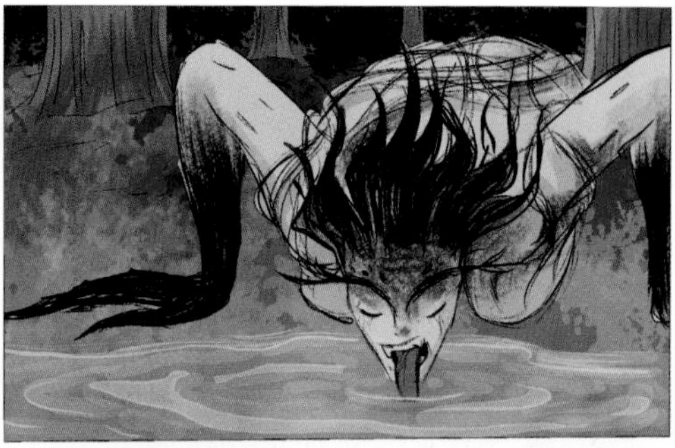
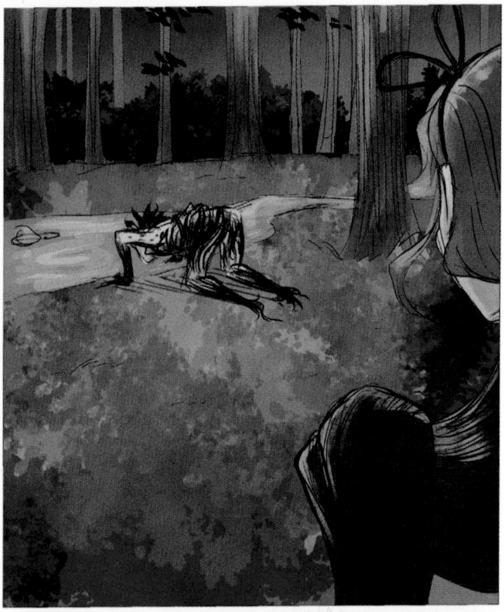
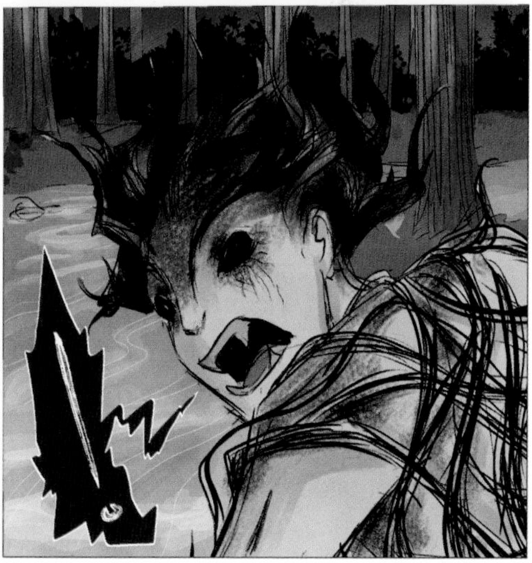

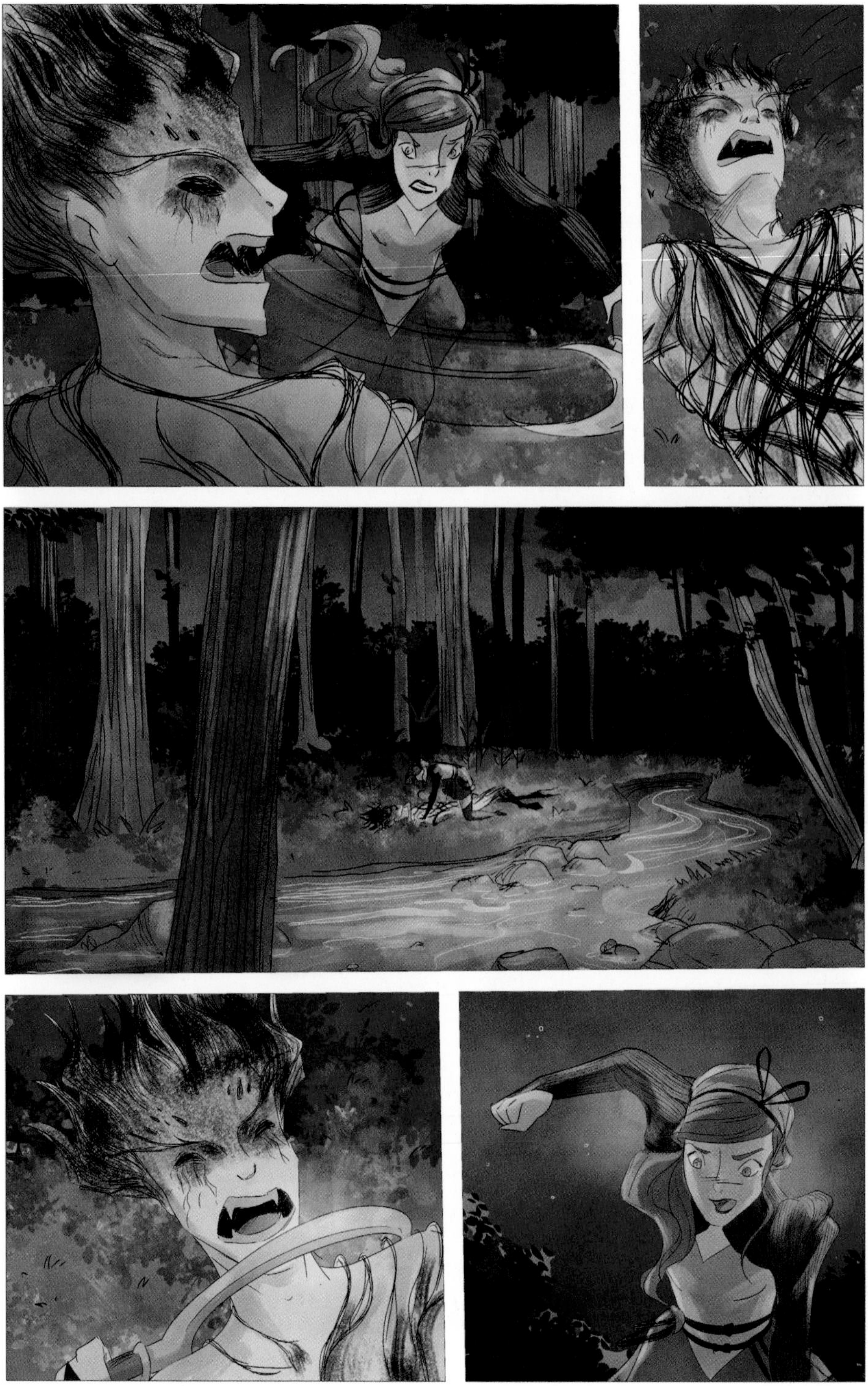

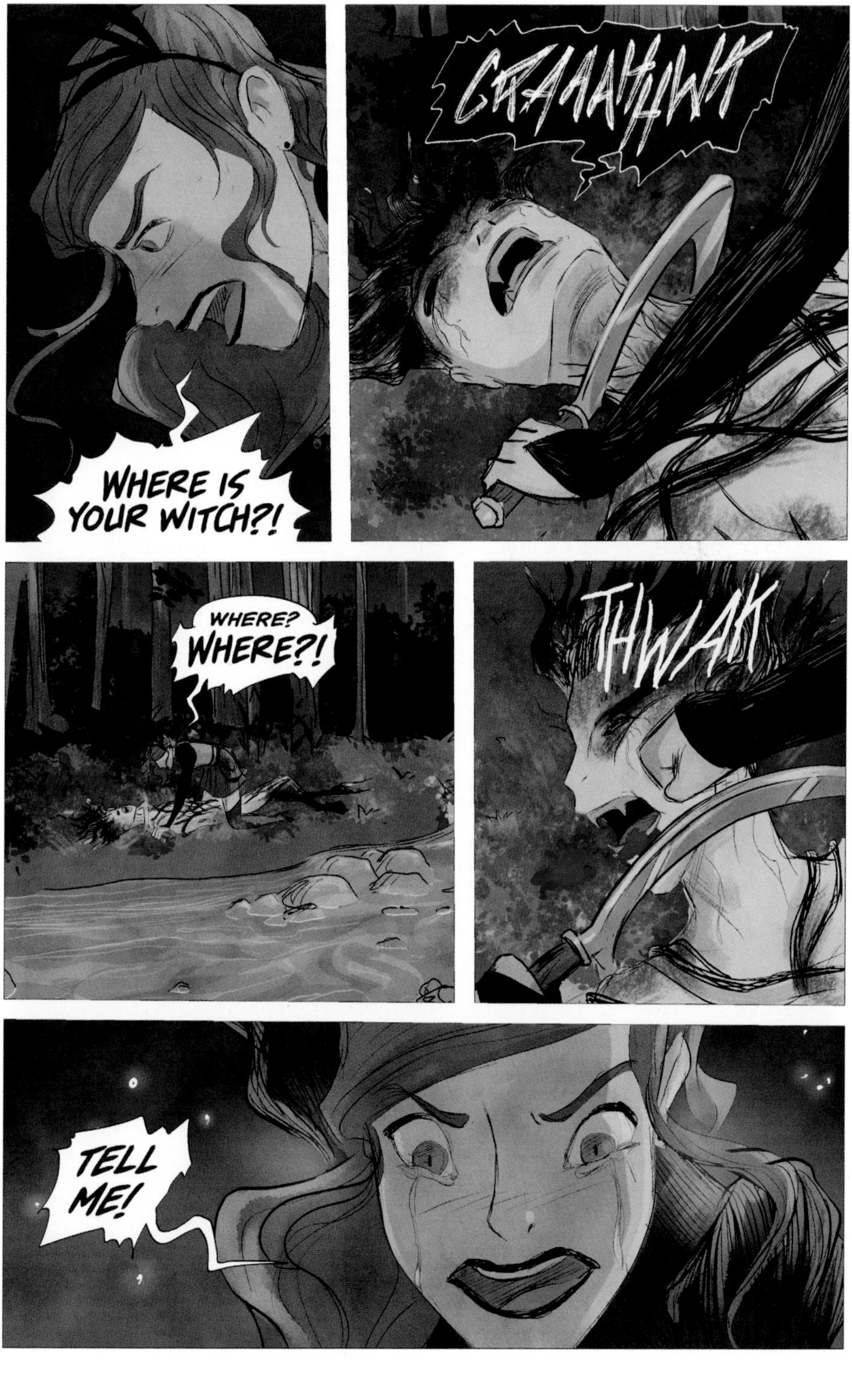
WHERE IS YOUR WITCH?!
GRAAAHHWK
WHERE? WHERE?!
THWAK
TELL ME!

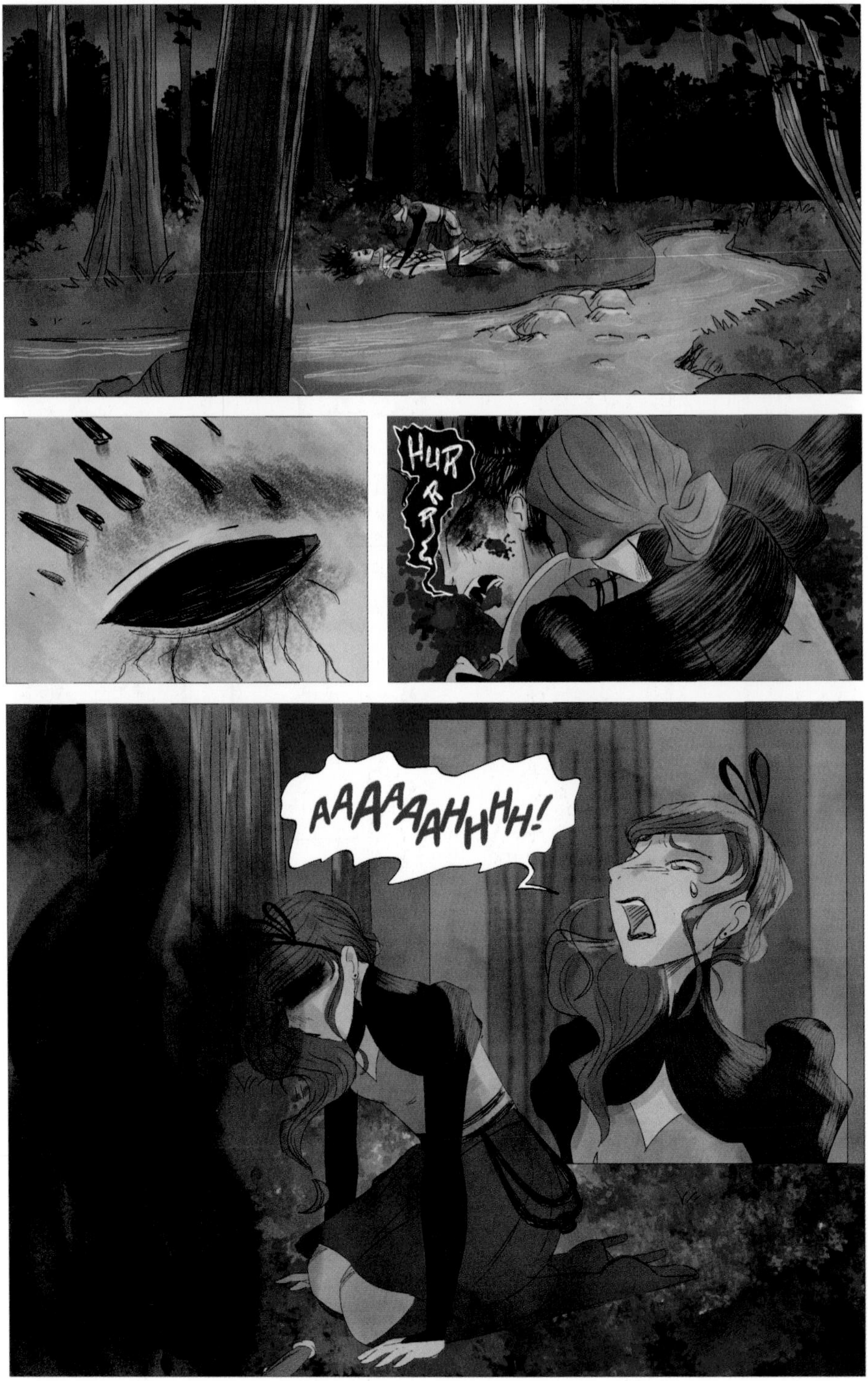
HURRRL
AAAAAAHHHH!

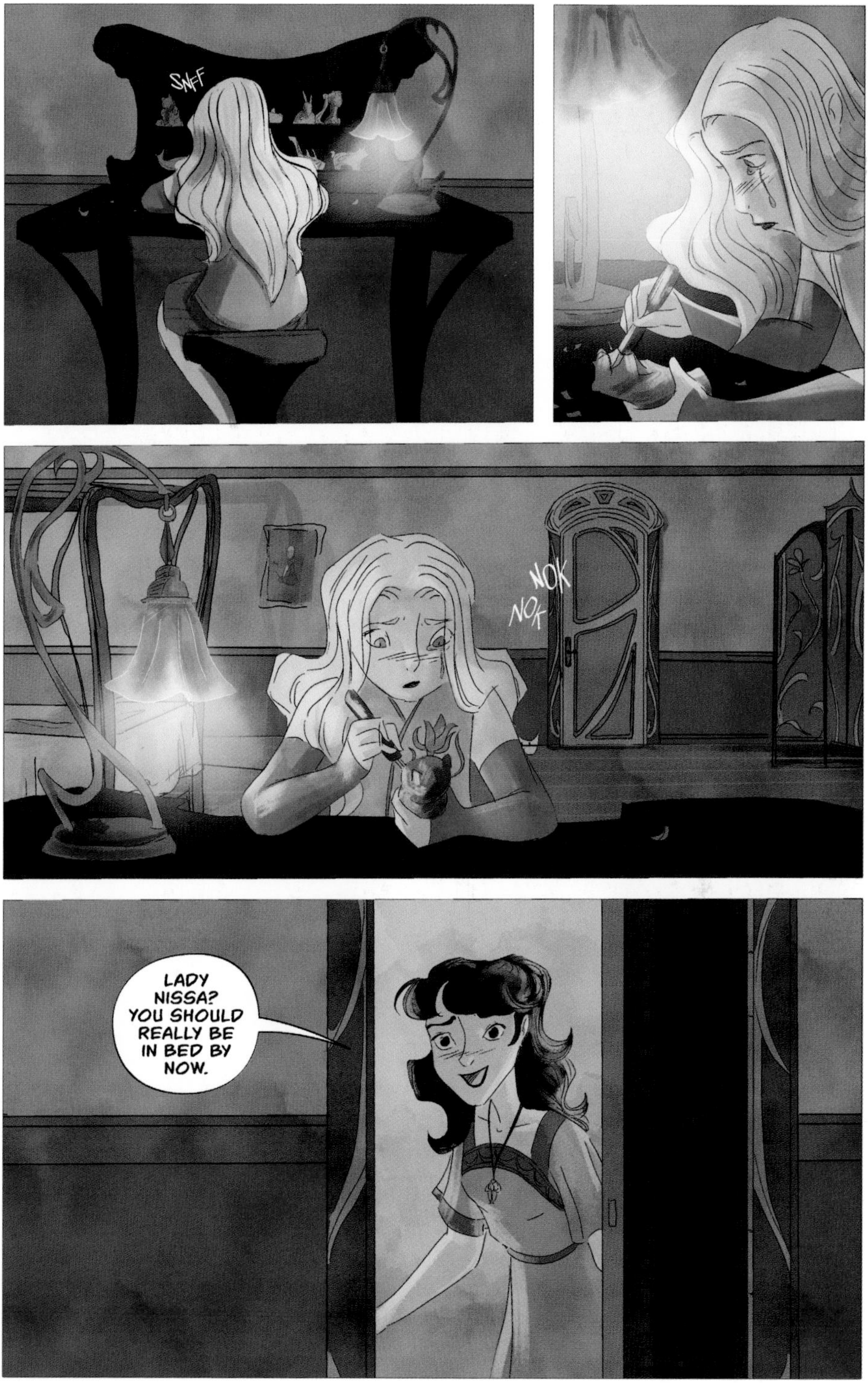
SNFF
NOK
NOK
LADY NISSA? YOU SHOULD REALLY BE IN BED BY NOW.

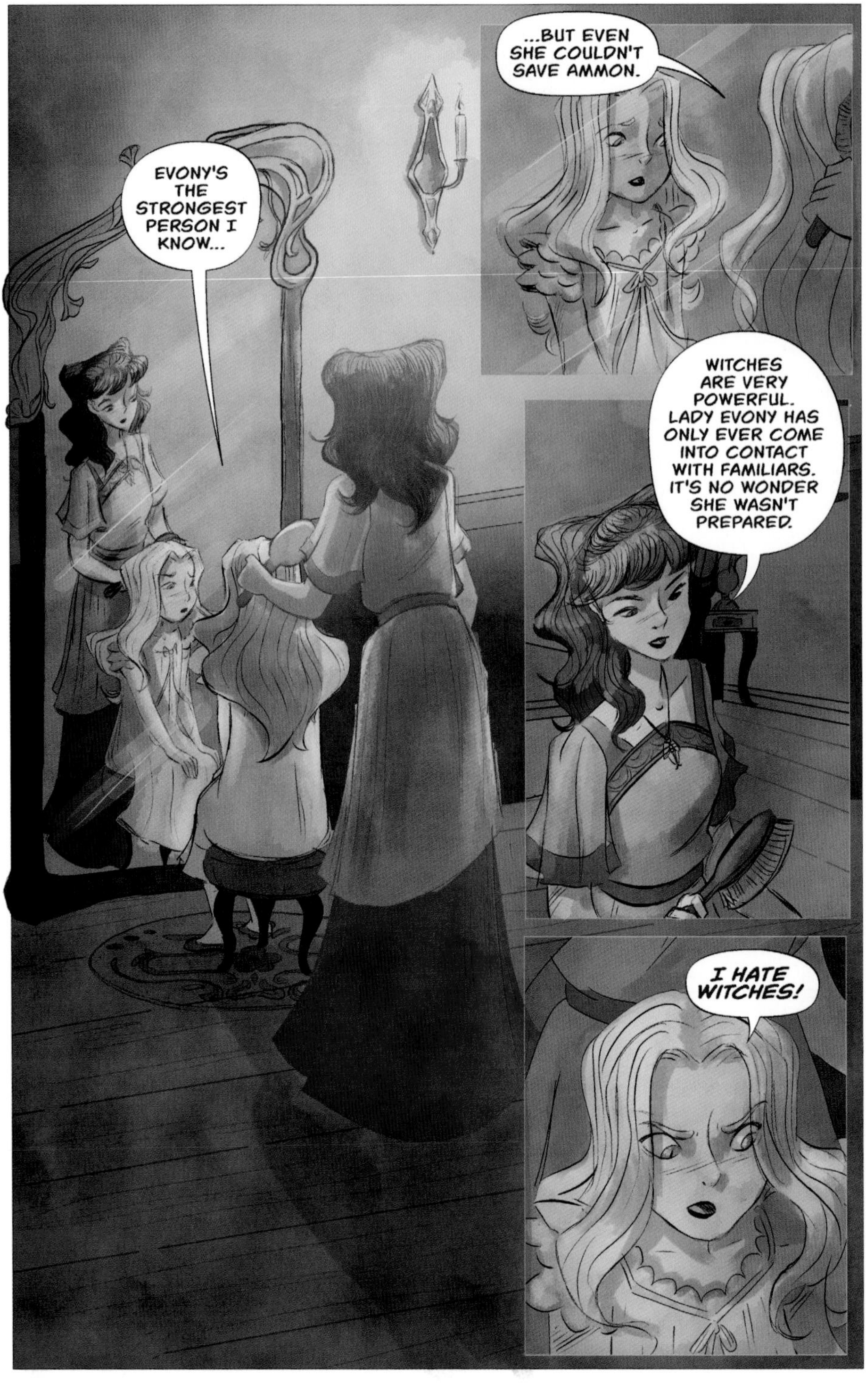
EVONY'S THE STRONGEST PERSON I KNOW...
...BUT EVEN SHE COULDN'T SAVE AMMON.
WITCHES ARE VERY POWERFUL. LADY EVONY HAS ONLY EVER COME INTO CONTACT WITH FAMILIARS. IT'S NO WONDER SHE WASN'T PREPARED.
I HATE WITCHES!

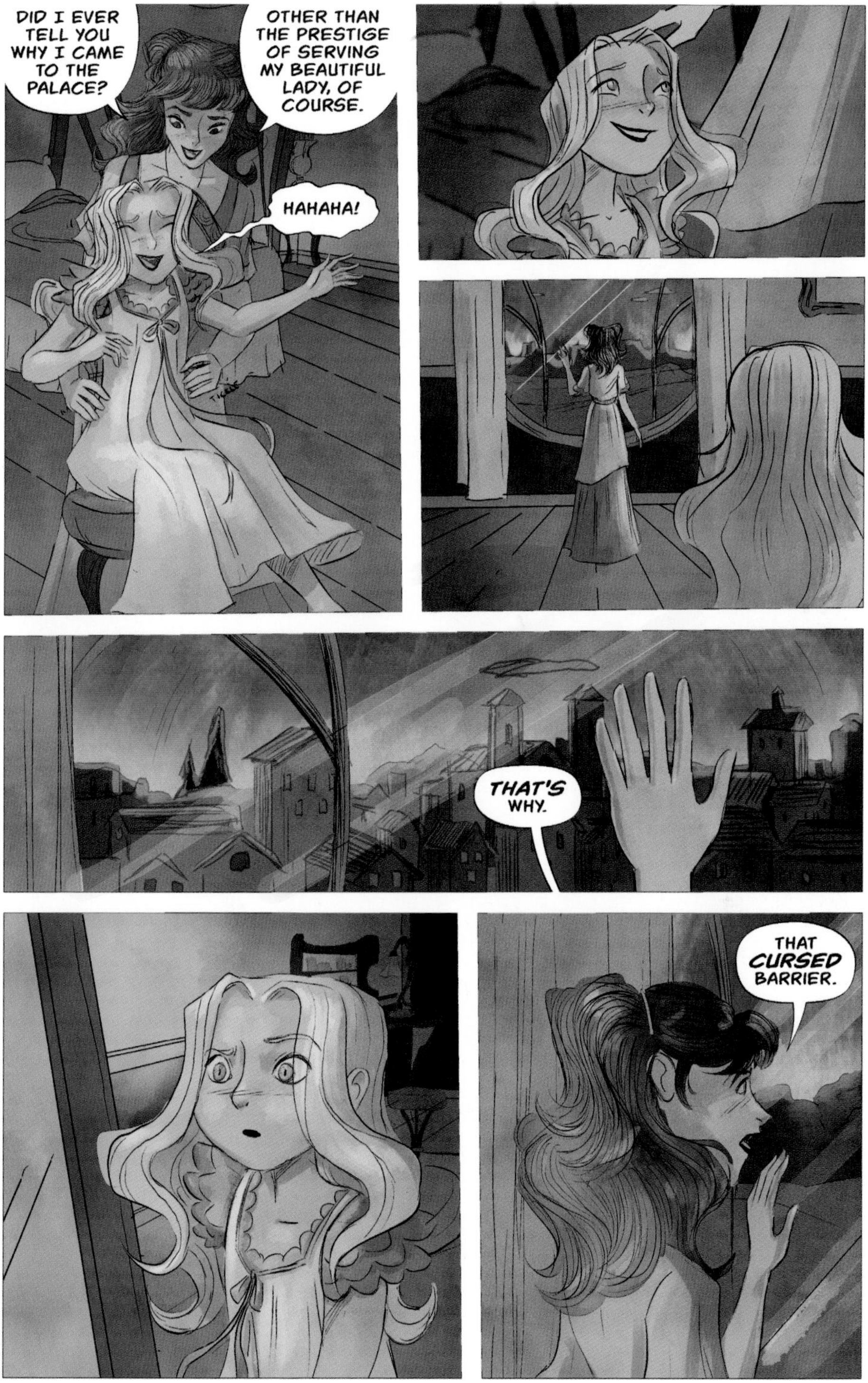
DID I EVER TELL YOU WHY I CAME TO THE PALACE?
OTHER THAN THE PRESTIGE OF SERVING MY BEAUTIFUL LADY, OF COURSE.
HAHAHA!
THAT'S WHY.
THAT CURSED BARRIER.

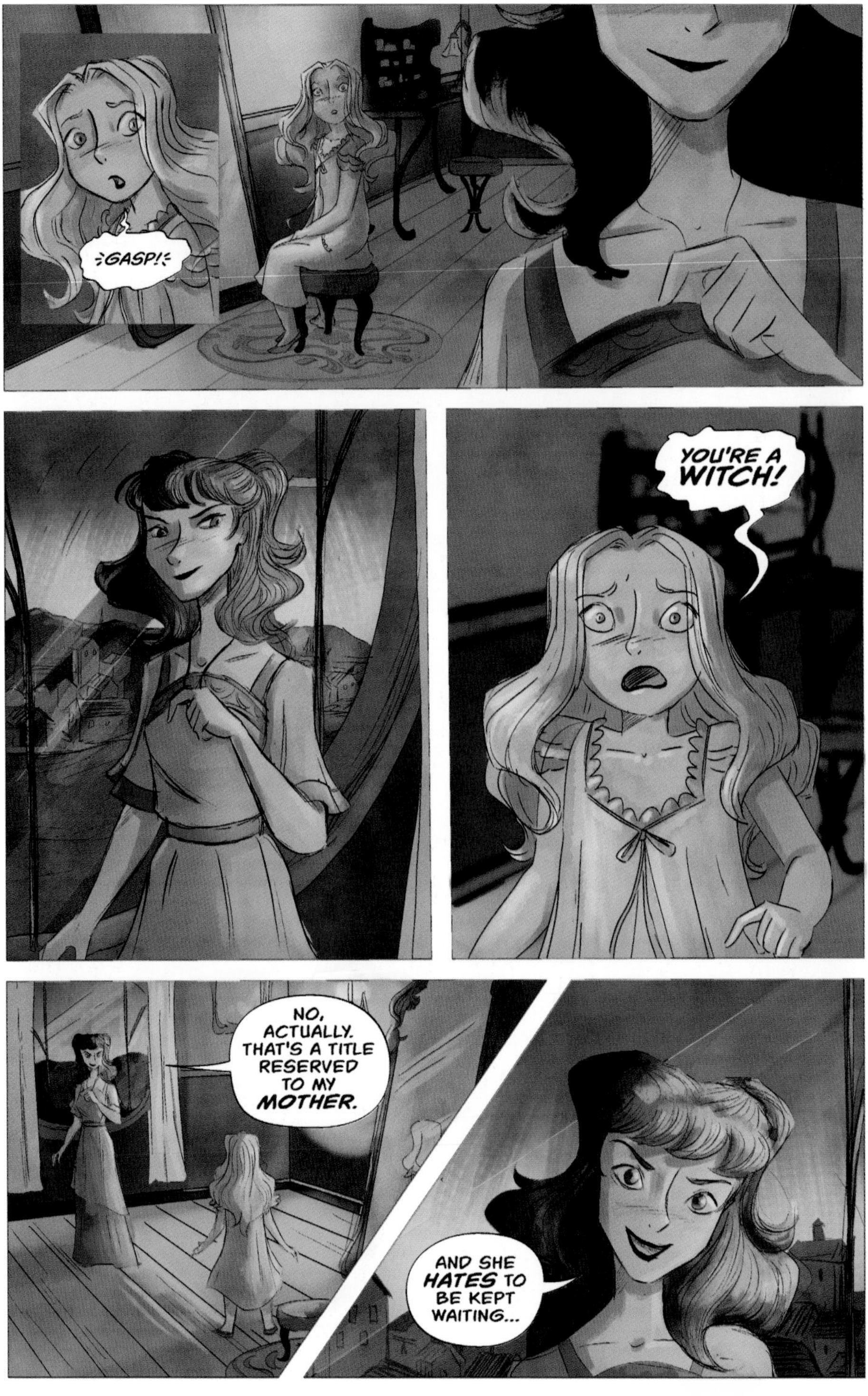

GASP!
YOU'RE A WITCH!
NO, ACTUALLY. THAT'S A TITLE RESERVED TO MY MOTHER.
AND SHE HATES TO BE KEPT WAITING...

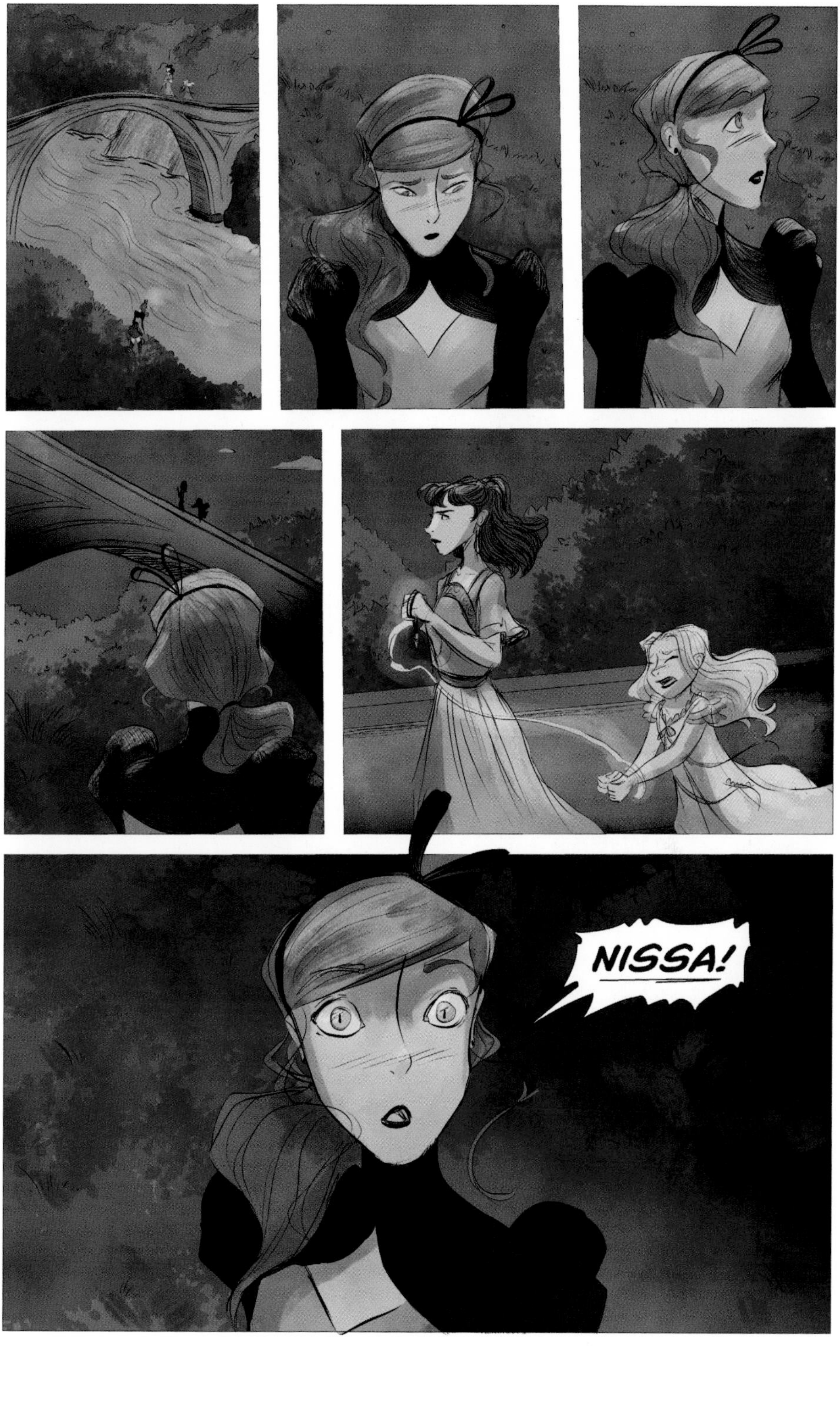
NISSA!

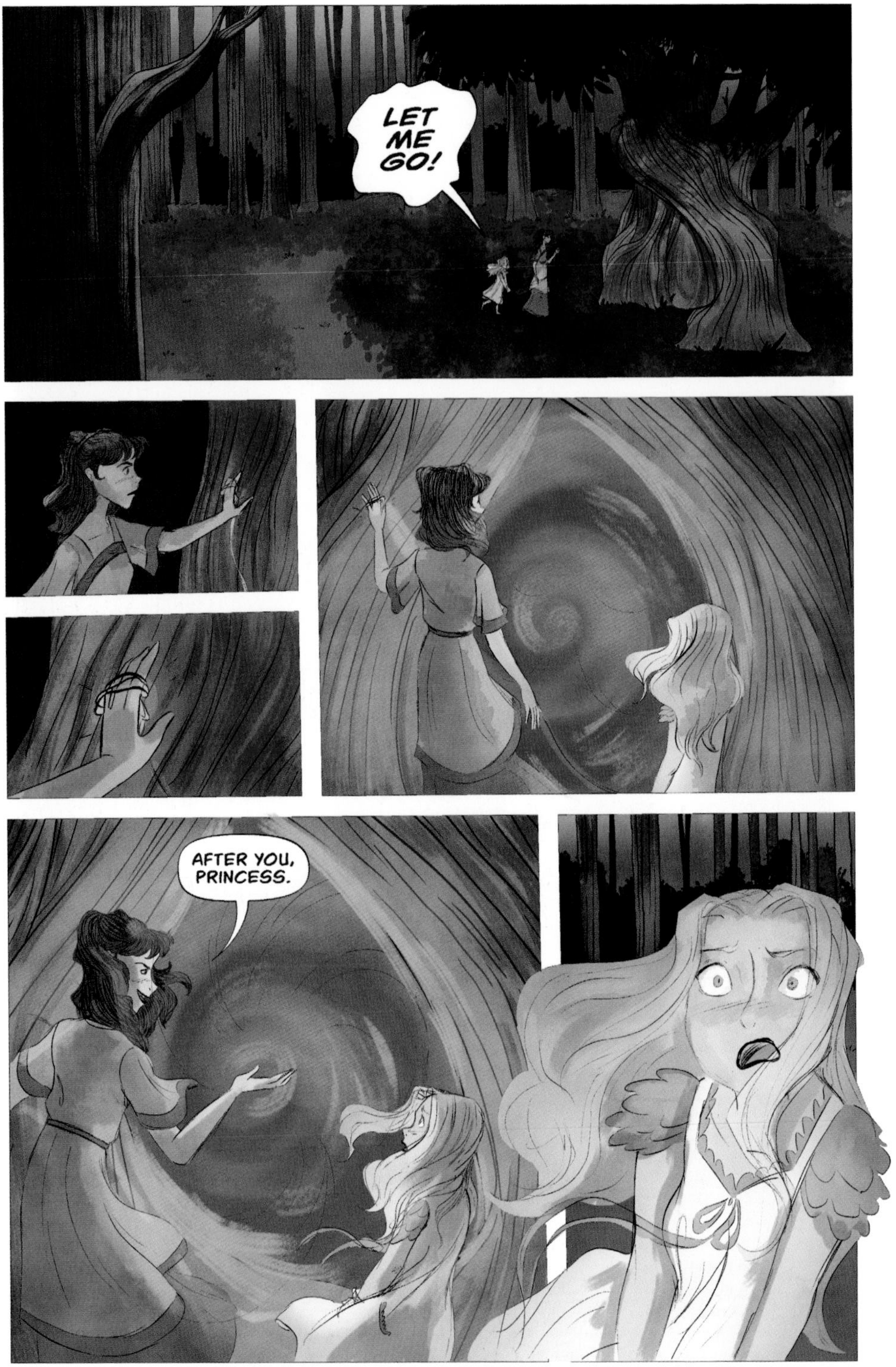
LET ME GO!
AFTER YOU, PRINCESS.

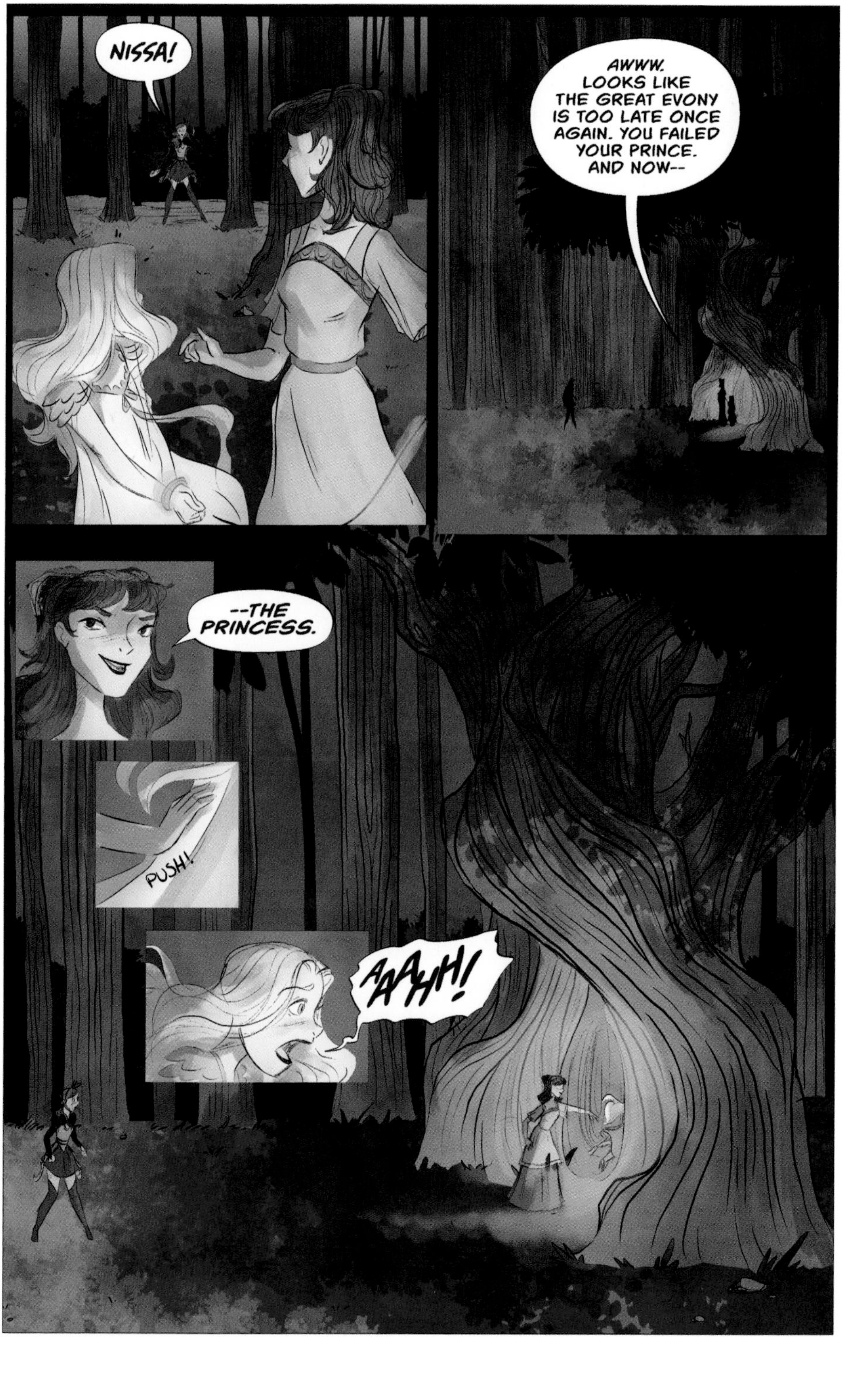
NISSA!
AWWW. LOOKS LIKE THE GREAT EVONY IS TOO LATE ONCE AGAIN. YOU FAILED YOUR PRINCE. AND NOW--
--THE PRINCESS.
PUSH!
AAAHH!

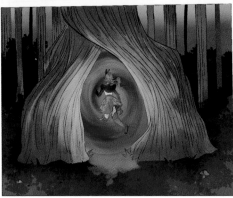

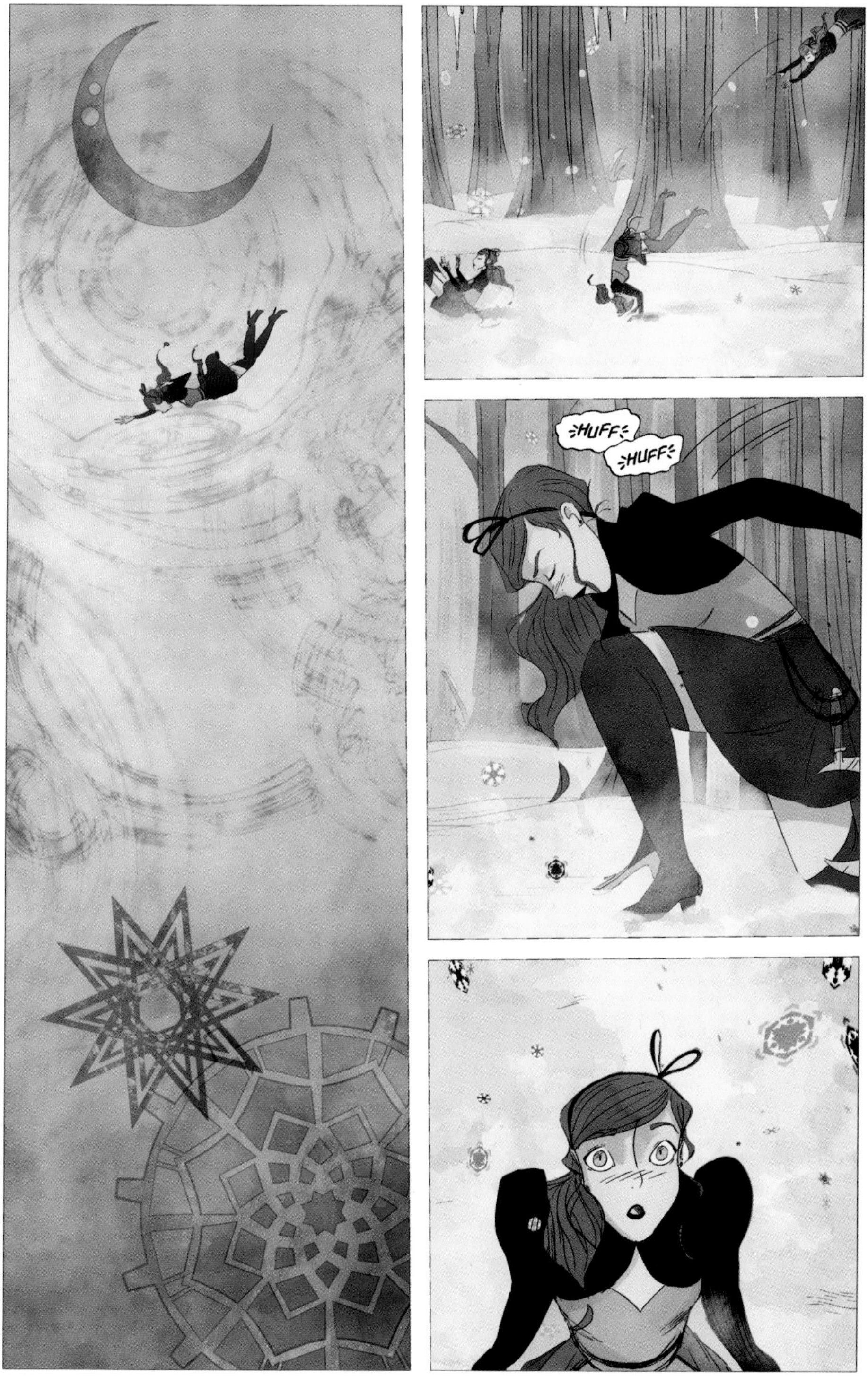
HUFF
HUFF

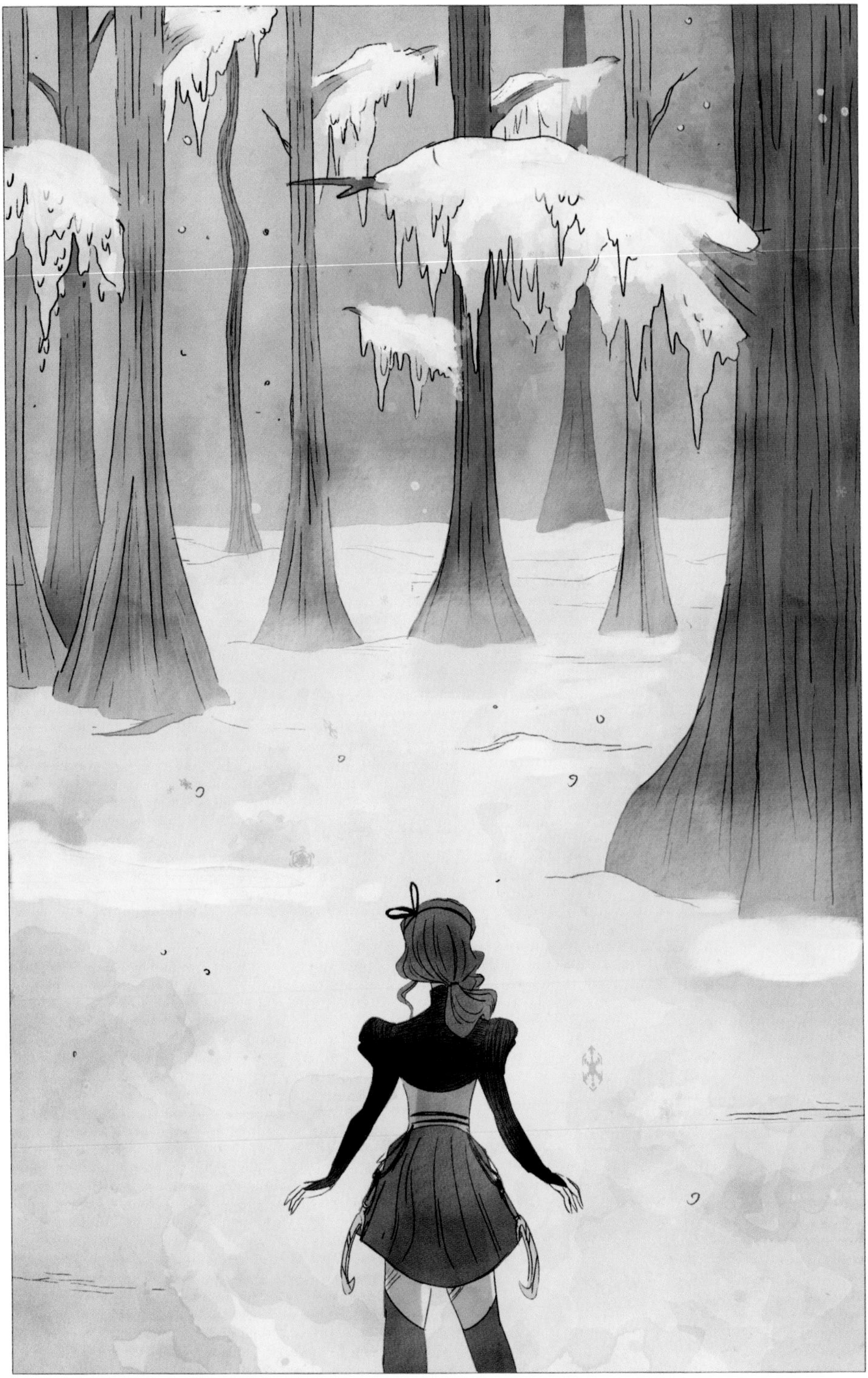

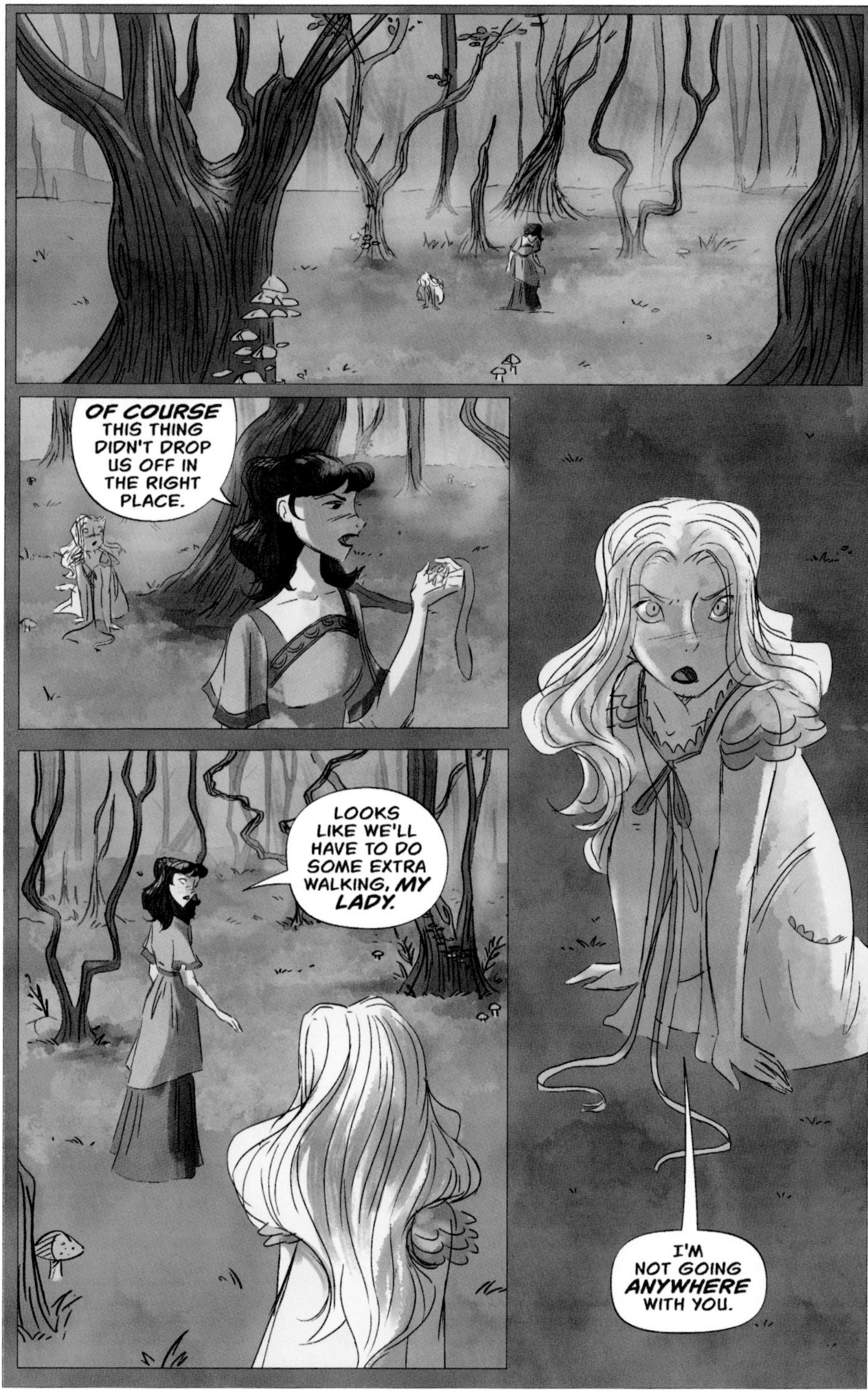
OF COURSE THIS THING DIDN'T DROP US OFF IN THE RIGHT PLACE.
LOOKS LIKE WE'LL HAVE TO DO SOME EXTRA WALKING, MY LADY.
I'M NOT GOING ANYWHERE WITH YOU.

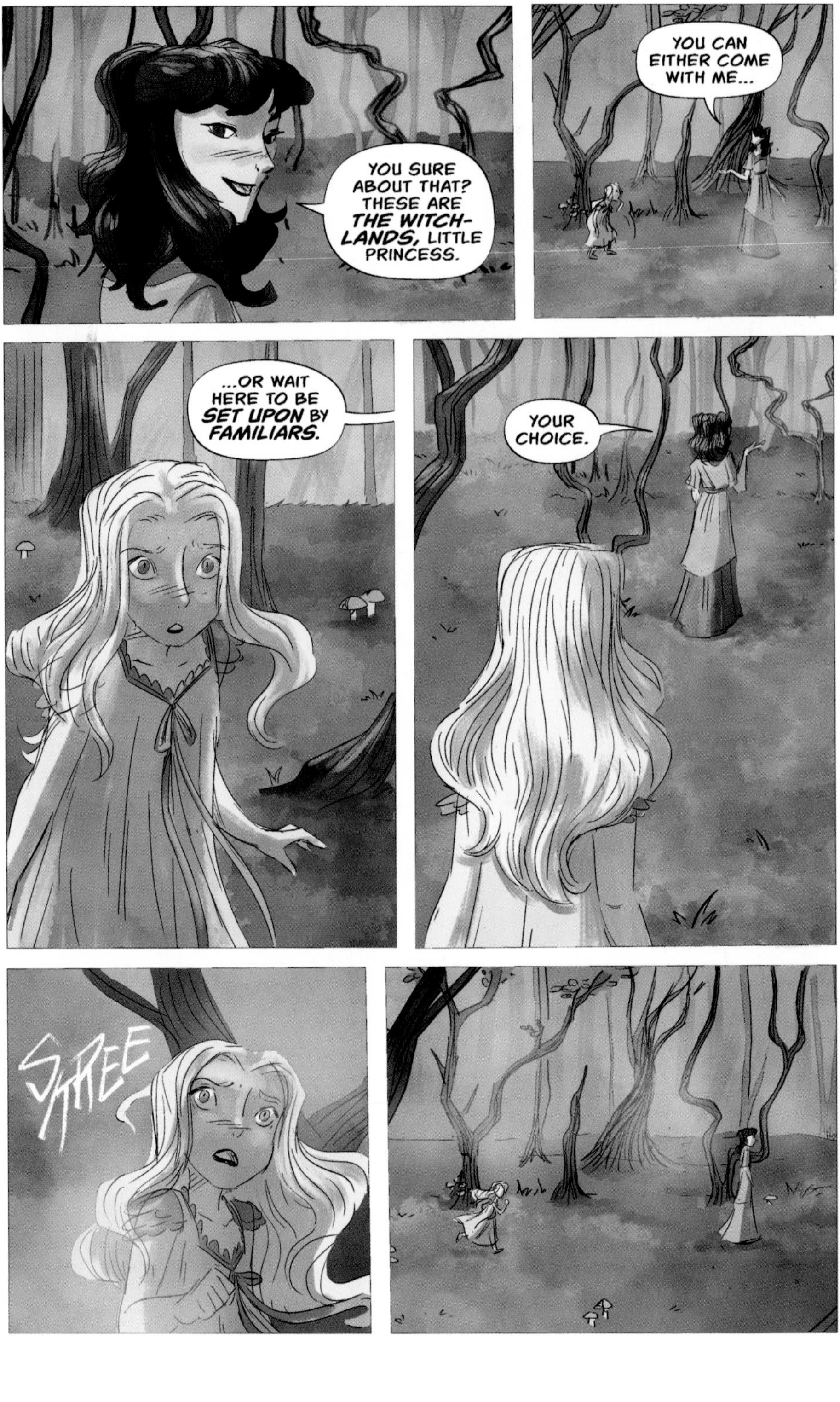
YOU SURE ABOUT THAT? THESE ARE THE WITCH-LANDS, LITTLE PRINCESS.
YOU CAN EITHER COME WITH ME...
...OR WAIT HERE TO BE SET UPON BY FAMILIARS.
YOUR CHOICE.
SKREE

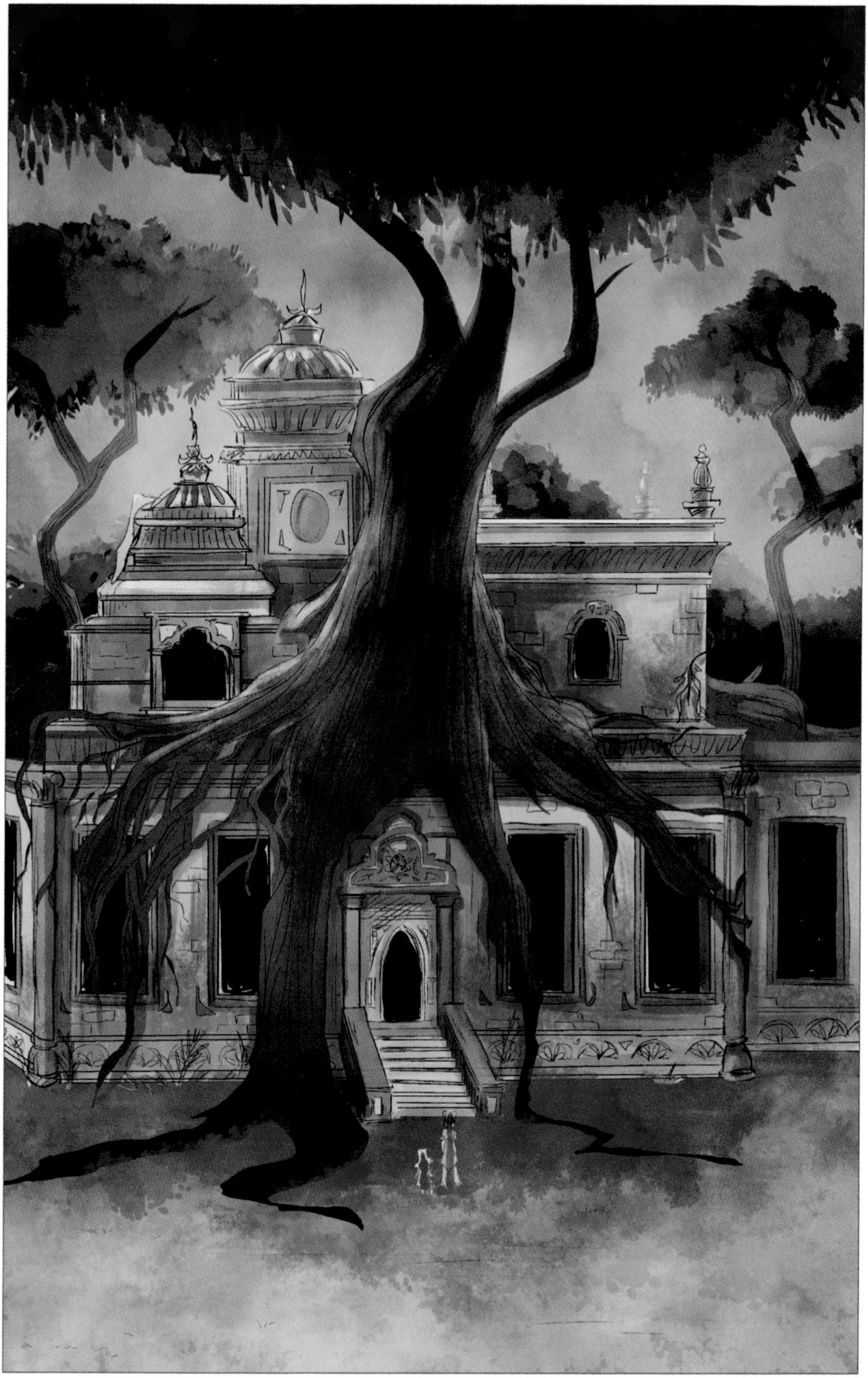

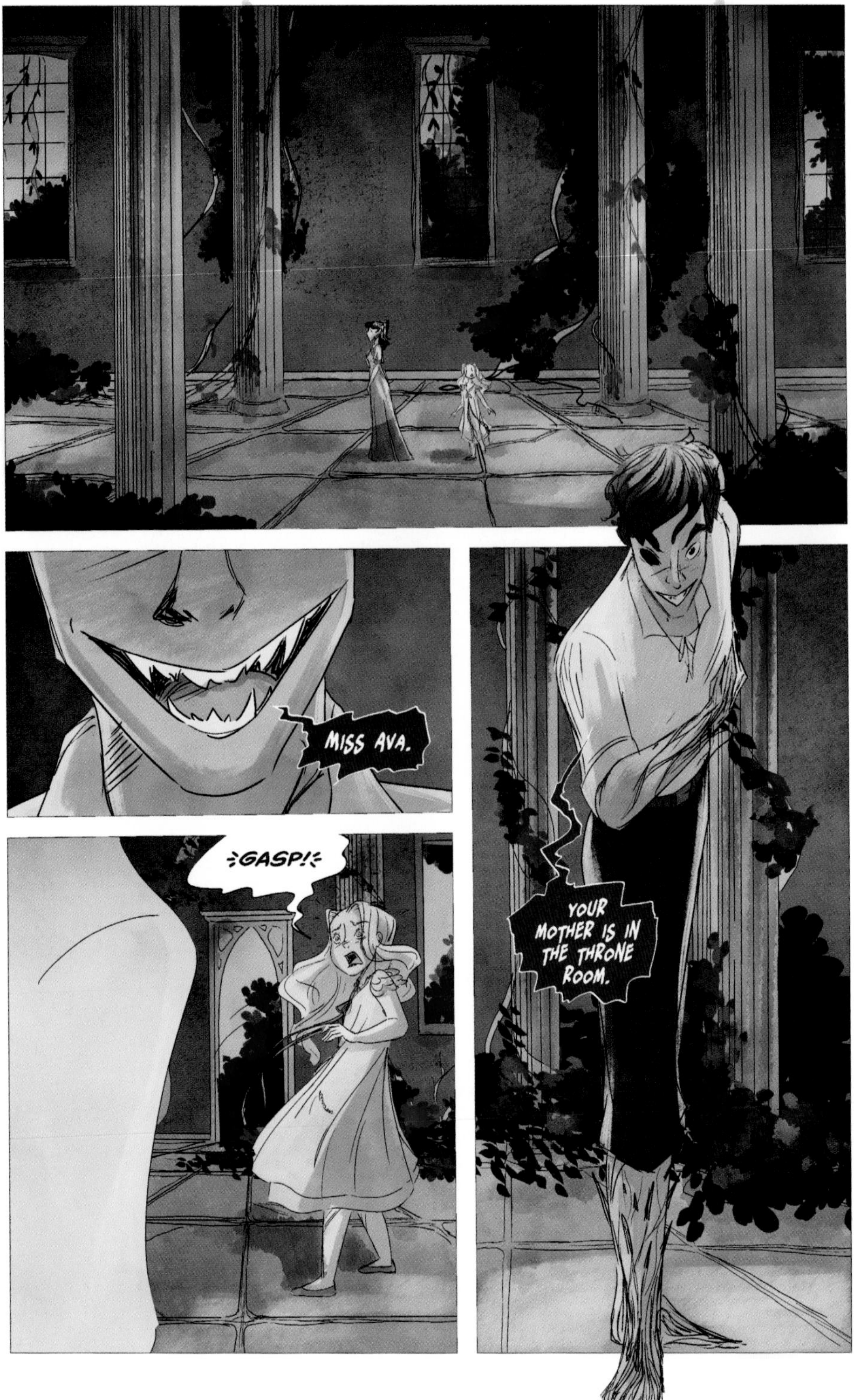
MISS AVA.
GASP!
YOUR MOTHER IS IN THE THRONE ROOM.

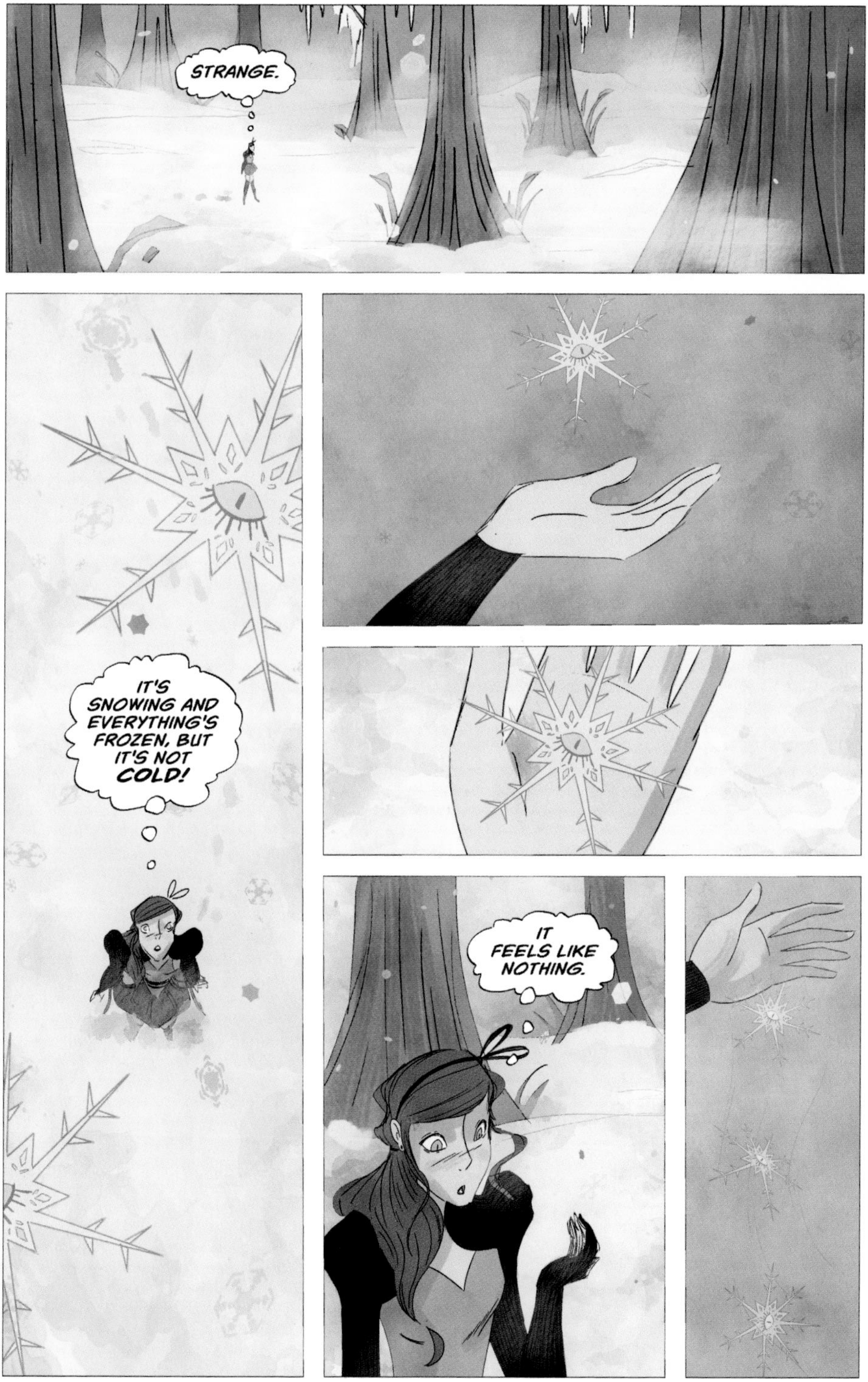
STRANGE.
IT'S SNOWING AND EVERYTHING'S FROZEN, BUT IT'S NOT COLD!
IT FEELS LIKE NOTHING.

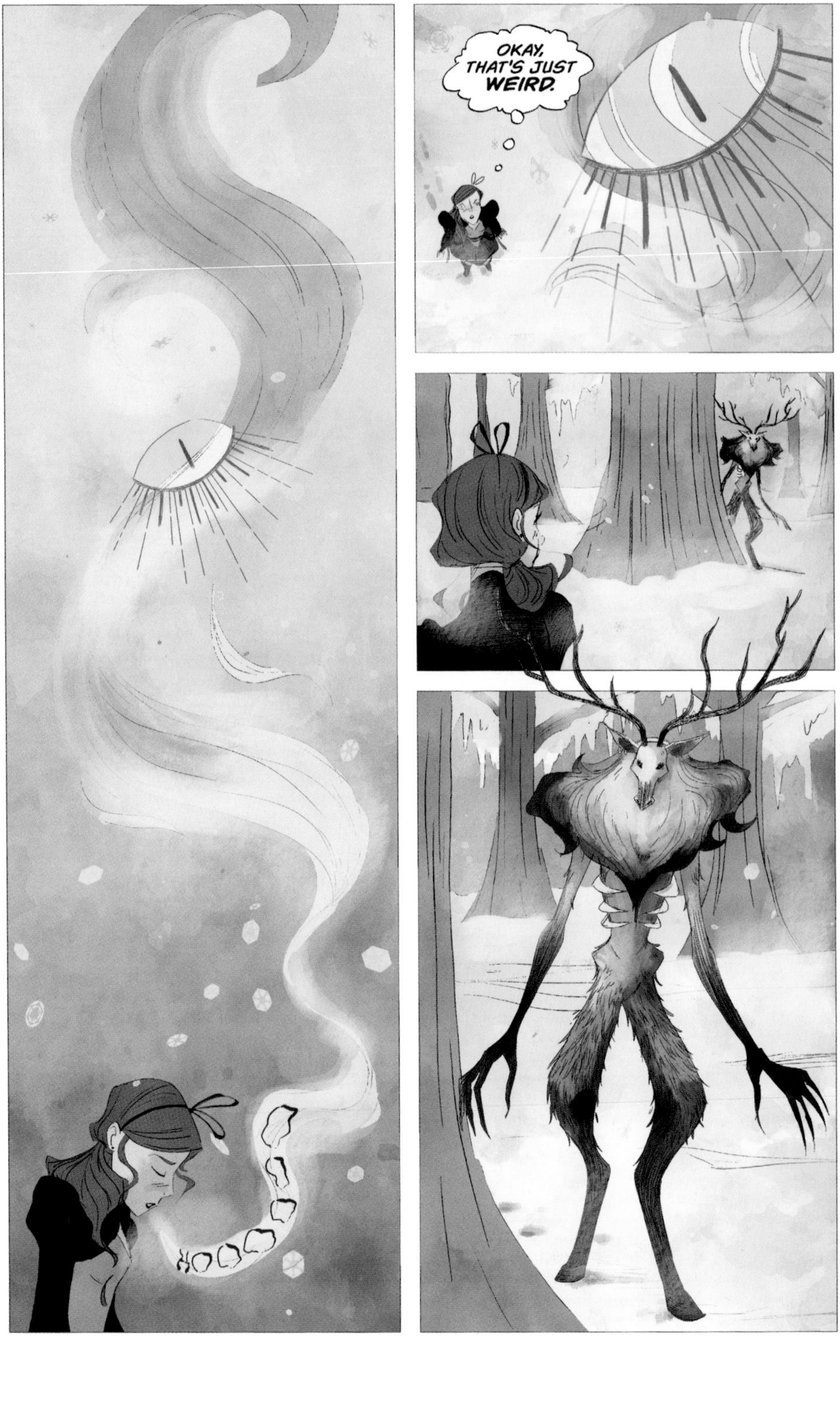
OKAY, THAT'S JUST WEIRD.

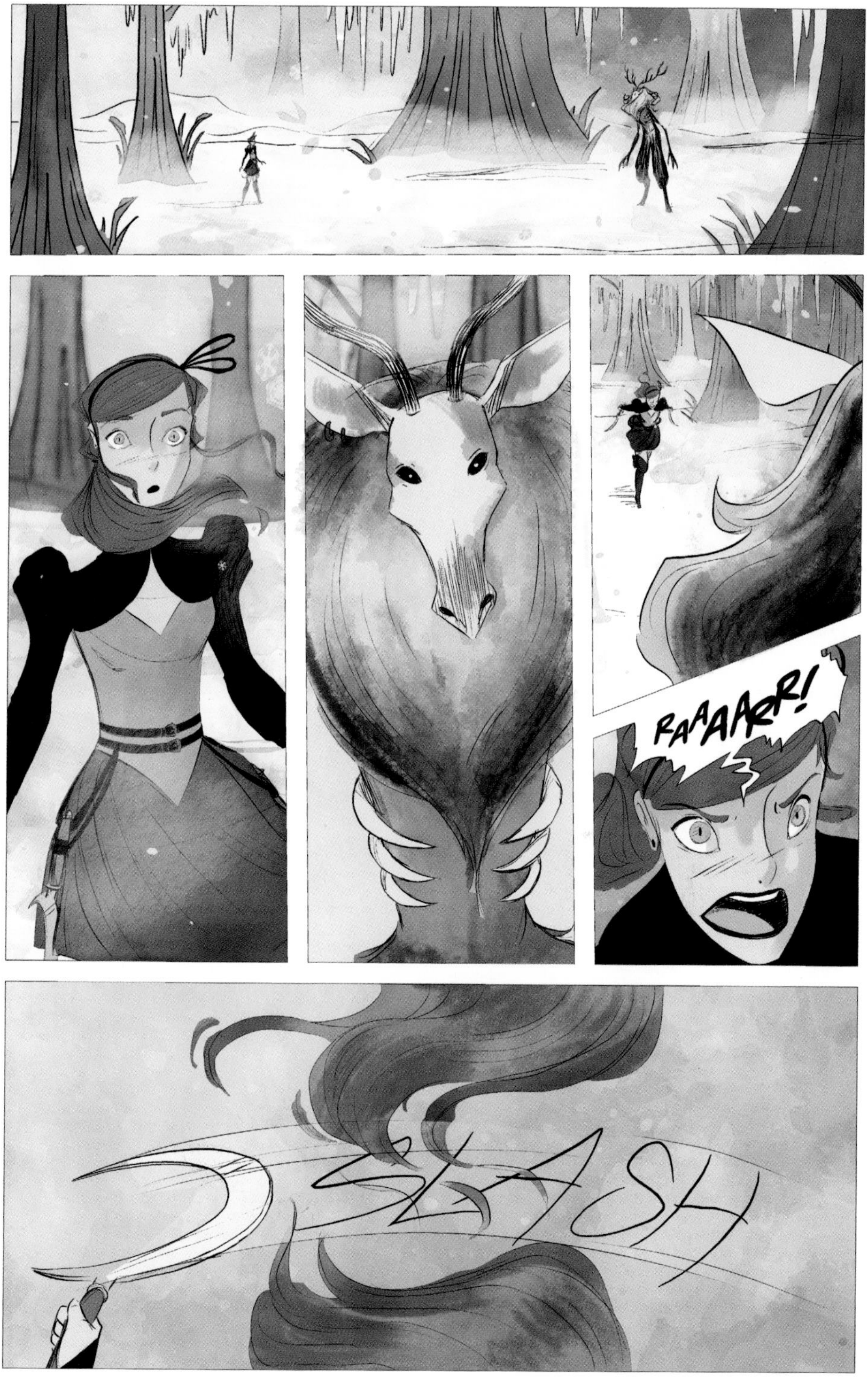
RAAAARR!
SLASH

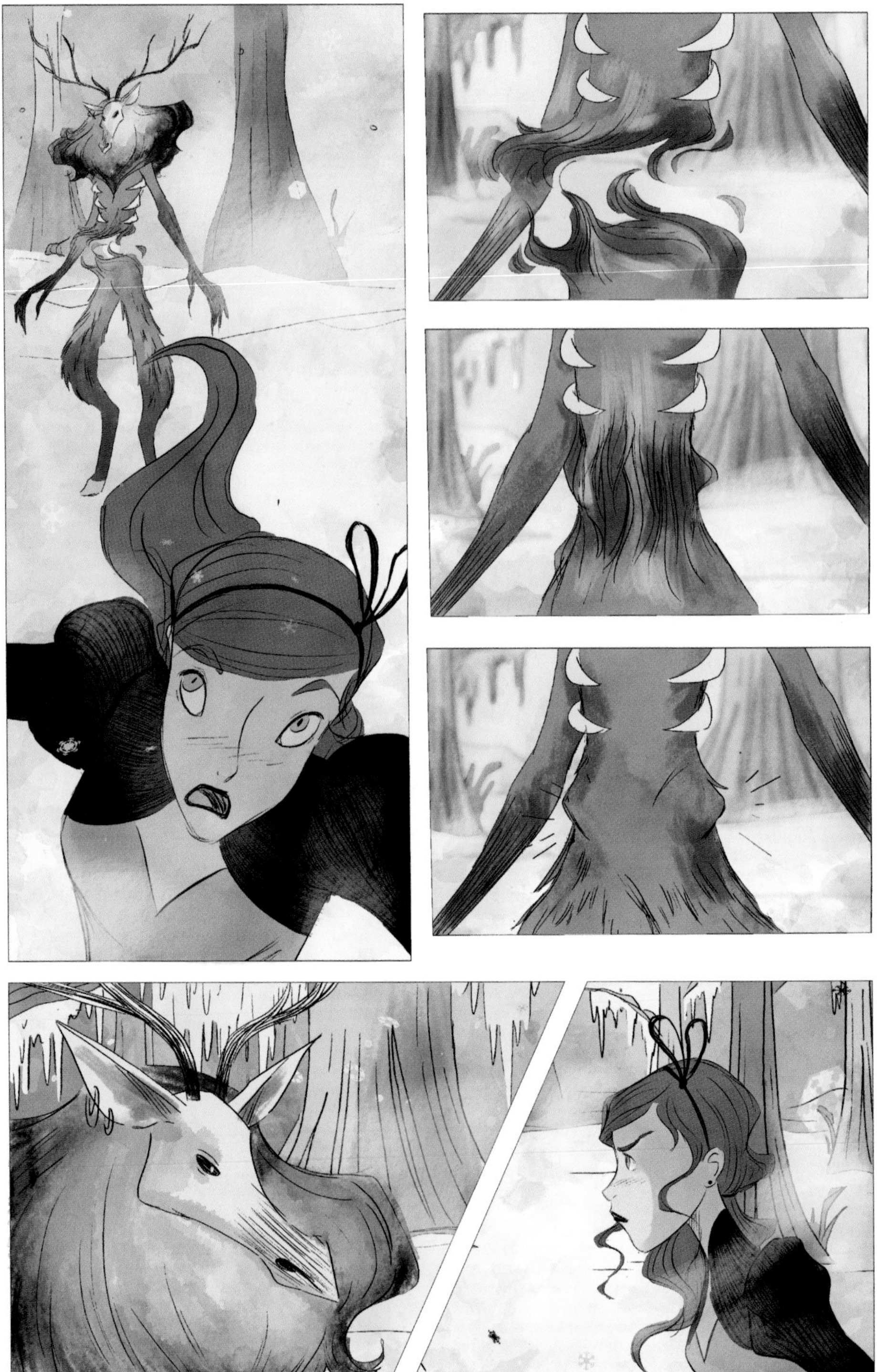

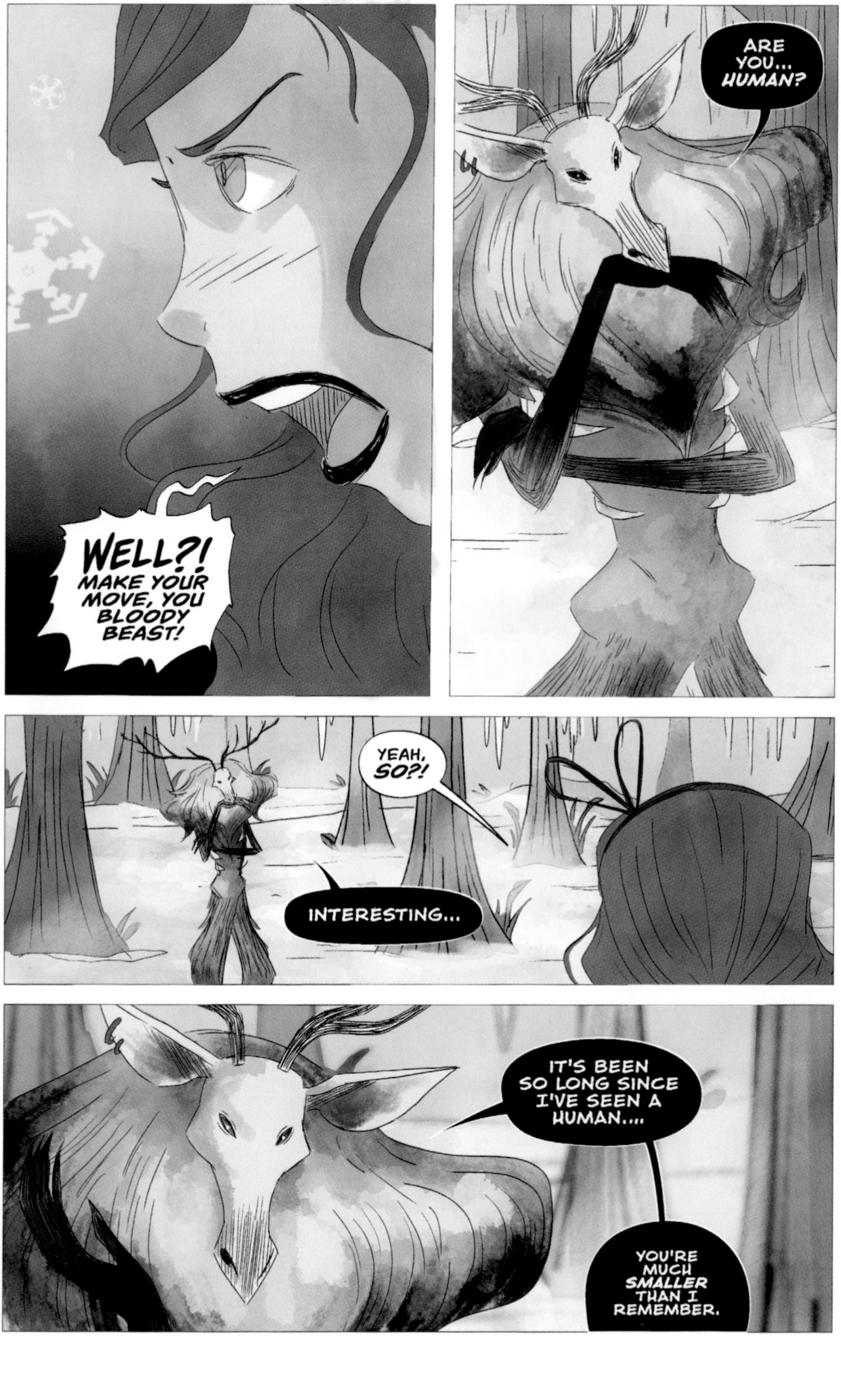
WELL?! MAKE YOUR MOVE, YOU BLOODY BEAST!
ARE YOU... HUMAN?
YEAH, SO?!
INTERESTING...
IT'S BEEN SO LONG SINCE I'VE SEEN A HUMAN....
YOU'RE MUCH SMALLER THAN I REMEMBER.

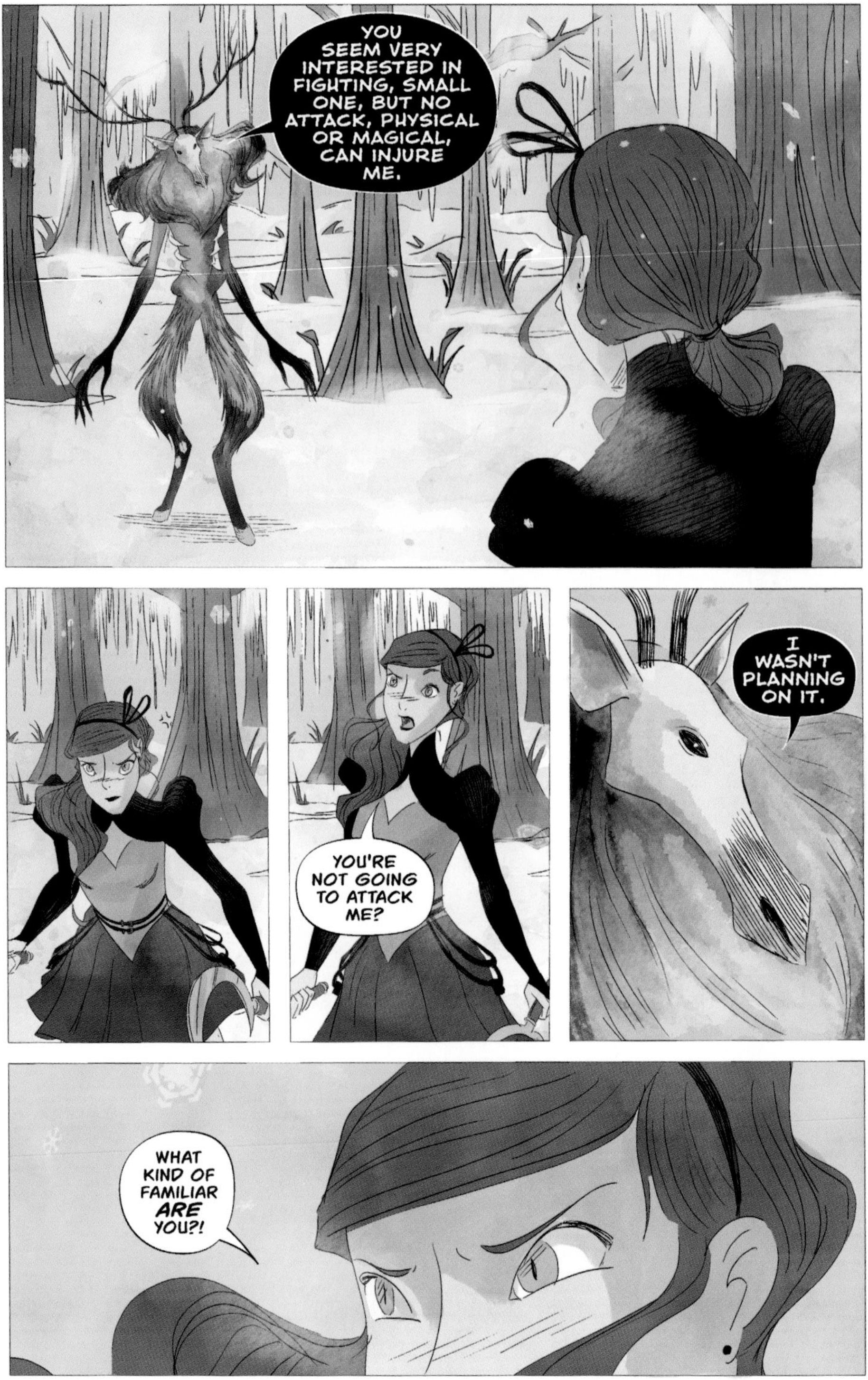
YOU SEEM VERY INTERESTED IN FIGHTING, SMALL ONE, BUT NO ATTACK, PHYSICAL OR MAGICAL, CAN INJURE ME.
YOU'RE NOT GOING TO ATTACK ME?
I WASN'T PLANNING ON IT.
WHAT KIND OF FAMILIAR *ARE* YOU?!

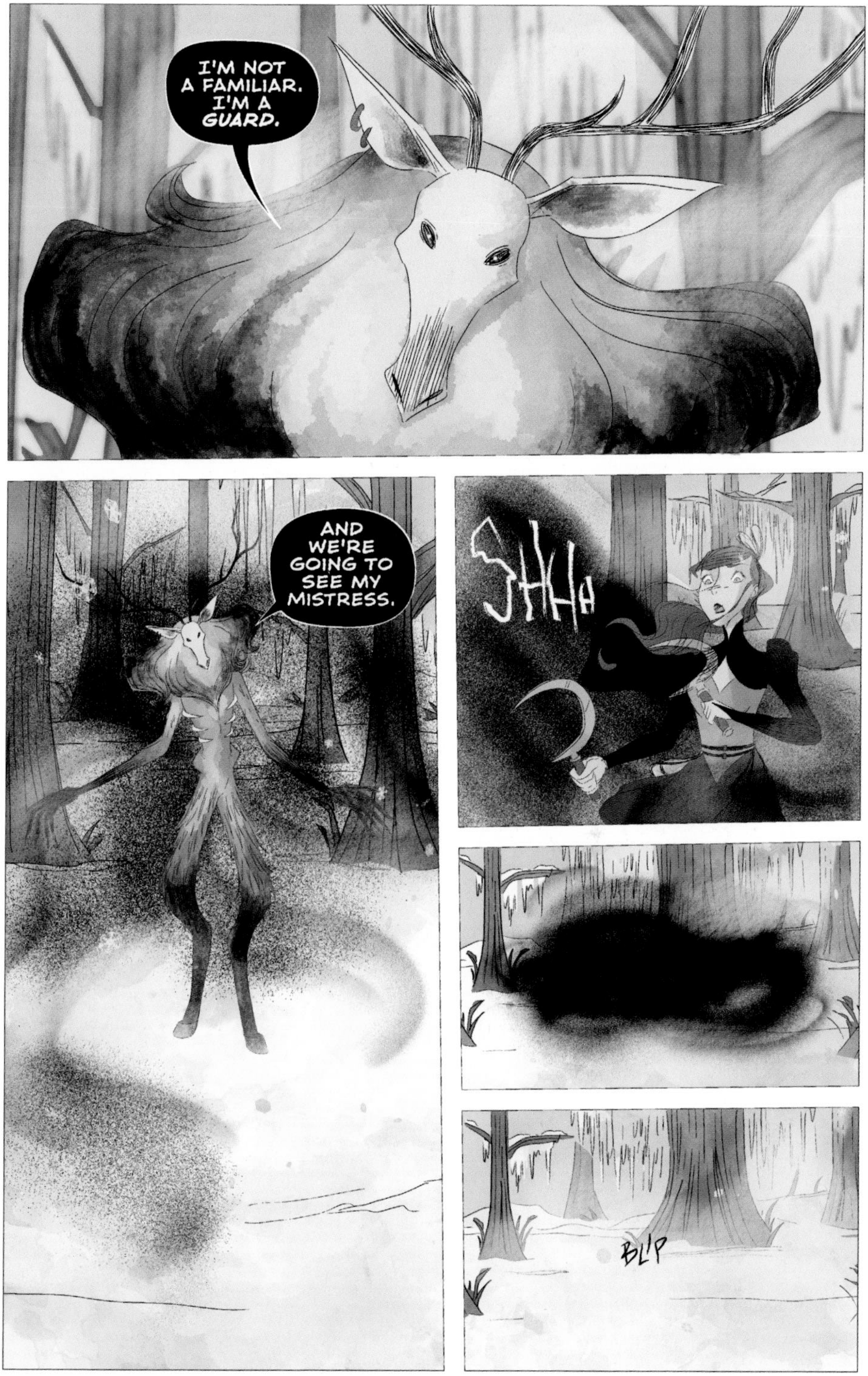
I'M NOT A FAMILIAR. I'M A GUARD.
AND WE'RE GOING TO SEE MY MISTRESS.
SHHH
BLIP

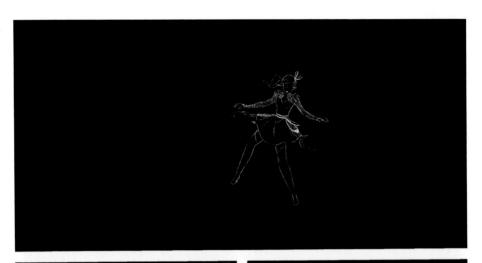

UMPH!

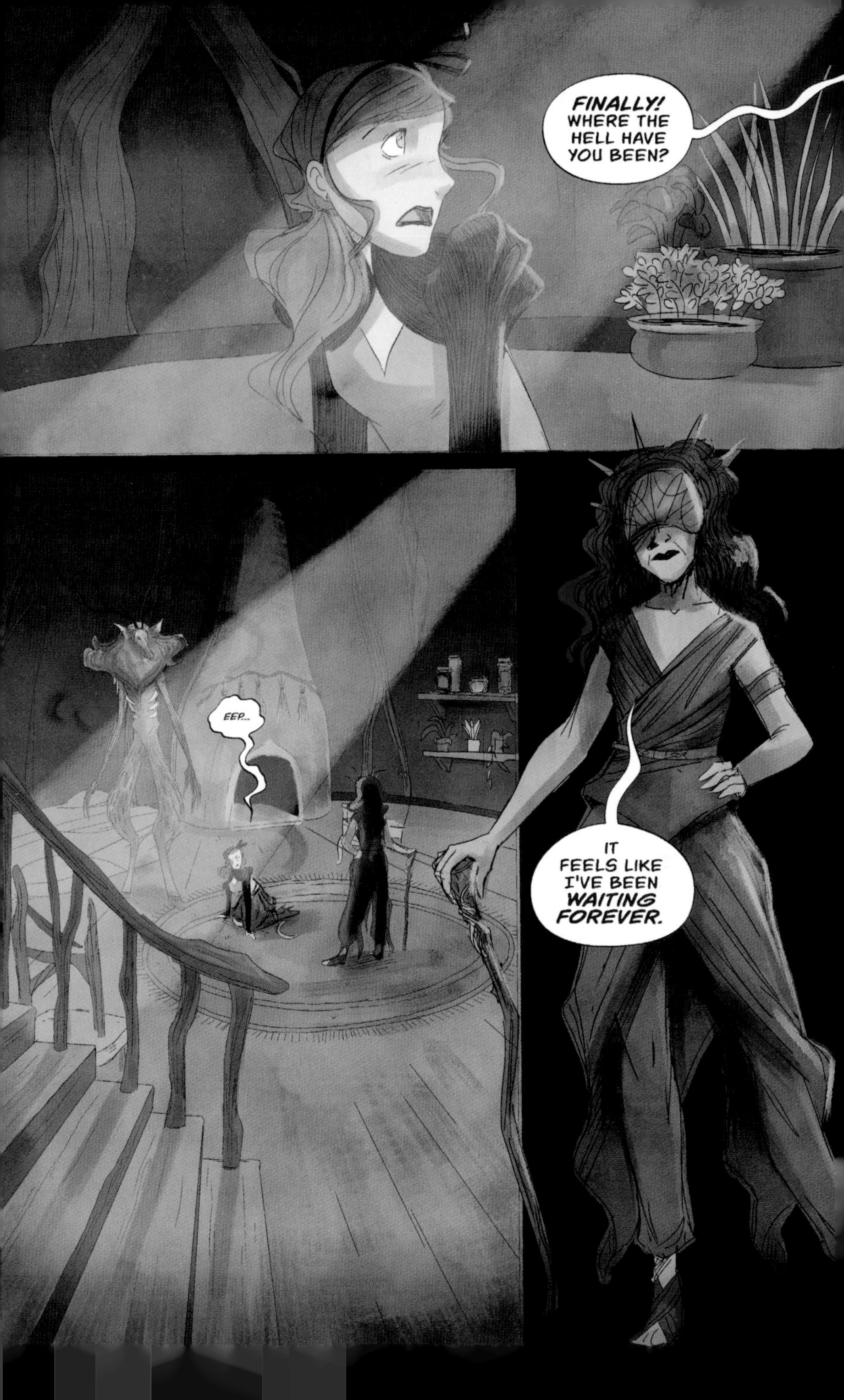
FINALLY! WHERE THE HELL HAVE YOU BEEN?
EEP...
IT FEELS LIKE I'VE BEEN WAITING FOREVER.

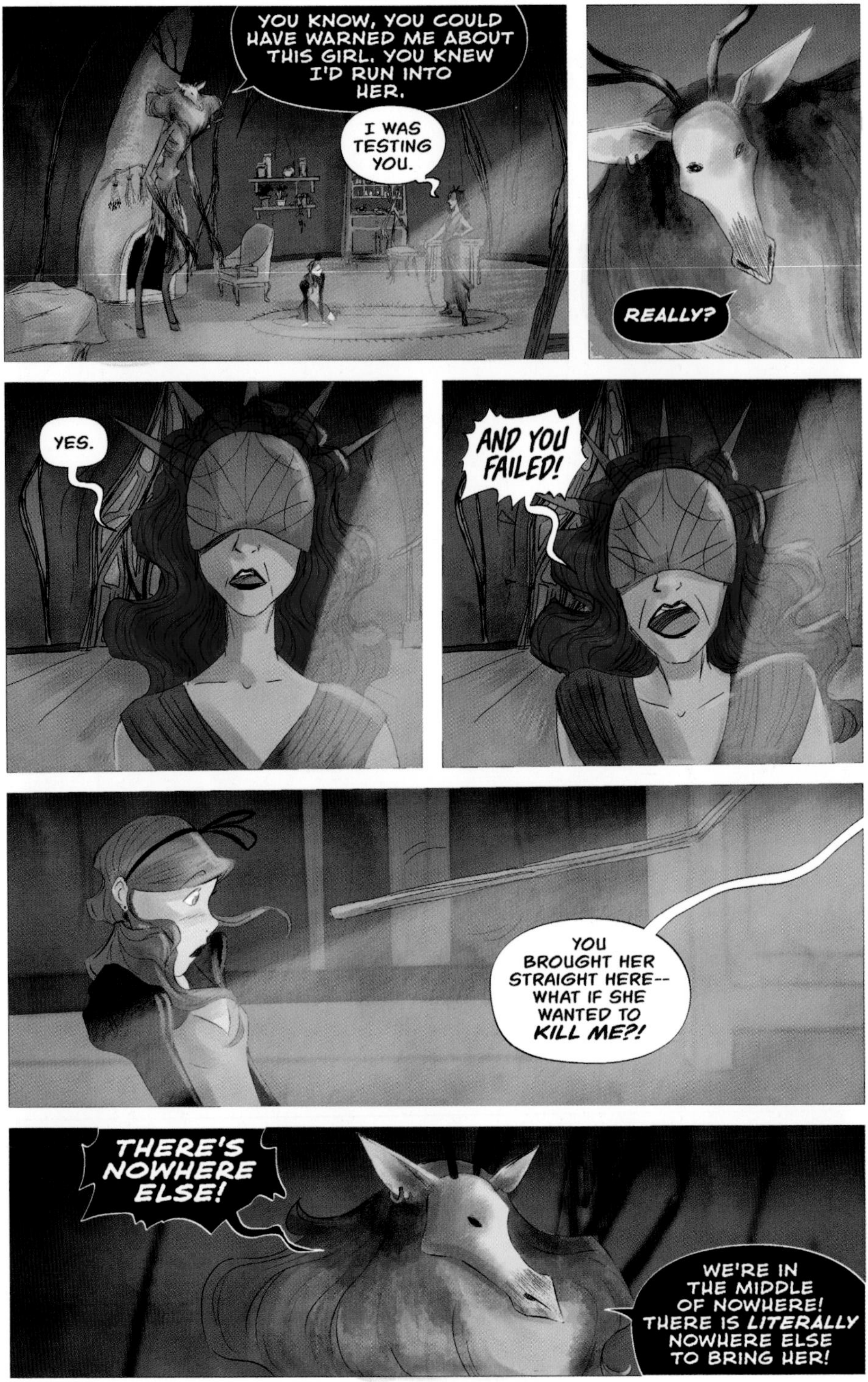
YOU KNOW, YOU COULD HAVE WARNED ME ABOUT THIS GIRL. YOU KNEW I'D RUN INTO HER.
I WAS TESTING YOU.
REALLY?
YES.
AND YOU FAILED!
YOU BROUGHT HER STRAIGHT HERE-- WHAT IF SHE WANTED TO KILL ME?!
THERE'S NOWHERE ELSE!
WE'RE IN THE MIDDLE OF NOWHERE! THERE IS LITERALLY NOWHERE ELSE TO BRING HER!

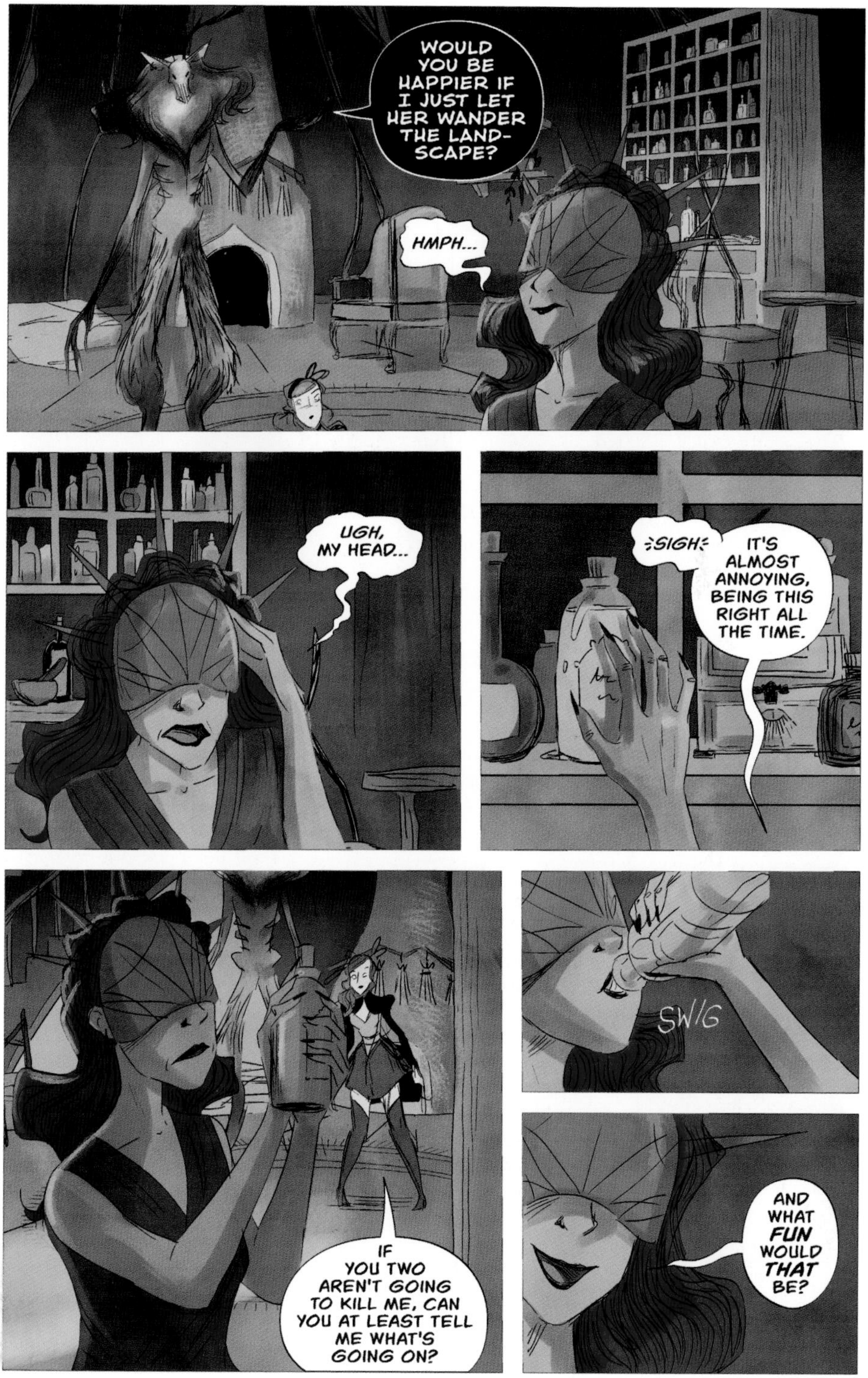
WOULD YOU BE HAPPIER IF I JUST LET HER WANDER THE LAND-SCAPE?
HMPH...
UGH, MY HEAD...
SIGH
IT'S ALMOST ANNOYING, BEING THIS RIGHT ALL THE TIME.
IF YOU TWO AREN'T GOING TO KILL ME, CAN YOU AT LEAST TELL ME WHAT'S GOING ON?
SWIG
AND WHAT FUN WOULD THAT BE?

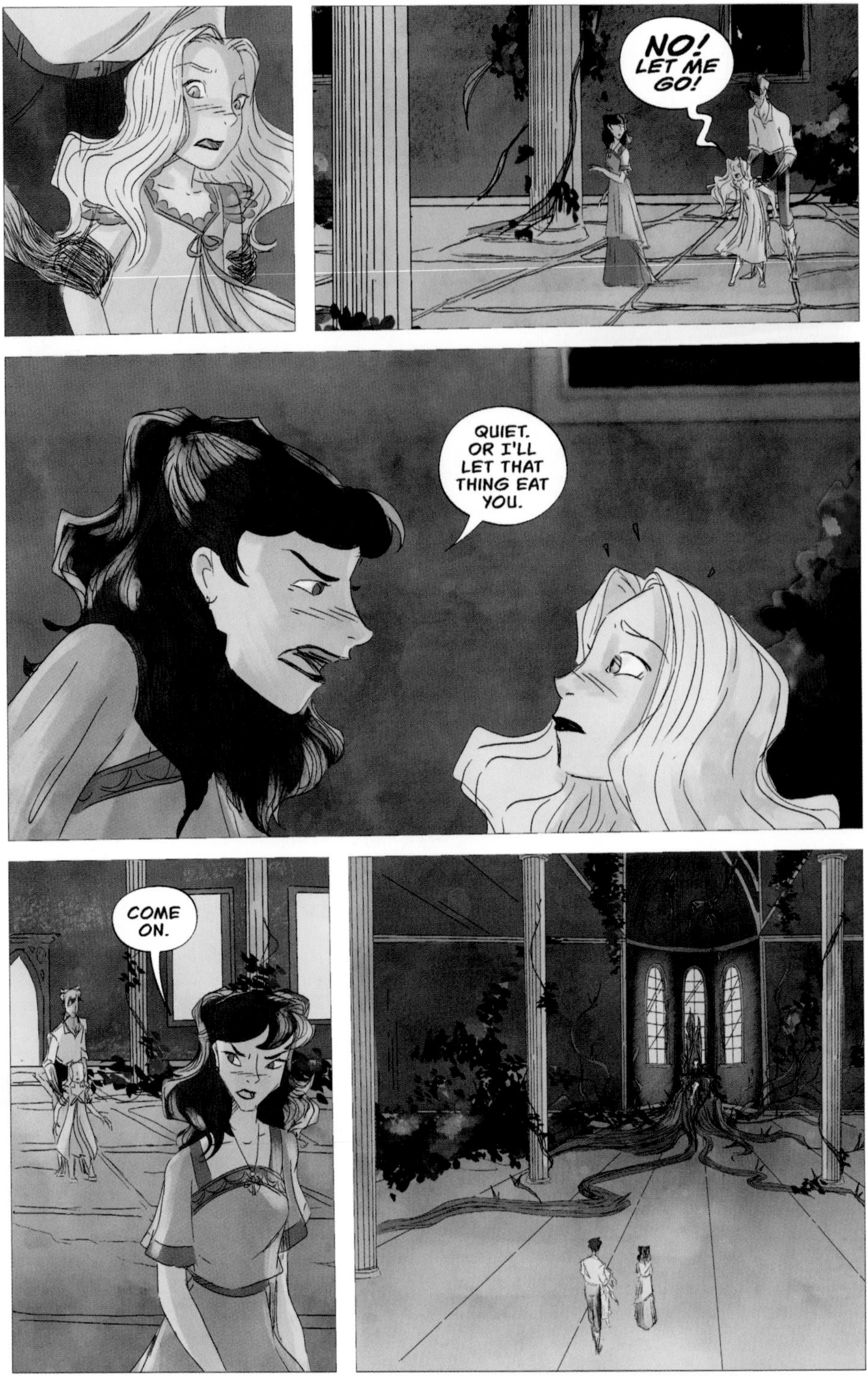
NO! LET ME GO!
QUIET. OR I'LL LET THAT THING EAT YOU.
COME ON.

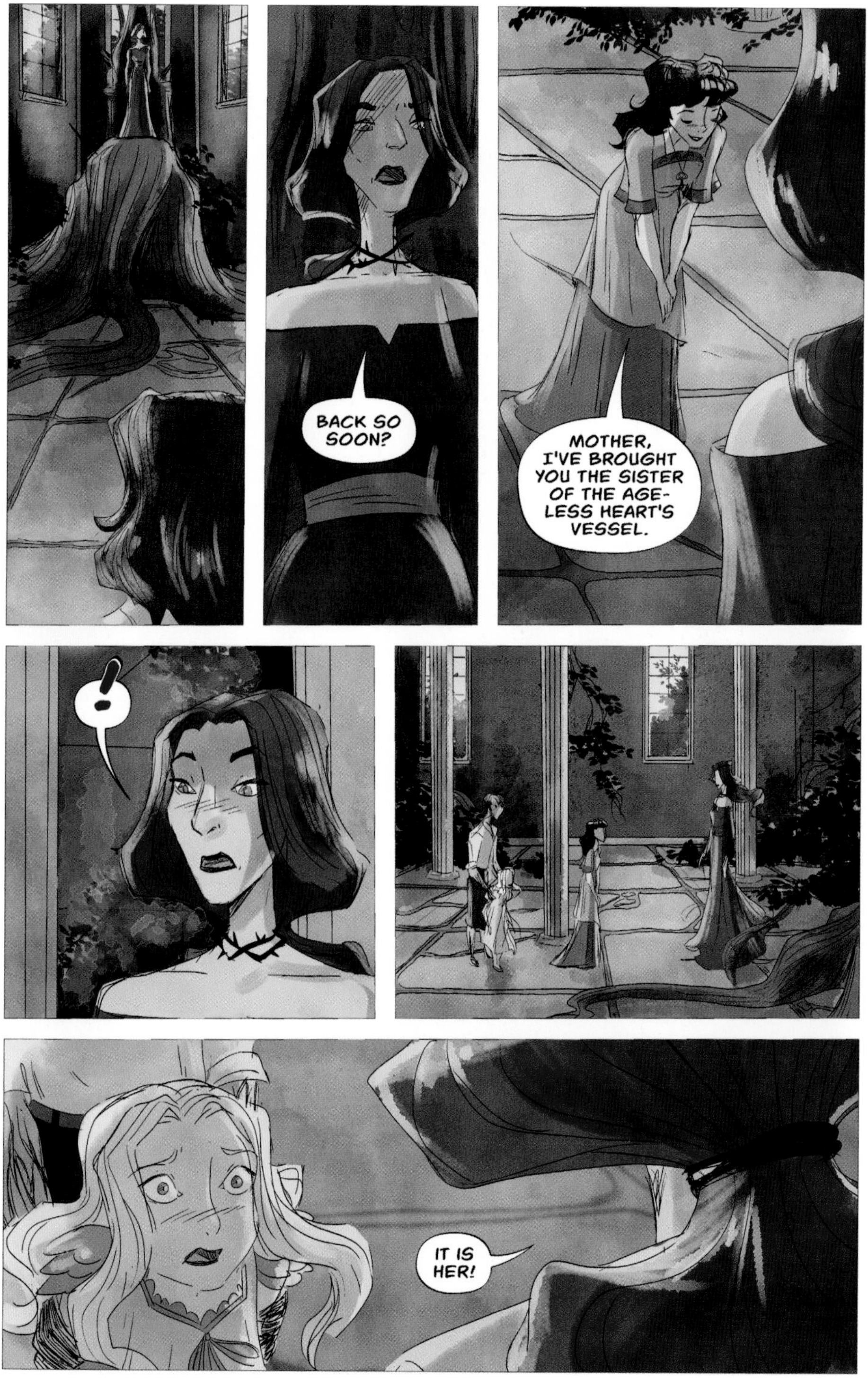
BACK SO SOON?
MOTHER, I'VE BROUGHT YOU THE SISTER OF THE AGE-LESS HEART'S VESSEL.
!
IT IS HER!

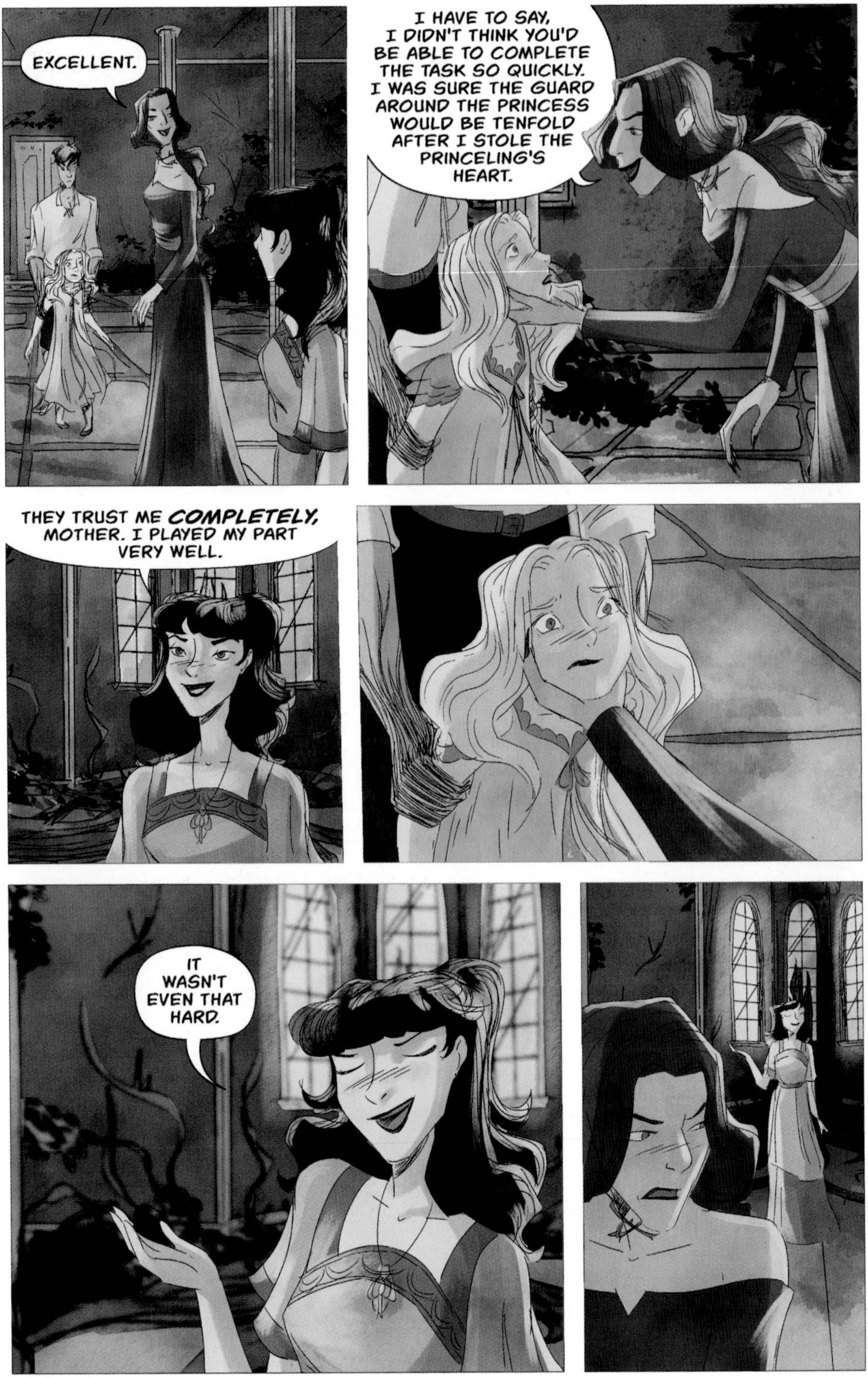
EXCELLENT.
I HAVE TO SAY, I DIDN'T THINK YOU'D BE ABLE TO COMPLETE THE TASK SO QUICKLY. I WAS SURE THE GUARD AROUND THE PRINCESS WOULD BE TENFOLD AFTER I STOLE THE PRINCELING'S HEART.
THEY TRUST ME *COMPLETELY*, MOTHER. I PLAYED MY PART VERY WELL.
IT WASN'T EVEN THAT HARD.

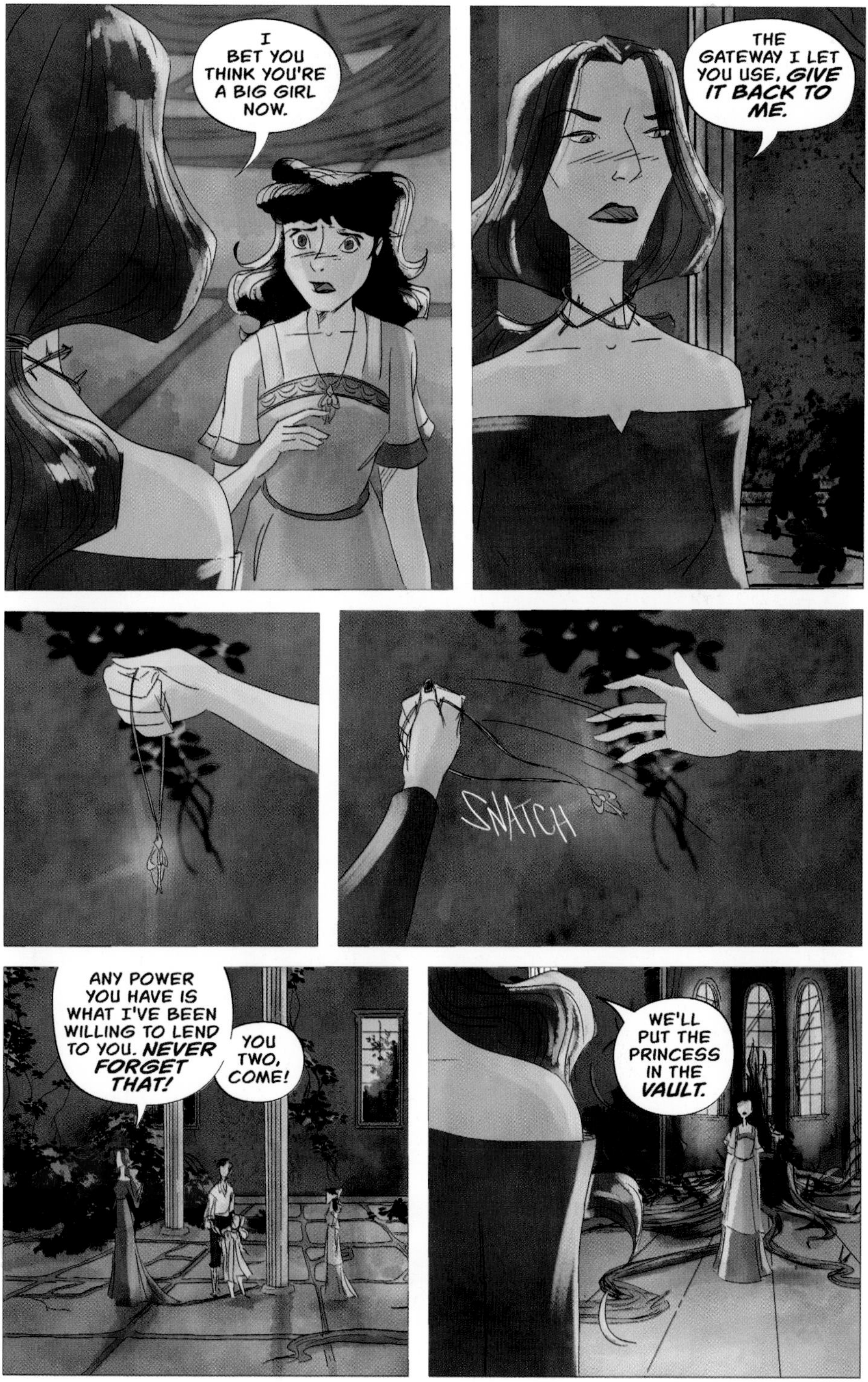
I BET YOU THINK YOU'RE A BIG GIRL NOW.
THE GATEWAY I LET YOU USE. GIVE IT BACK TO ME.
SNATCH
ANY POWER YOU HAVE IS WHAT I'VE BEEN WILLING TO LEND TO YOU. NEVER FORGET THAT!
YOU TWO, COME!
WE'LL PUT THE PRINCESS IN THE VAULT.

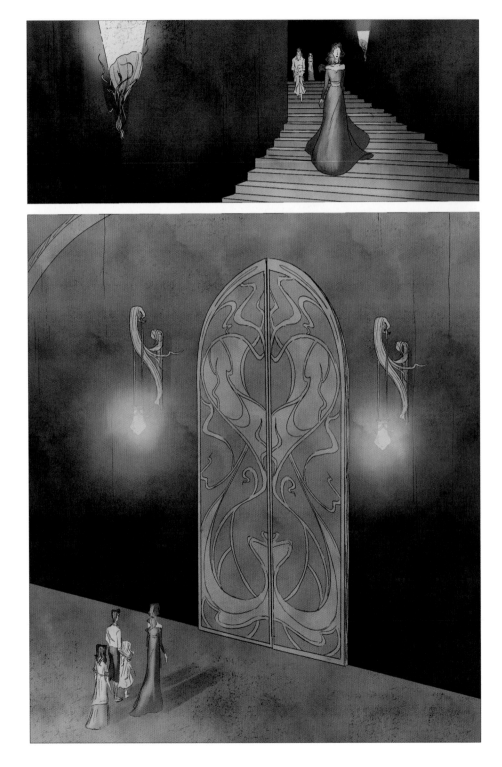

DAH-DUM

DAH-DUM

DAHDUM

DAHDUM

DAHDUM

DAHDUM

DAHDUM

DAHDUM

DAHDUM

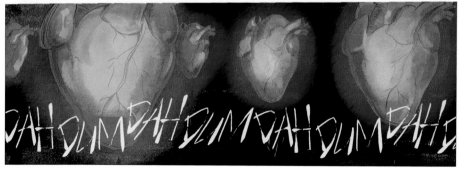

DAH-DUM DAH-DUM DAH-DUM DAH-

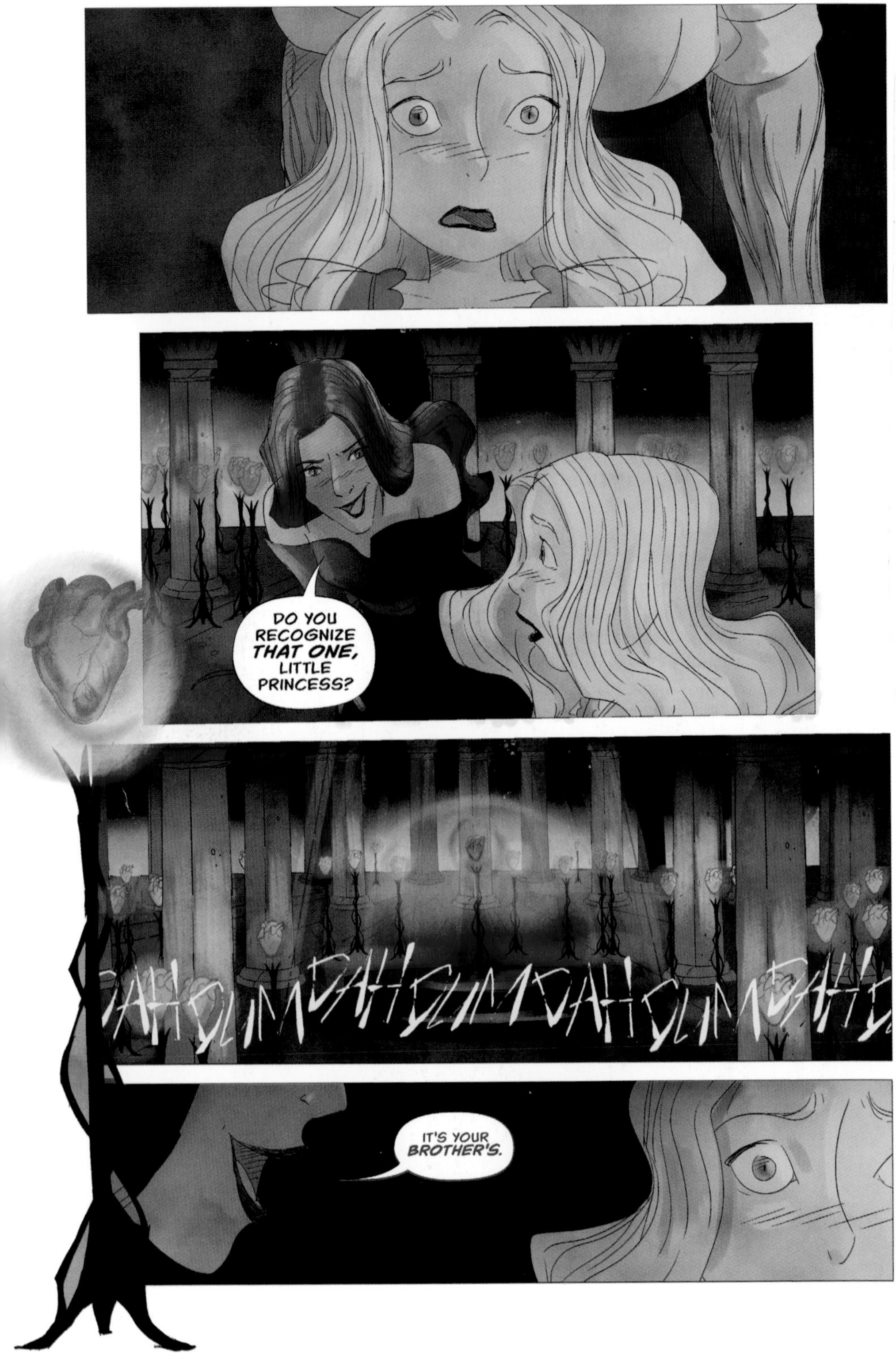
DO YOU RECOGNIZE *THAT ONE,* LITTLE PRINCESS?
DAH DUM DAH DUM DAH DUM DAH
IT'S YOUR *BROTHER'S.*

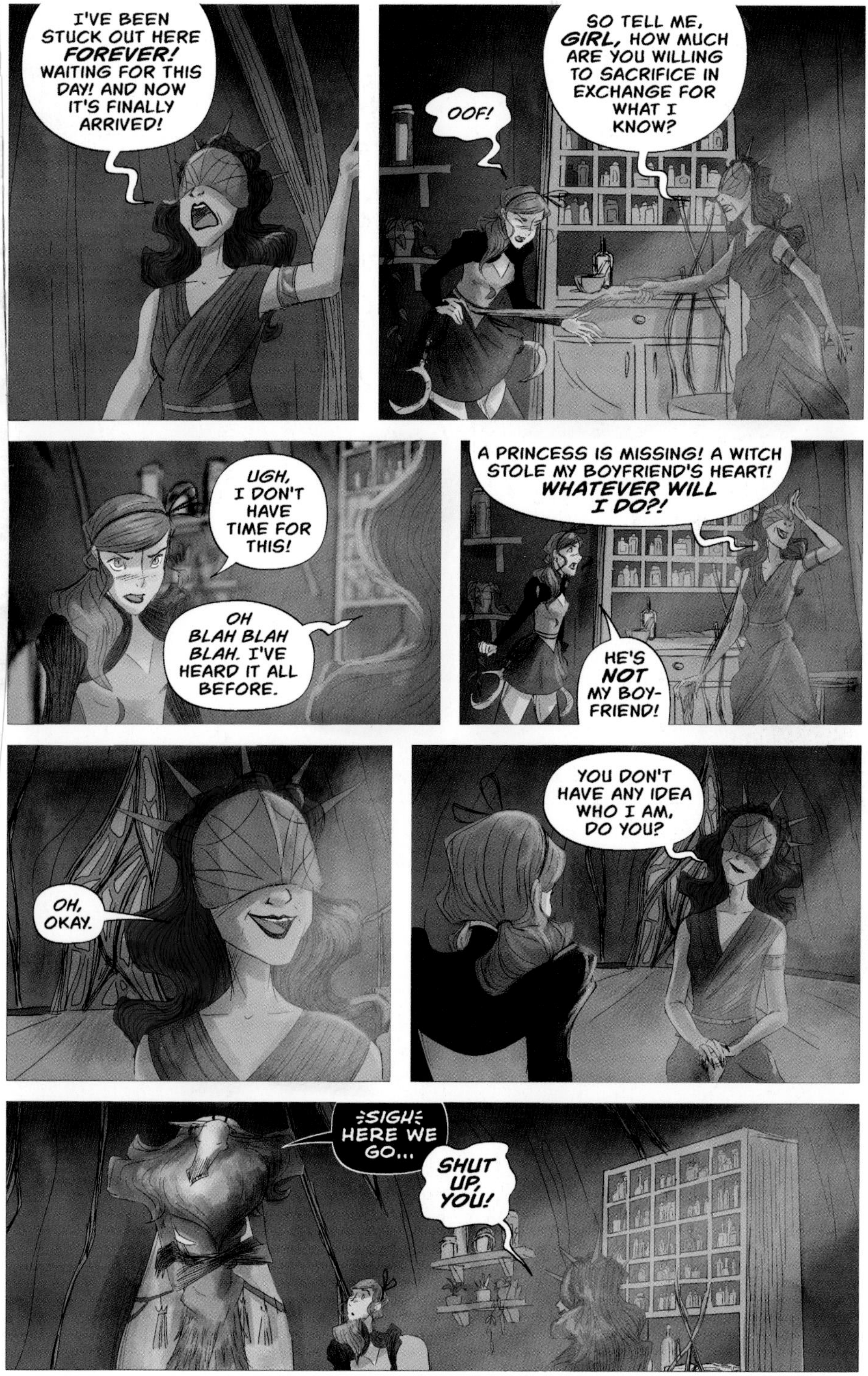
I'VE BEEN STUCK OUT HERE FOREVER! WAITING FOR THIS DAY! AND NOW IT'S FINALLY ARRIVED!
OOF!
SO TELL ME, GIRL, HOW MUCH ARE YOU WILLING TO SACRIFICE IN EXCHANGE FOR WHAT I KNOW?
UGH, I DON'T HAVE TIME FOR THIS!
OH BLAH BLAH BLAH. I'VE HEARD IT ALL BEFORE.
A PRINCESS IS MISSING! A WITCH STOLE MY BOYFRIEND'S HEART! WHATEVER WILL I DO?!
HE'S NOT MY BOY-FRIEND!
OH, OKAY.
YOU DON'T HAVE ANY IDEA WHO I AM, DO YOU?
SIGH HERE WE GO...
SHUT UP, YOU!

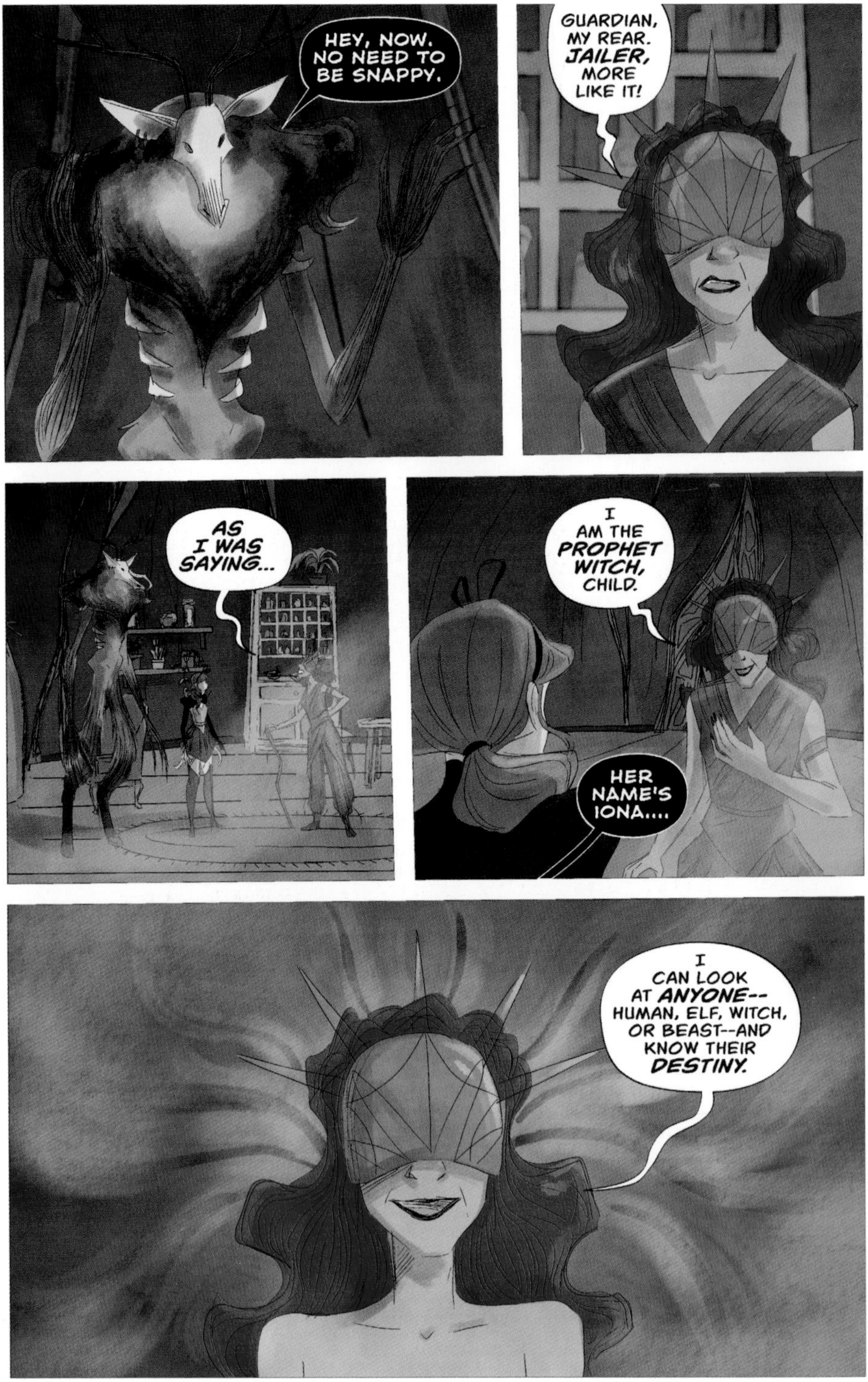
HEY, NOW. NO NEED TO BE SNAPPY.
GUARDIAN, MY REAR. JAILER, MORE LIKE IT!
AS I WAS SAYING...
I AM THE PROPHET WITCH, CHILD.
HER NAME'S IONA....
I CAN LOOK AT ANYONE--HUMAN, ELF, WITCH, OR BEAST--AND KNOW THEIR DESTINY.

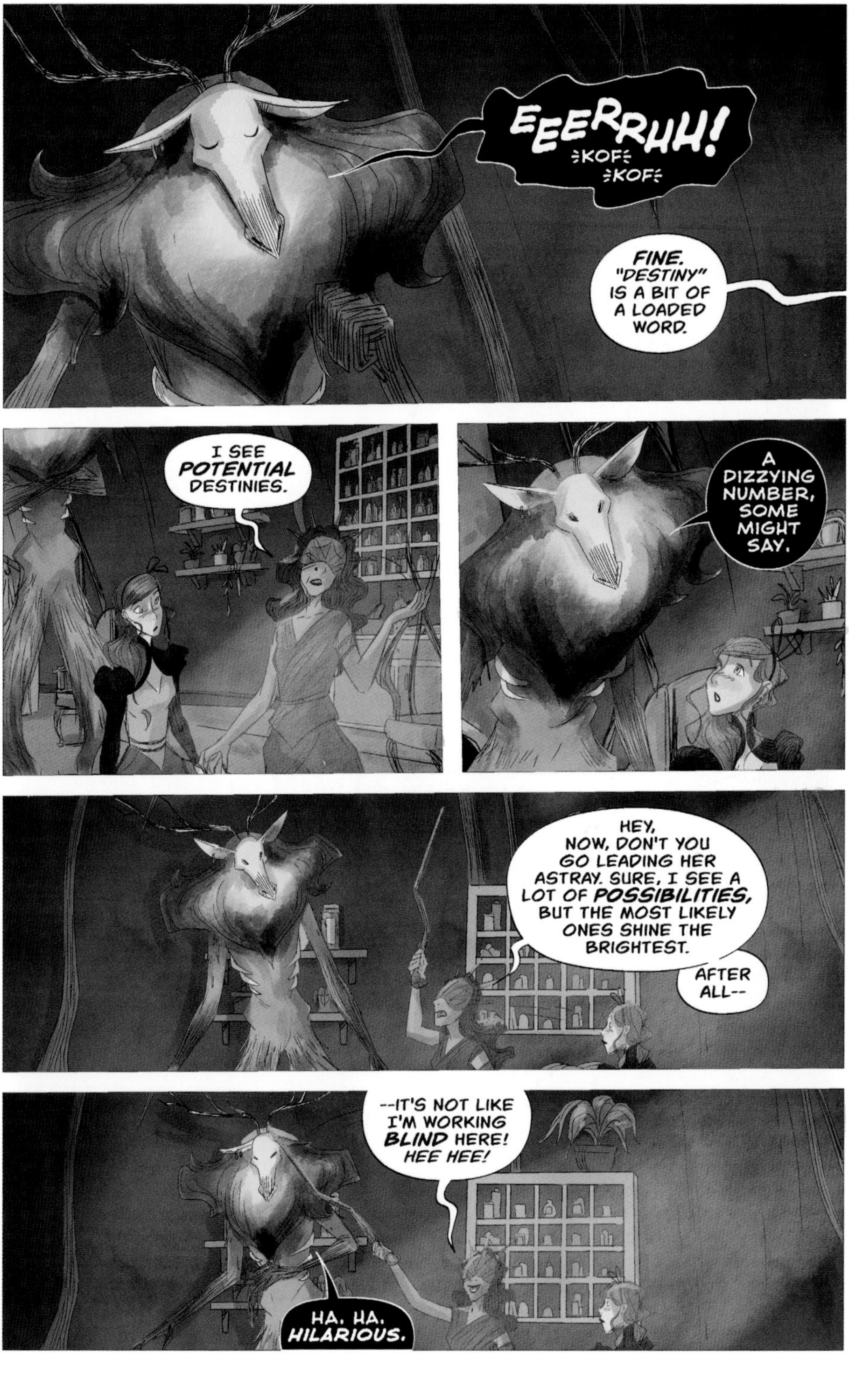

EEERRUH!
KOF KOF
FINE. "DESTINY" IS A BIT OF A LOADED WORD.
I SEE POTENTIAL DESTINIES.
A DIZZYING NUMBER, SOME MIGHT SAY.
HEY, NOW, DON'T YOU GO LEADING HER ASTRAY. SURE, I SEE A LOT OF POSSIBILITIES, BUT THE MOST LIKELY ONES SHINE THE BRIGHTEST.
AFTER ALL--
--IT'S NOT LIKE I'M WORKING BLIND HERE! HEE HEE!
HA. HA. HILARIOUS.

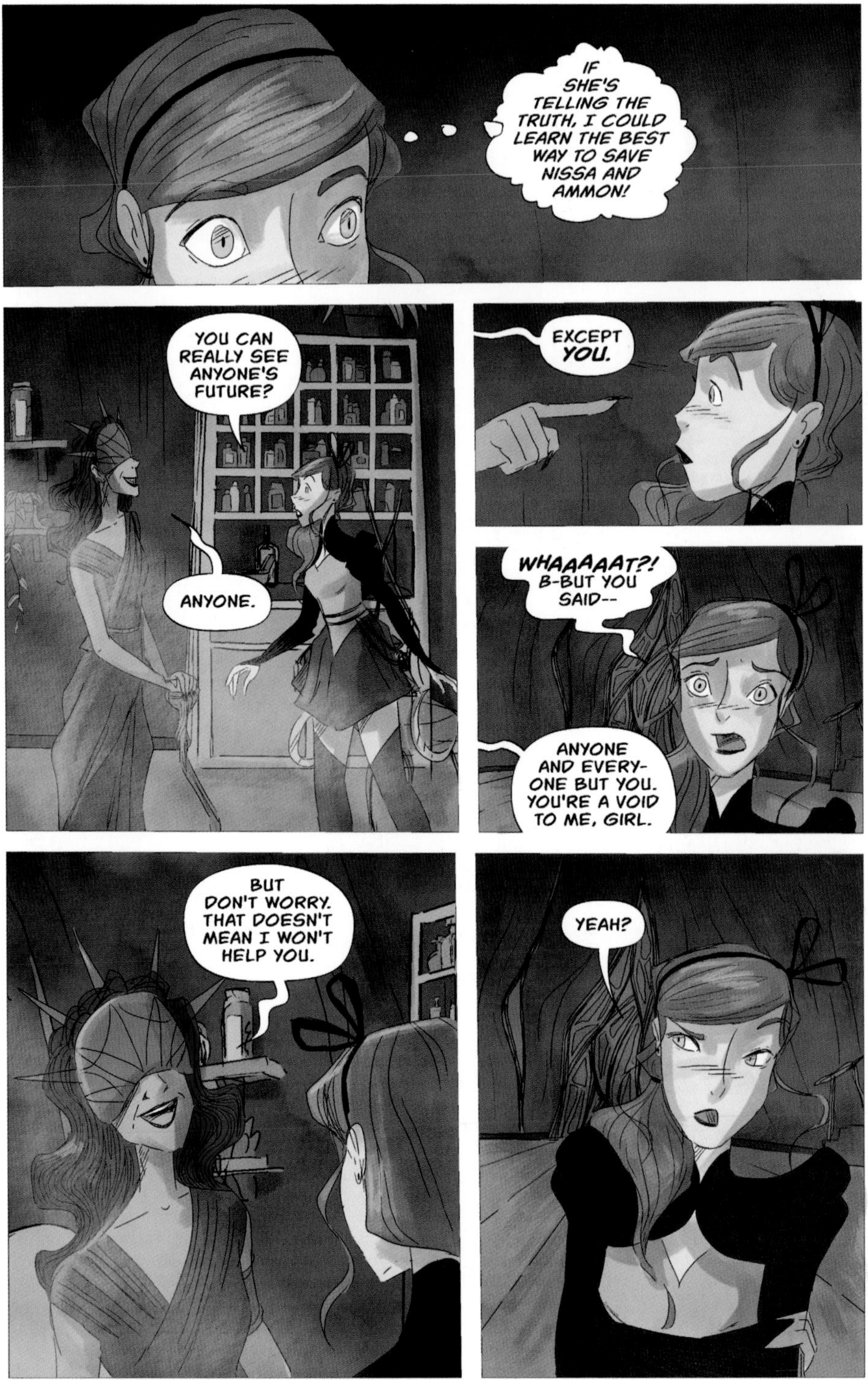
IF SHE'S TELLING THE TRUTH, I COULD LEARN THE BEST WAY TO SAVE NISSA AND AMMON!
YOU CAN REALLY SEE ANYONE'S FUTURE?
ANYONE.
EXCEPT *YOU.*
*WHAAAAAT?!* B-BUT YOU SAID--
ANYONE AND EVERYONE BUT YOU. YOU'RE A VOID TO ME, GIRL.
BUT DON'T WORRY. THAT DOESN'T MEAN I WON'T HELP YOU.
YEAH?

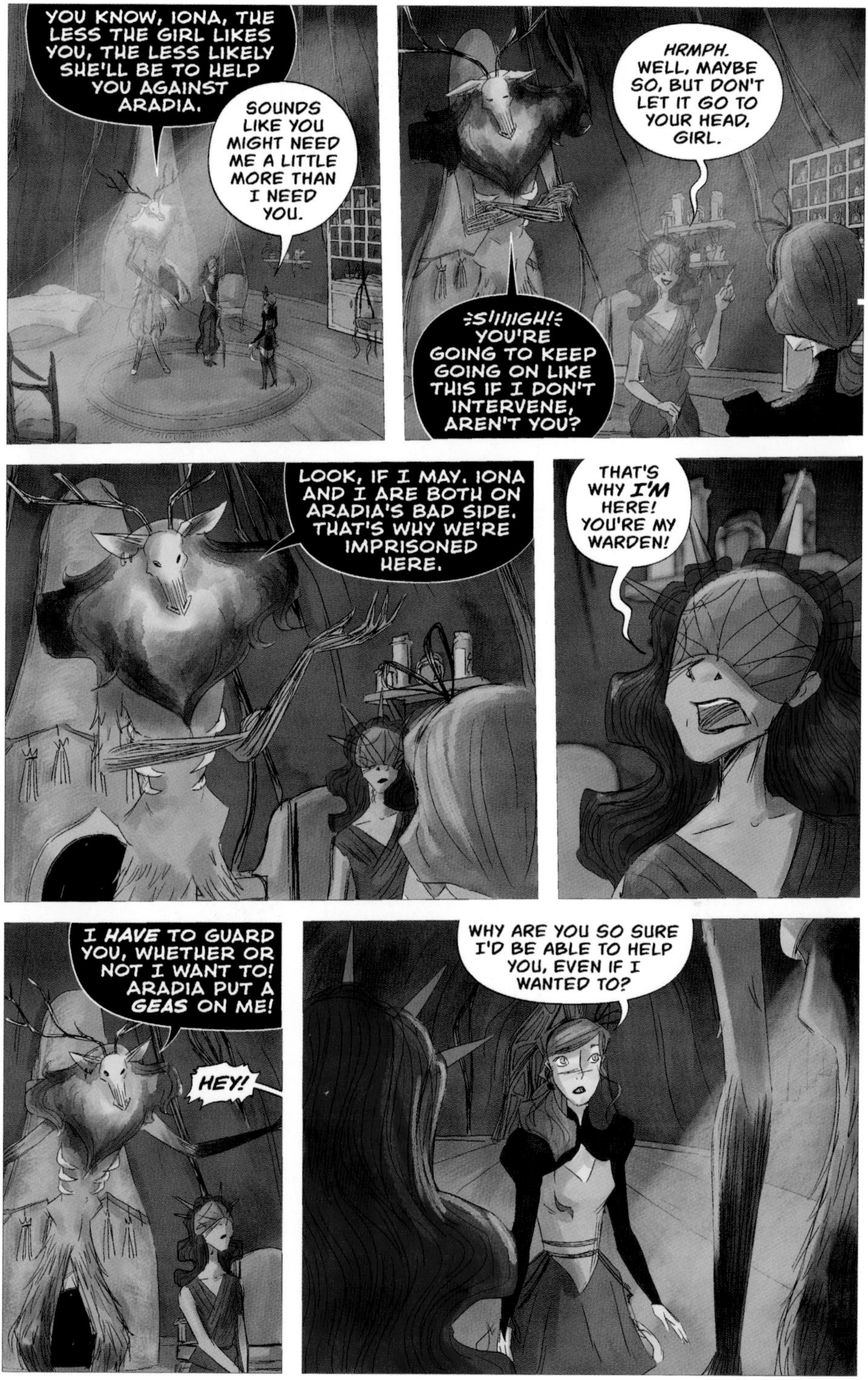
YOU KNOW, IONA, THE LESS THE GIRL LIKES YOU, THE LESS LIKELY SHE'LL BE TO HELP YOU AGAINST ARADIA.
SOUNDS LIKE YOU MIGHT NEED ME A LITTLE MORE THAN I NEED YOU.
HRMPH. WELL, MAYBE SO, BUT DON'T LET IT GO TO YOUR HEAD, GIRL.
SIIIIGH! YOU'RE GOING TO KEEP GOING ON LIKE THIS IF I DON'T INTERVENE, AREN'T YOU?
LOOK, IF I MAY. IONA AND I ARE BOTH ON ARADIA'S BAD SIDE. THAT'S WHY WE'RE IMPRISONED HERE.
THAT'S WHY I'M HERE! YOU'RE MY WARDEN!
I HAVE TO GUARD YOU, WHETHER OR NOT I WANT TO! ARADIA PUT A GEAS ON ME!
HEY!
WHY ARE YOU SO SURE I'D BE ABLE TO HELP YOU, EVEN IF I WANTED TO?

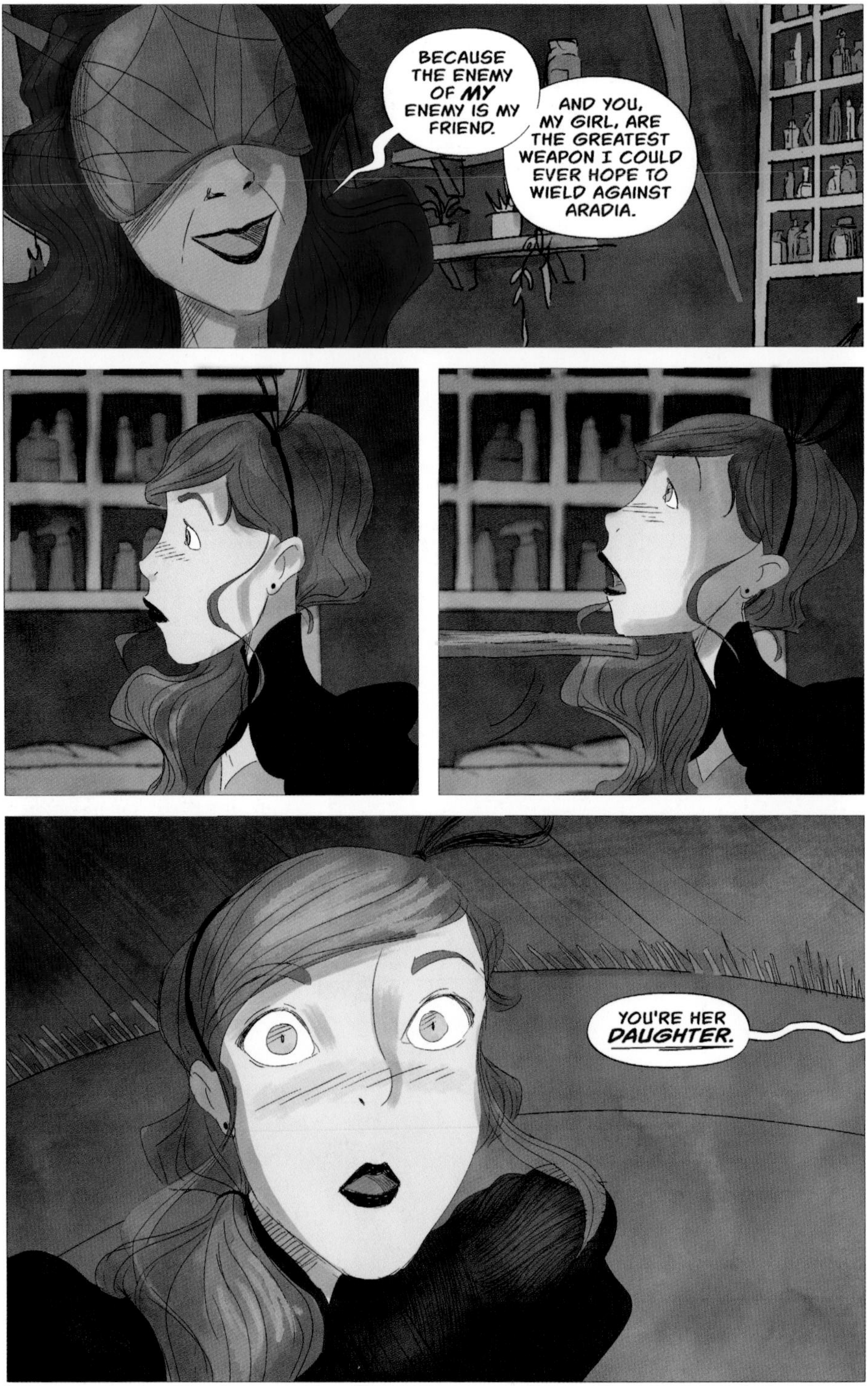
BECAUSE THE ENEMY OF MY ENEMY IS MY FRIEND.
AND YOU, MY GIRL, ARE THE GREATEST WEAPON I COULD EVER HOPE TO WIELD AGAINST ARADIA.
YOU'RE HER DAUGHTER.

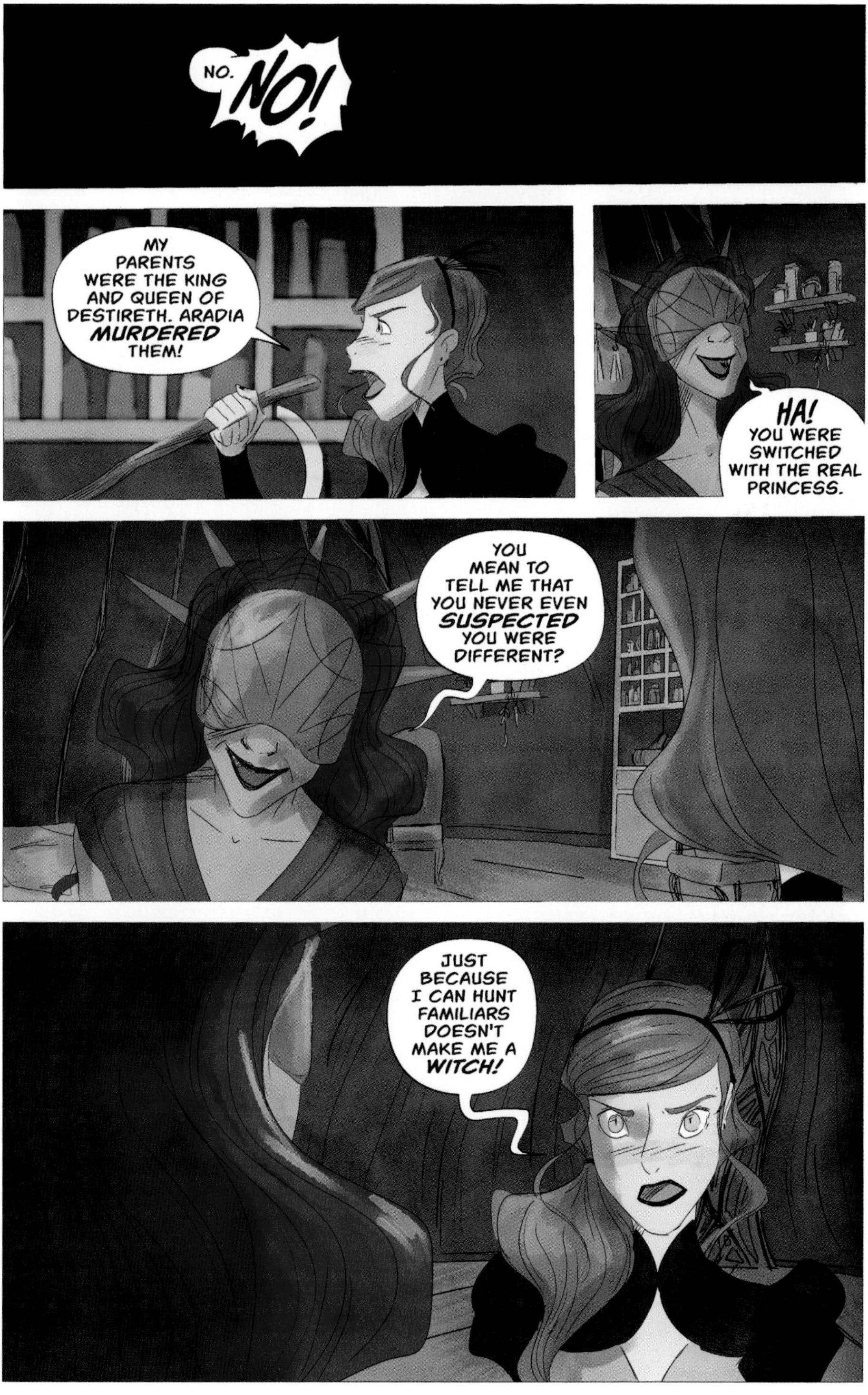

NO. NO!
MY PARENTS WERE THE KING AND QUEEN OF DESTIRETH. ARADIA MURDERED THEM!
HA! YOU WERE SWITCHED WITH THE REAL PRINCESS.
YOU MEAN TO TELL ME THAT YOU NEVER EVEN SUSPECTED YOU WERE DIFFERENT?
JUST BECAUSE I CAN HUNT FAMILIARS DOESN'T MAKE ME A WITCH!

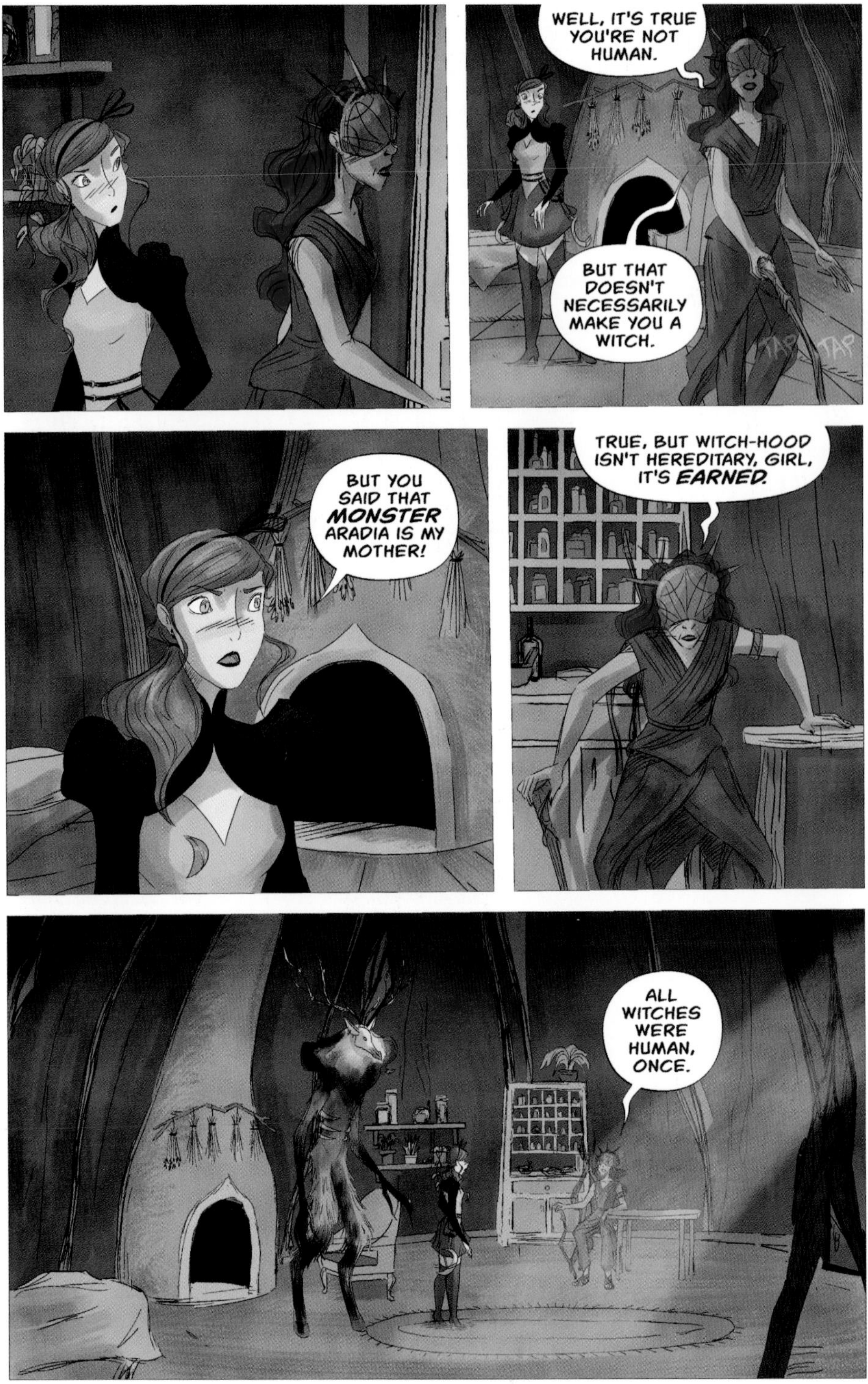
WELL, IT'S TRUE YOU'RE NOT HUMAN.
BUT THAT DOESN'T NECESSARILY MAKE YOU A WITCH.
TAP TAP
BUT YOU SAID THAT *MONSTER* ARADIA IS MY MOTHER!
TRUE, BUT WITCH-HOOD ISN'T HEREDITARY, GIRL, IT'S *EARNED.*
ALL WITCHES WERE HUMAN, ONCE.

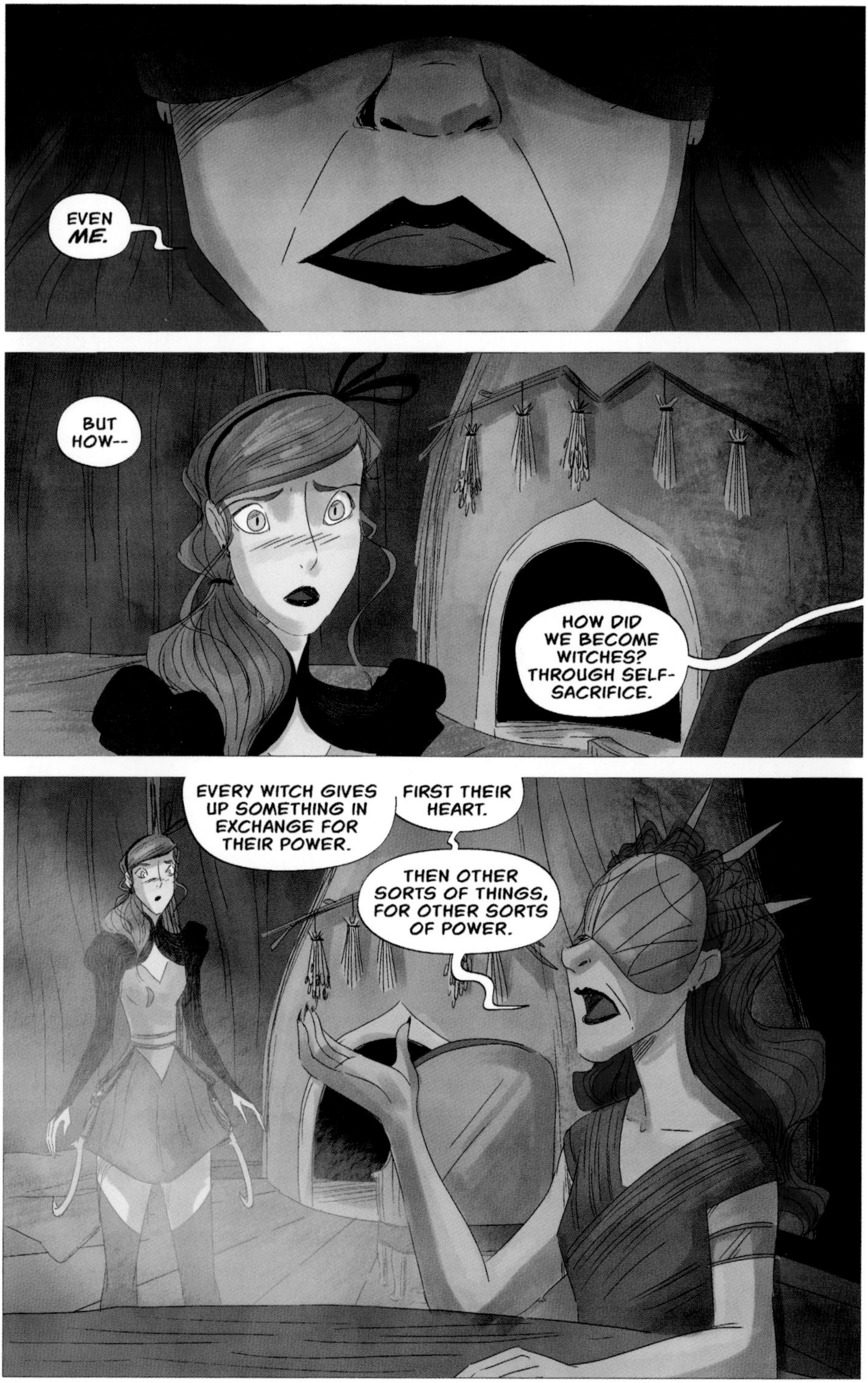
EVEN ME.
BUT HOW--
HOW DID WE BECOME WITCHES? THROUGH SELF-SACRIFICE.
EVERY WITCH GIVES UP SOMETHING IN EXCHANGE FOR THEIR POWER.
FIRST THEIR HEART.
THEN OTHER SORTS OF THINGS, FOR OTHER SORTS OF POWER.

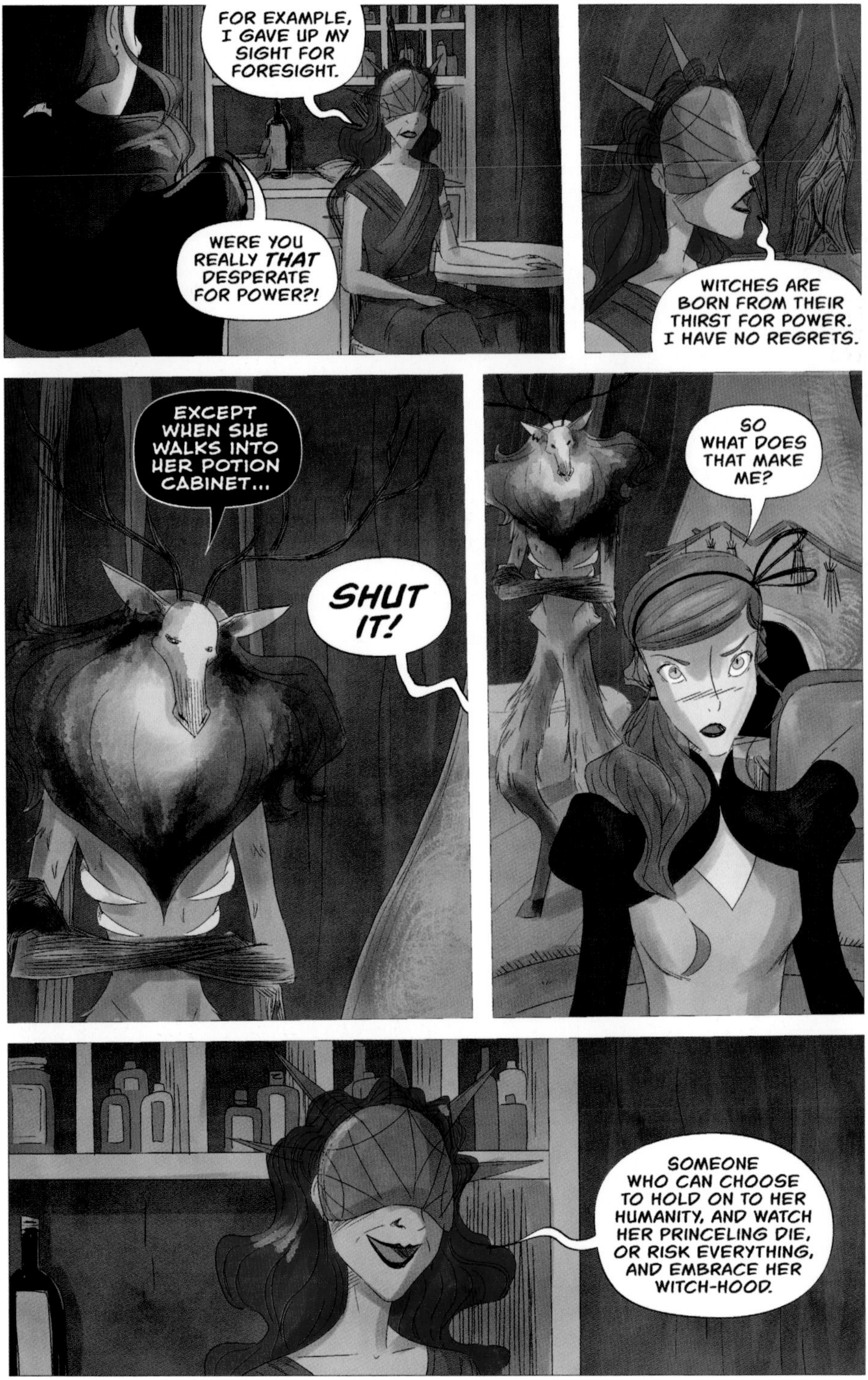
FOR EXAMPLE, I GAVE UP MY SIGHT FOR FORESIGHT.
WERE YOU REALLY *THAT* DESPERATE FOR POWER?!
WITCHES ARE BORN FROM THEIR THIRST FOR POWER. I HAVE NO REGRETS.
EXCEPT WHEN SHE WALKS INTO HER POTION CABINET...
SHUT IT!
SO WHAT DOES THAT MAKE ME?
SOMEONE WHO CAN CHOOSE TO HOLD ON TO HER HUMANITY, AND WATCH HER PRINCELING DIE, OR RISK EVERYTHING, AND EMBRACE HER WITCH-HOOD.

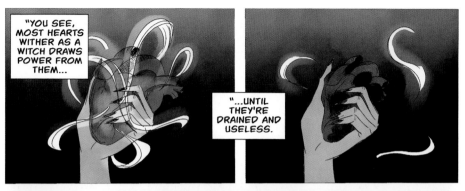

"YOU SEE, MOST HEARTS WITHER AS A WITCH DRAWS POWER FROM THEM...

"...UNTIL THEY'RE DRAINED AND USELESS.

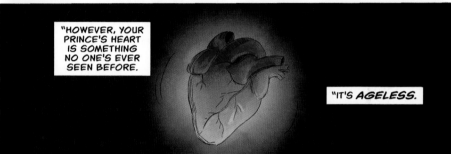

"HOWEVER, YOUR PRINCE'S HEART IS SOMETHING NO ONE'S EVER SEEN BEFORE.

"IT'S *AGELESS*.

"WHOEVER HOLDS AMMON'S HEART HAS IN HER HANDS THE KEY TO LIMITLESS MAGICAL POWER.

"MORE THAN ANYTHING, ARADIA WANTS A WAY TO HAVE POWER WITHOUT SACRIFICE."

AND THAT'S WHERE *YOU* COME IN.

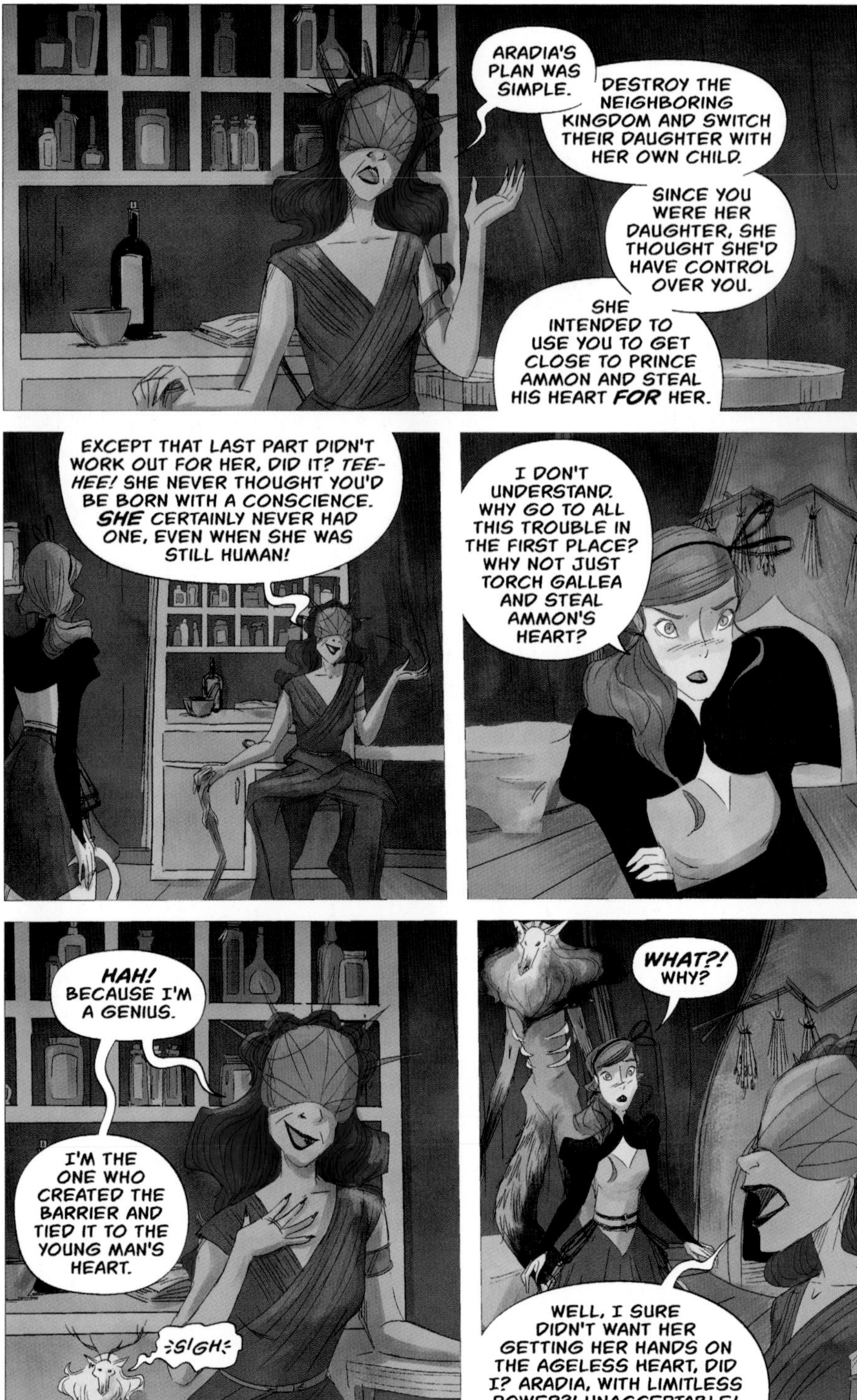
ARADIA'S PLAN WAS SIMPLE.
DESTROY THE NEIGHBORING KINGDOM AND SWITCH THEIR DAUGHTER WITH HER OWN CHILD.
SINCE YOU WERE HER DAUGHTER, SHE THOUGHT SHE'D HAVE CONTROL OVER YOU.
SHE INTENDED TO USE YOU TO GET CLOSE TO PRINCE AMMON AND STEAL HIS HEART *FOR* HER.
EXCEPT THAT LAST PART DIDN'T WORK OUT FOR HER, DID IT? *TEE-HEE!* SHE NEVER THOUGHT YOU'D BE BORN WITH A CONSCIENCE. *SHE* CERTAINLY NEVER HAD ONE, EVEN WHEN SHE WAS STILL HUMAN!
I DON'T UNDERSTAND. WHY GO TO ALL THIS TROUBLE IN THE FIRST PLACE? WHY NOT JUST TORCH GALLEA AND STEAL AMMON'S HEART?
*HAH!* BECAUSE I'M A GENIUS.
I'M THE ONE WHO CREATED THE BARRIER AND TIED IT TO THE YOUNG MAN'S HEART.
*SIGH*
*WHAT?!* WHY?
WELL, I SURE DIDN'T WANT HER GETTING HER HANDS ON THE AGELESS HEART, DID I? ARADIA, WITH LIMITLESS POWER?! UNACCEPTABLE!

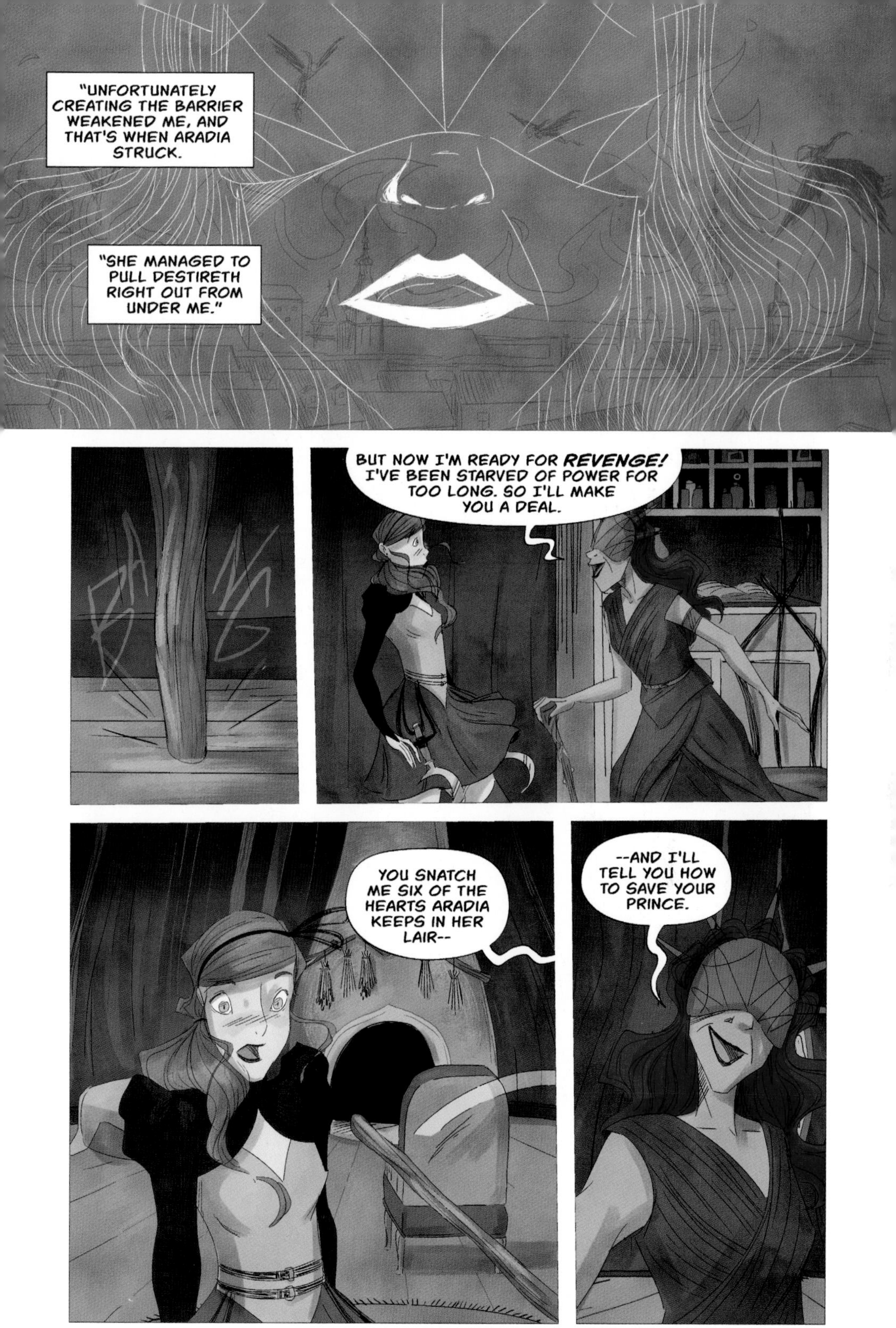
"UNFORTUNATELY CREATING THE BARRIER WEAKENED ME, AND THAT'S WHEN ARADIA STRUCK.
"SHE MANAGED TO PULL DESTIRETH RIGHT OUT FROM UNDER ME."
BANG
BUT NOW I'M READY FOR *REVENGE!* I'VE BEEN STARVED OF POWER FOR TOO LONG. SO I'LL MAKE YOU A DEAL.
YOU SNATCH ME SIX OF THE HEARTS ARADIA KEEPS IN HER LAIR--
--AND I'LL TELL YOU HOW TO SAVE YOUR PRINCE.

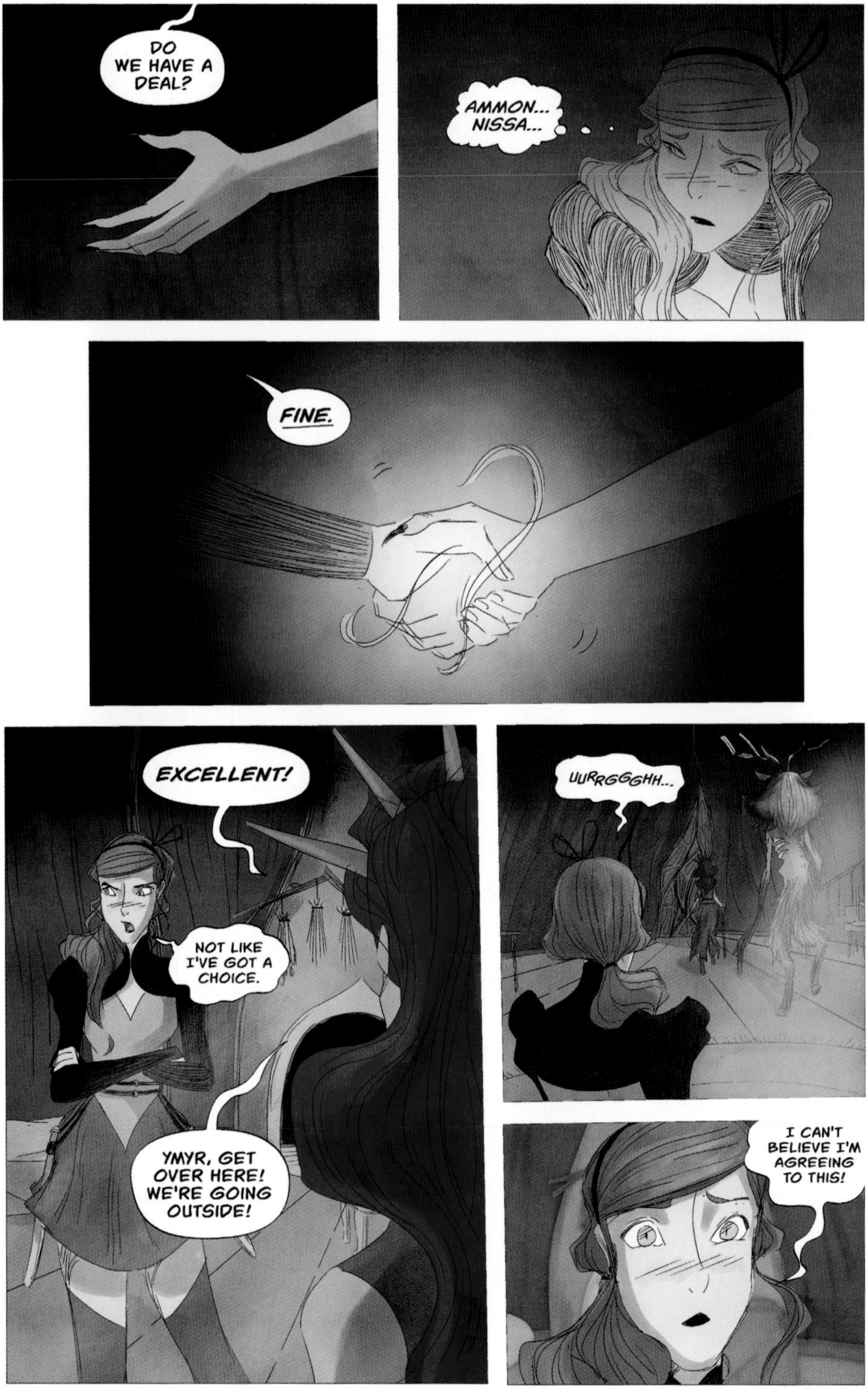
DO WE HAVE A DEAL?
AMMON... NISSA...
FINE.
EXCELLENT!
NOT LIKE I'VE GOT A CHOICE.
YMYR, GET OVER HERE! WE'RE GOING OUTSIDE!
UURRGGGHH...
I CAN'T BELIEVE I'M AGREEING TO THIS!

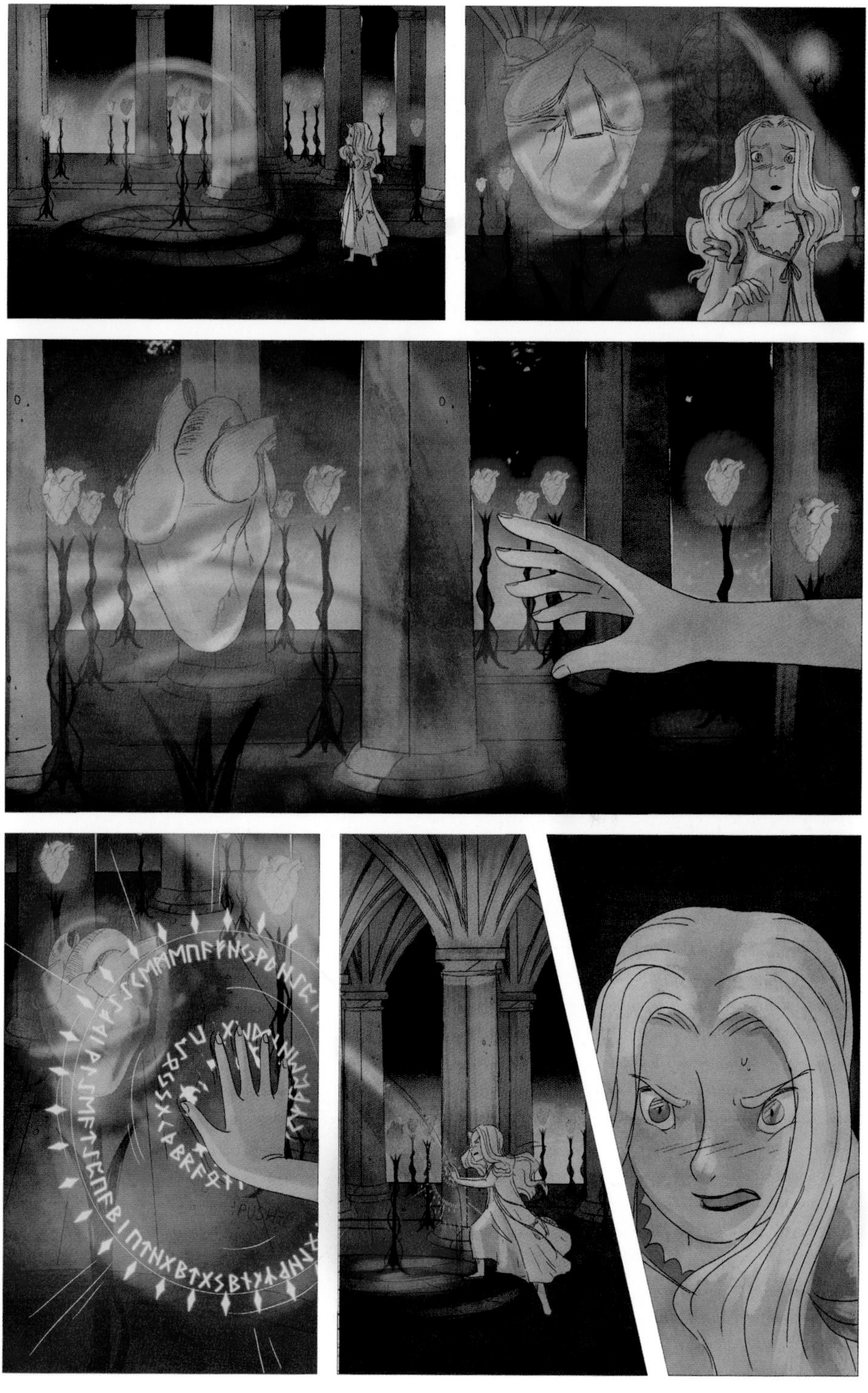

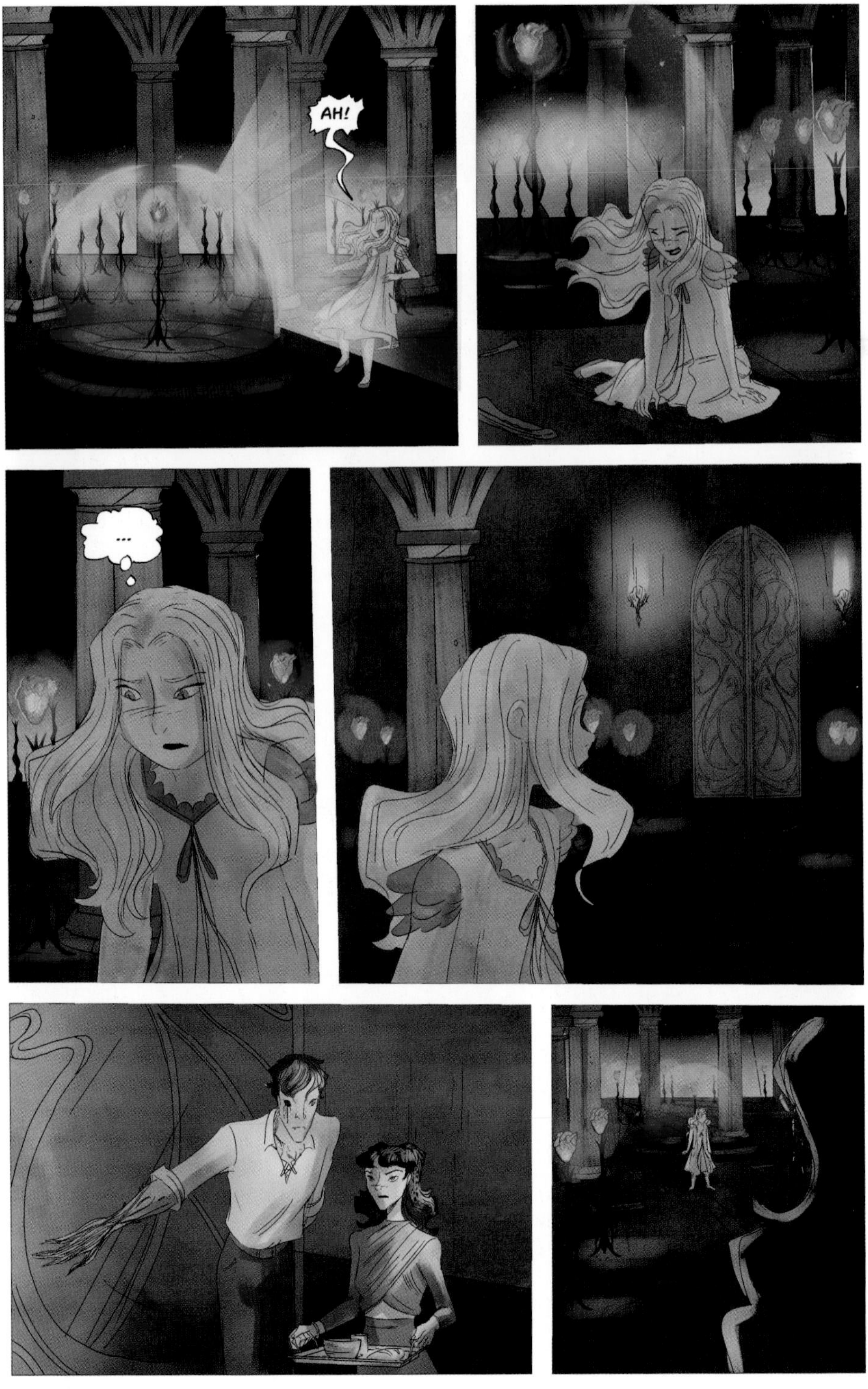
AH!
...

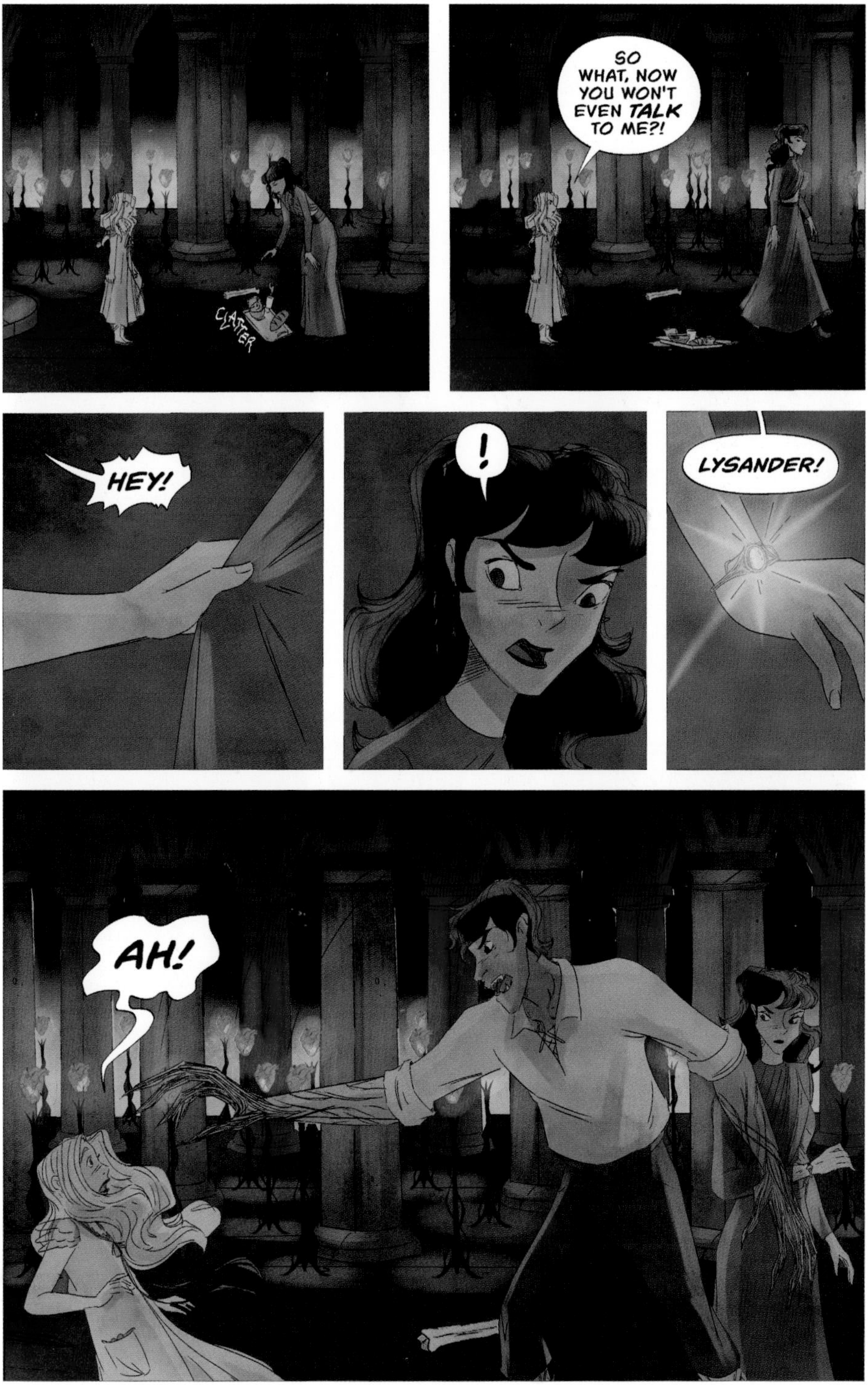
CLATTER
SO WHAT, NOW YOU WON'T EVEN TALK TO ME?!
HEY!
!
LYSANDER!
AH!

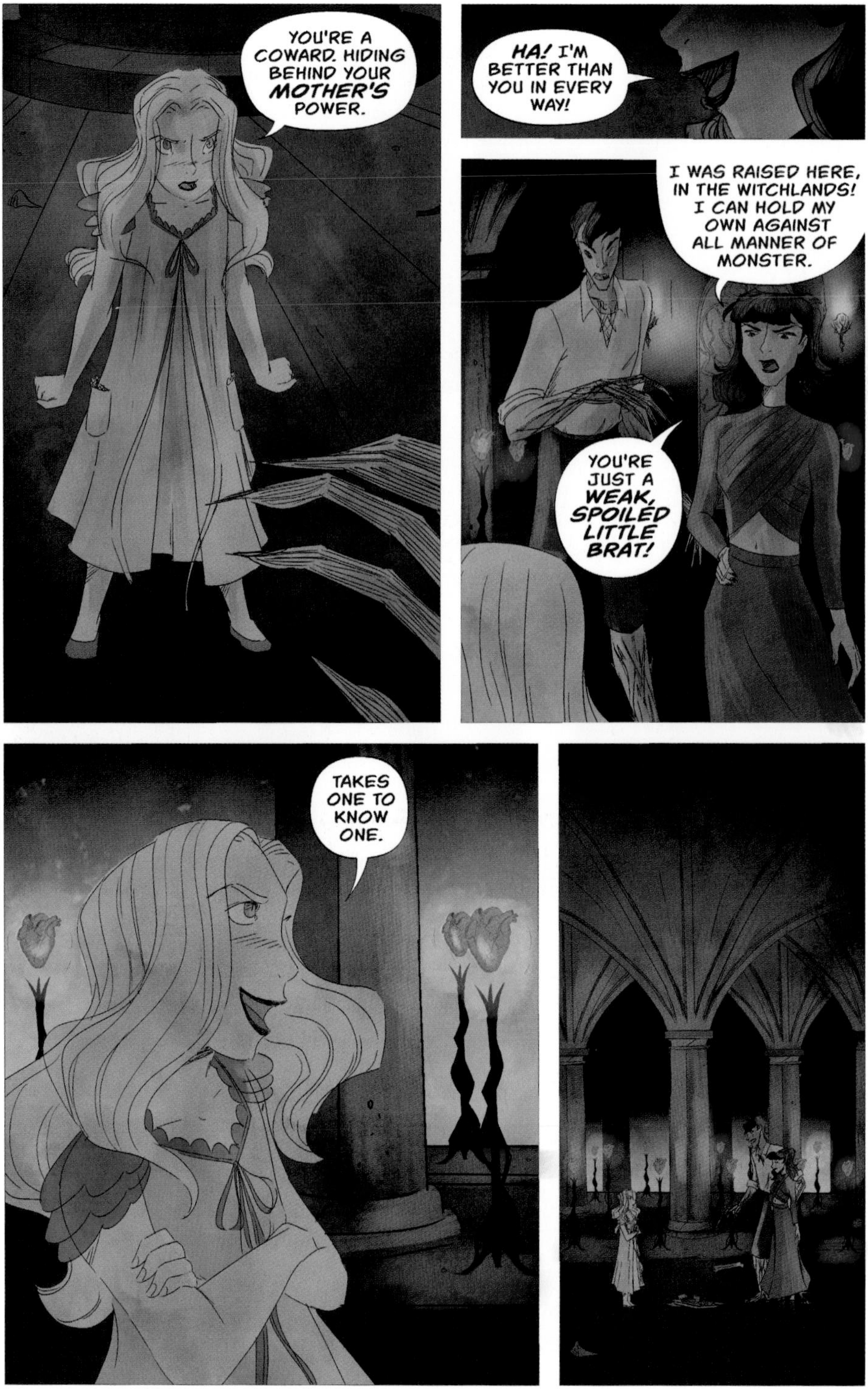

YOU'RE A COWARD. HIDING BEHIND YOUR MOTHER'S POWER.
HA! I'M BETTER THAN YOU IN EVERY WAY!
I WAS RAISED HERE, IN THE WITCHLANDS! I CAN HOLD MY OWN AGAINST ALL MANNER OF MONSTER.
YOU'RE JUST A WEAK, SPOILED LITTLE BRAT!
TAKES ONE TO KNOW ONE.

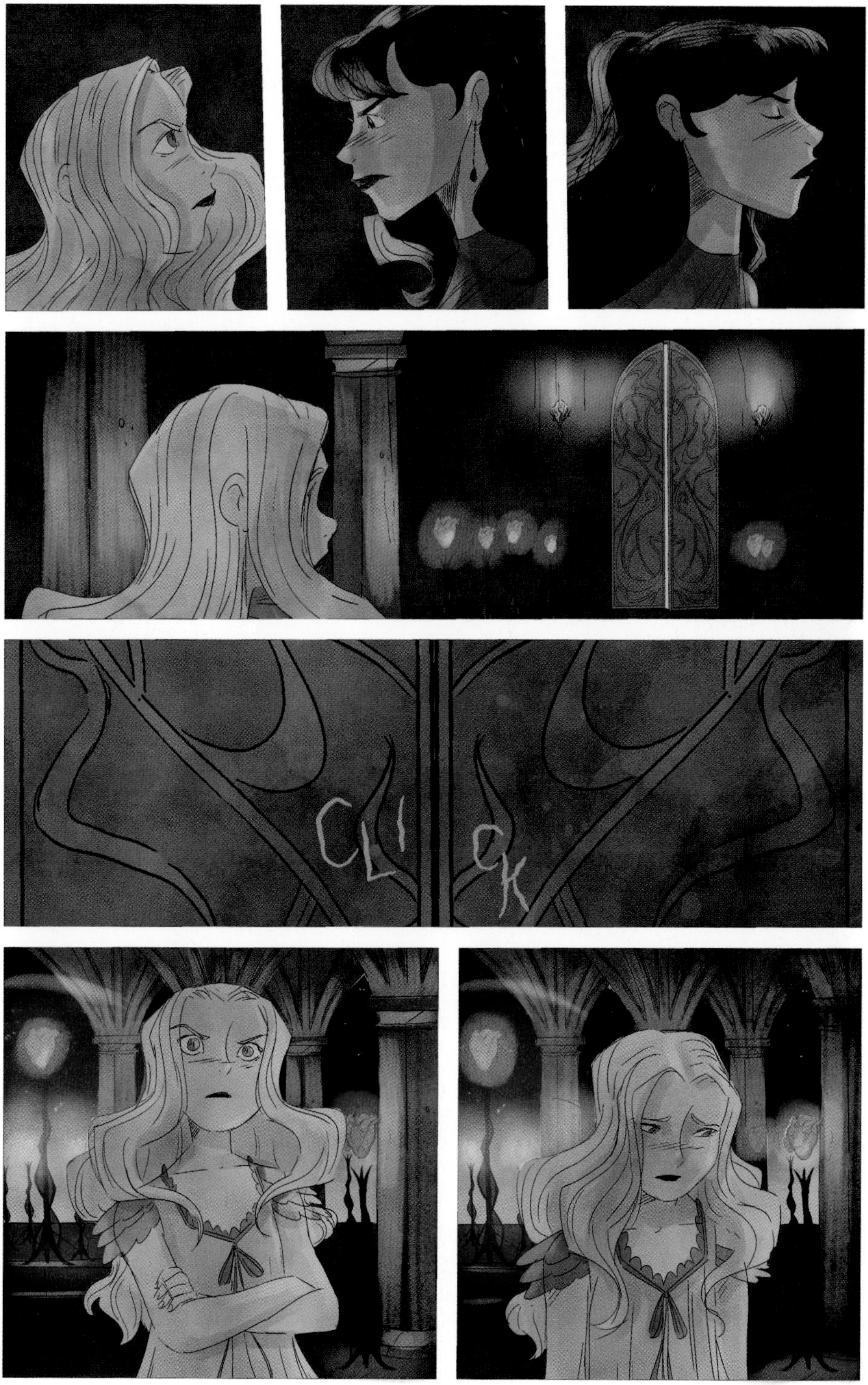
CLICK

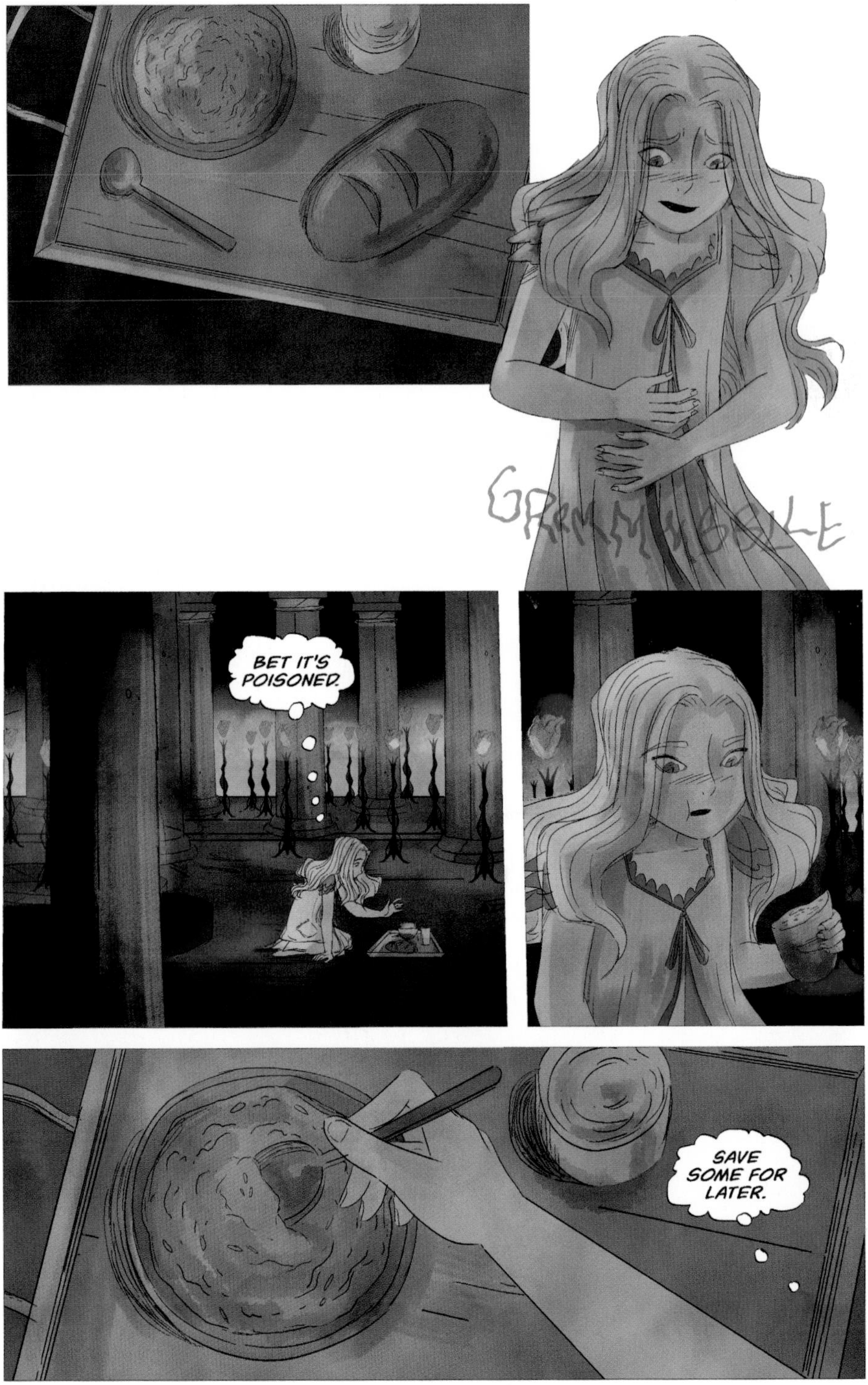
GRRMMMMBBLE
BET IT'S POISONED.
SAVE SOME FOR LATER.

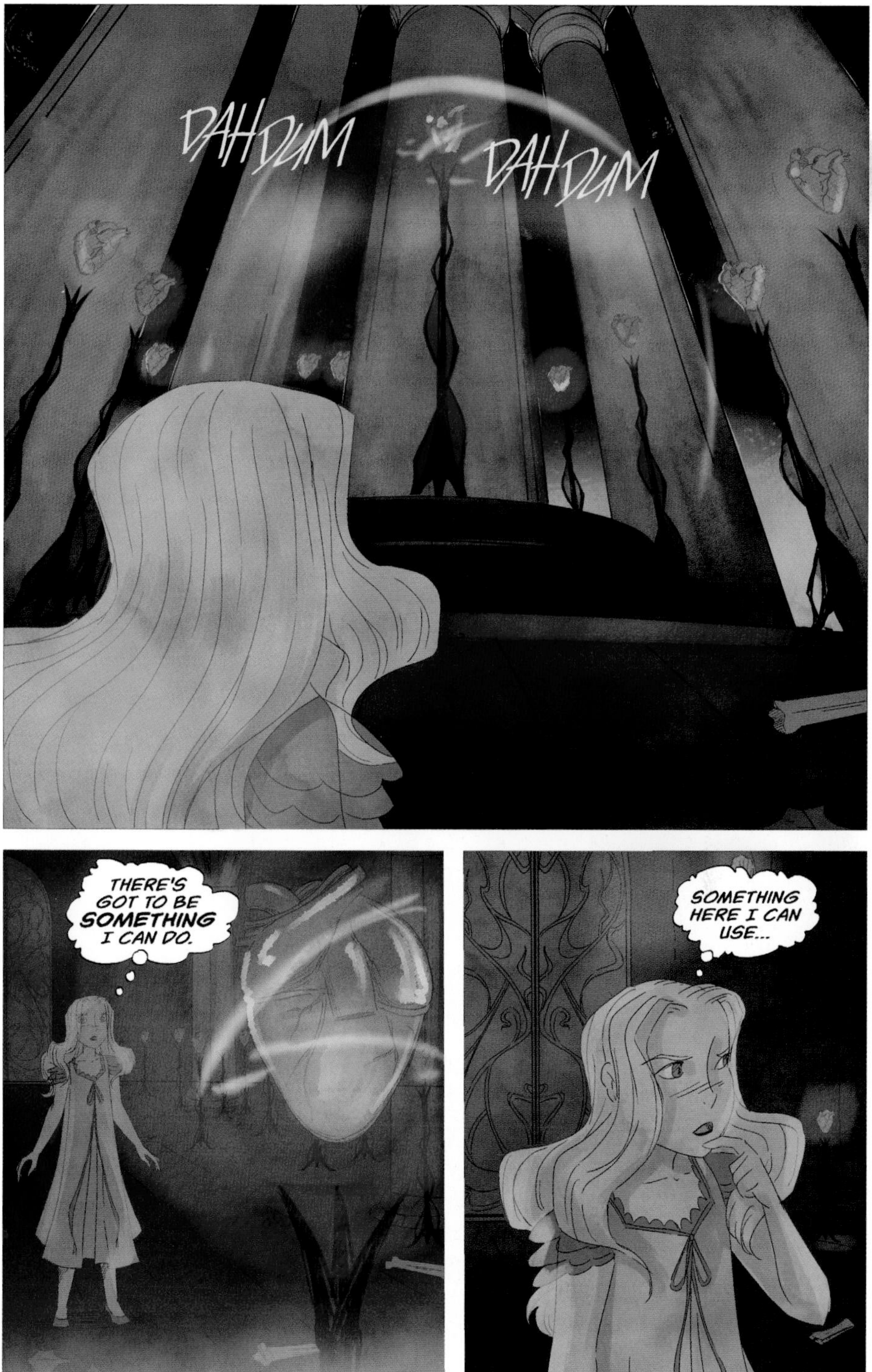
DAH DUM DAH DUM
THERE'S GOT TO BE SOMETHING I CAN DO.
SOMETHING HERE I CAN USE...

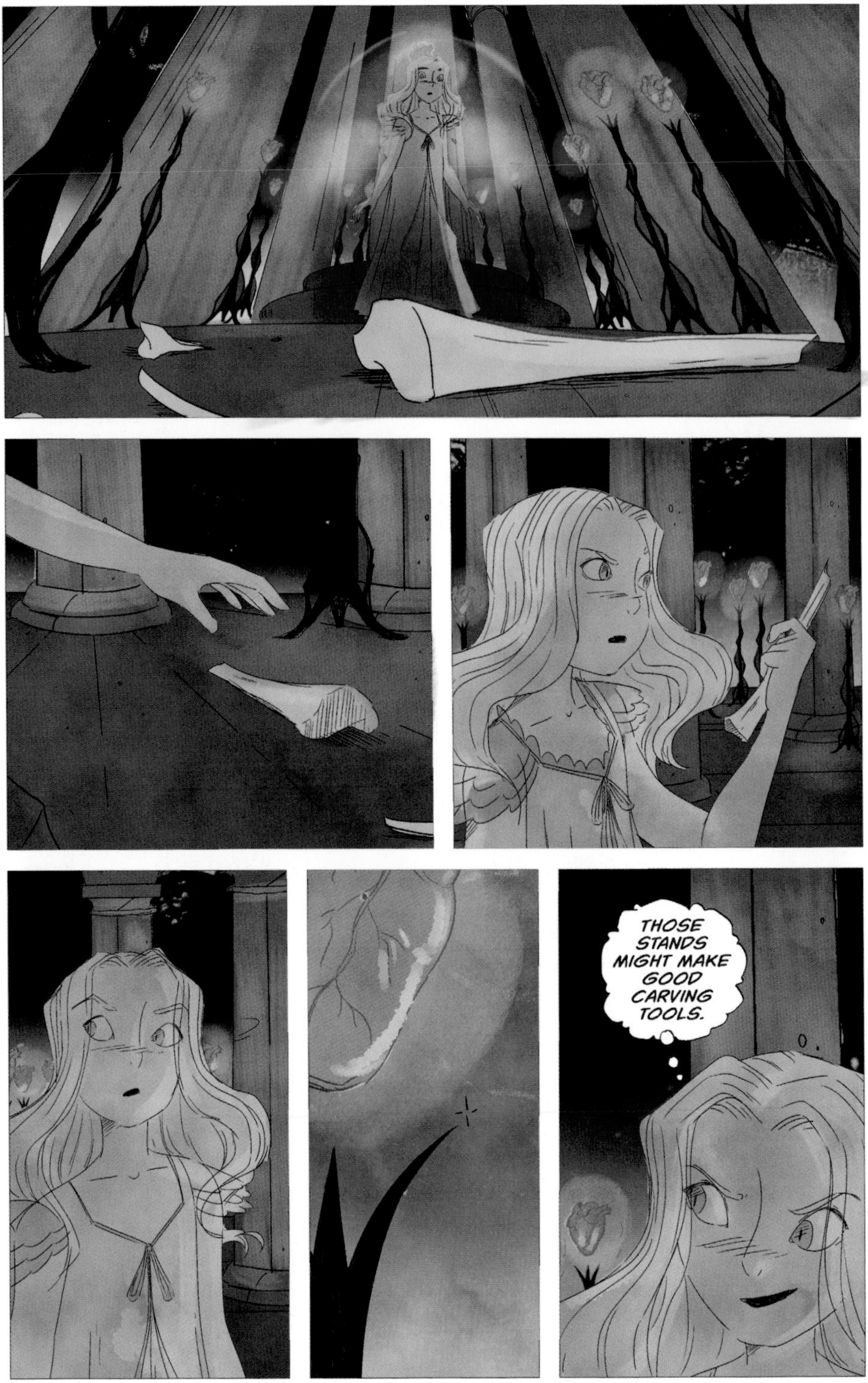
THOSE STANDS MIGHT MAKE GOOD CARVING TOOLS.

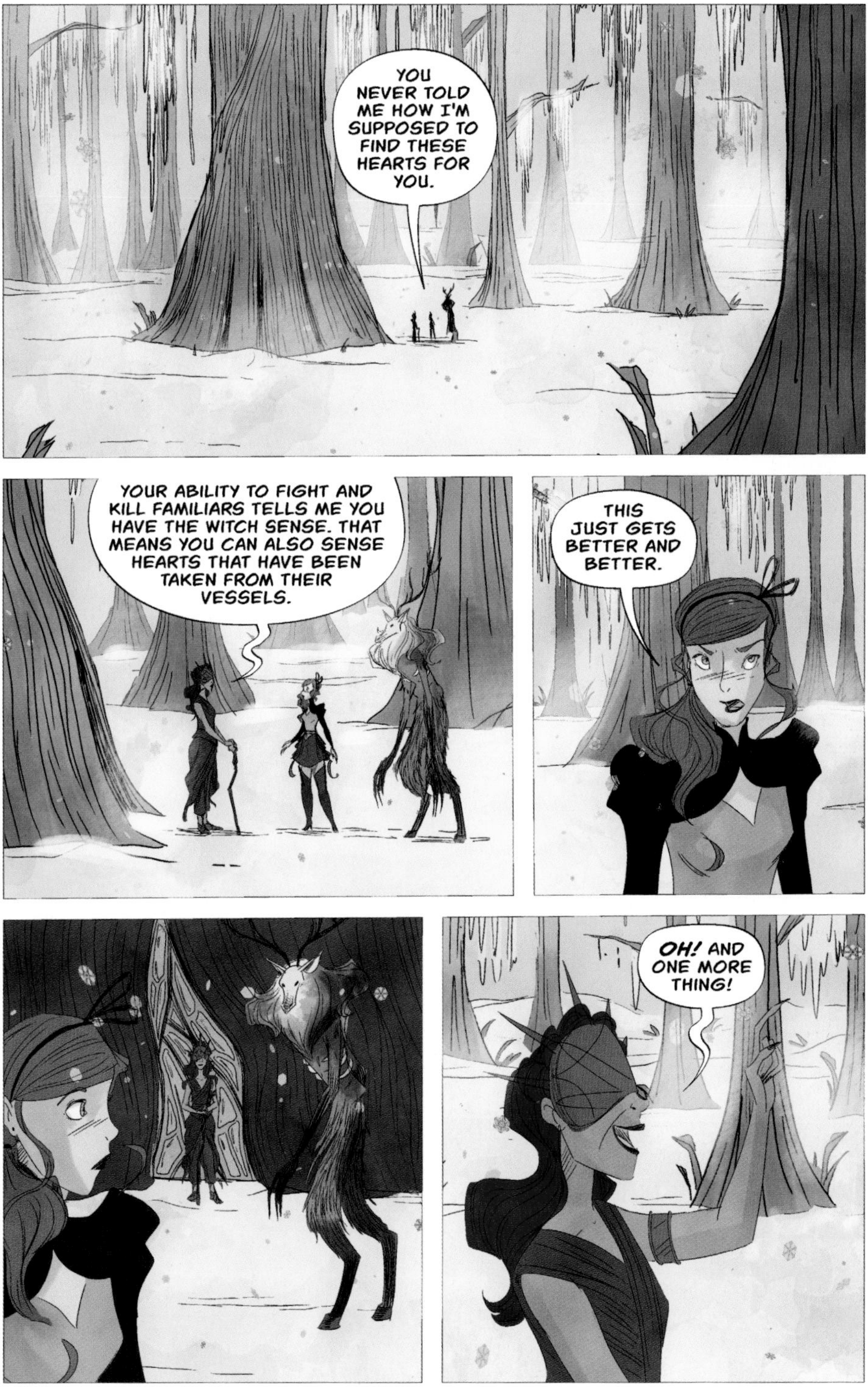
YOU NEVER TOLD ME HOW I'M SUPPOSED TO FIND THESE HEARTS FOR YOU.
YOUR ABILITY TO FIGHT AND KILL FAMILIARS TELLS ME YOU HAVE THE WITCH SENSE. THAT MEANS YOU CAN ALSO SENSE HEARTS THAT HAVE BEEN TAKEN FROM THEIR VESSELS.
THIS JUST GETS BETTER AND BETTER.
OH! AND ONE MORE THING!

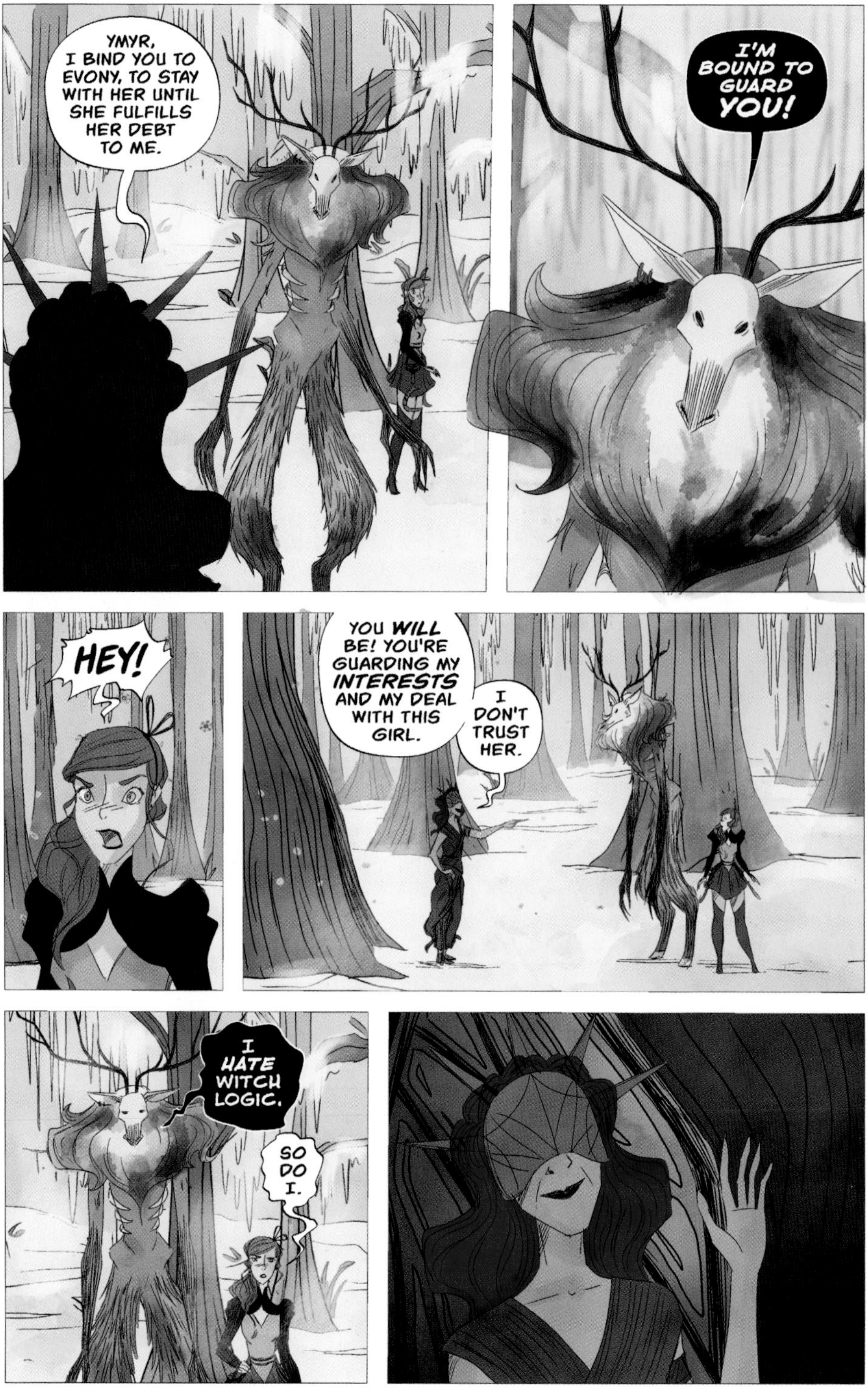
YMYR, I BIND YOU TO EVONY, TO STAY WITH HER UNTIL SHE FULFILLS HER DEBT TO ME.
I'M BOUND TO GUARD YOU!
HEY!
YOU WILL BE! YOU'RE GUARDING MY INTERESTS AND MY DEAL WITH THIS GIRL.
I DON'T TRUST HER.
I HATE WITCH LOGIC.
SO DO I.

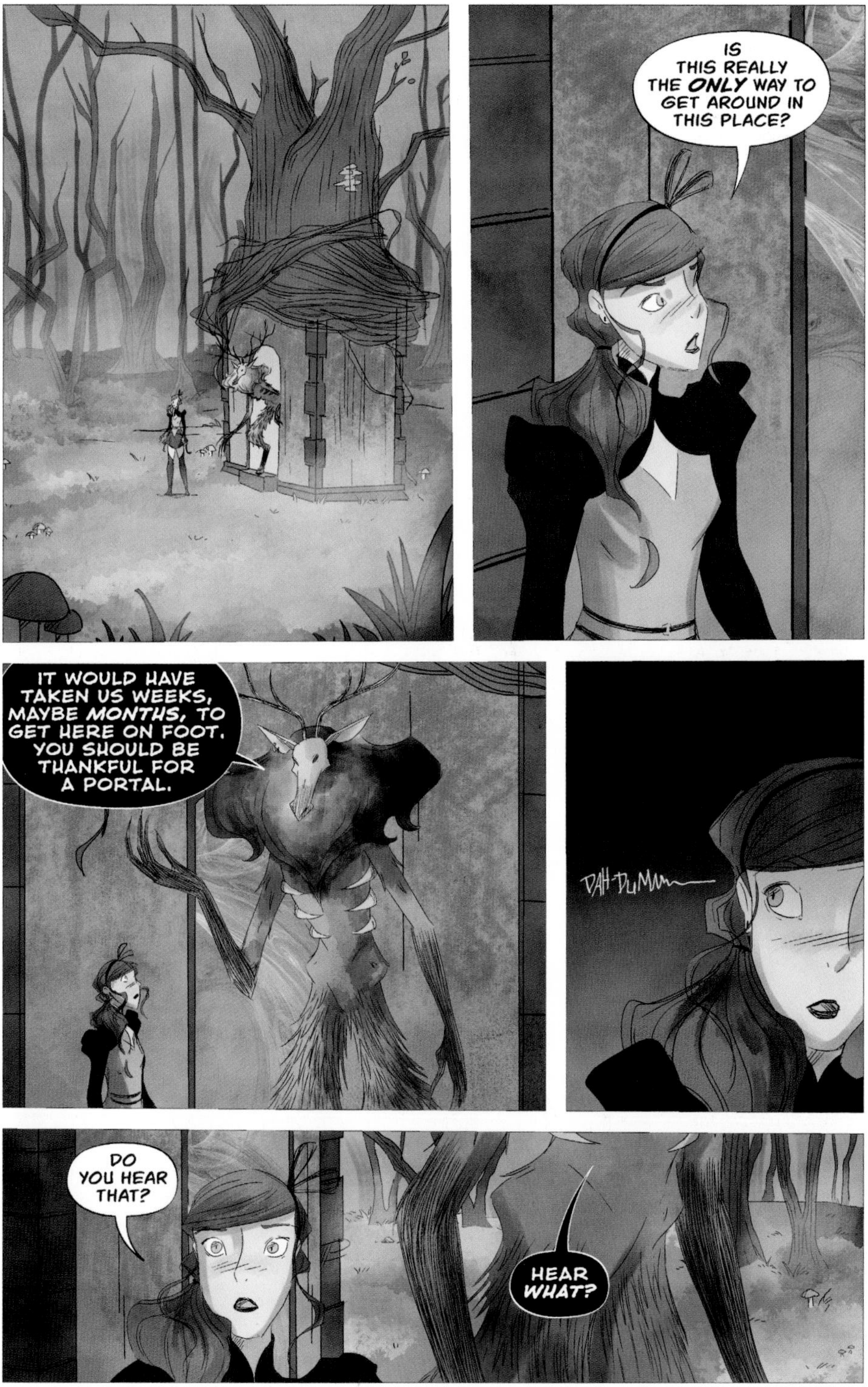
IS THIS REALLY THE ONLY WAY TO GET AROUND IN THIS PLACE?
IT WOULD HAVE TAKEN US WEEKS, MAYBE MONTHS, TO GET HERE ON FOOT. YOU SHOULD BE THANKFUL FOR A PORTAL.
DAH-DUMMM
DO YOU HEAR THAT?
HEAR WHAT?

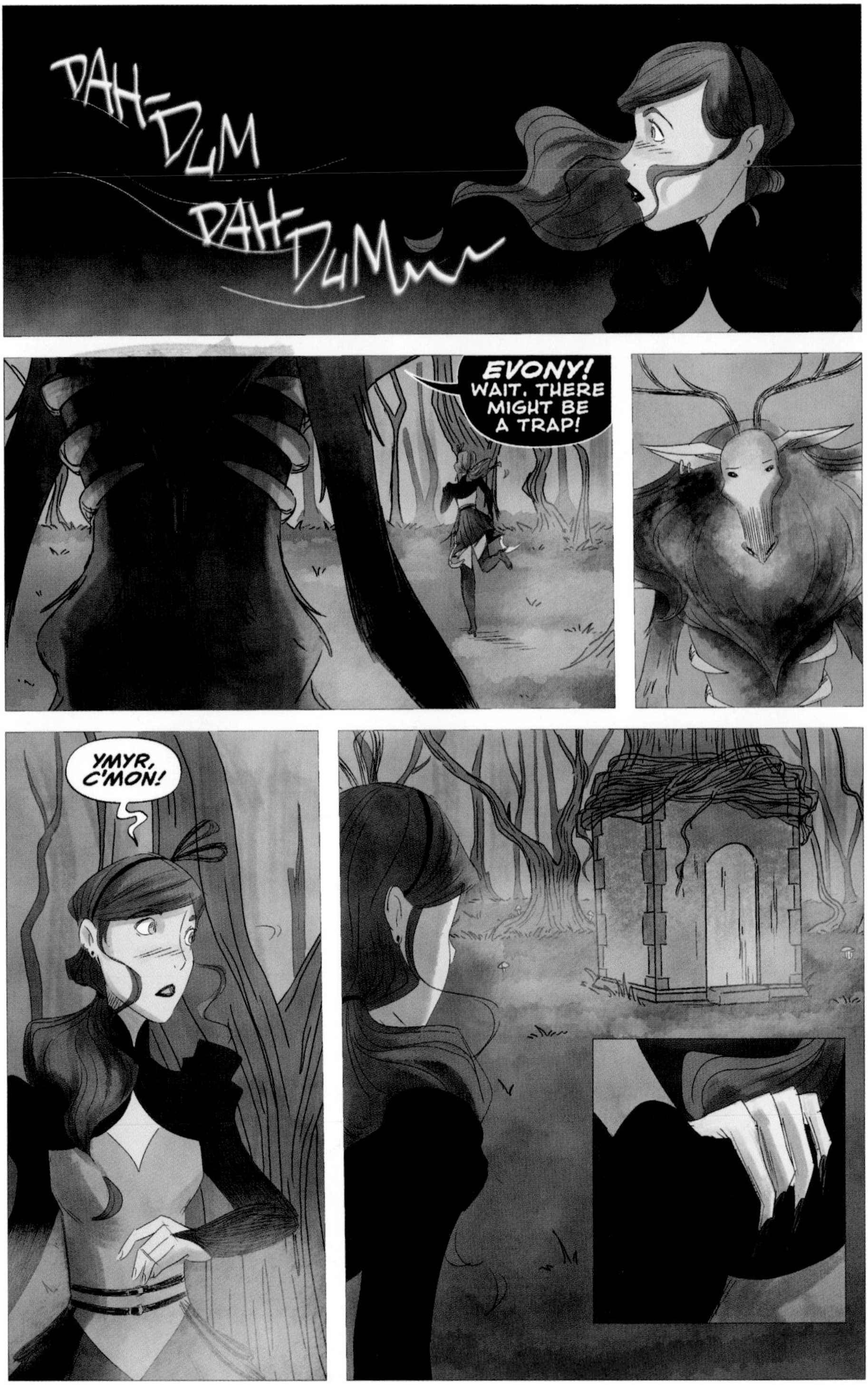
DAH-DUM
DAH-DUM
EVONY! WAIT, THERE MIGHT BE A TRAP!
YMYR, C'MON!

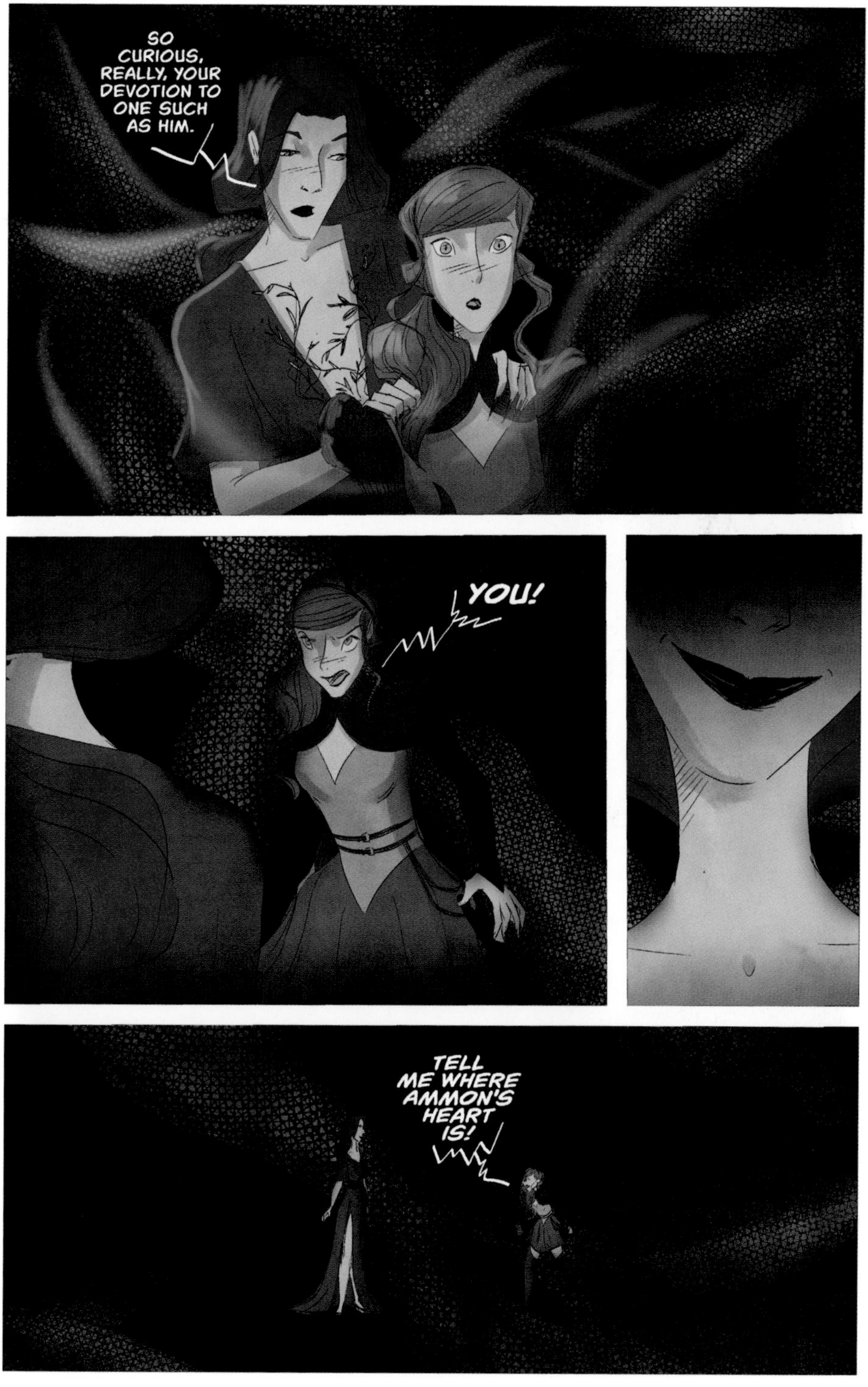
SO CURIOUS, REALLY, YOUR DEVOTION TO ONE SUCH AS HIM.
YOU!
TELL ME WHERE AMMON'S HEART IS!

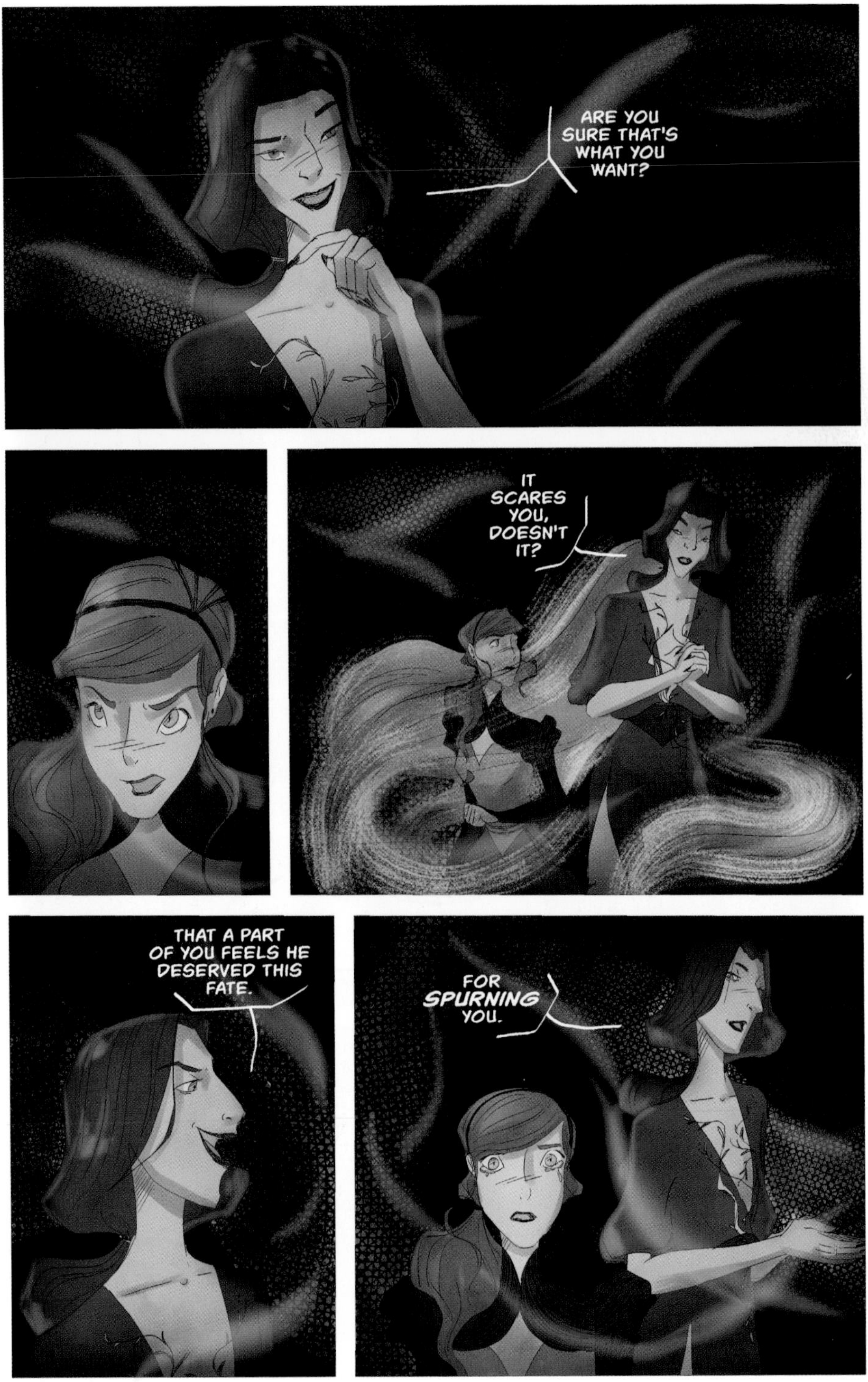
ARE YOU SURE THAT'S WHAT YOU WANT?
IT SCARES YOU, DOESN'T IT?
THAT A PART OF YOU FEELS HE DESERVED THIS FATE.
FOR *SPURNING* YOU.

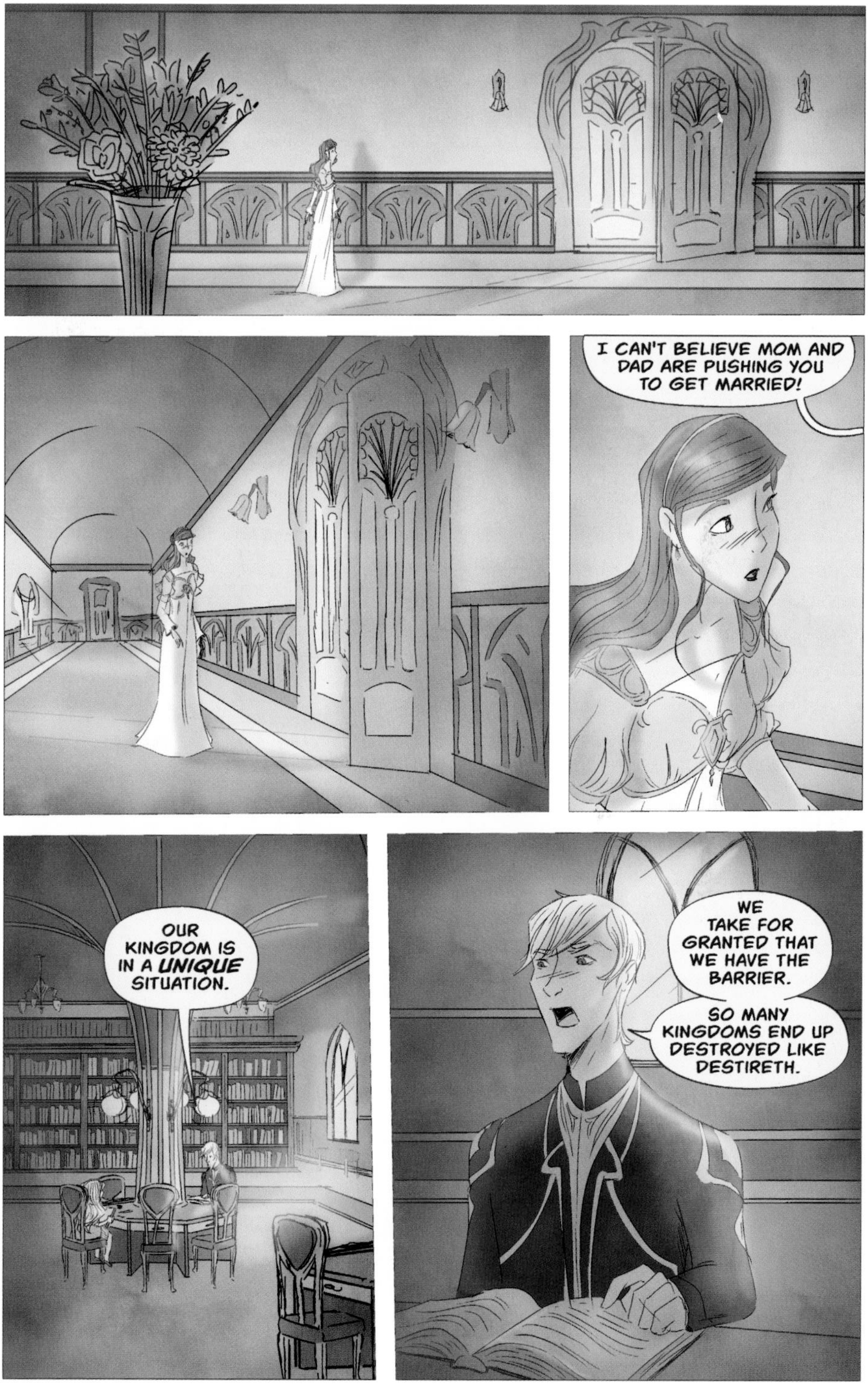
I CAN'T BELIEVE MOM AND DAD ARE PUSHING YOU TO GET MARRIED!
OUR KINGDOM IS IN A UNIQUE SITUATION.
WE TAKE FOR GRANTED THAT WE HAVE THE BARRIER.
SO MANY KINGDOMS END UP DESTROYED LIKE DESTIRETH.

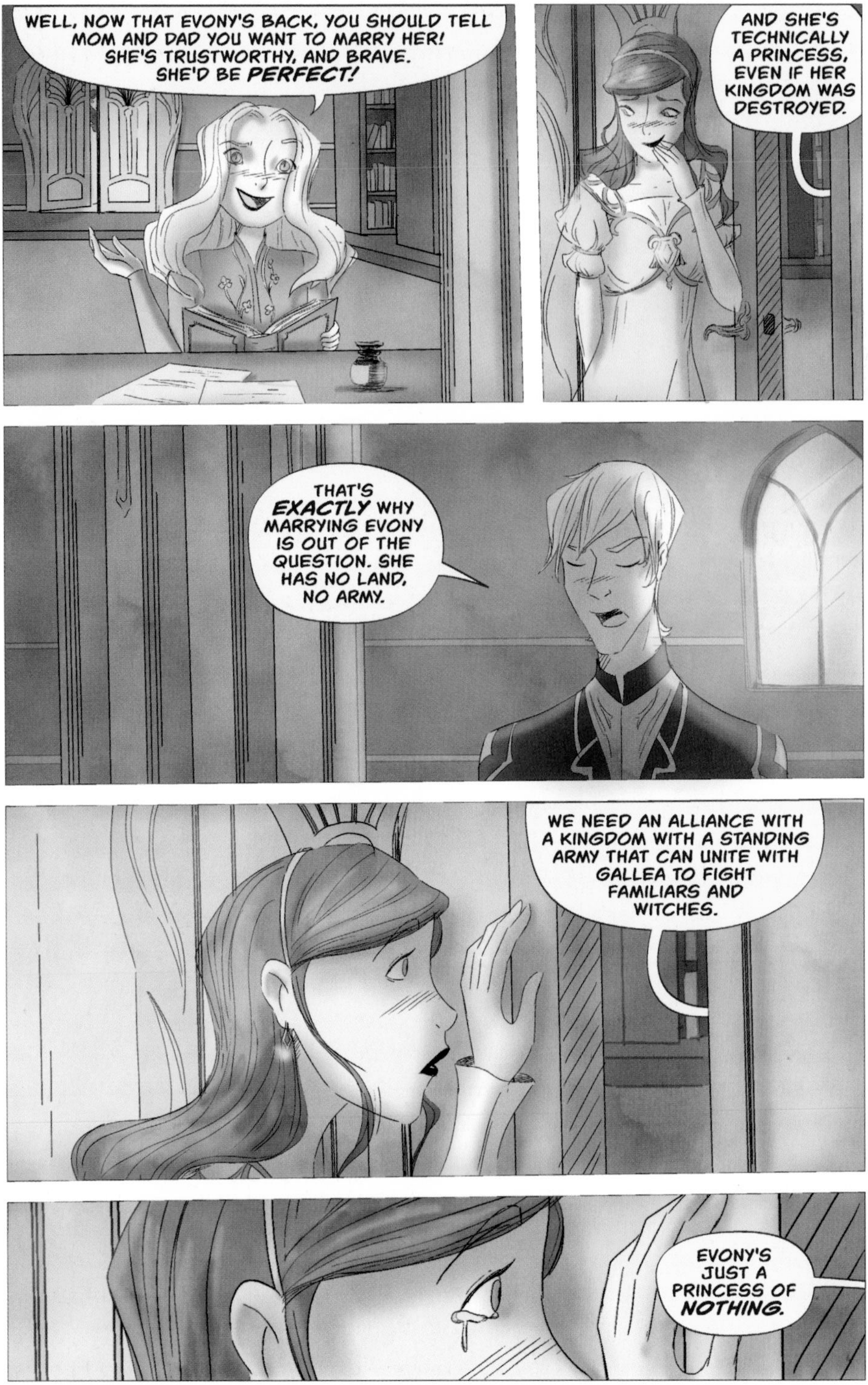
WELL, NOW THAT EVONY'S BACK, YOU SHOULD TELL MOM AND DAD YOU WANT TO MARRY HER! SHE'S TRUSTWORTHY, AND BRAVE. SHE'D BE PERFECT!
AND SHE'S TECHNICALLY A PRINCESS, EVEN IF HER KINGDOM WAS DESTROYED.
THAT'S EXACTLY WHY MARRYING EVONY IS OUT OF THE QUESTION. SHE HAS NO LAND, NO ARMY.
WE NEED AN ALLIANCE WITH A KINGDOM WITH A STANDING ARMY THAT CAN UNITE WITH GALLEA TO FIGHT FAMILIARS AND WITCHES.
EVONY'S JUST A PRINCESS OF NOTHING.

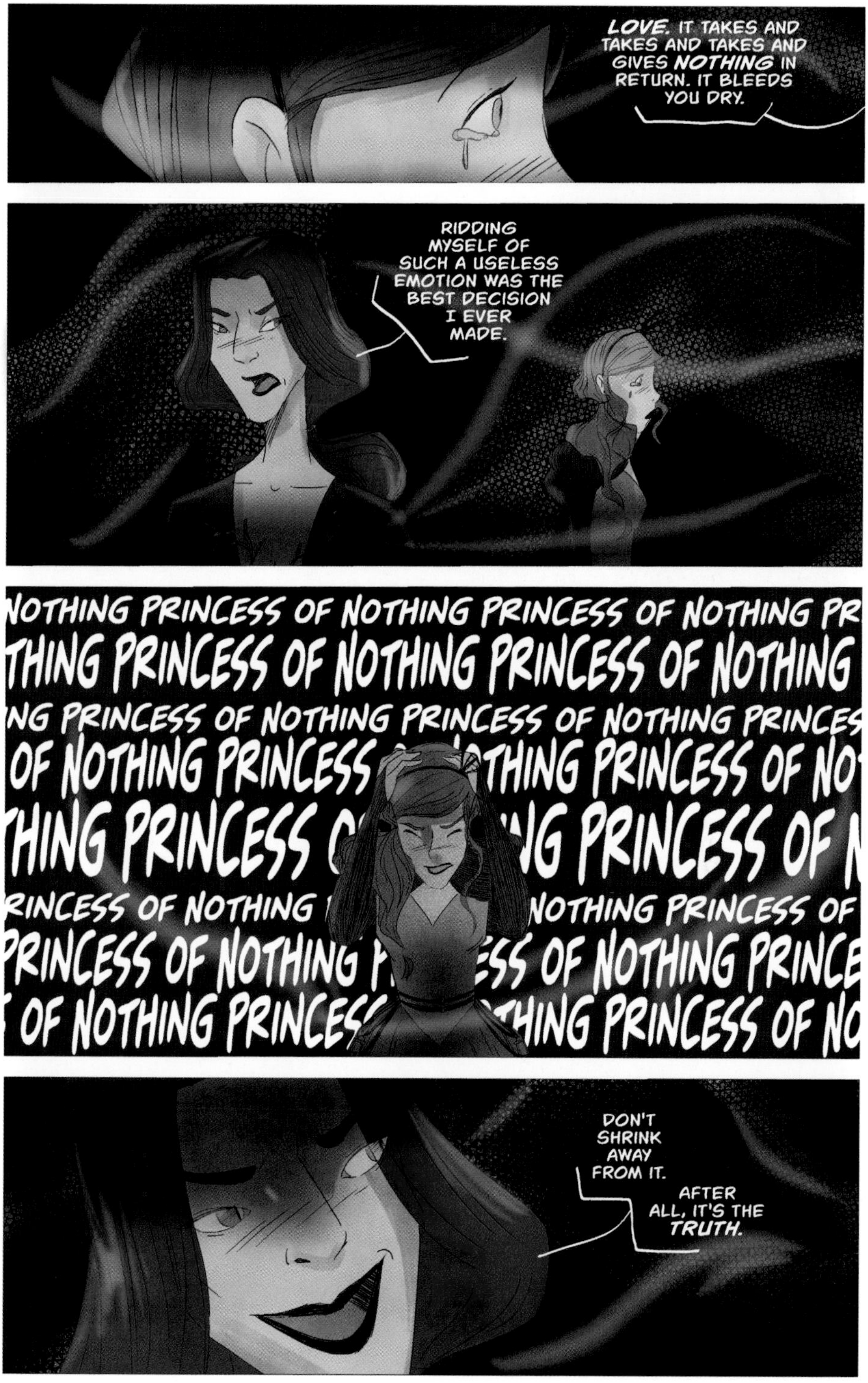

LOVE. IT TAKES AND TAKES AND TAKES AND GIVES NOTHING IN RETURN. IT BLEEDS YOU DRY.
RIDDING MYSELF OF SUCH A USELESS EMOTION WAS THE BEST DECISION I EVER MADE.
PRINCESS OF NOTHING PRINCESS OF NOTHING PRINCESS OF NOTHING
DON'T SHRINK AWAY FROM IT.
AFTER ALL, IT'S THE TRUTH.

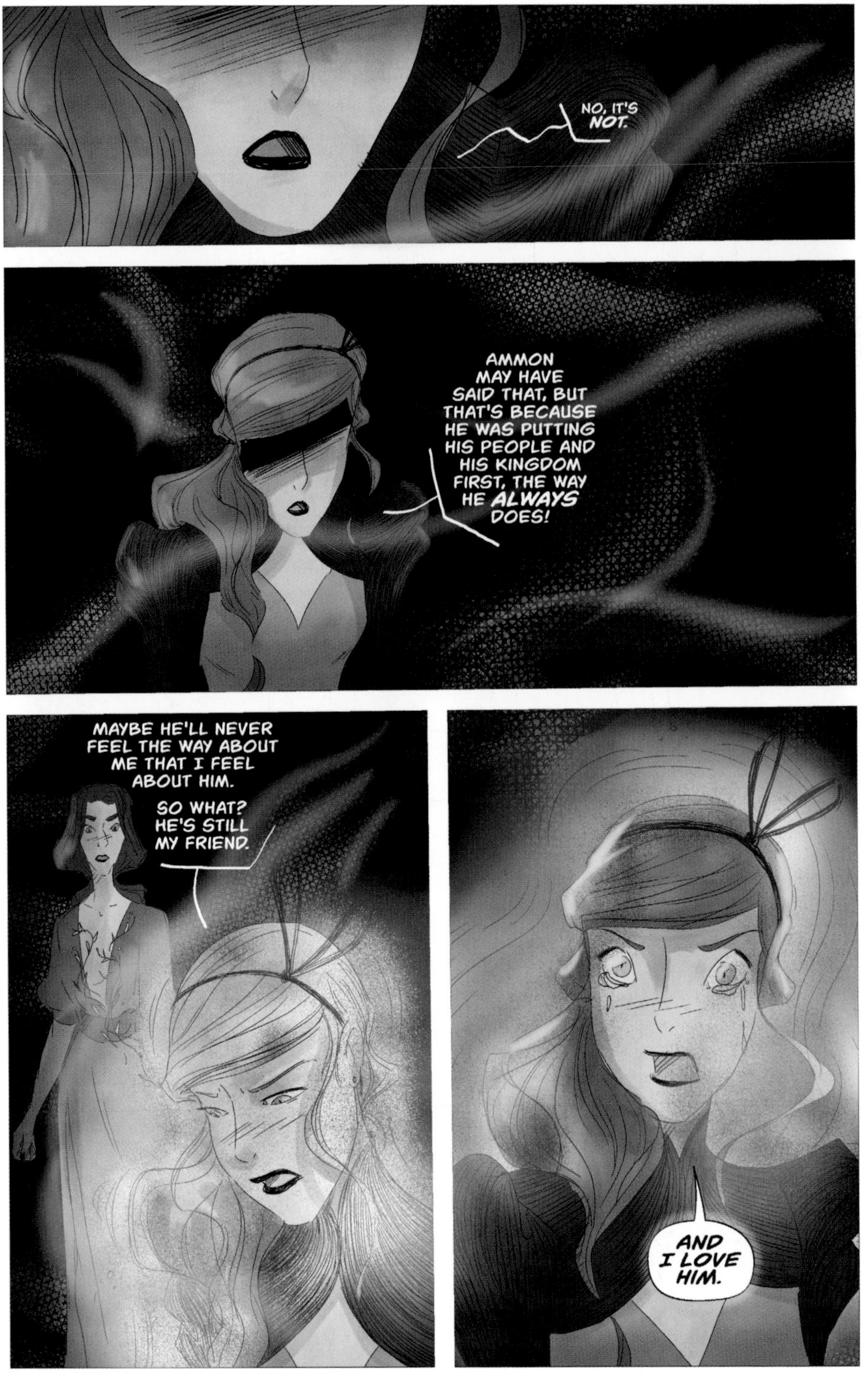
NO, IT'S NOT.
AMMON MAY HAVE SAID THAT, BUT THAT'S BECAUSE HE WAS PUTTING HIS PEOPLE AND HIS KINGDOM FIRST, THE WAY HE ALWAYS DOES!
MAYBE HE'LL NEVER FEEL THE WAY ABOUT ME THAT I FEEL ABOUT HIM.
SO WHAT? HE'S STILL MY FRIEND.
AND I LOVE HIM.

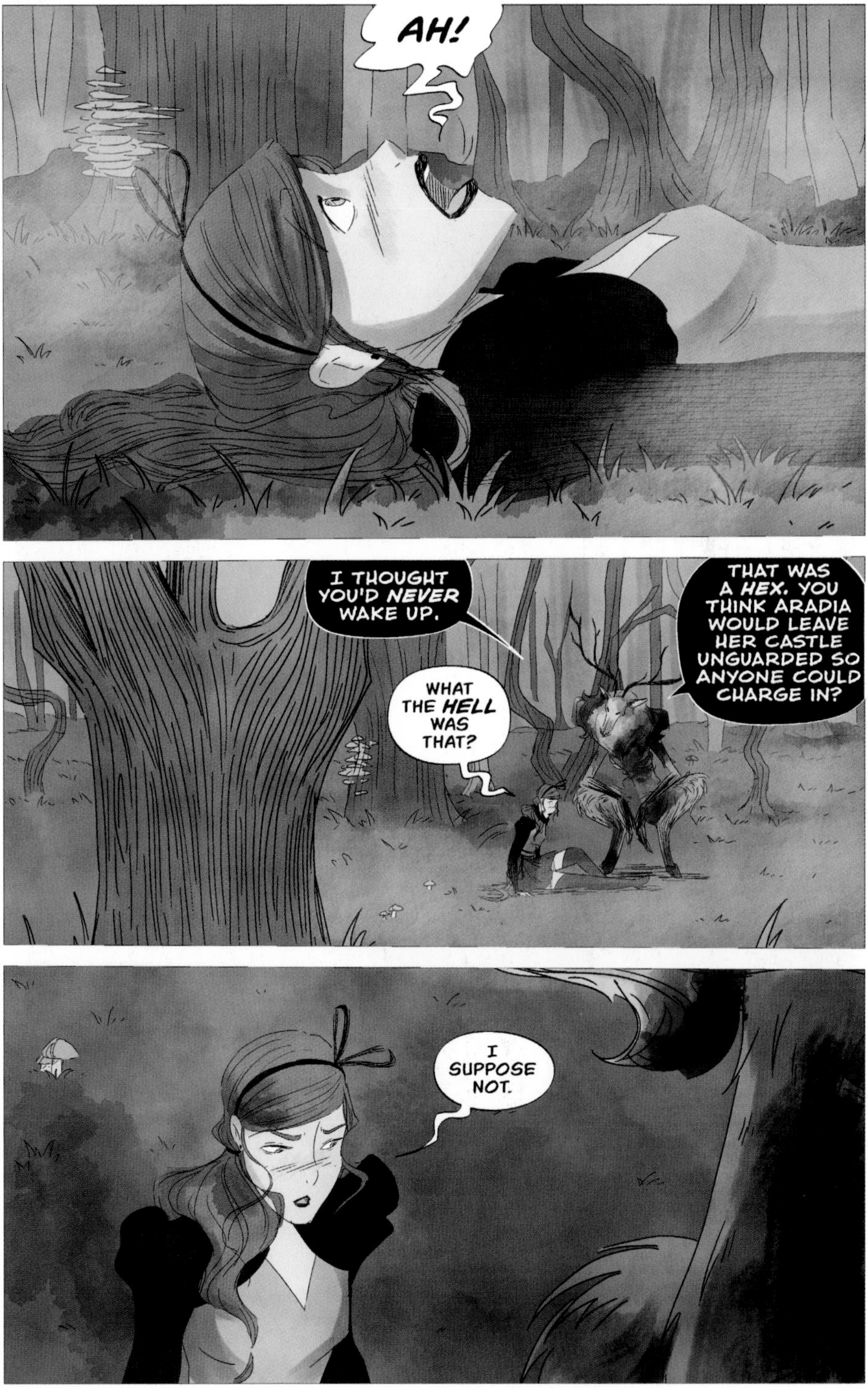
AH!
I THOUGHT YOU'D *NEVER* WAKE UP.
WHAT THE *HELL* WAS THAT?
THAT WAS A *HEX.* YOU THINK ARADIA WOULD LEAVE HER CASTLE UNGUARDED SO ANYONE COULD CHARGE IN?
I SUPPOSE NOT.

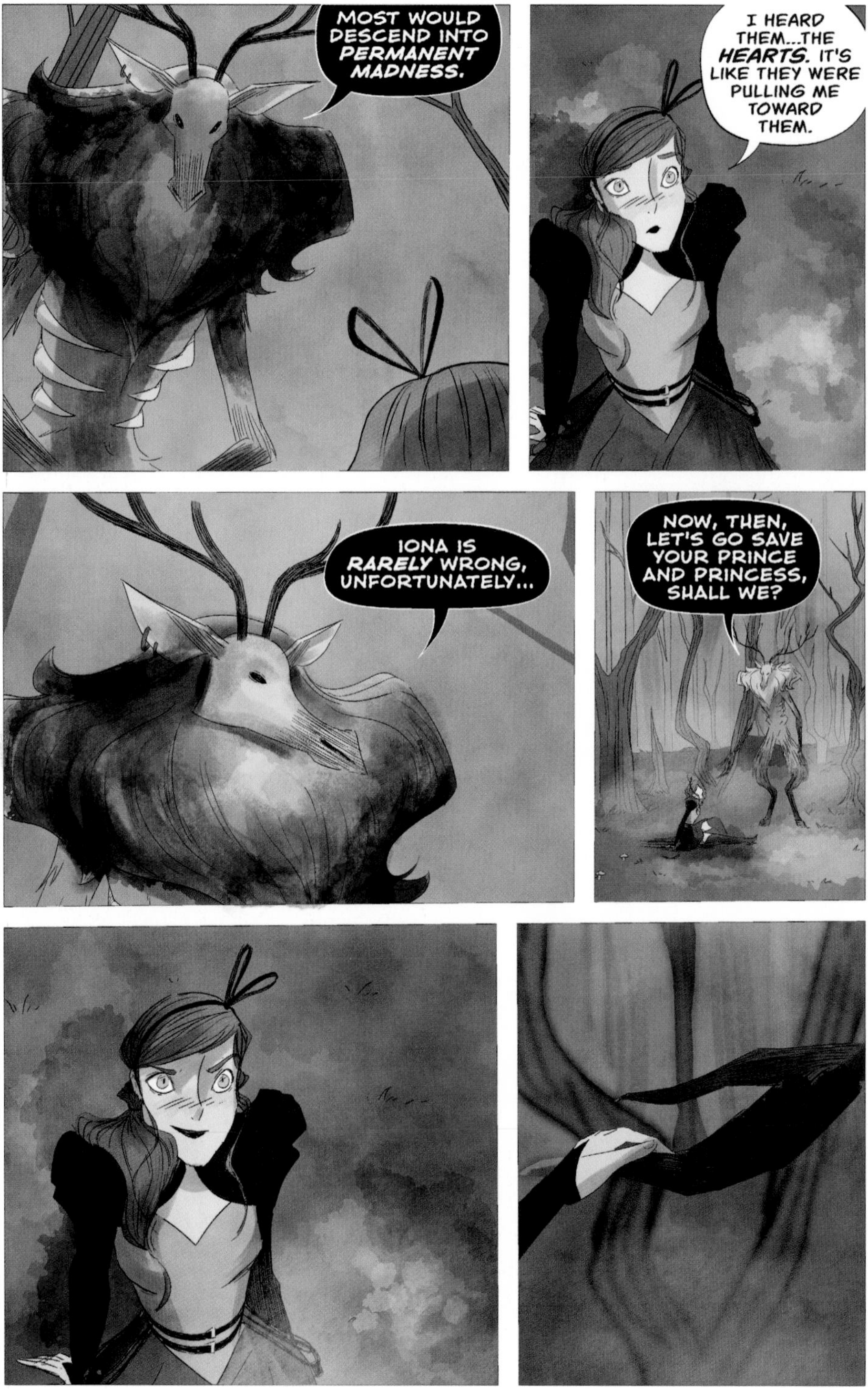
MOST WOULD DESCEND INTO PERMANENT MADNESS.
I HEARD THEM...THE HEARTS. IT'S LIKE THEY WERE PULLING ME TOWARD THEM.
IONA IS RARELY WRONG, UNFORTUNATELY...
NOW, THEN, LET'S GO SAVE YOUR PRINCE AND PRINCESS, SHALL WE?

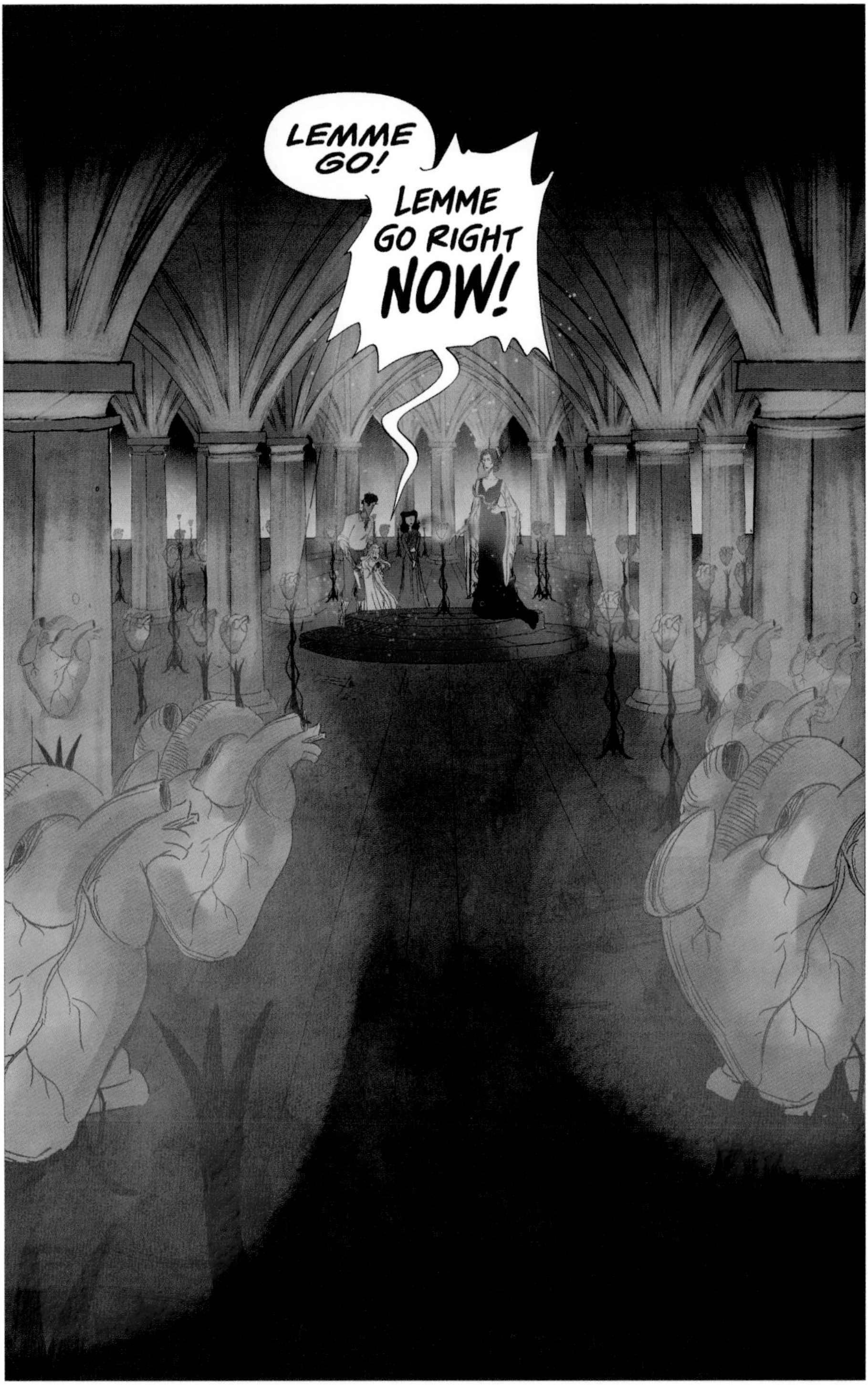
LEMME GO!
LEMME GO RIGHT NOW!

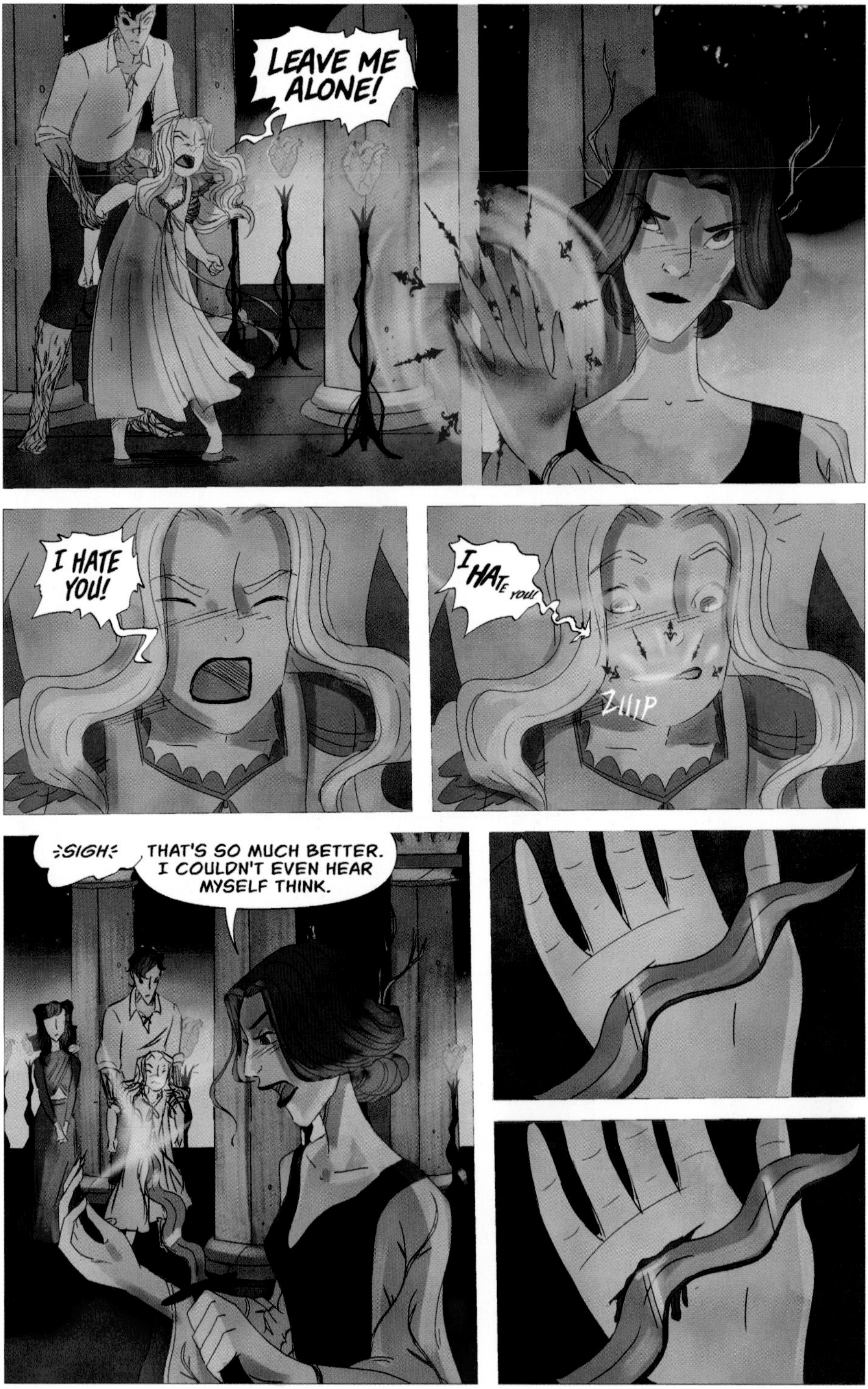
LEAVE ME ALONE!
I HATE YOU!
I HATE YOU!
ZIIIP
SIGH
THAT'S SO MUCH BETTER. I COULDN'T EVEN HEAR MYSELF THINK.

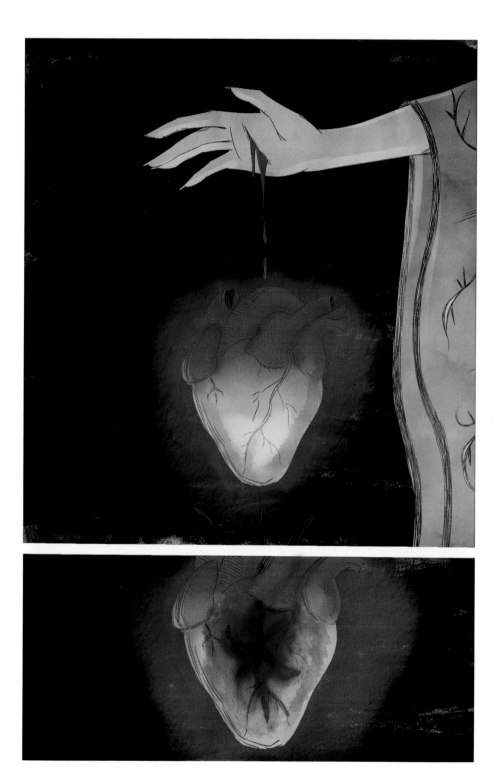

DON'T LET HER THRASH AROUND TOO MUCH.

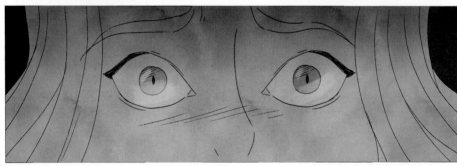

WE HAVE TO BE CLOSE--THE HEARTBEATS ARE *SO* LOUD!

DAH DUM DAH DUM DAH DUM DAH DU

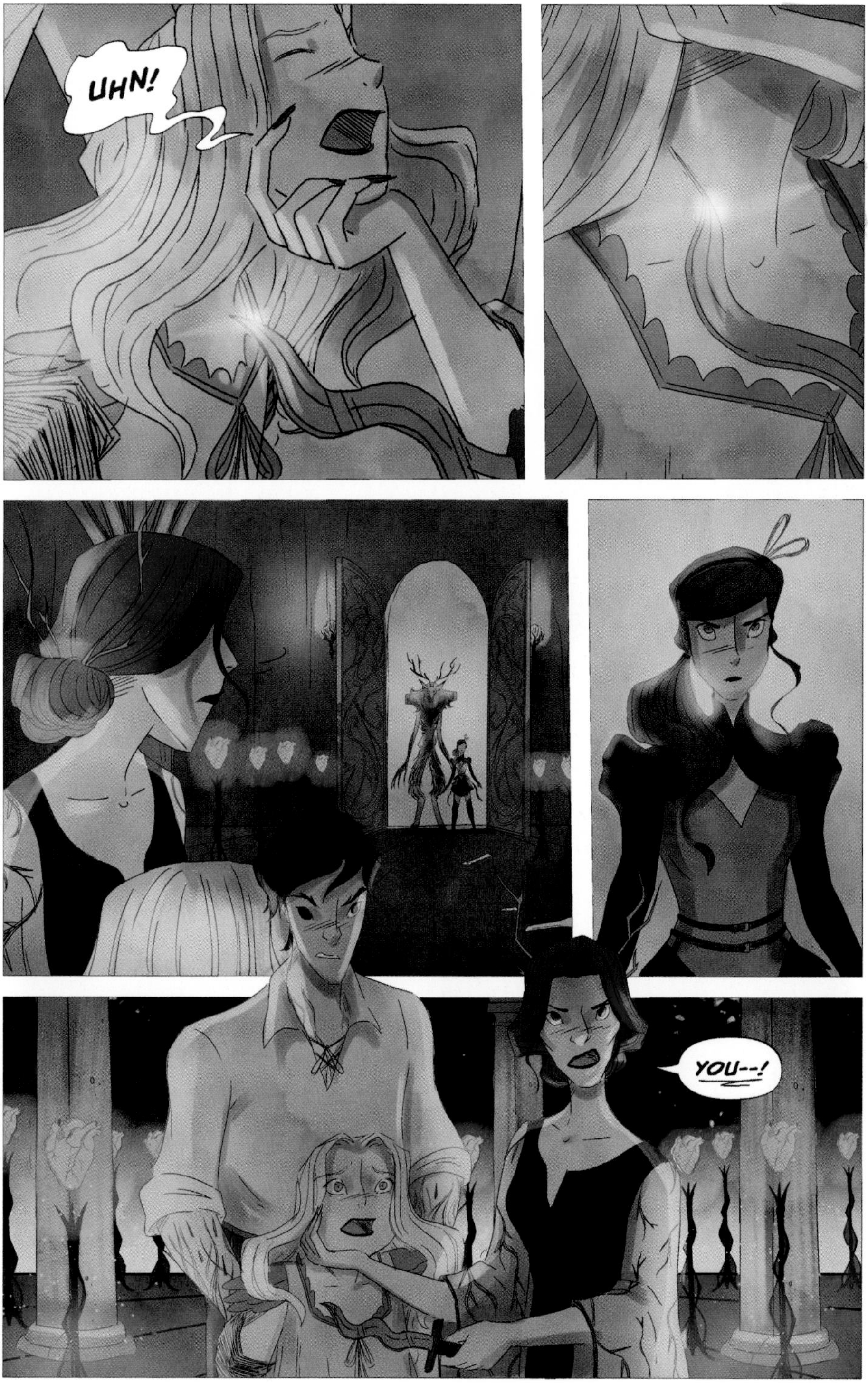
UHN!
YOU--!

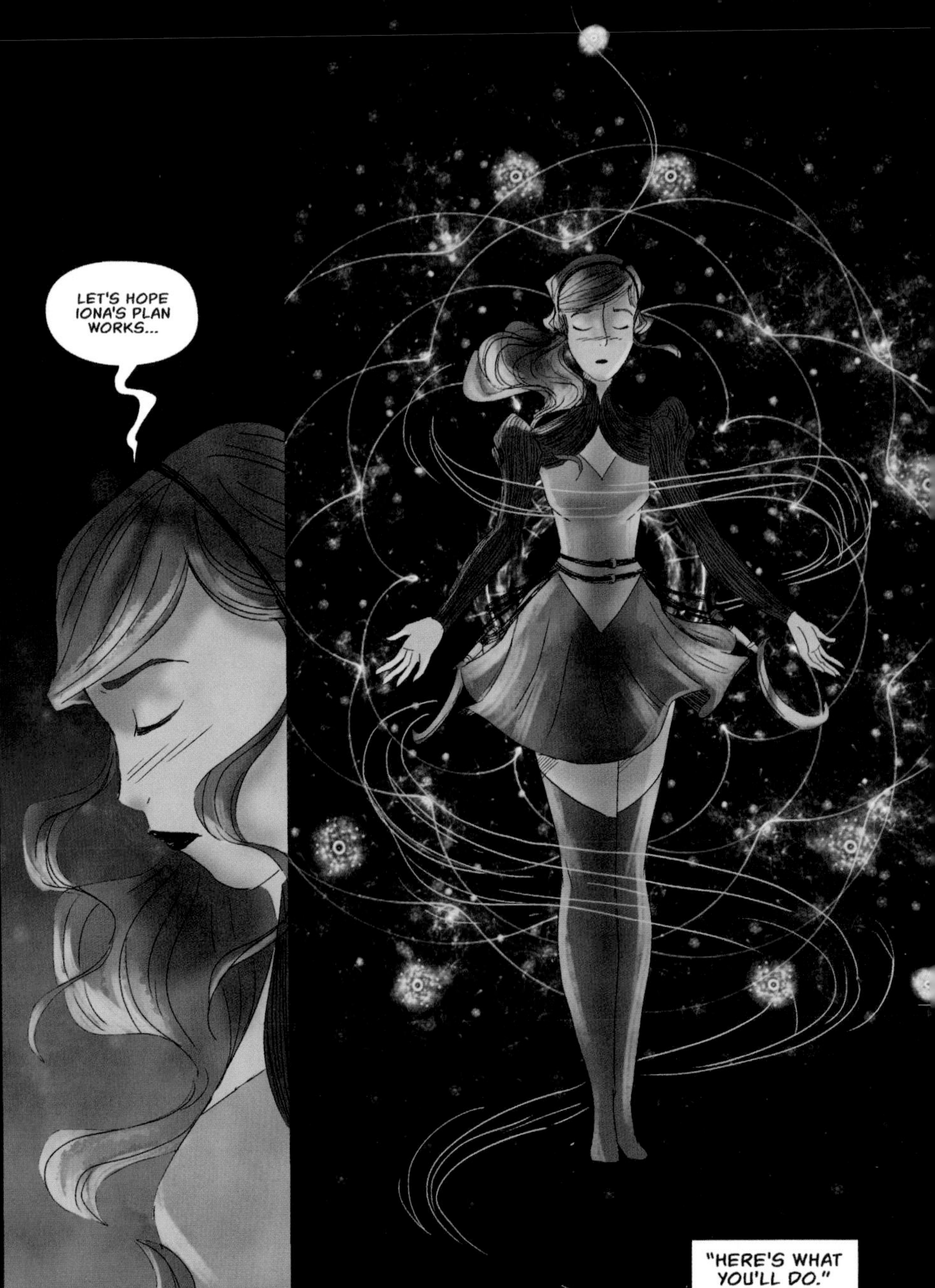
LET'S HOPE IONA'S PLAN WORKS...
"HERE'S WHAT YOU'LL DO."

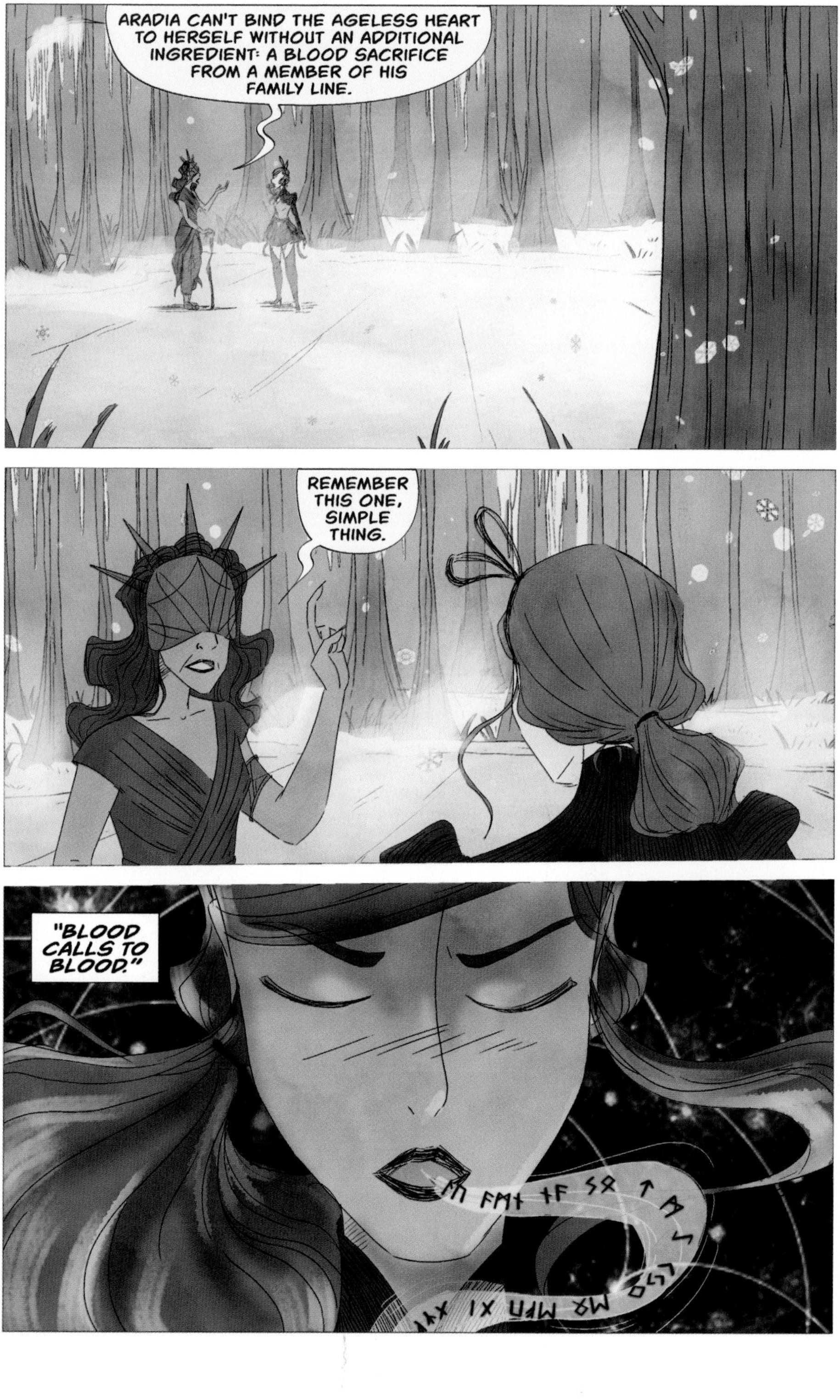
ARADIA CAN'T BIND THE AGELESS HEART TO HERSELF WITHOUT AN ADDITIONAL INGREDIENT: A BLOOD SACRIFICE FROM A MEMBER OF HIS FAMILY LINE.
REMEMBER THIS ONE, SIMPLE THING.
"BLOOD CALLS TO BLOOD."

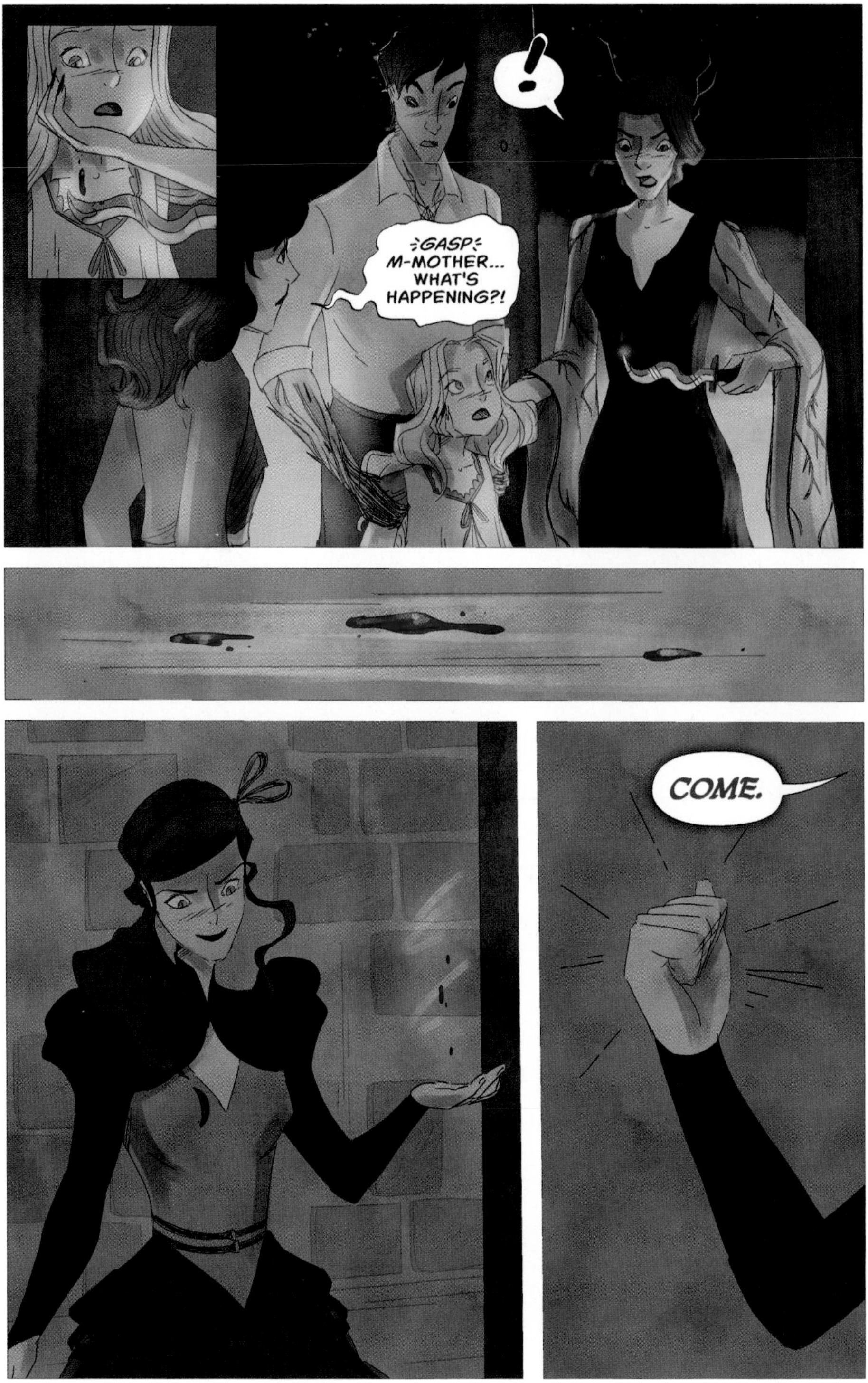
!
GASP
M-MOTHER... WHAT'S HAPPENING?!
COME.

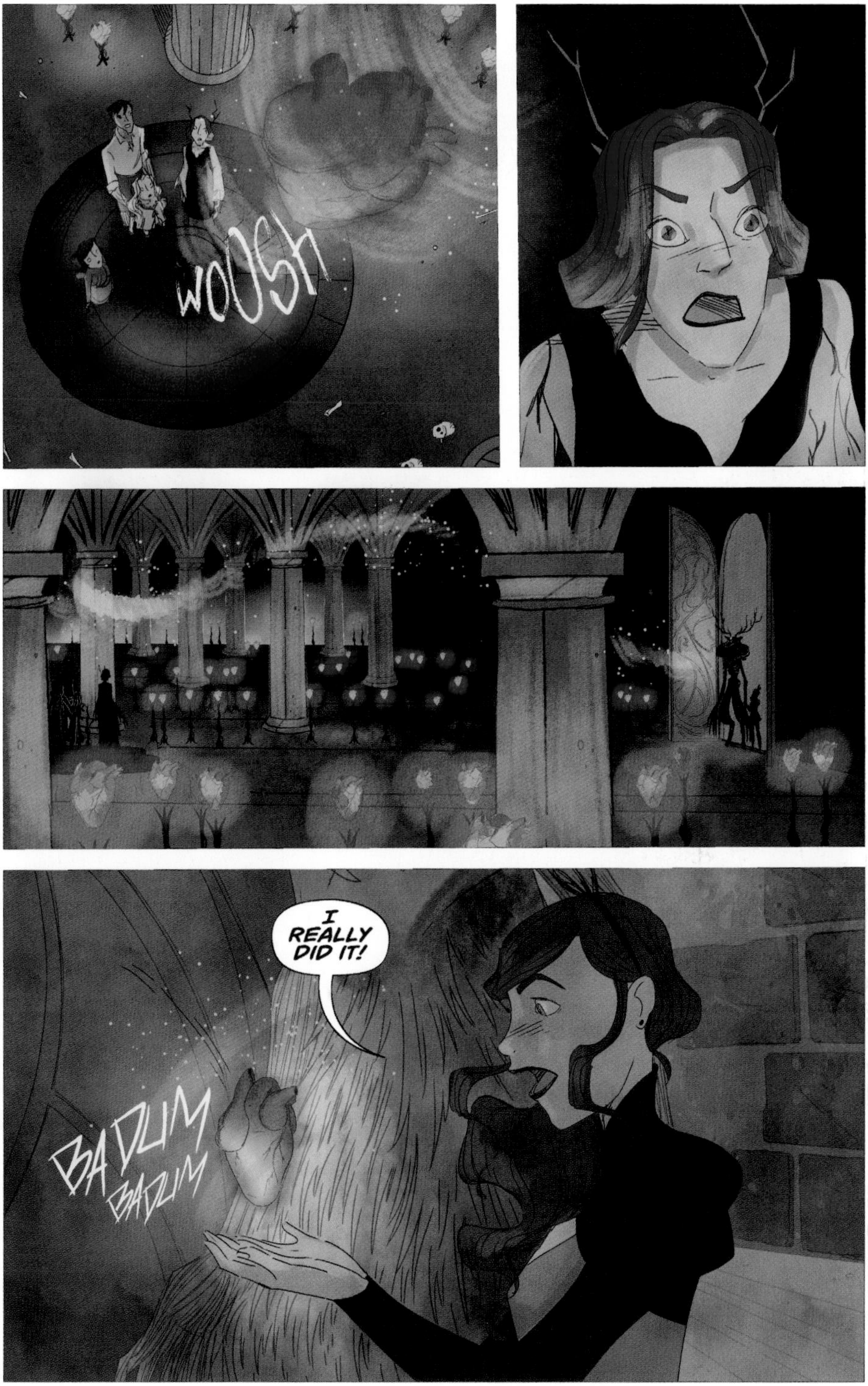
WOOSH
I REALLY DID IT!
BADUM
BADUM

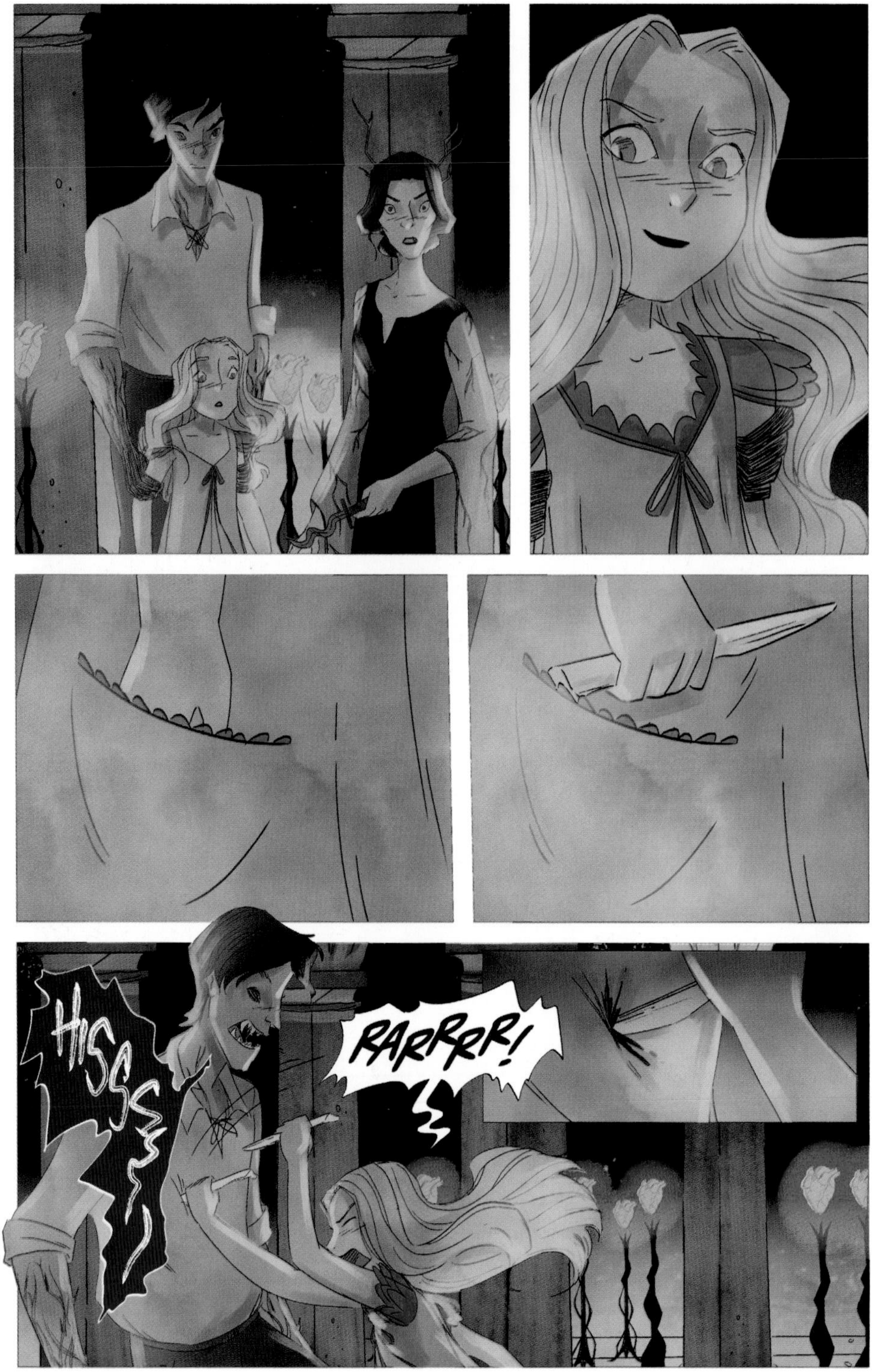
HISSSSS
RARRRR!

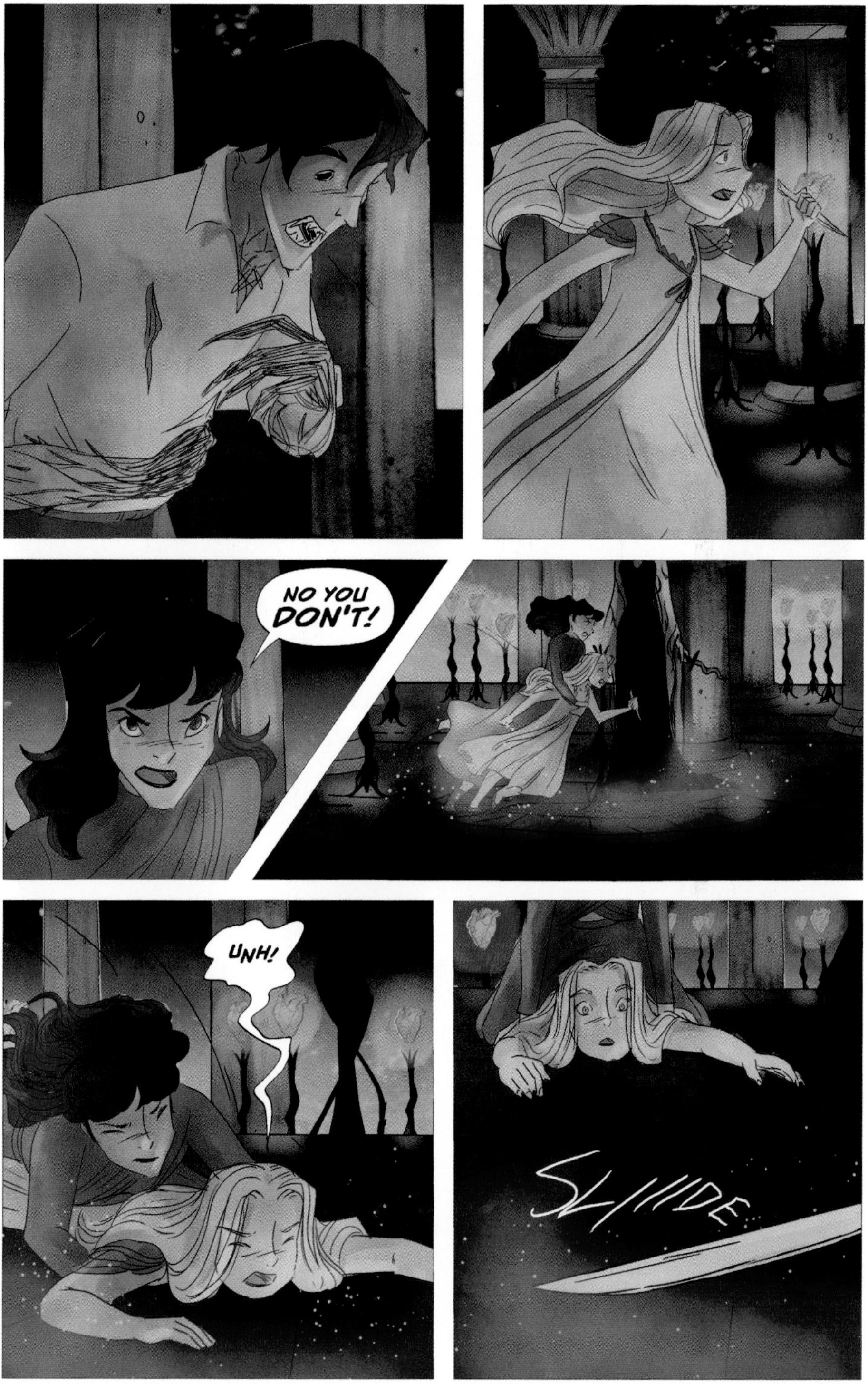
NO YOU DON'T!
UNH!
SLIIIDE

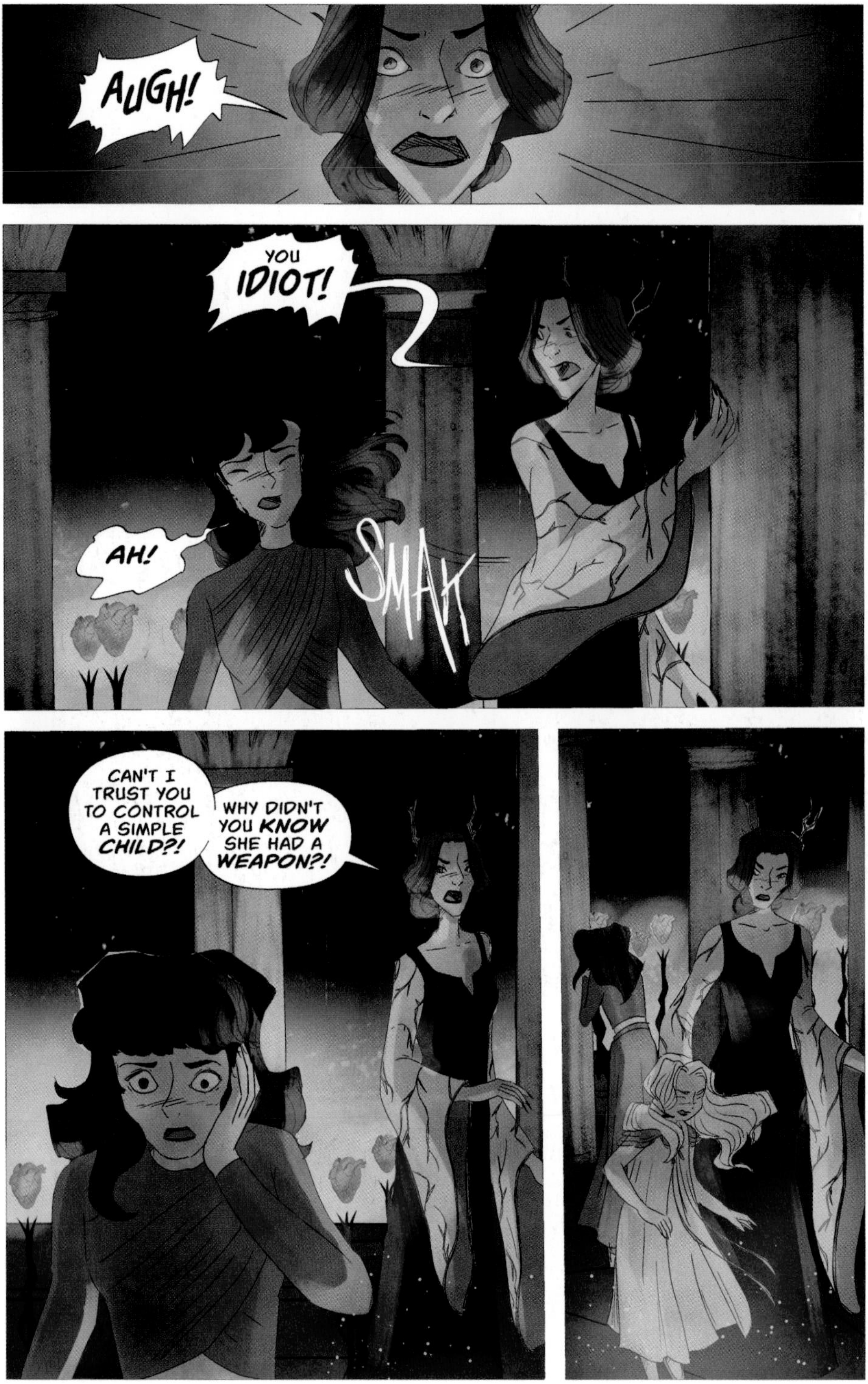
AUGH!
YOU IDIOT!
AH!
SMAK
CAN'T I TRUST YOU TO CONTROL A SIMPLE CHILD?!
WHY DIDN'T YOU KNOW SHE HAD A WEAPON?!

WELL. *THE PRINCESS OF NOTHING.* I GUESS I SHOULDN'T BE SURPRISED.

*OF COURSE* MY PROGENY HAS A LOT OF FIGHT IN HER.

TOO BAD YOU'RE WASTING YOUR EFFORT TRYING TO STEAL BACK SOMETHING THAT DOESN'T *REALLY* BELONG TO YOU.

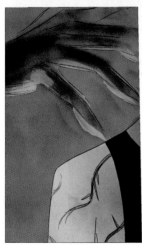

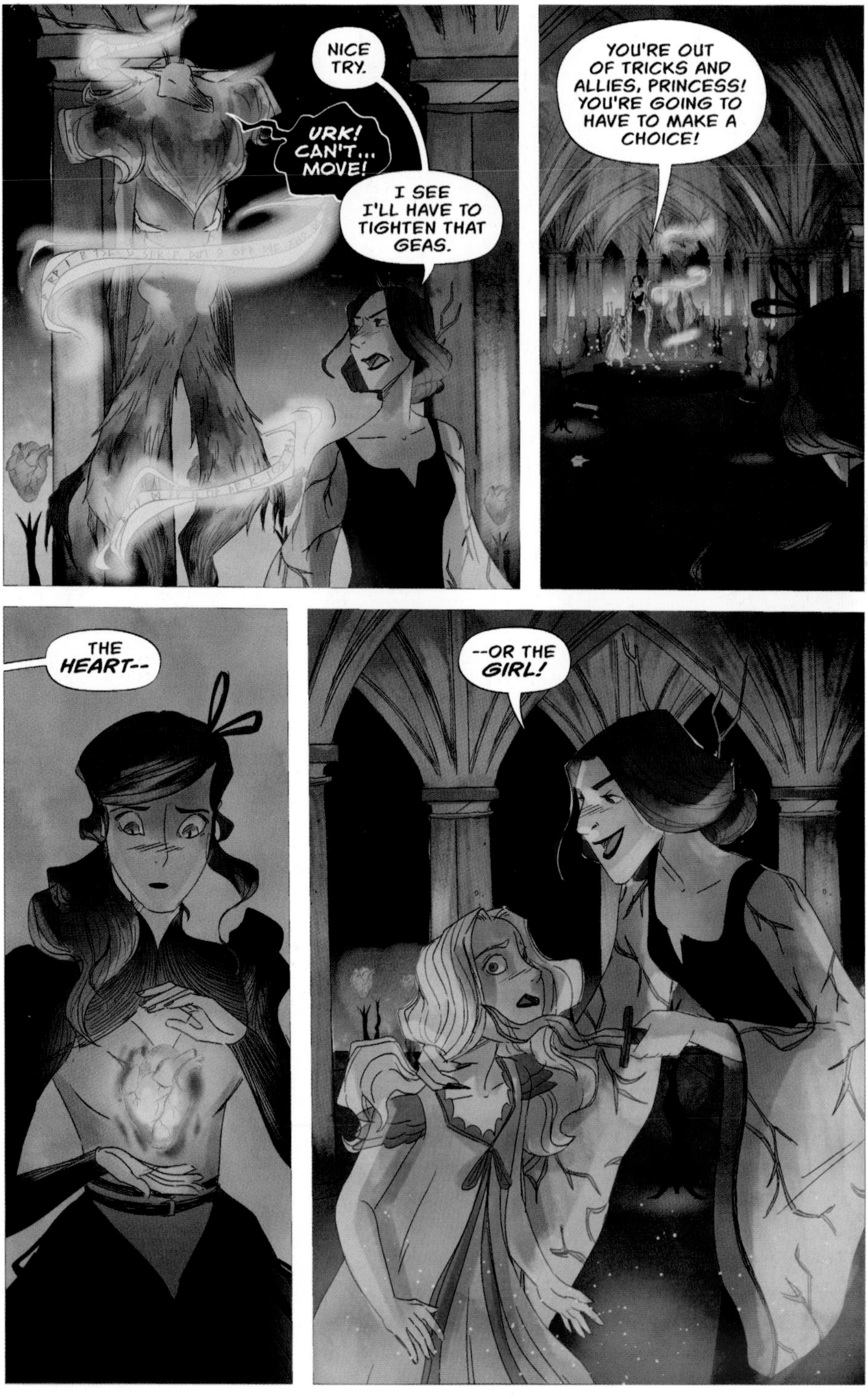
NICE TRY.
URK! CAN'T... MOVE!
I SEE I'LL HAVE TO TIGHTEN THAT GEAS.
YOU'RE OUT OF TRICKS AND ALLIES, PRINCESS! YOU'RE GOING TO HAVE TO MAKE A CHOICE!
THE HEART--
--OR THE GIRL!

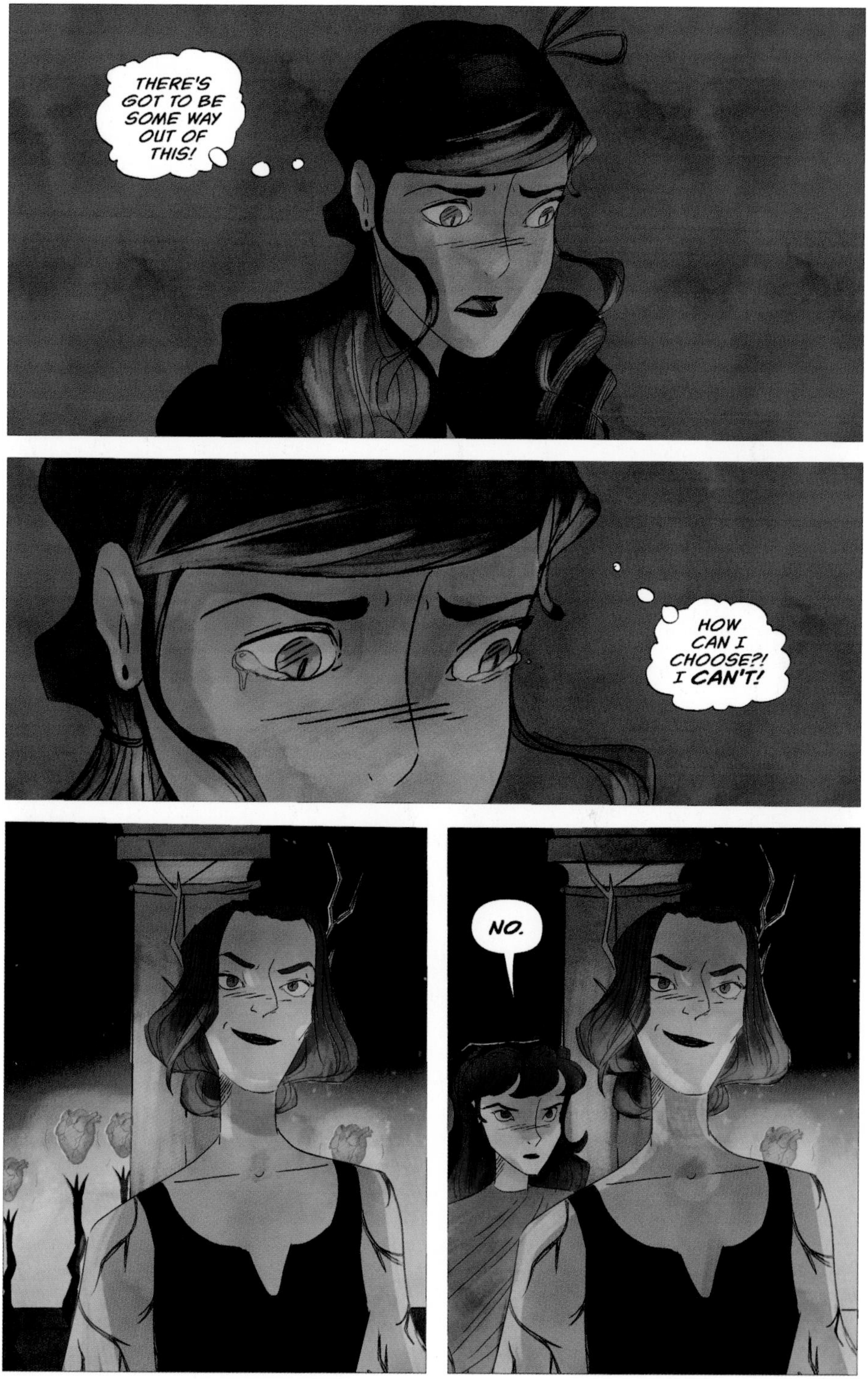
THERE'S GOT TO BE SOME WAY OUT OF THIS!
HOW CAN I CHOOSE?! I CAN'T!
NO.

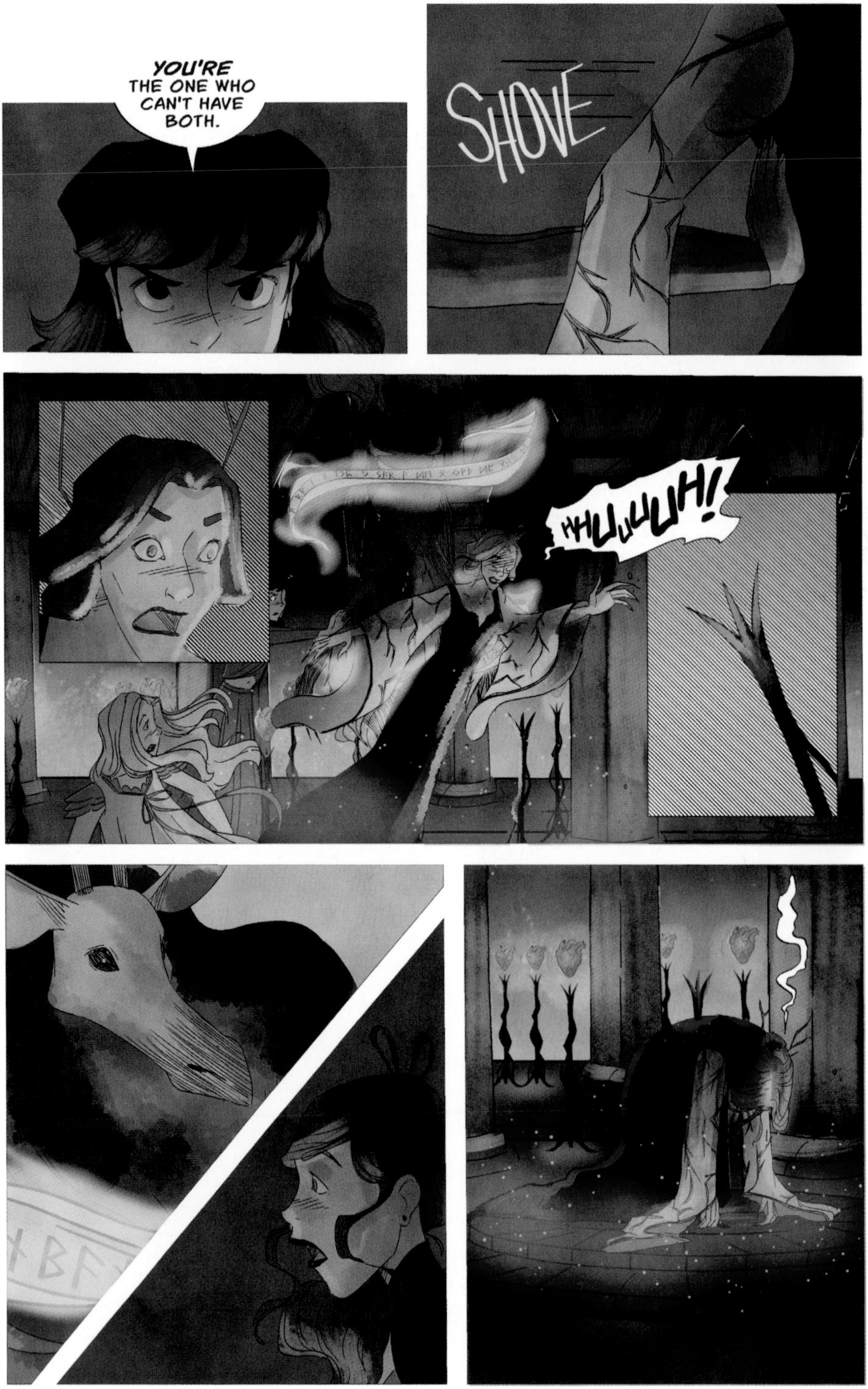
YOU'RE THE ONE WHO CAN'T HAVE BOTH.
SHOVE
HHUuuUH!

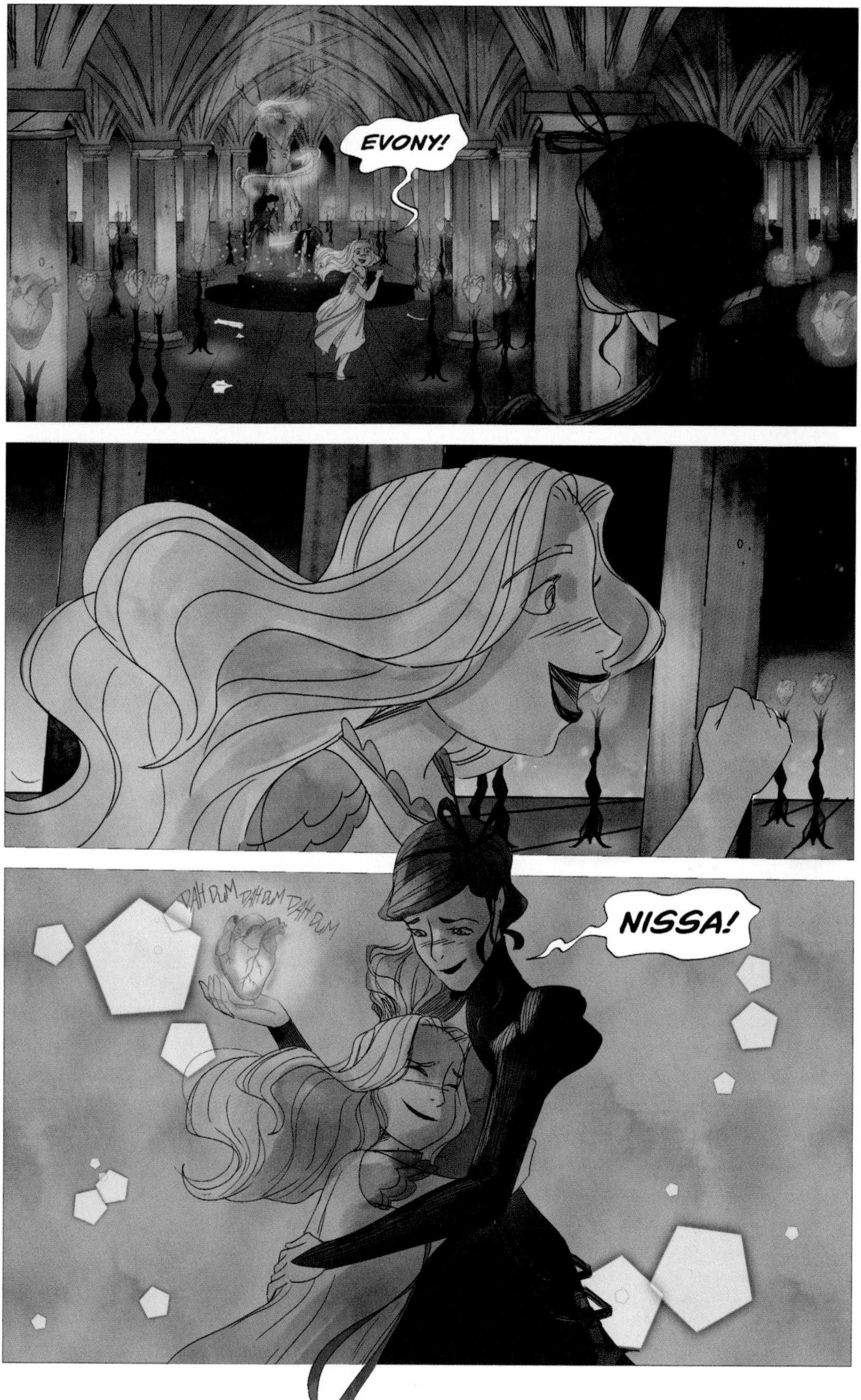
EVONY!
DAH DUM DAH DUM DAH DUM
NISSA!

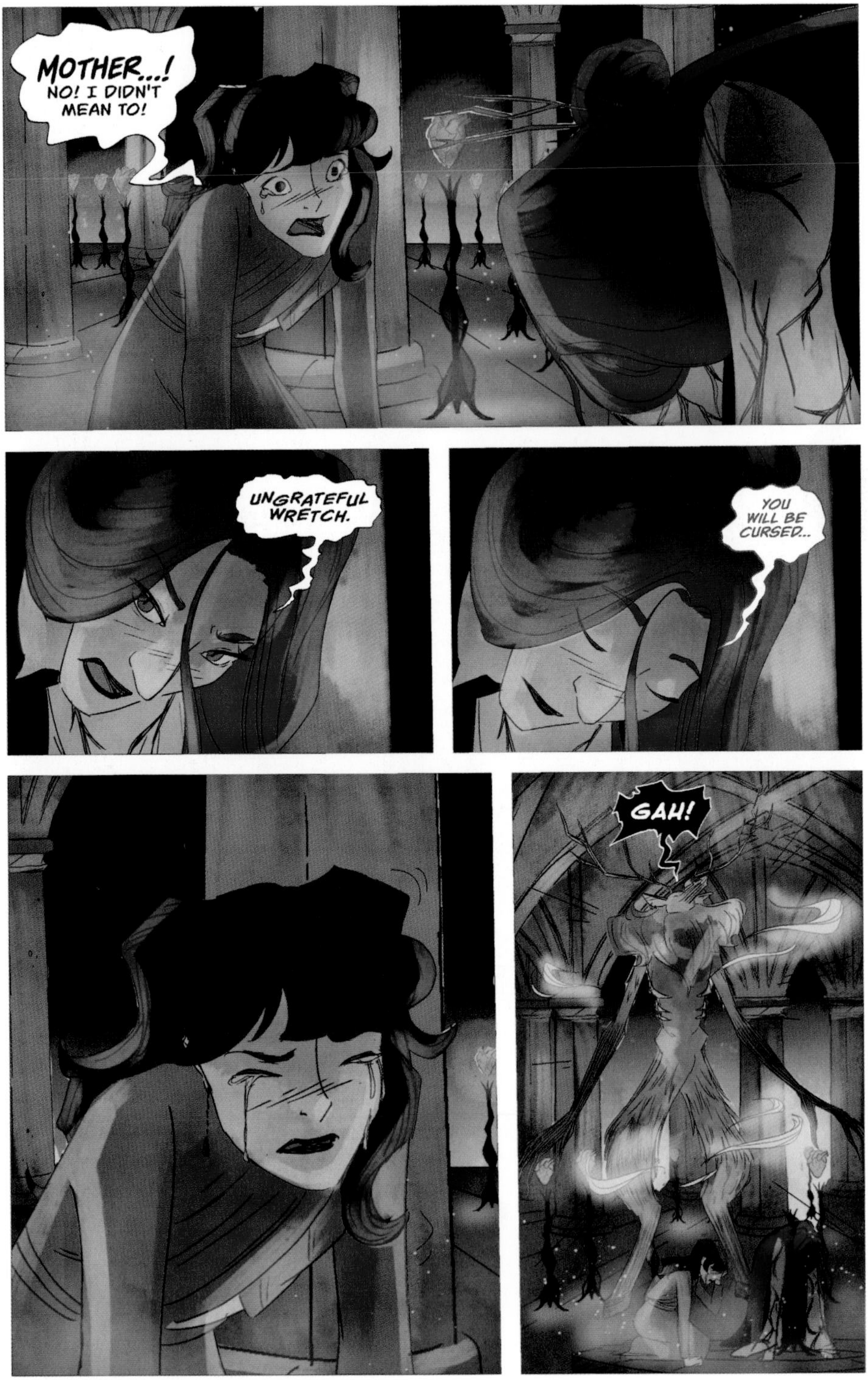
MOTHER...! NO! I DIDN'T MEAN TO!
UNGRATEFUL WRETCH.
YOU WILL BE CURSED...
GAH!

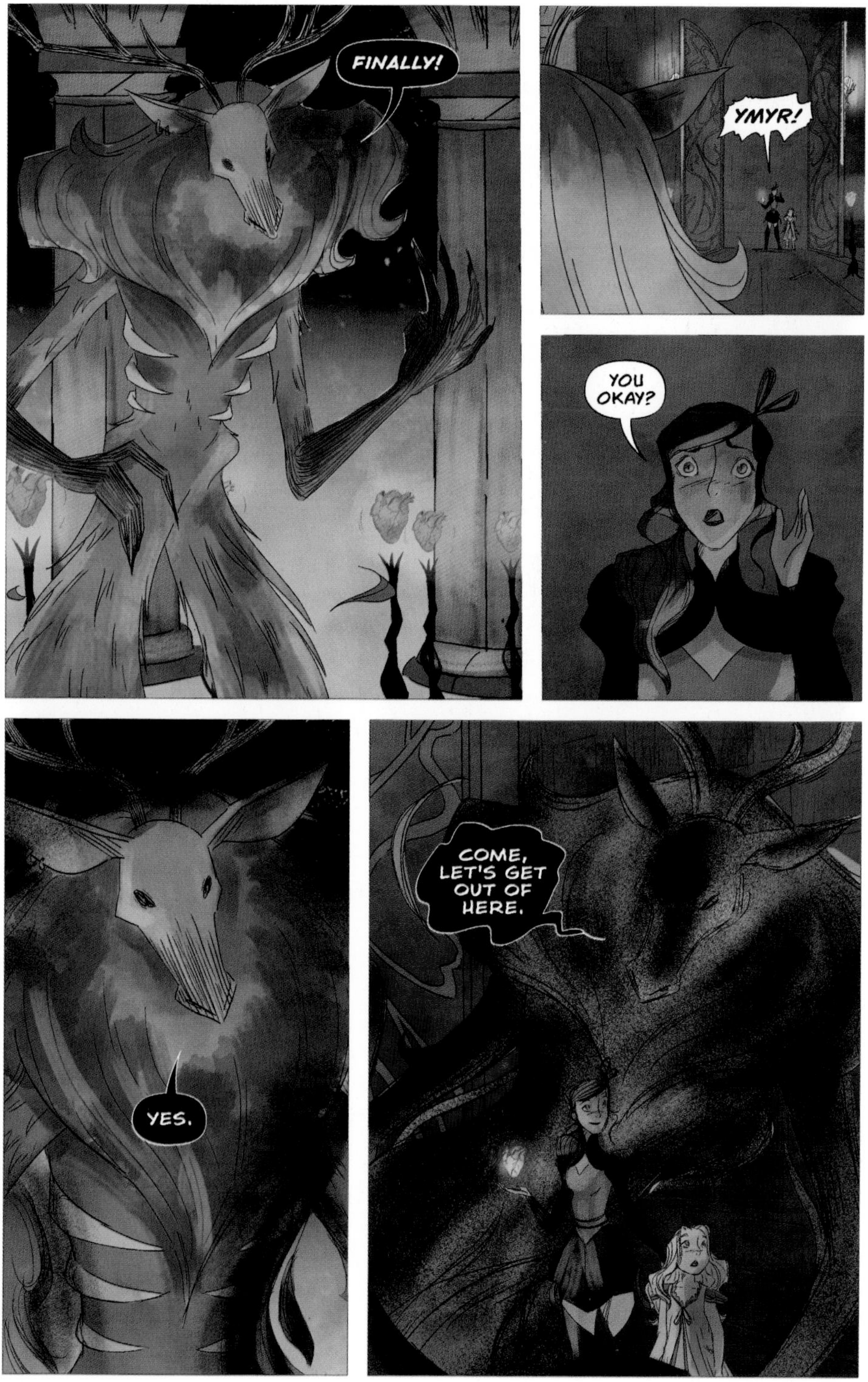
FINALLY!
YMYR!
YOU OKAY?
YES.
COME, LET'S GET OUT OF HERE.

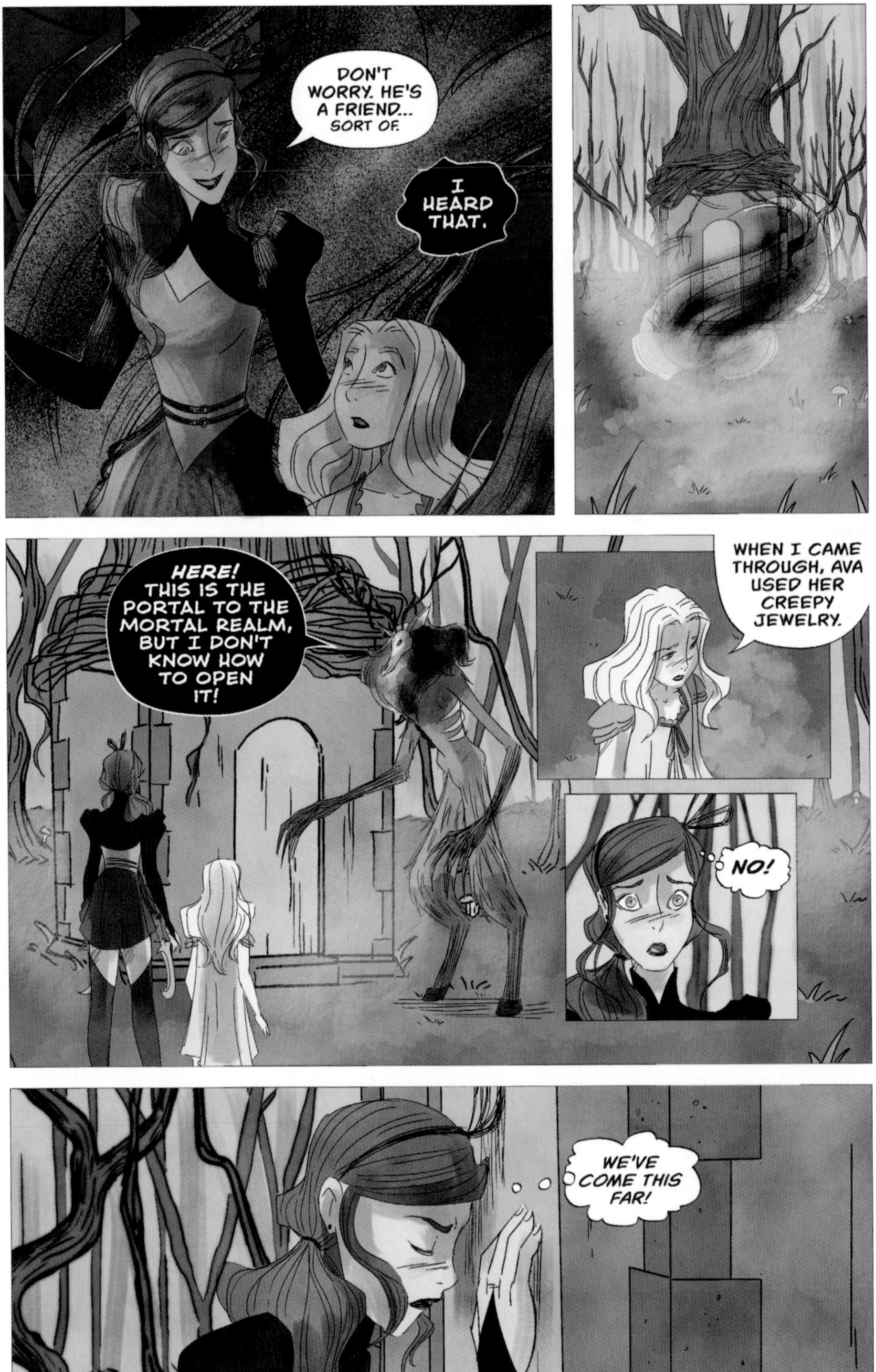
DON'T WORRY. HE'S A FRIEND... SORT OF.
I HEARD THAT.
HERE! THIS IS THE PORTAL TO THE MORTAL REALM, BUT I DON'T KNOW HOW TO OPEN IT!
WHEN I CAME THROUGH, AVA USED HER CREEPY JEWELRY.
NO!
WE'VE COME THIS FAR!

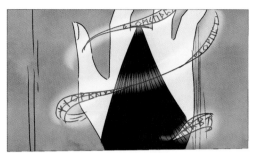

UH, EVONY?

YEAH?

WHOA...

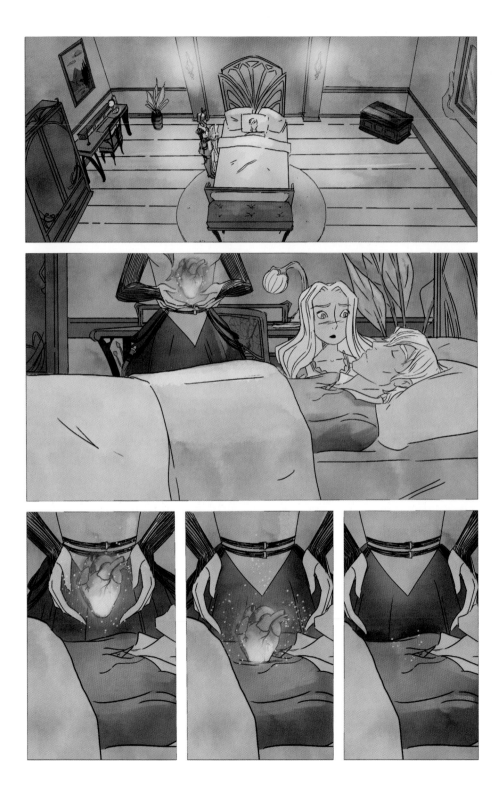

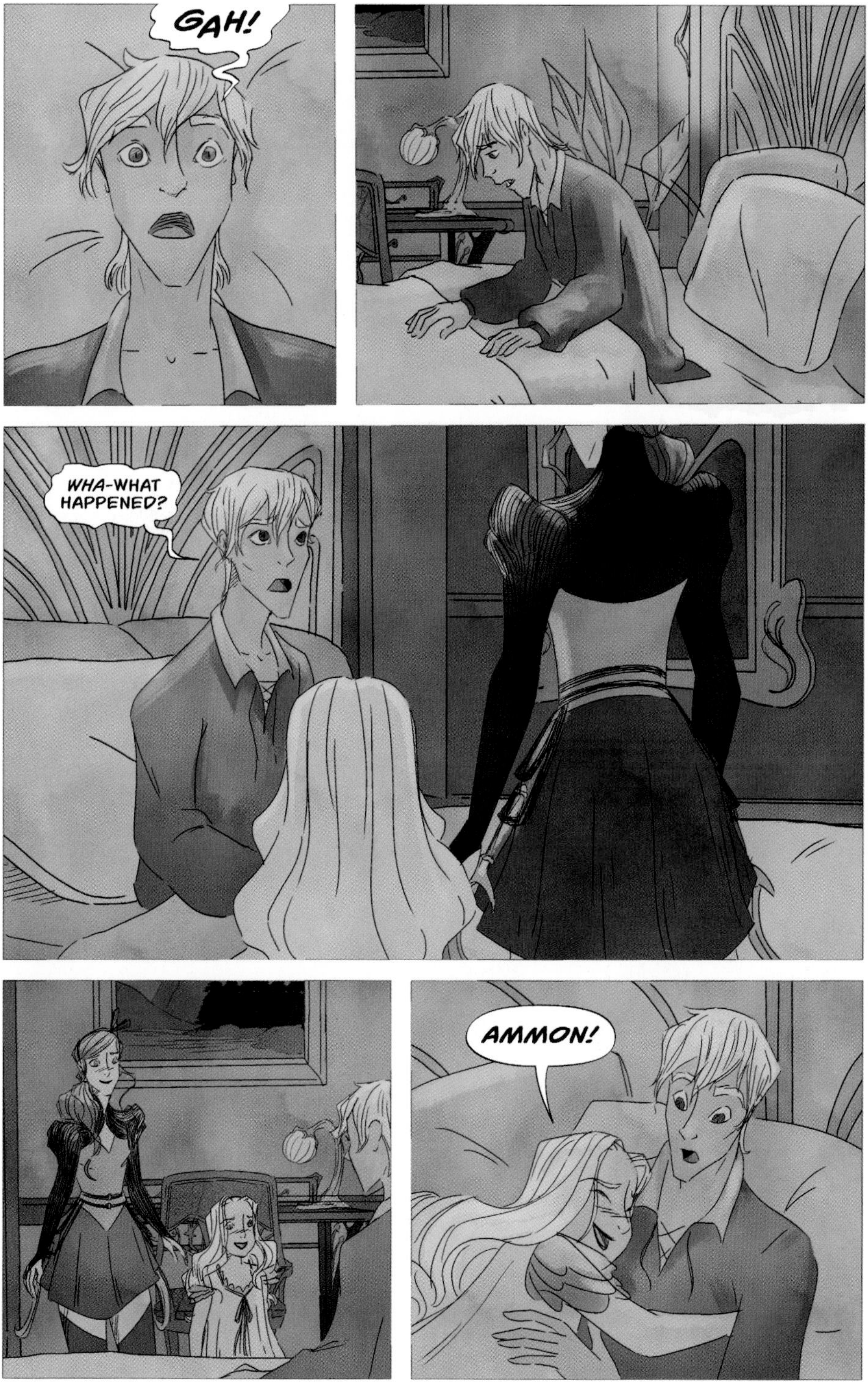
GAH!
WHA-WHAT HAPPENED?
AMMON!

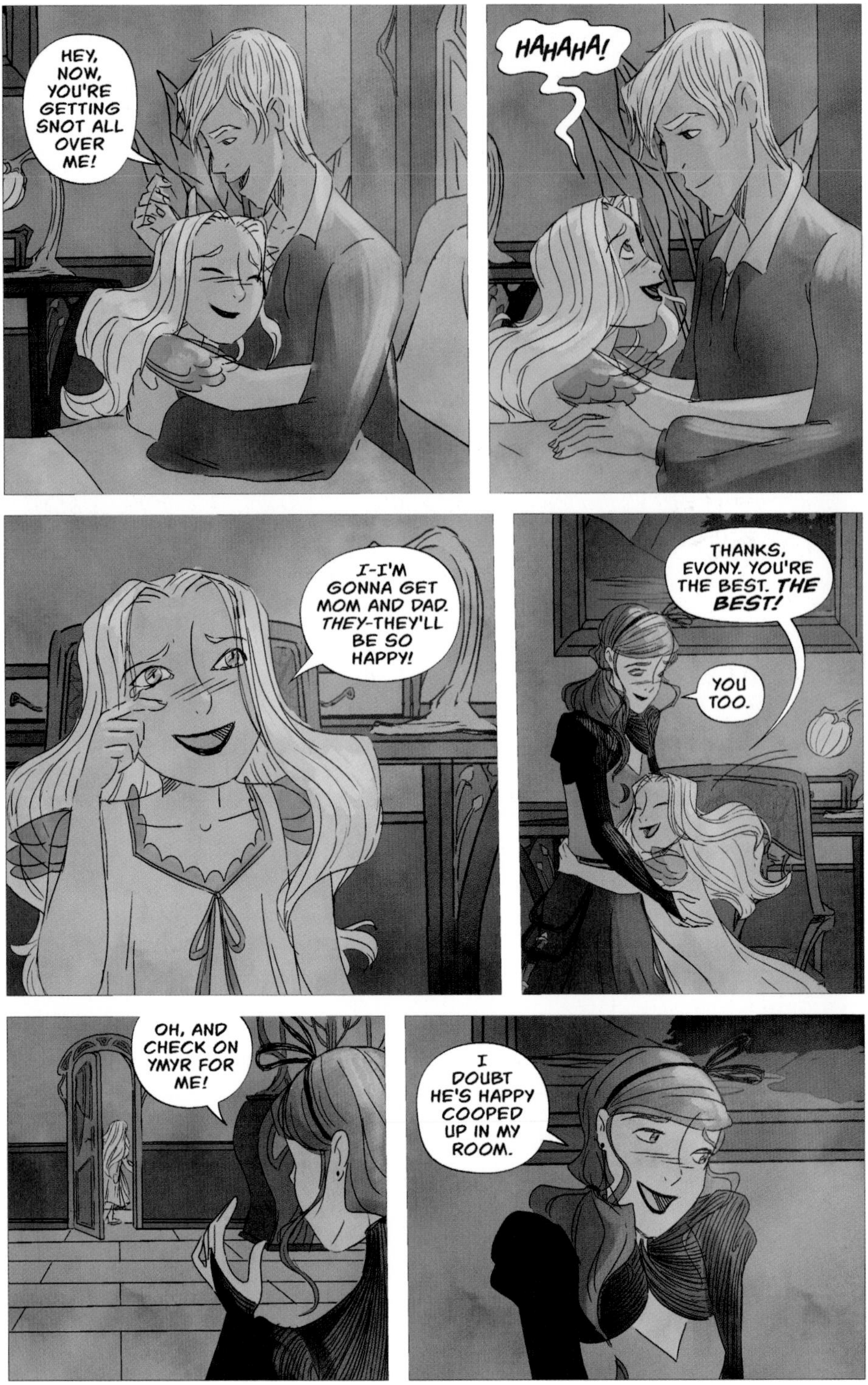
HEY, NOW, YOU'RE GETTING SNOT ALL OVER ME!
HAHAHA!
I-I'M GONNA GET MOM AND DAD. THEY-THEY'LL BE SO HAPPY!
THANKS, EVONY. YOU'RE THE BEST. THE BEST!
YOU TOO.
OH, AND CHECK ON YMYR FOR ME!
I DOUBT HE'S HAPPY COOPED UP IN MY ROOM.

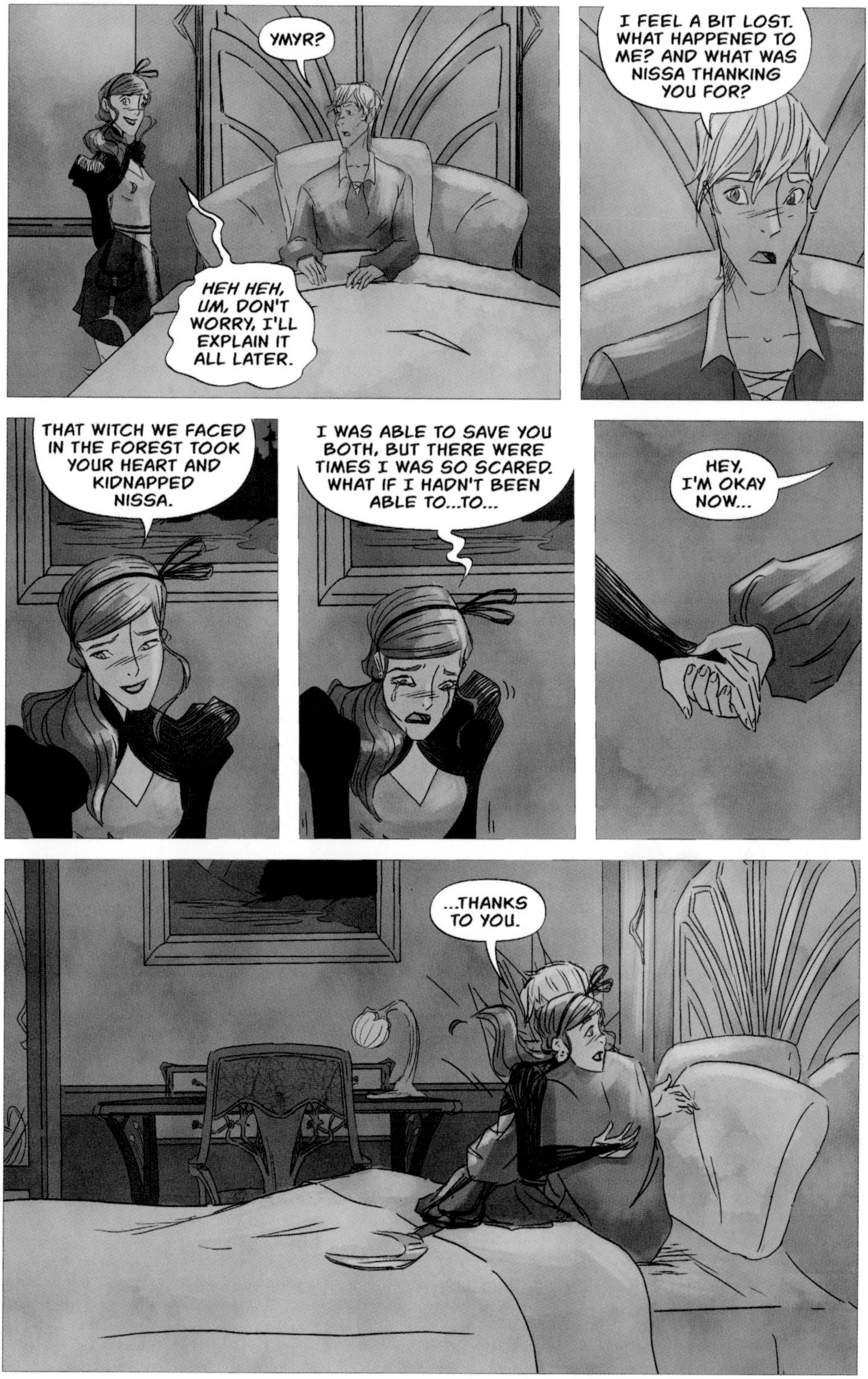
YMYR?
HEH HEH, UM, DON'T WORRY, I'LL EXPLAIN IT ALL LATER.
I FEEL A BIT LOST. WHAT HAPPENED TO ME? AND WHAT WAS NISSA THANKING YOU FOR?
THAT WITCH WE FACED IN THE FOREST TOOK YOUR HEART AND KIDNAPPED NISSA.
I WAS ABLE TO SAVE YOU BOTH, BUT THERE WERE TIMES I WAS SO SCARED. WHAT IF I HADN'T BEEN ABLE TO...TO...
HEY, I'M OKAY NOW...
...THANKS TO YOU.

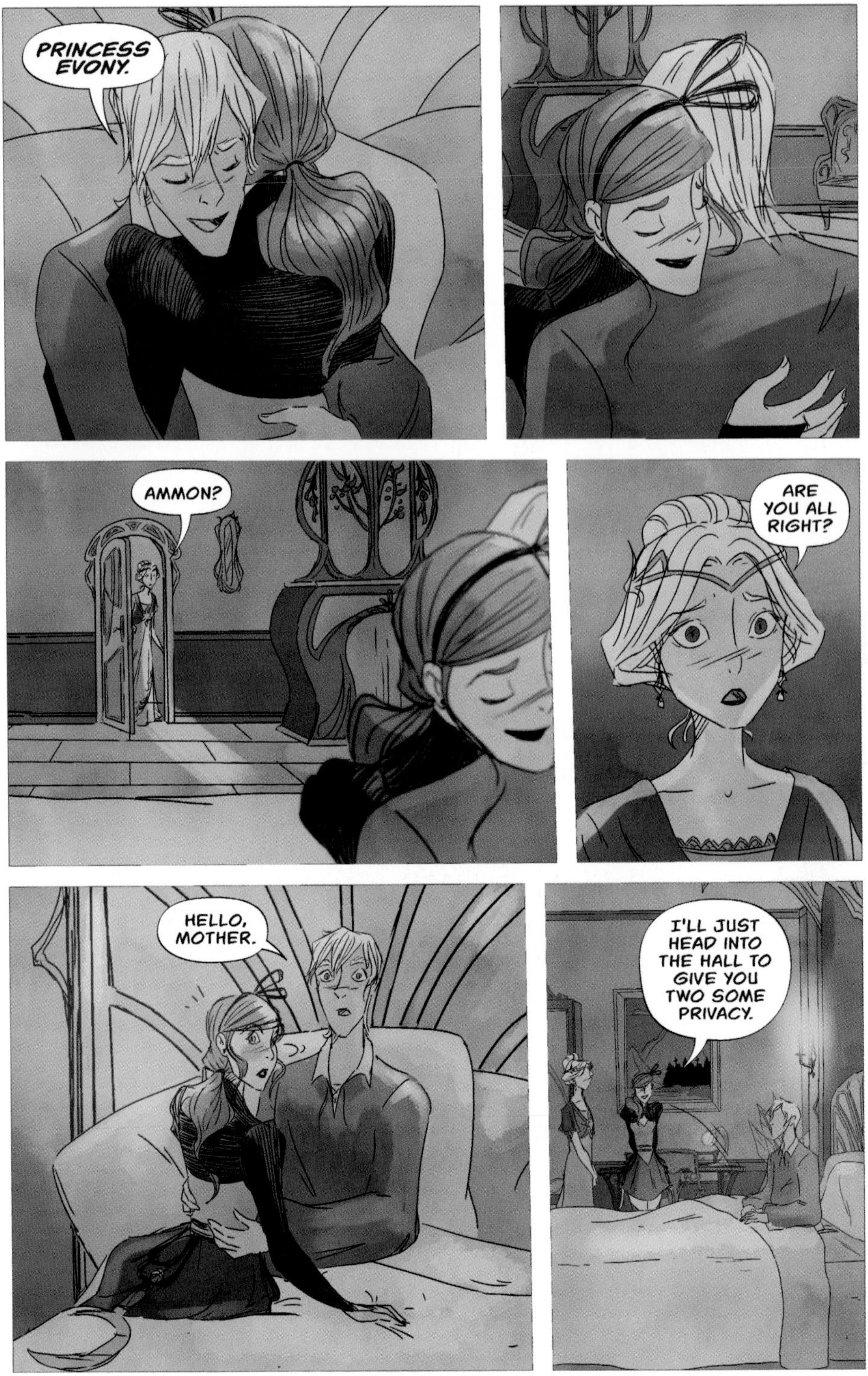
PRINCESS EVONY.
AMMON?
ARE YOU ALL RIGHT?
HELLO, MOTHER.
I'LL JUST HEAD INTO THE HALL TO GIVE YOU TWO SOME PRIVACY.

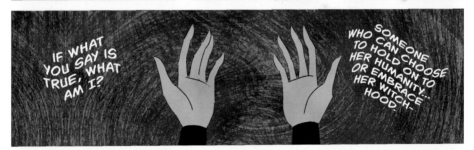

IF WHAT YOU SAY IS TRUE, WHAT AM I?

SOMEONE WHO CAN CHOOSE TO HOLD ON TO HER HUMANITY... OR EMBRACE HER WITCH-HOOD.

EVONY...

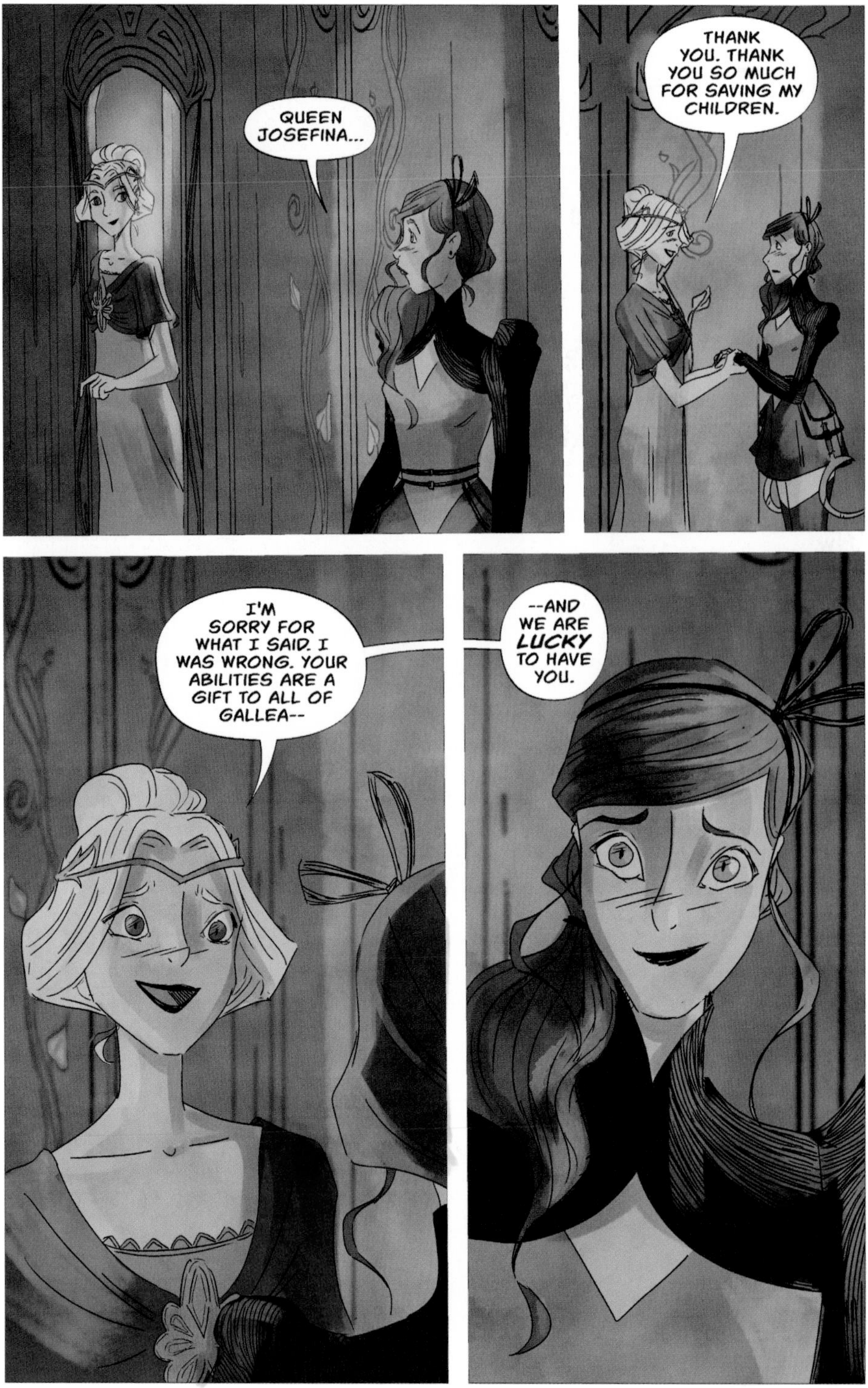
QUEEN JOSEFINA...
THANK YOU. THANK YOU SO MUCH FOR SAVING MY CHILDREN.
I'M SORRY FOR WHAT I SAID. I WAS WRONG. YOUR ABILITIES ARE A GIFT TO ALL OF GALLEA--
--AND WE ARE *LUCKY* TO HAVE YOU.

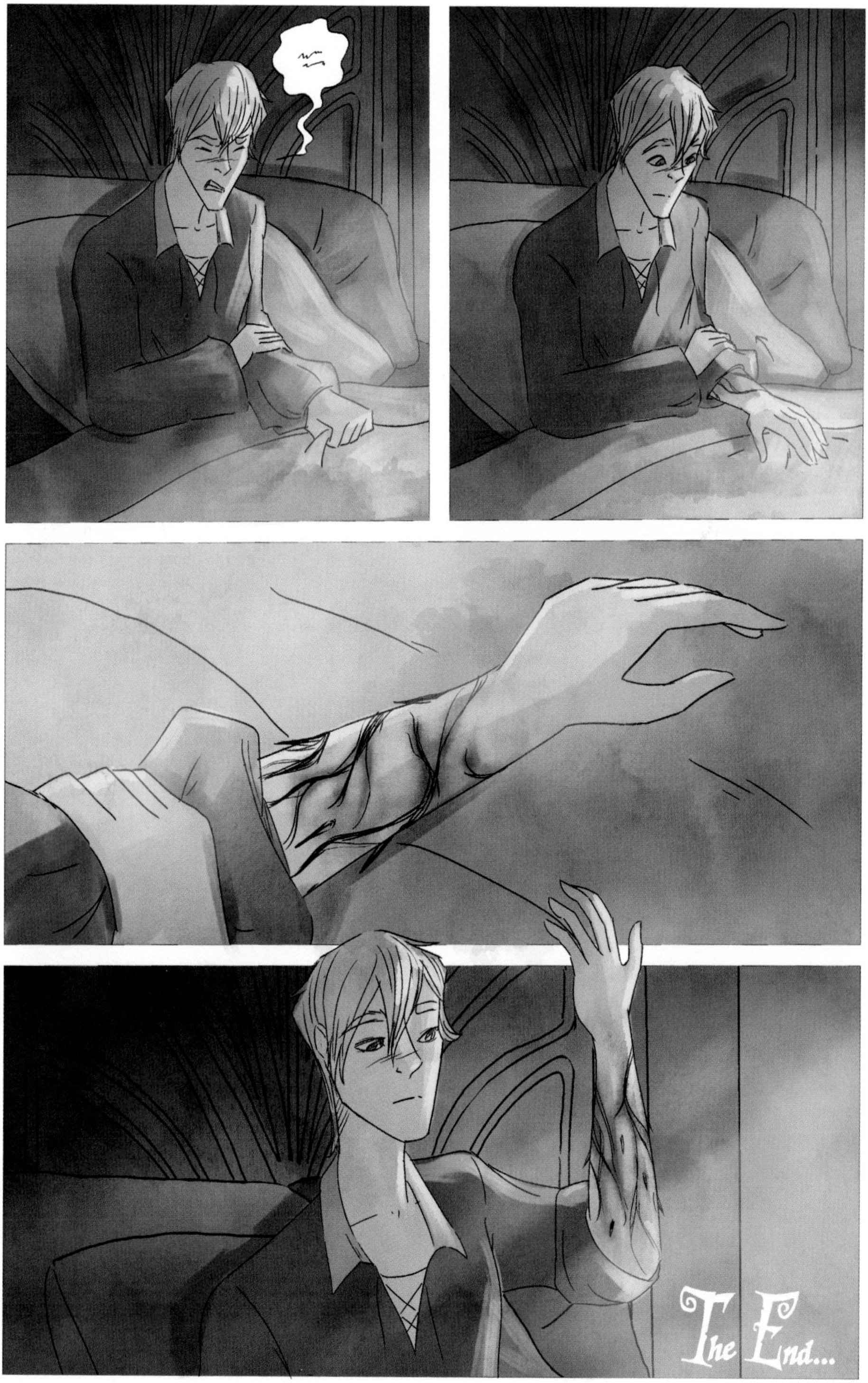
The End...

First Hardcover Edition, November 2021
First Paperback Edition, November 2021
10 9 8 7 6 5 4 3 2 1
FAC-034274-21288
Printed in the United States of America
Colors by Stelladia
Letters by Hassan Otsmane-Elhaou
This book is set in Buisnessland/Fontspring; OutofLine/Blambot; ShakyKane/Comicraft
Library of Congress Control Number for Hardcover: 2021933787
Hardcover ISBN 9781368028356
Paperback ISBN 9781368028363
Reinforced binding

Visit www.hyperionteens.com